PART 2

ASSASSIN

Spy Thriller

AGENT FOR HIRE

Intriguing New Series!

YONAH SAPIR

Tfutza
Publications

Assassin Part 2
Copyright © 2020 by Tfutza Publications
ISBN: 978-1-60091-784-4

Tfutza Publications
P.O.B. 50036
Beitar Illit 90500
Tel: 972-2-650-9400
info@tfutzapublications.com

Translation: C.S. Ben-Shachar
Cover design: Aviad Ben-Simon
Layout: Deena Weinberg

Distributed by:
Israel Bookshop Publications
501 Prospect Street
Lakewood, NJ 08701
Tel: (732) 901-3009
Fax: (732) 901-4012
www.israelbookshoppublications.com
info@israelbookshoppublications.com

Printed in Israel

Distributed in Israel by:
Tfutza Publications
P.O.B. 50036
Beitar Illit 90500
Tel: 972-2-650-9400
info@tfutzapublications.com

Distributed in Europe by:
Lehmanns
Unit E Viking Industrial Park
Rolling Mill Road,
Jarrow, Tyne & Wear NE32 3DP
44-191-430-0333

Distributed in Australia by:
Gold's Book & Gift Company
3-13 William Street
Balaclava 3183
613-9527-8775

Distributed in S. Africa by:
Kollel Bookshop
Ivy Common
107 William Rd., Norwood
Johannesburg 2192
27-11-728-1822

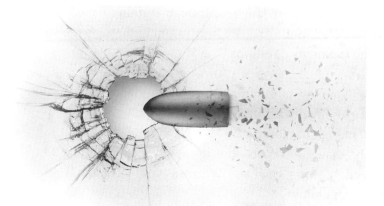

CHAPTER ONE

Gaza

Mark lowered his gaze, trying to avoid the beam of light projected directly into his eyes. It was a futile attempt; whoever was holding the flashlight was determined to keep him blinded.

"Your name," the unknown person said finally, his tone cold and calculated.

"Mark."

"Your *full* name."

"Mark Tyler."

"Where are you from?"

"Austria."

"What are you doing here in Gaza?"

"Humanitarian aid." The phrase was a good catchall. After all, professional humanitarians always single out certain groups for their aid – certain groups, and definitely not every one. So if Mark was essentially just helping himself – big deal. He was human, wasn't he?

The interrogator laughed, though it didn't sound like he was especially amused. "You've been walking through the streets and asking too many questions."

"I wanted to form my own impressions of the situation in Gaza."

"How did you get here?"

"Through the tunnels."

The man's eyebrows shot up in surprise, although Mark, still blinded, couldn't see that. "Who was your smuggler?"

"I don't know."

"You don't know who your smuggler was?" The interrogator sounded genuinely surprised. *This Mark hasn't undergone any training whatsoever*, he thought.

"Yes, because I..." Mark began, then stopped. He had fallen into a trap laid without even a drop of ingenuity. He had been on the verge of divulging Colin's role in this whole business, and if that happened...he didn't like to think where he might end up.

"Because you what? You're obviously not working alone here. So where are the others?"

"I don't know." It was the truth. He had no idea where they were based. If he were taken around the streets in a car and asked to point out their building, there was a good chance he would not be able to identify it, after the whole disorienting experience of being snatched like this.

The interrogator shook his head. "We have our ways of getting people to talk, young man. Let's say, for argument's sake, that you're a tourist here; I'm sure you'll agree that it would be a shame for you to have to suffer the tortures of the persecuted Palestinian people."

"How dare you talk about the persecution of the Palestinian people when you and your gang are the ones causing it!" The anger in Mark's voice was very real. He, like most of the youth in Europe, had been lapping up pro-Palestinian propaganda for years.

The interrogator and the man beside him exchanged glances. "Who do you think we are?" he asked.

"Mossad agents, or GSS, I suppose – one or the other, at any rate," Mark said with no attempt to conceal his disgust. "I know you have people working undercover in the occupied territories, so you can drop the pretense."

"So you're here to help the Palestinians? How are you planning on doing that?"

"That's not something that I'm going to tell you! You might be experienced at torture, but I promised to defend the persecuted Muslims of the world, and I'm not going to breach my vow." Mark knew his acting skills left much to be desired, but there was little else he could do.

"Quit the drama. You're among friends. We're Palestinians, though I can't tell you which faction we belong to."

"You're just saying that to get me to spill the beans, but I'm not going to tell you anything." Mark sat up straighter in an attempt to look at least somewhat imposing, even though he knew he was probably failing dismally.

"Okay, okay." The interrogator sounded weary. "So don't tell me. It doesn't sound like you have all that much to tell anyway. Whoever brought you in is pathetic, and so are you."

"It was Sami Al-Hasina," Mark said, confused, but finally figuring out that these guys truly weren't vicious, brutal Israelis.

"I'll speak to him." The interrogator stood up and walked out, leaving his partner to stand guard.

He returned just moments later, fuming. "Have you lost your mind?" he shouted. "This man is in the middle of an important intelligence operation, and you're disturbing him?!"

"He asked too many questions," the guard said. "We suspected that he was a plant. But nobody would be dumb enough to plant him here," he said derisively.

The interrogator ignored the barb. "And I suppose it didn't occur to you that whoever it might be would send us a blond, blue-eyed Austrian citizen to catch our attention? They don't have enough dark-skinned, dark-eyed citizens?" The interrogator was almost trembling with rage. "Use your head next time – if you have more than two brain cells in it, that is." The interrogator turned on the lights in the basement, and the man who had captured Mark quickly left. The interrogator then introduced himself as Khalil and apologized. "You'll forgive us, won't you?"

"Of course." Pale-faced Mark would have agreed to forgive the entire world just then.

The interrogator apologized again. "So sorry for all the discomfort. Really. As you can see, our men are a little too quick to react sometimes."

Mark took the Band-Aid that the other man extended to him. "Yes, I did notice that."

Ukraine

There was a lengthy silence in the jeep. Eyal exhaled deeply as a thousand thoughts flitted through his mind. But despite all that he wanted to say and all the questions he had, he chose to remain silent.

"Surprised?" The commander turned around from his seat next to the driver and looked at Eyal with an expression of curiosity coupled with derision.

"That wouldn't be the correct term." Who were these men? Dressed entirely in black, it was impossible to place them.

"So what would the correct term be?" the commander asked.

Eyal didn't reply. The jeep continued to speed ahead as his mind conjured up the words: "In pain." He was feeling a deep sense of pain and melancholy at the realization that so many people had been killed because of him. Not through him, but because of him.

"You're not asking who I am, where we're taking you, or what our goal is."

"I'm guessing that you don't need me to water your garden or feed your chickens."

"What a genius," the commander responded. He turned to the man sitting on Eyal's left. "John, put him to sleep."

There was no way for Eyal to avoid the needle prick in his arm. Within seconds his limbs grew leaden and his eyelids drooped. The commander eyed the slumbering captive with an inscrutable expression. Watching him earlier, running between the injured police officers and administering first aid to the very same men who had sought to have him arrested, he was filled with a sense of pride. He had seen Eyal ignore the blood flowing from his own wounds and overcome his fear of being returned to the torture of Ukrainian interrogation solely in order to do everything possible to spare the victims. They needed a man like him in Syria.

Gaza

"Thanks for everything."

They were at the entrance to the Rafah tunnel. The child had been put back to sleep and was now in Mark's arms. After Mark had briefly recounted the tale of his adventure, he had been duly castigated by Colin and penalized with the task of carrying the child throughout the next journey. It was a penalty that he accepted with good grace.

They had changed into clean, lightweight clothing. As they distanced themselves from the entrance of the tunnel, the air became cool and damp despite the relatively pleasant weather outside.

"We are grateful for your involvement," Abad, their escort

said as they marched onward. He wasn't the type to shed a tear, but his voice shook as he spoke. "I have family in Syria, and every night before I go to sleep I wonder if they'll still be alive in the morning. The situation in Gaza isn't exactly the best either, but it's not in the same league. If X can do something for my family and our Syrian brothers, I will be grateful to have had a part in all of this."

"There's no way of knowing if our plan will succeed at this early stage," Colin cautioned him. "But one thing is certain: X is doing everything in his power to fight for his nation."

"And this is the key to it all." Abad jerked his chin in the direction of the sleeping child.

"His father is, rather." Colin's lips closed suddenly, and he shook his head. "You're better off not knowing."

"I don't want to know."

"Better that way."

The tunnel was getting wider as they descended, and suddenly Abad gestured to a niche in the wall. They all turned and saw an electric scooter-car waiting for them. Abad grinned. "This time we travel in style. This tunnel has everything," he said proudly. "Water, electricity, ventilation – and refreshments for our guests."

They got inside and settled themselves in for the ride.

"The residents of Gaza smuggle everything through the tunnel network. Weapons, drugs (legal and otherwise), other forms of contraband, refugees. This tunnel, among others, is also used to smuggle vehicle components and sometimes entire vehicles."

Colin nodded. "It's impressive, I agree. Egypt doesn't agree, mind you. We heard about their attempts to sabotage the tunnels by filling them with sewage wastewater or salt water, but it's been a losing battle as far as they're concerned. There are just too many tunnels, and the residents of Gaza wouldn't manage without them."

"What are our plans?" Leon was frustrated over the fact that Colin insisted on keeping almost all the details of the mission to himself. "I don't want to find out at the last minute that my plane is leaving Egypt and making a detour to a fine Israeli prison."

"We're flying from Egypt to Ukraine. You understand, of course, why we've decided against flying out from an Israeli airport. Our reasoning includes the painfully tight security and the fact that this child's mother has probably told the authorities about the kidnapping despite our threats."

"So that's why we entered Gaza," Leon said. He took the child from Mark and absentmindedly stroked his hair where it grew long behind his ears. "But the Egyptians aren't on good terms with the tunnel diggers, as you just noted."

"True. But once we get out of here we won't be border smugglers. We'll be upright citizens flying to Ukraine for a family event."

"Who's going to give us the passports and tickets?" Leon asked.

"We have friends." Colin was vague as usual.

"Who?"

Leon, walking on Colin's right side, was treated to a glance of annoyance. "You really don't want to know."

"And what if I tell you I really do want to know?"

"It won't make the slightest difference," Colin said, completely unperturbed. He replaced his apathetic expression with an imploring look. "Leon, please understand that I'm not trying to be condescending. X has given his orders, and I am fulfilling those orders to the letter – to the best of my ability, that is. In order for me to fulfill my mission I need to know the details of our plan, and it's better that you do not. That's all there is to this."

Leon fell silent. Colin's explanation was far from satisfying, and he hated feeling that Colin was a step above him in the hierarchy of their group. But no one had asked his opinion on the matter. They continued to travel and eventually reached the tunnel's exit. "We're here, men," Colin said, skipping jauntily out of the electric scooter-car and starting to climb the last few yards by foot. "Welcome to Egypt."

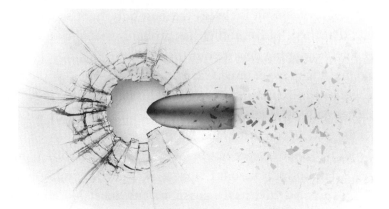

CHAPTER TWO

Ukraine

Eyal woke up and surveyed his surroundings. The room he was in was dark. His hands and feet had been un-shackled, and the wound on his leg had been tended to. His clothes were wrinkled and bloodstained and torn in places, probably from the fallout from the recent gunfight.

For ten seconds Eyal lay without moving. He looked at the room through half-open eyelids, enjoying the sensation of lying on a pillow and mattress. After too many days and nights lying on the concrete floor of a Ukrainian police cell with blinding light that penetrated even closed eyelids and the mind-numbing noise, the respite was intoxicating. And this room was heated, in stark contrast to the spine-tingling cold that he had endured while in prison. He absorbed the pleasant warmth, trying to imbibe a sense of tranquility.

For ten seconds – that was more than enough time to take it easy. Life wasn't supposed to be easy. Eyal sat up and gazed around the room with curiosity. The fact that he wasn't shackled to the bed was certainly cause for concern. Most of his captors over the years had not allowed him such freedom of movement, and certainly not if there was no one in the room keeping an eye on him with a finger on the trigger of some weapon. The room was five-star luxury compared to the prison cell he had only recently escaped, but based on his captors' performance on the previous day, these men seemed infinitely more dangerous.

Eyal noticed a night-light beside his bed, and he flicked the switch on. A pale glow illuminated the room, and Eyal frowned as he made a mental inventory of the furnishings. Aside from the wide bed he was sitting on, there were three chairs and a computer on a small desk. In the corner opposite him, a narrow door was ajar. Eyal stood up and went over to check it out. A bathroom.

Even without making an exhaustive inspection of the room, Eyal knew that there were certainly security cameras and listening devices keeping tabs on him. All the same, there were certain things a person could do even when under observation. Just maybe, making a bomb was one of them.

Eyal entered the bathroom, and his well-trained eyes scanned the contents of the room. It was possible to create a powerful bomb out of simple cleaning agents – he'd done that many times – but in this bathroom, for obvious reasons, there were no cleaning agents stored. His captors weren't so foolish as to leave acetone, grease remover, or any oxygen-based fluids lying around. There wasn't even a box of laundry detergent.

The mirror. Eyal peered at the image on the plated metal and smiled in grim distaste. Eli had been right; he truly looked awful. His left temple boasted a deep gash with patches of dried blood, and there was a huge blue bruise beneath his right eye. The remainder of his face was none too pretty either. All in all, he'd been through the wringer and it showed.

Eyal splashed water on his face and wiped it away carefully, wincing slightly as he did so. As he stepped out of the bathroom a knock on the door startled him. It was John, the man who had injected Eyal with anesthesia. "Come," he barked. "They're waiting for you."

Eyal tossed the towel onto the bed. "May I ask who it is that's waiting?"

"No." The man had his gun trained on Eyal, and now he tossed Eyal a pair of plastic handcuffs. "Cuff your hands."

With effort, Eyal fought down the sigh of despair threatening to burst from him. He placed his hands into the cuffs and snapped them shut with his teeth. "There's no way to get around having these on my hands?"

"With you, no. There's no way of knowing what ideas you'll get into that interesting head of yours." John gestured with his gun. "No escape attempts, in case I haven't made myself clear already, okay? Now start walking in front of me."

Eyal did as he was told. In any case, he wasn't about to make his escape before finding out exactly who his captors were.

John led Eyal down a long corridor, and Eyal looked around in surprise. Aside from the heavy-duty bars on the windows, the house could have been a regular family home.

Eyal was prodded into a large room in which were a dining room table, chairs, and three couches – a three-seater, a two-seater, and an armchair. Between the couches was a low table, and one of the walls of the room featured a huge plasma screen, now blank. Two men were seated on the couches, and they seemed to be waiting.

As soon as Eyal entered, the men rose to their feet, their gaze fixed on him.

"Welcome, Eyal," the first man, whom Eyal recognized as "the commander," said in English. "We've been waiting for you."

"How moving. But I don't know if I'll be able to meet your expectations."

"We're hoping that you will." The man offered a regal smile. "We've invested no small amount in you, only some of which you were privileged to witness yesterday."

Eyal tilted his head in an indecipherable gesture. "Murdering innocent people is considered an investment? That's a festive way of phrasing things."

The commander ignored his comment. "Sit down, please."

Eyal, still exhausted from his recent ordeal, readily accepted the offer, sinking into the single-seat armchair. His muscles protested at the movement, but he paid them no heed as he fixed the men before him with a questioning glance.

"I want to show you something." The commander lifted a remote control device, flicked it at the plasma screen, and pressed a button.

❦

Egypt

They stepped out into the fresh night air, looking up at a starry sky. A man of medium height, dressed in simple garb, approached. X had woven this mission together brilliantly, and he hadn't overlooked a single detail. Their latest contact smiled and offered the men drinks and sandwiches, then pointed to a Mazda parked nearby.

"Your tickets, passports, and luggage are already inside. The names on the passports are similar to your own, but for various reasons that I won't go into now, we needed to issue a girl's passport for the child. But that shouldn't be a problem. There's a small suitcase with makeup beneath the front seat. X told me that one of you is a professional makeup artist."

Mark looked at Leon. The man had worked for a Canadian

theater company for four years before deciding to leave the stage for more interesting pastures.

Colin, however, was disturbed over the change to the boy's passport. "X is aware of this?"

"Of course. Every part of this operation moves forward only through him." The man laughed. "Your flight from El Arish International Airport will be taking off in less than three hours. You have an hour's drive ahead of you, so I suggest that you get a move on. Have a safe trip."

"Will we have time to shop at the Duty Free?" Colin joked.

"You'll be disappointed by our Duty Free. This isn't Heathrow."

Colin glanced at the other man and saw the glint in his eyes. A suspicious gleam appeared in Colin's own eyes, and the other man smiled and winked. "I see that you're British," he said. "Speak in Arabic until tomorrow. Your accent's awful. Don't look at me like that, my friend. You can relax. I'm not an MI6 agent."

Colin placed his faith in X's know-how when it came to selecting smugglers. The men hurried to the car, and Colin sat at the wheel as Leon and Mark settled themselves in the back seat with Elitzafun lying across their laps.

Colin started to wind his way through Rafah's narrow streets until he reached the edge of town. As soon as he turned onto Highway 40 he stepped down hard on the gas, and his passengers jerked back in their seats.

"Careful on the road." Leon wiped his brow. "I'd rather not end up on a respirator in an Egyptian hospital. Why should we suffer just because that guy got you nervous?"

"I'm not nervous," Colin said through clenched teeth. "We need to make our flight."

"We're not going to make it if we get smashed up in a car accident," Mark said. "Slow down, Colin."

"Cowards!" Colin hit the gas harder, and the car sped even

faster. "If we miss that flight, that's the end of the story. No more tickets, no more flights. We will end up being one big failure, and nobody here cares about failures. So, you two, start getting our girl ready. We'll be reaching our destination pretty soon."

"Who was that guy in Rafah?" Mark asked.

Colin groaned. "Think a bit about what you've been through up to this point, and then maybe you'll be able to figure out why I'm not going to answer that one."

"Well, I'm not to be blamed for the fact that he's an idiot," Leon complained as Mark offered him a playful punch. "Let's see you do a better job, my hero."

"True." Colin turned the steering wheel sharply, passing a huge truck. "The less you know, the better. Start putting on the makeup already! We'll be there within half an hour."

Leon bent down to retrieve the suitcase with the makeup in it from under the front seat. He surveyed the contents and pulled out a bag full of cotton wadding.

"Shouldn't we start with the hair?" Mark asked nervously. Unlike Leon, he had never been a member of the world of theater. "Doesn't that take longer?"

Leon pulled tiny tufts of cotton out of the wad in the bag, balled them up, and wedged them between the child's gums and jaw. "There's a wig inside. It'll take us exactly two minutes to deal with the hair. Three minutes if that grass growing on the kid's head doesn't adhere properly."

Mark looked at the "grass" on the child's small head and shook his head. Something about the innocence in the boy's face was taking his breath away, but he resolutely paid it no attention.

Leon eyed him suspiciously. "Did something happen?"

"Nothing." Mark had never been an actor, but he knew how to adapt to circumstances. There was a reason he numbered among X's men and had been chosen as a member of the kidnapping team. "Should I start with the eyes?" he asked purposefully.

"No. I'll do the eyes. You just pass me things as I ask for

them. I'll need the sponges too. We only have another thirty minutes."

"Twenty-five," Colin called out, eyeing the Waze monitor. In another two miles he needed to turn onto Highway 55. The El Arish military hospital was already visible in the distance. "There's no traffic at this hour. We should be able to fly down the road."

"We're supposed to fly," Mark murmured. Suddenly he noticed the logo on the makeup box, and a look of appreciation appeared in his eyes. He had always known that X was liberal when it came to expenses, but apparently this project was much more important than he had imagined if X was investing so much in even the most seemingly negligible of details.

Ukraine

"Where's my mother?" Elitzafun called out of the huge screen. A steel fist wedged its way into Eyal's heart, and his breath seemed to be trapped somewhere between his ribs. *Ribono shel olam!* he screamed silently. *This can't be happening! You have to help! I don't know how, but You have to help me!* He wasn't easily shocked, but the image on the screen had caused his face to turn ashen. *Ribono shel olam, what do they want of Your child? What do You want me to do?*

"We're going to bring you to your father very soon," a voice was heard saying – the image was blurred. "Do you want a nosh?"

"Yeah. But there's no kosher symbol," Elitzafun was now saying. "And you don't look like you're religious. I want my mother!"

"Your father's no good?" the voice asked.

"My father is good but...but I want my mother..."

"You'll be seeing your father in another few hours, kid. In the meantime, we'll try to find you something that you like."

"Fine." The child rattled off his list of favorite snacks. "I like onion Bissli, potato chips, Nacho Doritos...and I like red Bamba the best. Oh, and gum, and milk chocolate without nuts."

"I wrote it all down." The voice sounded amused at the child's list.

The commander stopped the playback and turned to stare at Eyal. Eyal's expression was hidden – he was holding his head between his handcuffed hands, his eyes clenched shut.

"Eyal," the commander said gently.

"What do you want?"

The commander smiled. "You've reached that point so quickly? You're not asking anything about your child?"

"There's nothing to ask."

"Why?"

Eyal looked up and his green eyes shot daggers. "Because creatures who kidnap children for their own needs are not in the category of human beings."

"Oh, but didn't you take note of how humane we are? You should give us credit for our foresight. Your child is being given everything he wants. From the video you can see just how kindly he's being treated! Somewhat better treatment than what you experienced at the hands of the Ukrainian police, don't you think?"

"You're breaking my heart." Derision, fury, and fear mingled together in Eyal's voice.

"Okay. Let's get straight to the point. We need you, Eyal, and in order to encourage your cooperation, we've taken a small and beloved hostage whose father will do anything and everything to have him released."

"What do you want?"

"This." The commander pointed to the screen, which now showed a picture of a large structure. "In about two weeks' time, the latest UN peace conference will take place in this building. One of the subjects that will be discussed will be the state of fighting in Syria. But aside from eating caviar and drinking champagne, nothing useful will get done. So we want to shake them up a bit."

"Who will be at the conference?" Eyal maintained an inscrutable expression, as though he hadn't promised Bentzy that... A thought entered his mind, draining him with its potency. This battle to win him over via the kidnapping of his son had not been waged by chance. There was great intelligence in its making, and every last detail had been carefully planned.

"You're not asking how we want you to shake them up."

"I'm guessing you don't want me to air a documentary on the horrors of war."

"A genius indeed," the commander said. "What would you do if we gave you free choice on how to go about things?"

"Who will be at the conference?" Eyal repeated his previous question, ignoring the commander's words.

"Lots of fat and useless fish. Millionaires who are pouring their money into the wrong mouths, the German chancellor, the Russian president, the Ukrainian prime minister, the UN secretary-general, and most important of all, the US president."

"You want to get them all in one package deal?"

"No. I think that would be too much. Even for you."

A bitter smile. "I'm happy you realize that my capabilities are limited."

The commander leaned forward. "We'll make do with one. The man you promised to provide security for during your trip to Ukraine. Remember?"

Eyal's heart sank. Until now he'd been acting as if he were clueless, in the hope that they knew nothing about him and the security he had promised to provide for the president. But there had been a reason behind that shootout with the police officers, and this kidnapping. They knew everything.

"Your promise to provide security makes things so simple. Everything has already been put in place in order for us to be able to reap the rewards." A smile. "And for you to have your son returned to you alive."

Eyal said nothing.

"Eyal?"

When Eyal finally opened his mouth, the voice that emerged was barely audible. "I don't think I can do it."

"Oh, don't underestimate yourself. We will provide you with everything you could possibly need. Just remember what is hanging in the balance, and you'll find your creativity flourishing. And do please bear in mind that if you don't do as we ask, your son will not be returning to his mother – ever."

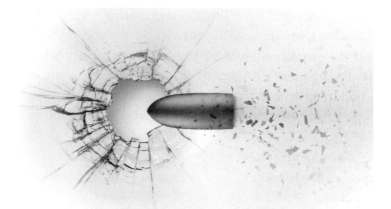

CHAPTER THREE

Ukraine

Aheavy silence filled the large room. The commander looked at Eyal, keeping his gaze steady, and it took a full minute for Eyal to respond. "You're seriously expecting me to capture the US president without an alias – to just walk in there, a known figure, and do what you're asking? I'll never be able to pull it off."

"Eyal, I have made extensive investigations into your past," the commander said. "I know what you are capable of. You've managed to get yourself out of some very nasty places – such as Ukrainian prisons, if you don't object to being reminded. So this time you'll make another breakout and add that feather to your cap. It will make for interesting story time for your kids in another twenty years. And it's the least you can do for my countrymen."

"Your countrymen?" Eyal echoed.

"Yes. My fellow Syrian citizens are being murdered – massacred. I'm sure you know what's going on there."

Eyal, whose sarcasm had been sharpened by his feelings of fear and fury, responded swiftly. "Everyone murders everyone there, no? Assad's army is pitted against the rebels and the rebels are against the pro-Assad citizens. The Iranians and Hezbollah murder Al Qaeda men and the Americans murder members of ISIS. The Turks murder the Kurds, the Russians murder everyone, and the Israelis take care of the weapon convoys. Is there anyone that I missed out?"

"You're an expert analyst," the commander said. "And the way things work in Israel is this: The Israelis murder the Palestinians in Judea and Samaria, the Gazans retaliate, while Israeli Arabs join the fray with knives and tractors. The Europeans defend them in their war of words and the Americans tread the fine line of supposed neutrality, which is mostly a farce. The Iranians meddle when it suits them, and the Russians keep their feet dry even as their hands drip blood. Is there anyone that I missed out?"

"Very funny."

"Like all Westerners, there's something you don't understand. But it's one thing for the Americans and Europeans to make this mistake, and another thing entirely for an Israeli to do the same. Assad is a born dictator. The Syrians wanted him ousted from power the same way that Mubarak was overthrown in Egypt and Gaddafi was knocked out in Libya. But in Syria things took a different turn, and for whatever reason, the world prefers to shut its eyes and say that things will take time but they'll pass. And in the meantime my countrymen are experiencing a holocaust. A holocaust!" The man's eyes were on fire.

"The United States thinks they're the police force of the world. They had Saddam Hussein killed because of his personal feud with President Bush senior, so why can't they take care of the mass murderer in Syria? Where has the American system of ethics disappeared to? American soldiers were murdered in Iraq and Afghanistan, so why is Syria different? I need the American president's involvement for our benefit."

"I think I understand," Eyal said, his eyes narrowed. "Correct me if I'm wrong. Of the nearly one hundred various terrorist organizations currently operating in Syria, you're going to be the one to change things in that war-torn country."

"I owe it to my fellow citizens and to myself to try. I can't just sit idly by as my countrymen are murdered. Wouldn't you do the same thing if you had been in Europe eighty years ago? Or would you have sat around and done nothing while your brothers were slaughtered, even though you knew that you were capable of assisting them?"

Eyal fell silent and studied the plasma screen. What a noble endeavor. Halting the Syrian holocaust. Only it was his son stuck in the middle of it all.

"What are you going to do to him?" he asked quietly.

"To your son?" the commander asked. "Right now he's enjoying himself. My men have been running around in search of red Bamba with a good kosher symbol."

"Not my son," Eyal's voice reflected his exhaustion and fatigue. "To the president."

"We're not going to murder him. He'll be useless once he's dead. All that would happen if we killed him is that the Americans would lower their flags to half-mast for a day or a week, and another president would be selected in his place. No – we want to shake him up, and we can't do that while he's sitting in the Oval Office."

"Who is 'we'? Which militia do you belong to?"

"You're moving into uncharted territory. We will supply you with whatever you say is necessary for this mission, but we will not provide you with any unnecessary information." The commander looked at his watch. "You will meet your son in another hour and a half, or perhaps two hours. I hope all of the border transfers have passed without incident. And I also hope that you will be wise enough to make your son's stay here pleasant, so that he feels no trauma from his kidnapping. This can be the opportunity of a lifetime. He'll be granted as many snacks as he wants, and he'll have quality time with his father. We've already ordered him a Playmobil castle."

Eyal didn't respond.

"John, take Eyal to his room and remove his handcuffs. After the video he saw I believe he'll be wise enough not to try and flee. Eyal, we are at your service. We have less than two weeks at our disposal, which is a very short window of time to prepare for this mission. If all goes well it will not fail, but if things do not go well it may end in a bloodbath. Our best men will be available to you, and if you want anything related to food, drink, or a specific type of cigar or passion-fruit-scented soap, just say the word and you'll have it."

John approached Eyal without uttering a word. Eyal rose, and the man led him back down the corridor to the room he had occupied before. The door was of plain wood. *No metal bars or sophisticated locks*, Eyal thought. As he stepped through the doorway John tapped him on the shoulder, and when he turned around, the man sliced open the cuffs with a razor blade. *Right*, Eyal thought bitterly. *They know me too well. No cuffs needed when they have a far better way to manipulate me. Obviously, I won't be going anywhere while Elitzafun is in their clutches.*

John closed the door to the room and disappeared. Eyal looked around. His heart was beating wildly, and a million thoughts danced around his head. Before he could recover, there was a knock and the door opened.

The commander stood on the threshold. "I didn't properly introduce myself earlier, and that was impolite. My name is X. Don't be insulted by the fact that I am not divulging my true name. X is the name that my men know me by too. Is your room to your satisfaction, Eyal? There are kosher wines in a small bar under the table, and snacks as well. From what I understand, you haven't exactly eaten much during the past few days. Enjoy."

Eyal looked at X but said nothing.

"Rest up for an hour, and then we'll talk again," X said. "And... Eyal?"

Eyal eyed him wordlessly still, a question mark in his eyes.

"Don't do anything stupid. Remember what's hanging in the balance."

Eyal's voice, when he finally deigned to respond, was bitter. "I remember."

Ukraine

Eli sat slumped down in the driver's seat of the car, confused and exhausted. Their plan had gone completely haywire. Eyal had been captured again, and there seemed to be no options left. Eli, usually so creative and upbeat, now sighed in frustration and despair. And then his phone rang.

"Hello?" Eli was shocked when the voice of his direct superior, Uri Shabtai, came over the line.

"Uri, what happened?" He couldn't recall a single instance when they had spoken over an unsecured line.

"Eli, where are you?" His superior's voice had an urgent, almost alarmed quality to it.

"I'm in my car. It kind of became home for now. I can't go back to the apartment."

"Call me back from Delta Street." Uri hung up and Eli shook his head. "Delta Street" meant a public phone somewhere discreet. It wasn't ideal, but then, nothing could possibly be ideal right now with all the things that had already gone wrong.

He turned the key in the ignition and made his way to the nearest town. Dawn would be breaking soon, but the streets were still empty. He cruised along slowly, scanning the streets for a phone booth. There. He parked right next to it so that he could, if necessary, make a swift exit within two seconds if necessary, and dialed a number.

"Uri? What happened."

"Have you been following the news?" his commander asked.

"Uri – seriously? I should ask the same of you. The short answer is *no*. What happened?"

"Two things. Let's start with the less-bad news: Unidentified agents attacked the police escort taking Eyal back to prison. Six officers were murdered, the others were injured, and Eyal has disappeared. The Ukrainian police force is fuming, and they've decided to cast the blame for this on Israel."

"Eyal has disappeared?" Eli choked. "And that's the *less-bad* piece of news?"

"Yes. Are you sitting down?"

"Enough already! What happened?"

"Elitzafun's been kidnapped."

"What?" Eli shrieked. "Elitzafun Gilboa?"

"Do you know of anyone else with that name?" Uri's voice was filled with bitter fury.

"How? When? Where? Why?"

"We don't have a lot of information. The kidnapper warned the child's grandfather not to contact us, which limits us, because we don't want them to know that we're involved."

"What do they want?"

"They want something from Eyal, and they're using his son as a means of extortion. But we don't know what it is that they want of him. Not yet, that is."

Eli wiped beads of sweat from his forehead, despite the sub-zero temperature. "Trouble comes in leaps and bounds," he murmured. "I was almost planning on visiting Eyal in prison, but now it looks like there'll be no one to visit."

"You wanted to visit him in prison?" Uri shouted. "I thought you had some sense, Eli. Don't you realize that they're baying for your blood? The Ukrainians are convinced that you orchestrated

Eyal's escape. They want to roast you alive!"

"Wonderful." Eli swallowed hard. Through no fault of his own, Ukraine had turned into enemy territory for him as well. "So, Eyal has disappeared, his son has disappeared, I've become a wanted man, and we don't have a single clue to go on. Just wonderful."

Ukraine

A gentle rapping on the door woke Eyal. He'd been so sure that he wouldn't fall asleep – not with so much preying on his mind – but his experiences in prison, the interrogations, the beatings, and the fact that he'd barely slept in the last few days, had all left their mark on him. And so, despite the rage, fear, and pain that he was feeling, he did fall asleep, almost immediately. He hadn't even made the most cursory perusal of his surroundings to check for a possible escape route. He was, after all, only human; even if his captors were trying to ascribe superhuman traits to him, such as…

Such as abducting the president. If it weren't so sad, it would have been laughable. It was impossible to capture the president! The security around him was impossible to breach. Dozens of eyes kept watch on him every minute of the day, and he was protected by the very best that technology could provide. The notion that somehow Eyal could engineer his abduction was so far-fetched that he would have dismissed it out of hand, if not… if not for Elitzafun.

The knocking persisted, and Eyal stumbled out of bed and went to open the door. X stood in the doorway, a huge grin on his face. "The last hurdle has been overcome," he said. "Your son is on his way here right now, as we speak."

A bitter taste filled Eyal's mouth. He realized that he had been hoping that Hashem would send messengers, in the form of Israeli security agents, to stop the kidnappers in their tracks, but now it was too late for that. X's men, whoever they were, were real professionals. Despair threatened to engulf him entirely – and then, suddenly, the image of Rabbi Shindelheim's illuminating smile and piercing gaze appeared before him. "The Creator conducts this world in a much better fashion than we can ever imagine, Eyal. Even if we think that things would be better off one way or another, He – and only He – knows what is truly best for us."

And what is best for you, Eyal, is that they've managed to smuggle your son over the border, a voice echoed in his mind. *Everything that has transpired over the last few months has been for your good. Even the past few days, as difficult as they have been, were also custom-designed for you by Hashem.*

Eyal drew a deep breath. He wasn't alone. Despite the fear and confusion and the ever-present danger, Hashem was with him. Nothing had happened by chance. It was all being orchestrated by his Father in Heaven.

"Would you like to see him?"' X asked.

Eyal fixed him with a scornful look and said nothing. He would save his words for Elitzafun.

X stepped away from the door. "Leon, Colin."

A sound. An elevator door opened and two men came out carrying Elitzafun between them.

Tears filled Eyal's eyes. Leon set the boy down on his feet, and he ran toward Eyal with outstretched arms.

Eyal lifted Elitzafun and hugged him. As he embraced his son and drew him close to his heart, the physical pain from his beatings in prison seemed to melt away. He stroked his stepson's hair and fingered his *kippah* and *peyos*. "How are you, Elitzafun?" he asked softly.

"I'm okay," the boy said. "These people are really strange, but they brought me everything I wanted on my way here. Why am I here? For a trip?"

"Yes." Eyal tried to stabilize his voice. "It's a kind of trip."

"Yay! So much fun that it's just the two of us!" Elitzafun pulled his face away from his father's. "What happened to you?"

"What do you mean?" Eyal was relieved that most of his injuries were beneath the surface, and he was even more relieved that he had thought to wash his face earlier, so he looked at least a bit more presentable.

"That...that bruise...and that blood."

"Well, I fell." He had fallen. Among other things.

"It hurt you?" Elitzafun asked.

Eyal smiled gently. "A bit." He hugged his son again. "But when you're here, nothing hurts."

"So, it's just you and me?"

"Yes."

"That's so much fun," Elitzafun said. "Now Chagelet won't tell me what to do, and Elishama won't interrupt and ask you to tell him stories. So when are we going to go to the zoo?"

"Maybe tomorrow," X said. "Come, Elitzafun. We've prepared a beautiful room for you."

Elitzafun shook his head. "I want to sleep in my father's room."

"Your father is busy right now. He needs to recuperate from his fall. After that you can meet each other again."

Elitzafun looked at his father, who nodded in consent to the question in his eyes. Intuitively the boy understood that his father had no control over the situation, and he allowed himself to be smothered with another hug before turning to follow Colin down the corridor and then around a corner and out of sight.

"It is as we said," X said, a satisfied expression on his face. "He's feeling fine, and he's calm and happy. He's not going to be lacking for anything as long as you fulfill our request."

"You leave him alone," Eyal said, his voice breaking. "He's only five years old."

"True. But his father holds the key to everything that we need. So...what can I say, Eyal? The temptation was just too great."

CHAPTER FOUR

Ukraine

Eyal tried to relax. He opened the fridge in his room and pulled out a sandwich roll wrapped in sealed plastic with a *hechsher* on the wrapping, an apple, a banana, and a bottle of mineral water. He washed his hands and ate the modest meal, slowly and thoughtfully. Aside from the apples that he had found in the car he had requisitioned, many long hours had passed without food – so many that he had lost track. Eyal had been tested with periods of prolonged fasting while undergoing intelligence training, and then again during fieldwork, but the experience was never easy – it was something that was impossible to get used to. The knowledge that X and his cohorts were watching his every move was unpleasant, but he knew that he had to eat. With every bite he took, he resented even more the fact that by partaking of the food that they had provided for him he was succumbing to their will and playing by their rules.

But he had no choice. And he also had no choice but to strategize the president's capture.

After *bentching*, Eyal walked slowly around the room, running his fingertips along the walls, pictures, and windows. It was pointless, of course, but it was his second nature. It also served as a ridiculous sort of reassurance that at least he knew the positions of the cameras that were tracking his every move.

Eyal completed his inspection and opened the fridge again, examining the beverages there. They all had kosher seals on them. X had done his homework well, and Eyal was impressed by the psychological methods that were being employed. They could have chosen to break him, providing him with nothing but dry crusts of bread and water, and their treatment would still have been an improvement over his prison conditions. And he would still have been subservient to them so long as they had Elitzafun in their clutches. He wondered whether he was supposed to feel grateful that they had opted for the velvet glove approach, and he decided that, yes – he would thank Hashem for this measure of comfort. He certainly felt that he needed it.

Eyal peered closer at the bottles of wine and beer. Their alcohol content was low, but still enough to create a blaze. Open electrical wires would provide the spark, and the window curtains would be the fuel. He could burn the room down within minutes, but they knew that he wouldn't dare.

Eyal's prison clothes were ripped and bloodstained, and the closet was full of replacement items for him – all in his size and preferred style. How very considerate.

Eyal decided not to change out of his prison uniform. Instead, he went over to the bathroom and took another look around. The faucet could serve as a weapon if necessary, and the shower rod could be ripped out of its socket to serve whatever purpose he wanted it to serve. But he knew it was futile. His search of the room had already revealed the anticipated results: listening devices – two – and security cameras – three of them. The chances of his being able to assemble a bomb in such conditions were virtually nil. Or rather, they were *precisely* nil.

He needed to sleep and make up for some of the hours his body had been deprived of. He needed to recoup his strength. He lay down on the bed, filthy clothes on pristine bed linen, and the silence seemed to echo in his ears. It was such a stark contrast to the sirens that had wailed ceaselessly in his prison cell.

Despite his exhaustion, sleep would not overtake him, and he almost wondered if some substance had been mixed into something he had eaten or drunk. More likely, however, it was simply his deep yearning that was keeping him awake. He thought of his small home in the north of the country – the people he loved so deeply, the little *yishuv* that was so close to his heart – and anxiety gripped him.

They had been pursuing him, and that was why all of this had happened. Eyal turned onto his side, briefly letting the fear and anguish overpower him. What he wouldn't give to speak to Efrat, even briefly…

Eyal sat up and held his head in his hands. Regret for his past deeds stabbed at him like daggers. He had created a powerful name for himself, and that strength was what had led the president to appoint him as his chief bodyguard. That strength was also what had led these men to drag him into exile and to blackmail him in a manner that rendered him utterly helpless.

Weapons, technology, information, and even accomplices were simple to assemble. He could easily come up with a plan that would jolt the entire United States. As the president's bodyguard he would be granted free access almost everywhere, and X would provide him with anything the Americans couldn't or wouldn't. He could pull it off. And only his conscience, his freedom, and his family would pay the price.

"Eyal?" a voice whispered into the darkness and the door opened a crack. "Can I come in?"

It wasn't a question. There was no point in X pretending that he was trying to respect Eyal's privacy when his room was under constant surveillance, with not a single blind spot to exploit. Eyal looked away.

"I see that you can't fall asleep." X entered the room and flicked on the light. "Is it this mission that's disturbing you, or is it the safety of your wife and children?"

Eyal jumped off the bed, his eyes flashing. "Don't play the part of the compassionate professional, Mr. X. You're a bigger criminal than those Ukrainian interrogators. They beat my body and starved and tortured me, while you're plying me with fine drinks and soft linens, but they were doing their jobs and were on the right side of the law, while you're nothing more than a heartless criminal."

"So you want to return to prison?" X's emotions were masked.

"It would be better than working for you."

"Look here, Eyal." X signaled for him to sit down and face him. "I have no interest in torturing you, either physically or emotional-ly. I'm simply desperate here. You need to realize that."

"Desperate," Eyal repeated the word mockingly. Instead of re-sponding to X's motion for him to sit, he remained standing, fury blazing from his eyes.

"Exactly. I must – I absolutely need to do this."

"No one is forcing you to do anything."

"My brothers' blood is calling out to me. I've already explained that, Eyal. Hundreds of thousands, perhaps even millions, of peo-ple are being slaughtered in Syria, and no one cares. We've thought up a way to shift public opinion. It may not be easy, but I want you to acknowledge the fact that we have tried to do whatever we could to make this simpler for you."

"How very moving."

"I don't need you to be moved. I need you to understand my reasoning. Those interrogators, whom you claim were on the right side of the law, were acting out of egotistical considerations. They didn't beat you just because they thought that you were a murderer. They beat you because they wanted to get a confession out of you in order to close your file. They abused you because you were getting in their way. I, on the other hand, have chosen, voluntarily, to live a persecuted existence, in order to help other people build new lives."

"The end does not justify the means." Eyal said the words in Hebrew, and X looked at him in confusion. "What?"

"Nothing," Eyal whispered. He was emotionally drained. "Don't start trying to manipulate my feelings, okay? Because if I promise to work for you, you won't release my child just because of that promise."

"True. If we release him just because of a promise, then you'll do all that you can in order to escape." X smiled. "There's a reason we've chosen you. We've read about your past missions. You are a master of escapes. Among other things. We needed a bargaining chip, and we worked hard to get one. You wouldn't have acted any differently."

"I would never have toyed with the life of a child."

X shrugged. "We're treating him well. He doesn't have to emerge traumatized from this. But if you weigh one Israeli child's life against the lives of tens of thousands of Syrian children, then your question is moot, wouldn't you say?"

❧

Daylight was filtering in through the window, finally some proof that Eyal had fallen asleep at some point. He'd probably collapsed onto the bed a few minutes after X had left the room, though at that moment, he couldn't recall. After everything he'd been through, it was no wonder that his memory lapsed a bit. He washed his hands and got up to gaze through the bars on his window at the shining sun. If he knew where he was, perhaps he would be able to direct Eli and the Mossad team that he hoped beyond hope would be sent to extricate him.

No sun. Instead, a huge, ugly stone building blocked his view. The courtyard below was in an abandoned state, with wild grass poking out between the cracked paving stones. There was no way that he could see of identifying his location, and no way for him to contact anyone and let them know where he was.

A reassuring thought suddenly entered his mind: *There is Someone Who knows where you are...*

"Eyal?" X opened the door, and Eyal eyed the man with loathing as he sat down on a chair. "I understand that you hate me more than you've ever hated anyone else on the planet." X tried to soften his words with a beaming smile.

"How brilliant of you to reach such a realization." Eyal's words were laced with cold fury. "You are absolutely, completely on the mark."

"I'm going to try not to take this personally."

"Which would be a shame, because this is very personal."

"In that case, let's get to the point and stop wasting time on such personal and essentially petty matters. Our technology experts are currently meeting, and I think it's a good idea that you make their acquaintance."

"I don't remember offering to cooperate with you."

"Eyal," X said, his voice calm and patient. "Until now, you did seem to realize how serious we are. We will supply you with everything you ask for. We even brought your child here to see you. But we are very stubborn people."

"You'll provide me with everything I ask for?" There was a change in Eyal's tone of voice.

"Yes. Granted, of course, that you don't ask us to release the boy, or anything else that could enable your escape."

"In that case, I want to speak to my wife."

"Your wife?" X looked at him in surprise.

"Why are you so surprised? I haven't spoken to her since my arrest. She was worried enough about my disappearance, but now you've kidnapped her son. Can't you understand that what I want more than anything else is to calm her down?" He smiled bitterly. "As much as is possible, of course, under the circumstances."

X visibly wavered. "You know what? Come with me to our supply room, where you will find everything that you need to make the call." He moved toward the door. "Are you coming?"

Eyal followed X into an elevator with a concealed number panel. From what Eyal had been able to tell from his glance out the window, his room was two stories above ground level, but now the elevator went down at least three stories, which meant that they were in a basement of some sort.

The elevator door opened, and X led the way down a narrow corridor and into a medium-sized room that was full of equipment. X motioned to a chair and then gestured toward a man standing nearby, stiff as a statue. The man left the room. X fixed Eyal with a piercing stare. "Not a word, nor even a hint, of where exactly we are. You know the price you could pay for such stupidity. What language will you speak in?"

"I'll speak in English, and it's not like I know where I am anyway. But I won't hint at anything or give her any sort of clue," Eyal said wearily. "I would never play with my child's life in that manner."

"As far as we're concerned, you are free to converse in Hebrew. We have two people here who speak the language."

"It's fine." Eyal shrugged. He and Efrat both spoke a first-rate English. And he had his reasons for choosing that language.

X nodded in agreement, and a fully-armed man entered the room with a satellite phone.

"Telephone number," X said.

Eyal gave the number, and the armed man dialed. X handed him the receiver.

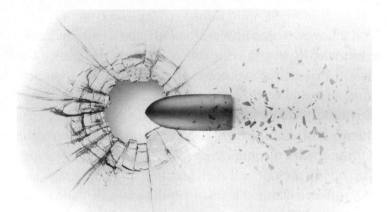

CHAPTER FIVE

Ukraine

One ring. Two. Three. Four. Eyal's heart beat wildly. He had never in his life been this nervous before speaking to another person. What would he tell her? What could he say?

"Shalom." Efrat's voice came on the line, and Eyal felt like he might collapse. This one phone call was about to accomplish what dozens of sessions of interrogation hadn't managed to achieve.

The blood drained from his face, and Eyal opened his parched lips. "Efrat," he said quietly.

"Yes. Who is this?" His voice was unclear over the secure line.

"It's me." Eyal said the words in English. He wanted X to understand every word.

"Eyal?" The fact that he had spoken in English almost certainly meant that someone was listening in to the conversation. But who might that person be? Efrat had no idea. Was this conversation going to be used against her, or Eyal? Maybe she was better off saying nothing with an eavesdropper?

"Yes."

"Where are you? What's happening to you? I heard—" Eavesdropper or not, she couldn't hold her words back. "Do you know...?" Suddenly, she stopped. Maybe he didn't know, and by asking, she would reveal the fact that she had told the intelligence agencies about Elitzafun's kidnapping.

Unaware of this aspect of the story, Eyal figured out immediately what she meant. "Yes. I know. He's here with me. He's fine. Totally fine. I promise you. And...I'm sorry." The word was so woefully inadequate that it was pitiful.

"With you? How? Why?" Efrat's relief was mingled with terrible fear.

"Yes, here in Ukraine. They kidnapped him because they want something from me. And I'm going to give it to them, so you don't have to worry. I give you my word that he's fine. I—" Should he apologize again? "Sorry" was such a wretched word.

"But...when are they going to release him? Is he really okay? Did you see him?"

"I saw him. And he's really, truly fine. He's getting food, snacks, and toys, and he has no idea that he's become a bargaining chip. He thinks he's on some kind of vacation. So...I'll be doing some work for these guys, and then he'll come home, *im yirtzeh Hashem*."

"What are they asking you—"

"Something that's difficult, complicated – it needs a lot of planning, but it will be okay. Everything will be fine. Don't worry, Efrat. Elitzafun is really okay. I'm okay. I...I'm really sorry that this happened."

"Don't blame yourself for being too good," she said. Her voice sounded choked, and he realized that she was holding back tears. His heart pounded with agony. What a mistake she had made in marrying him. "How are you managing to call me?"

"They allowed me to call you and speak to you, but they're listening to every word."

"Don't they have feelings? How can they play with the life of a five-year-old? How can they hurt a mother like this and blackmail a father?" It was clear to both Efrat and Eyal that she was speaking to the kidnappers, not to her husband.

"I'm sorry to have to hurt you, Mrs. Gilboa." X took the phone from Eyal's hand, and his powerful voice filled the room. "But you need to understand us. I am also a father, and I understand what a father's concern means. My children, my six-year-old, my four-year-old, and my one-year-old were killed a little over three years ago. In November of 2014 Assad's army wiped out my home, my children, and my life. Your child will return, I hope, but my children never will. My country is going through a holocaust, and no one cares."

X breathed heavily into the phone and Eyal tried to guess what was going through the man's mind. Certainly he had many painful memories that he would rather be able to forget.

"So, we found a way to shake up the world, and your husband is one of several people who can help us. Isn't that worth your child being slightly inconvenienced? I promise you that he won't come to any harm. He might be a bit shaken up, but we haven't laid a finger on him, other than to provide for his needs. We gave him toys and sweets and brought him to his father. If your nation had had the choice of causing one set of parents some discomfort eighty years ago, wouldn't they have chosen that over the tortures of the Holocaust?"

Efrat was not in a state of mind for considering philosophical questions. "If you want to prove to me that you're so humane, then release Elitzafun and accept my husband's promise that he will do whatever it is you're asking of him. There's no need to cause an innocent child to suffer!"

X shook his head. "Much experience has taught me that words alone are worthless. A father will do a much better job when his child's life is hanging in the balance."

"Eyal?" Efrat gave up trying to influence the kidnapper directly.

"Yes, Efrat?" It was hard for Eyal to get the words out.

"Come home safely." Her voice had a strong and unflinching quality to it now. "I'm praying for you."

"Thank you, Efrat. I'm sorry."

"Goodbye, Eyal."

There was the sound of the phone line disconnecting, and X looked at Eyal. "Satisfied?"

"It's ludicrous to describe what I felt as satisfaction, but it was okay."

"Are you now prepared to begin working on this project?"

Eyal nodded his head listlessly, his shoulders slumped in resignation.

"Good," X said briskly. He led Eyal into a conference room, and Eyal sat down at the head of the table, as X had instructed him. Eight men were seated around the table, and they eyed him with interest but refrained from addressing him directly.

"This is our man," X said curtly, before dismissing them. "Their work is largely done already," he noted, gesturing to the stacks of documents and maps on the table. "This is where you step in." X flicked a switch, and a large screen on the wall came to life. "First, you will review the president's movements as they have been summarized by my people. Then you will map out the various routes he takes when traveling to a variety of locations, with an eye out for spotting potential security breaches."

"You really think the president's security team will overlook a security breach?"

X smiled. "I didn't phrase myself precisely. You won't be finding the breach – you'll be creating it."

"Where's the list of presidential escorts?"

"Here."

Eyal looked over the names on the list. Aside from the president and a few choice cabinet members, there were journalists, drivers, security guards, and two doctors.

More lists were handed over to Eyal, and he focused on absorbing the information. The vehicles that would be used in the president's convoy, the types of weapons, the routes used...X's best men had compiled the information, and they had done an excellent job. Any information that might be useful in any sort of capacity was there. That in itself was suspicious – it suggested a leak from the president's inner circle, no less. Maybe the breach already existed and just needed to be widened and then exploited.

Hours passed. Eyal sifted through the information, separating the significant from the trivial, highlighting the most critical facts and setting aside pictures of important people.

"So," X said, sitting back down across from Eyal, several hours later. "Dazzle us with your plan. What have you come up with?"

"No – what have *you* come up with?" Eyal responded. "You surely gathered this information with a purpose in mind."

"I'm much more interested in hearing your ideas first."

Eyal shrugged. "There are several weak points in the president's plans." Eyal spoke quietly, knowing that he was digging a hole for himself by speaking and that if the president's team continued to overlook the points he had noted, his plan would "succeed" and he would most likely never see the light of day again. "The president's security measures are consistently tight, regardless of time or place. You know that. They keep every area covered, and it will make no difference if I'm just a member of the president's security team or his personal bodyguard. The Americans don't grant a single guard, and certainly not a newly arrived guard, enough authority to make any major decisions."

"So what have you come up with?"

"The compartmentalization is a weak spot. The president's bodyguards aren't told via what route the president will travel until the very last moment, and sometimes that could be too late. The men on the president's security team work in sync within the team, but across the entire staff, compartmentalization is their weak spot."

"Why?"

"Because if I alter the slightest bit of information being fed to each guard, no one will know the difference. The various members of the security team will accept any last-minute changes that I make at face value, because they're used to the fact that the president's route is subject to constant change, even, and perhaps especially, in the last few hours before he actually sets out. So, I believe that with extensive and coordinated advance preparation and cyberwarfare, we will be able to draw the president into our trap."

"An interesting plan." X leaned back and examined Eyal with satisfaction. "I didn't make a mistake in choosing you."

"It was the president's choice, not yours."

"True." X paused. "But the fact is that the president's capture won't be achieved according to the plan that you've just proposed. Instead, we have a much simpler plan in mind. You will booby-trap the hall with hidden explosives, using the methods that you've taught dozens of Mossad agents to use. And you will ignore that which you will see on the day of the conference."

Eyal fell silent. "When will you set the bomb to go off?"

"A beautiful question, to which your conscience wishes to know the answer, due to the fact that hundreds of people will be in attendance at the conference. Rest assured, however, that no one will be harmed."

"And what will I see on the day of the conference that you'd like me to ignore?"

"Ten or twelve armed men, whom you will allow into the hall. After you do that, your mission will be over. This is a big mission, but keep in mind that the starring role belongs to me. The spotlight will be on me alone, and I only need you to deal with the props, stage lights, sound, and pyrotechnics. The backdrop needs to suit the scene, because this will be one of the most exciting dramas the world has ever known."

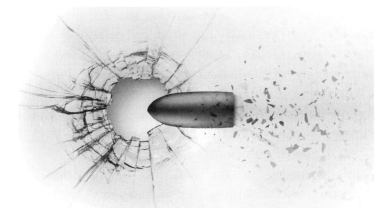

CHAPTER SIX

Israel

E frat choked back her tears and anguish as she placed an MP3 player, earphones, apple, and water bottle into her purse.

The phone call from Eyal had upended her emotional equilibrium, but it had been somewhat comforting as well. She had heard her husband's voice, and he had promised to do everything in his power to bring Elitzafun home. Her belief in his capabilities was what was calming her down now, even if that calm was extremely tenuous.

"You're going out?" her father asked.

"Yes."

"Good luck," he said quietly. "I don't know where you're going, and it's probably better that I don't know, but you should only have good *mazal* wherever you go."

"Thank you, Abba. I may not return until tomorrow. You'll send the children off to school, right?"

"Everything will be just fine, Efrati."

"Thanks, Abba. *L'hitra'ot.*" Efrat stepped outside. Her beautiful house, once the background to a tranquil life, had been built by Shemaryahu. She had spent so many peaceful years in that home, and now a storm was brewing there. Shemaryahu had built the house with a huge glass window, and Eyal had replaced the regular glass with bulletproof glass. He had also installed sophisticated security cameras on the roof, and he had mounted sensors all around. He had replaced the pens, papers, and batteries in the drawers with guns, bullets, and cartridges.

Life as she had known it had changed drastically upon her marriage to Eyal.

It was time to go.

As she approached her car, Efrat noticed her father-in-law standing nearby, a compassionate expression on his face.

"Hello," she said, startled.

"You're going out?" Her father had asked her the same question only minutes ago, but her father-in-law said the same words with an entirely different tone.

"Er...yes."

"Where to?"

"Central Israel."

"Why?"

The questions unnerved her, and she swallowed down her angry frustration as she reminded herself just how full of heartache her father-in-law's life was. She had been a partner to this lifestyle for less than two years, but her father-in-law had been experiencing similar emotions for many long years before that. She recalled how Eyal once told her about a cake that he had planned to make for his mother's birthday. He had been only ten at the time, and he had taken his father's car to get to the grocery store in order to buy the necessary ingredients...

It was safe to assume that Eyal had caused his parents quite a bit more heartache than what she herself had suffered.

Efrat shook herself and returned to the present. "Eyal called," she said quietly.

"*What?*" The almost shrill outburst didn't suit Menachem's quiet and reserved nature in the slightest. Efrat silently reprimanded herself for not telling her father-in-law earlier. She had almost forgotten that her husband had a tense and terrified father.

"I...I'm sorry I didn't tell you before. This only just happened, and I'm going to headquarters now in order to hand over the conversation. Not that I think it will help much, because the kidnappers gave Eyal a secure line to use, and they obviously didn't allow him to drop a single hint as to his exact whereabouts, but maybe they'll manage to find something there all the same."

"How did he call? Did he tell you that?"

"His captors allowed him to make the call. He didn't say much, but he did say that Elitzafun is okay and that he's with him."

"I see."

Efrat opened her car door. "If there are any new developments, please keep me posted," Menachem said.

"Of course," she said. "*Im yirtzeh Hashem.*" She fired the engine and headed down the street, gazing morosely through the windshield at the pristine peaks of Mount Gilboa, looming in the distance. "Oh, how the mighty have fallen. Eyal and Elitzafun, gone..." The road suddenly grew blurry before her eyes, and Efrat maneuvered onto the hard shoulder and stopped, in an attempt to pull herself together.

Removing a package of tissues from the glove compartment, Efrat dabbed at her eyes until she was calm enough to return to the road. Just before turning onto the Trans-Israel Highway, in an additional effort to calm down, she turned on some classical music.

When she reached the Kesem Interchange she paused. Should she continue along this route or keep going until the Nachshonim

Interchange? There were many ways of reaching the city of Petach Tikva, and even without Waze, which she hadn't turned on for fear of being tracked, she knew what her options were.

She knew exactly where the Mossad headquarters were located, as Eyal had given the information to her in the event that she would need it one day.

That day had now arrived.

Efrat passed the Yarkonim shopping center and turned right into the Segula industrial zone. How would she make contact with anyone at headquarters? The building wasn't accessible to regular citizens.

As she passed Rechov Alexander Yanai, Efrat noticed for the first time that a car was following her. Her eyes slid to the side, where she saw a motorcycle closing the distance between them. Two. Maybe more.

She was fairly confident that she could identify her trackers – again, because Eyal had explained the precise methods trackers used. "Trackers don't simply act as a tail," he had told her. "When someone is being tracked, there's a team at work. It's not a single person following, but rather multiple tails who are keeping track of the target and synchronizing their positions by radio. They rotate their roles, and as soon as one tracker leaves his position another tracker takes over, then a third and a fourth. By the time the first tracker reappears, the target has already forgotten what he looks like."

"So how can a layman figure out that he's being tracked?" Efrat had asked.

"By doing one of two things: Choice one, go on a shopping trip."

"Not bad."

"In a shopping center, or on any street with lots of businesses around, trackers will need to appear on the scene two or three times, or more. The longer the errand, the more trackers will be needed in order to remain undetected. No team has an endless supply of trackers, and so the longer the route, the more times the trackers will have to expose themselves. If you see the same blue Mazda, or man in sunglasses, four times, then you're most likely being followed."

"What is choice two?" Efrat had asked.

"Find a tracking detection spot – a spot where you can remain in for hours, which is also somewhere the tracker can't pass without exposing himself. There's an art in tracking someone. You don't just need to know how to track him; you also need to know when to back down so as to avoid detection."

At that point Efrat had grown impatient. "Enough," she had said. "The lesson on espionage is over for today."

Eyal had smiled, and Efrat remembered that smile now even as her heart missed a beat. Where was Eyal today?

So, Efrat was clearly being followed. Her trackers were making no attempt to conceal themselves. Only now did she recall that the motorcyclist had been close by since she passed the Kesem Interchange, and now there was a car too.

Her heart beat faster. She was on friendly territory, but...

On Rechov Habursekai the car's driver honked. Smiling, he gestured toward a stone building concealed by shrubs.

Relief, tinged with anger, filled her. She was sick of the espionage games.

The car passed her and motioned to the guard at the gate to let her in. As Efrat's car entered the compound, the motorcycle clung to her side like a shadow.

Car driver and motorcyclist both left their vehicles and approached Efrat's window. She opened it slowly.

"They're waiting for you," the car driver said.

"On the third floor in the room with the white door," the motorcyclist added.

She felt as though she were being manipulated and cheated, but still she felt happy. They had known that she would come, and they had set out in order to bring her in.

She stepped into the elevator, and, upon reaching the third floor, she looked out for the white door and knocked.

"Please come in, Mrs. Gilboa," a voice called out. Gingerly, Efrat pushed open the door and saw two men sitting across from each other at a desk.

The first man smiled. "My name is Zev Avshalom. I'm assuming you know who I am."

Efrat nodded.

"I'm Shaul Lerner," the second man introduced himself. "GSS head."

Efrat looked at the second man uncomprehendingly. "You're working together?" From what she had heard, there was no love lost between the Mossad and the GSS.

"Sometimes, when it becomes necessary, we do that," the Mossad chief said.

"For instance, in the case of a former Mossad agent sent on a mission for the GSS," Lerner commented. "Which is something so strange that it could only happen to Eyal."

"We anticipated that you would come here to ask about what we're doing for your son," Zev Avshalom said.

"I didn't come here to ask questions," Efrat said, pulling her MP3 player out of her bag. "I came to give you information."

The two men exchanged surprised glances, and Efrat pressed the playback button.

As Eyal's voice echoed through the room, the two men started, shocked. Frowning hard in concentration, they listened to the recording.

"What do you have to say about this?" Efrat asked, after the soundtrack had finished.

"Eyal hasn't left us a single clue," Zev Avshalom said.

"So I noticed."

"He was obviously worried for his son." Lerner sighed. "And of course, there's no background noise or static."

"There is someone who might be able to help us with this,"

Avshalom said slowly. "But he's in Ukraine, putting a search team together for Eyal."

"Eli," Efrat said quickly.

"Exactly. He and your husband have been together on so many missions in the past that perhaps he'll be able to pick up something in Eyal's words that is suggestive, something we are overlooking."

"That's why I'm here," Efrat said. "Because I thought you might be able to identify a clue. You trained Eyal. You created the legend called Eyal Gilboa. You know him better than his own father. I was hoping that one of you would be able to spot something between the lines."

Ukrainian-Israeli Phone Line

"Eli." It was rare for Mossad Chief Zev Avshalom to dial his agent's number.

"Have you heard from Eyal?" In his excitement, Eli knocked over his cup of coffee. He hurriedly picked up the papers beside it so they wouldn't get soaked through.

"How did you guess?"

"Why else would you call?" Eli quickly placed the papers on a nearby chair.

"We have a recording that we need you to listen to. Try to see if you can make out some sort of hint." Zev Avshalom had Eren, from the communications department, send the recording directly to Eli's computer.

Tense as a spring, Eli opened the audio file and listened. "Are you really so dense?" he shouted when it finished. "He told you exactly what to do!"

"What?" Zev Avshalom and Shaul Lerner asked.

"His son is with him, and that's the clue that he planted. Eyal's being tracked by the Angels of Peace. If they know where he is, then they know where Elitzafun is too."

"Yes. But Ford wasn't exactly cooperative when it came to your tracking Eyal down via him."

"True, but he'll cooperate now, because a kidnapped child won't look good in the photos. And I'll blame his organization in the media. Anything related to the kidnapping, and to his sending Eyal to commit a murder, will be lumped together. Some people might be tempted to suggest that he brought this upon himself and that he deserved this, and more, but all the rules have changed now that there's a child in the picture."

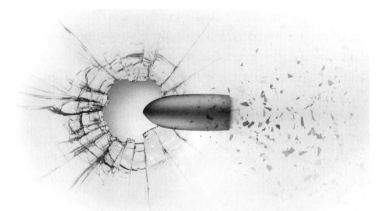

CHAPTER SEVEN

Ukraine

In his new safe house – or rather, apartment – Eli slumped down on a chair and frowned. He wasn't satisfied with the security arrangements here, and without Eyal's reassuring presence at his side, he was wracked with doubts. He was 94 percent certain that he hadn't been tracked to this new hideout, and business was too urgent to worry about the other six percent. In time, he would try to take care of it. In the meantime, he had to run the risk.

He grimaced at the computer on the desk and then opened it. It was Eyal's laptop and he knew the passwords. And he was furious. These men had trapped Eyal, sending him from one prison to another for their own purposes. They had to be stopped, somehow. If only he knew how…

He activated the first code, then the second and the third.

Finally, he opened the program and sent a high-priority message to Ford: *If you don't tell me where Eyal is I will publicize the fact that you are connected to this kidnapping.*

Ford's response came within minutes.

Ford: *What are you talking about?*

Eli: *Don't pretend to be innocent. Your people have kidnapped Eyal's son.*

Ford: *No, we haven't.*

Eli: *Are you so sure about that? Why does it seem to me that you're involved here?*

Ford: *You are mistaken.*

Eli: *So it's not your organization then. But you're tracking Eyal's every move. Tell me where he is at this minute, so I can find him and release his son.*

Ford: *I can do no such thing.*

Eli: *Either you tell me where he is, or tomorrow morning the fact that the Fraternity is connected to the kidnapping of the child will appear in every newspaper in the world.*

Ford: *Allow us to consider the various factors at play here, and we will let you know.*

Eli: *My fingers are hovering over the keyboard. You have ten minutes to reach a decision.*

Ford's name blinked and faded, and Eli waited impatiently for ten minutes to pass. A demon within him was hoping that Ford wouldn't give in to his demands, so that the story of the Fraternity could finally be splashed across the world. Cold logic, however, told him that if that happened, Eyal would be the first to suffer and Elitzafun would be the second.

Nine minutes and fifty seconds.

Ford's name flashed across the screen.

Ford: *We have decided that we cannot tell you where Eyal is. Before publicizing everything that you know, however, sip slowly from a cool glass of water and calm down. Making this story known will cause unimaginable damage, as I assume that the moment the kidnapping becomes public knowledge, the kidnappers will murder the child involved.*

Furious, Eli slammed the computer shut, nearly smashing the screen. With trembling fingers he dialed Uri's number.

"Uri, Ford won't cooperate."

"So forget about him and that bunch of posers. We'll send you a team of men and we'll locate him for you. It shouldn't be difficult to discover where he is. What will be difficult is finding a way to release him."

Eli sighed. "So I'm finally going to meet our agents in the Ukraine?"

"We have many collaborators, and I wouldn't trust all of them with such a sensitive mission. But there is one wonderful agent by the name of Vitali Lamberg. He holds a senior position in Rubinov's mafia. Be in touch with him, and maybe he'll suggest some trustworthy locals as well."

Boris, Eli thought.

"Once we figure out where the kidnappers are located, we'll send you all the technical help you need. Just don't do anything stupid on your own. I know I can usually trust you, Eli, but this time your emotions are controlling you, and remember what your training taught you about that."

Spare me the speech, Eli thought. But because he wanted to spare himself the pep talk – "Rule number one for a spy who's emotions have gotten the better of him..." – he said nothing.

"Where will I meet him?" he asked quietly.

"He'll contact you."

"I'll be waiting for the phone call," Eli said. He was unapologetic regarding the clear breach of Mossad authority.

Ukraine

"You forgot something." There was undeniable admiration in X's eyes, but Eyal was unmoved. Eli would have said that Eyal was simply accustomed to being admired all the time, but that wasn't it. *I'm unimpressed by X's admiration,* Eyal told the Eli in his mind, *not because this man is a wicked kidnapper and I don't want admiration from a lowly creature of that sort, but because the source of that admiration is what got me – and Elitzafun – into this mess in the first place.*

"I know," Eyal said weakly. "I forgot to tell the president that I'm providing him with security."

X was astonished. "How did you know?"

Eyal shrugged. "I could guess. If Russia says I killed Rubinov, then America makes a point of not believing it. Otherwise, we could have assumed that the assignment is off. That would make more sense, but not when you account for conspiracy theories and certain high-placed members of the president's inner circle who are heavily influenced by such notions. And so..." Eyal sighed. "It's not over yet."

There was a knock on the door of the conference room, and John opened it. Leon was standing there with Elitzafun at his side. X raised his eyebrows questioningly.

"We told the boy that his father is busy, but he insisted on seeing him," Leon said.

"Good, good." X relaxed his stiff shoulders. "It's important that we make sure the child stays happy. There is no reason to cause him any pain."

Elitzafun glanced at X and then ran toward his father and sat down on his lap. Eyal winced as Elitzafun's foot brushed painfully against an injured spot, but he said nothing, hugging his stepson to him and allowing him to rest his small head on his shoulder.

"Are you bored, Elitzafun?"

"No. There are more toys here than we have at home. But I missed you."

"So how about bringing one of your games here to play."

"Okay." Elitzafun slid off Eyal's lap and hurried to the door. "You're very busy, right, Abba?"

"Yes, I am. Very, very busy."

"You always are." The child sighed with resignation. "I'll be back, Abba. Don't worry."

Elitzafun disappeared, and X fixed Eyal with a look of pride and satisfaction. "You see? We're looking after your child wonderfully. We have absolutely no intention of harming him."

"You have me moved to tears, as usual," Eyal said.

"Back to the point. We need you to call Bentzy to tell him that everything is fine. You've run away from prison, and you will be providing the president with security as planned."

"Bentzy isn't a baby. One phone call to the Mossad and he'll figure out everything that's going on."

"Your wife was warned against letting anyone know."

"I think you're smart enough to realize that she contacted the Mossad regardless. You can be as furious as you like, but someone at the Mossad knows what's going on – no doubt about it. You would never remain silent if it was your own child who had been kidnapped."

"If the kidnappers threatened me—"

"Then you still wouldn't sit around and do nothing. I'm working on the assumption that my wife went to the Mossad and that therefore Bentzy will realize, within moments, that I'm being blackmailed."

"So what do you suggest in that case? No one is going to pay any attention to an anonymous message sent to the White House."

"Let me think of an inconspicuous way to get the message to Bentzy."

Elitzafun chose that moment to return with a Lego police station. He scattered the pieces about beside his father's feet and began his construction in silence. Eyal and X spoke in hushed tones.

"You've disqualified my plan," X said. "So now come up with one of your own."

"I'm going to speak to Bentzy," Eyal said, carefully examining the thoughts running through his mind. "But I won't tell him that I managed to run away. I'll tell him that I'm still in hiding, and that he shouldn't tell anyone that he spoke to me. Then I'll ask him to get everything ready for my arrival."

X wrinkled his forehead. He was suspicious of any plan that Eyal came up with independently. His talents were what had caused the president, and himself, to select him, but those very same talents demanded caution. "He'll listen?" X said.

"Yes. Bentzy trusts me. He won't say anything to anyone."

"And he won't be wary of your not turning up in the end?" X asked, gratefully accepting a cup of black coffee that one of his men held out to him. He pointed to the beverage and asked Eyal if he wanted a cup of his own.

"No," Eyal said shortly, getting back to the subject at hand. "Bentzy knows me. If I tell him I'm coming, then as long as I'm alive I will come."

"Good." X handed Eyal his satellite phone. "Call Bentzy."

"Now?"

"Now."

A flash of hesitation appeared on Eyal's face, but he took the phone and dialed the number.

"Hello." An enthusiastic voice greeted him.

Eyal drew a deep breath. "Hello, Agent Shein. This is Eyal Gilboa speaking."

A moment of shock and then a shriek. "Eyal!! Where are you calling from?!"

"It doesn't matter. I'm not in jail anymore, but I'm not exactly a free man either. Don't tell a soul – not my wife, and certainly no one from the Mossad – that you spoke to me.

The satellite phone might have been distorting the sound waves, but Eyal's use of certain terms that he and Bentzy had agreed upon years ago left no room for doubt. The man on the other end of the line was certainly Eyal Gilboa.

"Fine. But Eyal, why?"

"I'll explain it to you when we meet."

"Meet? We're going to meet?" Bentzy made no attempt to hide

his excitement. "Are you serious? Where are you?"

"I'm between the shards and the bullets, like in days gone by. And *im yirtzeh Hashem*, I'll be in the United States in a few days' time to act as the president's bodyguard, just as we originally planned."

"Eyal, just yesterday the president handed the job over to Bernie." Bentzy said. The head of the president's personal security team wasn't someone he wanted to confront.

"I see. Please remind the president of his request for me to come and provide him with secuirty. Tell him that I'm willing to do him a favor and come. I'll call again in a few hours to find out if I should cancel my tickets because Bernie will be in charge, or if everything is ready for my arrival."

"I'll find out."

"Thanks, Bentzy. And I need not repeat that this is classified, right?"

"What if the president asks?" Bentzy said.

"Tell him that things are compartmentalized. He knows how much compartmentalization goes on at the Mossad." A light chuckle. "Even if you're not a Mossad agent anymore."

"Eyal, it doesn't work that way with the president," Bentzy said.

"There's compartmentalization within the CIA as well, and as I see it, he wants me on his team very, very badly."

"You're seeing correctly."

One of X's fully armed silent men brought Eyal back to his room. Surrounded by sophisticated equipment and an array of maps, Eyal pored over the information that he needed. On a small bed on the other side of the room, Elitzafun lay asleep. Looking from the computer to his son, Eyal felt a tremor overtake him. He had been the one to ask for the child's bed to be moved into his room, and he had paid for that request by being moved into a different room with a steel door and a triple lock. X had explained that Eyal couldn't remain in a room with a wooden door together with his son because he could so easily bust the door open and escape with him. And so Eyal had happily agreed to be locked into a room, if only to remain with the boy.

Slowly, Eyal approached his stepson's bed, sitting down gently at the edge and stroking his hair. None of the escape maneuvers and drills that he had executed over the course of his career had included a child. And this child was his. When he married Efrat he had agreed to take care of her children as his own. He needed to bring this child home safely, and it made no difference what price he would have to pay.

Eyal's gentle strokes woke Elitzafun up. "Abba," he said drowsily.

"Yes, sweetie."

"Where's Ima?"

"Ima…" Eyal attempted to inject a note of gaiety into his voice. "She's not here. It's just you and me here right now."

"When will we see Ima?"

"In another few days. I need to be here for work, and I missed you so much that I asked them to bring you here."

"But I miss Ima," Elitzafun said. "You saw me enough already. Now I want to go back to Ima."

"In another few days," Eyal repeated. His heart felt as though it were breaking. "I don't have anyone to send you with in the meantime. So we need to wait until I finish here, and then we'll go back together."

"We can't do things a different way?" A part of Elitzafun understood, either from maturity or from naivete, that there was no different way.

Eyal smiled in an attempt to cover his anguish, fears, and pain. "There is no other way."

"You know, Abba…" Elitzafun shook himself slightly and looked at his father, fully awake now. "My friend Neria was surprised when he heard that I call you Abba. He doesn't call his father Abba. He calls him Yishai."

"Why?"

"Because Yishai isn't Neria's real father. He just married his mother. And you're also not my real father."

Eyal was stunned. Of all the children, Elitzafun hadn't batted an eyelash when he had been asked to call Eyal "Abba." He had been just three years old when he lost his father, and Eyal had assumed that he'd replaced the void almost seamlessly. Eyal hadn't thought, not for a moment, that Elitzafun didn't consider him to be his father. Elitzafun had always innocently accepted their relationship and made it seem so natural! He touched his son's hair and stroked his soft cheek. "I am your father. I adopted you when I married your mother."

"Right. But Neria, and other kids like him, don't call their stepfather Abba. They call them by their real names."

"And you?"

"I don't want to do that." Elitzafun lay back down on his bed. "I don't want to call you Eyal. I want to call you Abba. Because you are my father. You're my only father in the world, and I love you."

"I'm glad."

Elitzafun closed his eyes. "Because you don't have children, right?"

"I'm not happy for me. I'm happy for you. Because it makes you happy." But Eyal found himself speaking to himself. Elitzafun had fallen asleep. And Eyal remained awake, gently stroking his child's cheek. His child who loved him.

CHAPTER EIGHT

Ukrainian-Israel Phone Line

I just want you to know what your son-in-law is going through." Eli had called Eyal's house hoping that his father-in-law, not his wife, would answer the phone. In the end it had been Elishama who had picked up the phone, and he passed it on to his grandfather.

Rafi, outside and weeding the garden to pass the time, scowled when he heard what the man on the other end of the line wanted. This agent was searching for his grandson, and he also just so happened to be one of his son-in-law's best friends.

"I don't want to hear it." Rafi's voice was a mixture of bitterness and fury.

"Just listen to what I have to say," Eli said. He was pacing around his safe house like a caged lion. As he passed from the door to the window and back to the door, the walls of the small apartment seemed to close in on him. As soon as he'd heard Uri mention that Eyal's father-in-law was blaming Eyal himelf for his grandson's kidnapping, Eli had decided to throw caution to the winds and speak to Rafi. "I'm sure you can do with some regards from your family."

"Fine," Rafi said shortly, putting down the weed hacker. A lot of good that work in the garden would do for his daughter, who was currently disassociated from anything and everything. "When did you see him?"

"I saw him in prison, after he'd been through two days of torture."

A crack appeared in the otherwise icy demeanor. "Why? Who tortured him?"

"Ukrainian police interrogators. They're all KGB expats, and they were determined to get a confession out of him at all costs, as well as whatever other information they could get."

"They wanted him to confess to murder." The crack in Rafi's voice froze over again. "I heard about that." The few words failed to do justice to the shock he had felt upon hearing the media report about his son-in-law's arrest for the murder of one of the world's most influential political leaders. Rafi balled up his fist. And that had been before Elitzafun's kidnapping... *Plenty of nachas we're seeing from this son-in-law*, he thought wryly.

"Eyal did not commit the murder that he was indicted for. Trust me."

"Oh, really?" About ten notes of disbelief barged into Rafi's voice. "So, the entire Ukrainian security establishment is wrong, and only you are right?"

Eli gritted his teeth in an effort to remain calm. "Actually, yes. I was there, and I know."

"In that case, why aren't you doing anything with your superior knowledge?" Rafi said, his tone of voice ambiguous, leaving Eli trying to figure out if his words had been spoken with hope or with scorn.

"Because as of yet, I have no concrete proof. That's why I'm still here – to find evidence, hard evidence that the Ukrainians will accept."

"Looks like there's no point in that anymore." Rafi kicked at the dirt in the flower beds. "Unless he's still in Ukrainian hands, which seems unlikely."

"Yes, but…that isn't why I decided to call you. I wanted to tell you about my meeting with Eyal when he was still in prison."

Rafi sat down on a bench and gazed unseeingly into the distance. "So tell me," he said, still trying to maintain the scornful note in his voice even as his innards shrank.

"I won't bother to describe the bruises on his face and arms, which told me something about the way he'd been treated. And I won't tell you about how they were starving him – how he hadn't eaten for two days. I'm sure you're not interested either in how he was kept in handcuffs twenty-four hours a day. And yet, despite his suffering, the first thing he asked of me wasn't to hire him a top lawyer or to try to get the Ukrainians to ease up on his prison conditions. No – all he wanted to tell me was to make sure to call his wife to put her mind somewhat at rest, because he couldn't call her as he had promised he would."

Rafi's fingers gripped the phone tightly. He got up and started to pace around the garden, nausea overtaking him. "Just…just bruises? Nothing worse?"

"Hearing all the gory details won't be good for your heart. So just pray that he comes home in one piece so he can tell you about it himself."

"But Elitzafun…"

"Yes, Elitzafun," Eli said. "We are doing everything we can to bring him back, but – Mr. Frisher – please don't blame my friend. Because he, more than anyone else, would be doing his absolute best, and more, in order to bring your grandson home safely."

"If he wasn't…" Rafi couldn't find the words.

"If he wasn't such a walking intelligence agent legend? Is that what you want to say? That if his reputation wasn't what it is, this wouldn't have happened? That may be true, but it's unreasonable to blame a person for being too good."

"I'm not looking to blame Eyal," Rafi said. "I just want to see my grandson come back home safely, and I'm angry at anyone and anything related to his disappearance."

"I hope we'll manage to release him, so that your son-in-law doesn't have to pay a high price," Eli said quietly, choosing his words with care. "Because there is no price that he wouldn't pay for Elitzafun, and that includes his freedom and his life."

Israel

Evening came, but with no accompanying sense of calm. Efrat's mother had prepared her grandchildren's favorite meal – spicy shakshuka, freshly squeezed orange juice, and home-baked pitas.

The fragrant smells brought her grandchildren bounding into the kitchen.

"What did you make, Savta?"

Reut turned away from her grandchildren so as not to notice the absence of the youngest one. Elitzafun was the most mischievous of Efrat's children. She could easily picture him scampering onto the counter and peeking curiously into the frying pan – unless a butterfly had suddenly caught his attention and he was hopping from chair to chair in order to capture it. Where was the owner of the sweet voice who would now be saying: "I don't like it with so many spices, Savta." Where was that child?

"*Pitot* with onions and shakshuka!" She tried to inject a note of joy into her voice, but failed. "Who's going to wash first?"

Chagelet and Elishama raced toward the sink and then sat down to eat. "When will Abba be back, Ima?" Chagelet asked her mother. "I haven't spoken to him in so long."

If only he could speak, Efrat thought. *If only he could say something, give us a sign of life.*

"I hope he'll be calling soon," she told her daughter, an exaggerated note of nonchalance in her voice. "You know how busy he is."

"He's always busy," Chagelet grumbled into her orange juice. "It's too much!"

Absolutely, dear daughter. It's too much for me too.

"He's doing important things," Efrat said, but even she knew that her voice lacked conviction. "You know that he loves you a lot more than his work, but sometimes his work does take him far away. He's sorry about that too, sweetie. A lot sorrier than you are."

"Fine," Chagelet said. "But let him at least call!"

The children finished eating, and after *Krias Shema* and a story that should have been full of suspense but was instead boring and choppy sounding, they fell asleep.

Back in the kitchen, Reut noted that Efrat's plate was still full. Efrat, sitting on the couch in the living room, was folding laundry with glazed eyes that only came into focus when she saw Elitzafun's socks.

Watching her daughter from the kitchen, Reut's heart clenched in fear. Maybe they should hide Elitzfun's clothes somewhere, so that...

Enough!! Despite the fact that the shout hadn't emerged from her lips, it felt almost real. *Stop it!* Reut chided herself. *Elitzafun will be back! He'll be back!!*

Entering the living room, Reut approached her daughter with faltering steps. "Efrat," she said, "you need to eat something."

Efrat looked up with dull eyes. "How do you expect me to eat when I don't know what, or if, my son is eating?"

Reut pursed her lips in order to contain her sigh and tears. As Efrat's mother, she needed to be the strong one. "You said that Eyal told you they're treating him decently," she said quietly. "Maybe go out for a short walk to calm down, and then come back. Call Galit and ask her to go with you. The fresh air will do you a world of good."

"Maybe." Efrat pursed her lips together, revealing the stubborn streak she had displayed since childhood. "Ima, one of Eyal's friends called Abba to tell him that he saw him in jail. He said that Eyal had been tortured and starved for days. Even now, I don't know how his captors are treating him. They're treating Elitzafun well, but who knows what they're doing with Eyal himself? How can I eat fancy food while he's not even being allowed a drink of water? How can I take a walk in the fresh air while he's shut up in a basement somewhere? I can't do it, Ima. I just can't."

"Abba told you this?" Reut said, wondering at the wisdom of sharing such information with their daughter.

"No, but I heard him on the phone." Unbeknownst to her father, she had listened in on the conversation, lifting the phone after it rang and staying on the line even though she immediately realized that the conversation wasn't meant for her ears. What she had done was quite wrong, she knew, but she hadn't been able to stop herself.

"How many times have I told you not to eavesdrop," her mother said, forgetting momentarily that her daughter was no longer a ten-year-old, or a teenager.

"Ima, this is about my husband and my son. Until they return, I have no life. I'm a living widow and a bereft mother of a living child. This is no life!"

"But you need to go on living," Reut said. "Efrati, if not for yourself, then you need to be strong for your other two children."

Efrat trembled. "I hope the children haven't figured out the truth." They had decided to tell them that Eyal had traveled abroad for his work and that Elitzafun had gone to his uncle Menashe's home in Yerushalayim. The children had immediately protested this blatant display of favoritism, and so she had promised to give them each their own turn to make the special trip as well.

"I'm sure they realize that something is going on, but they're children, and as long as you do your best to create an atmosphere of calm strength, they'll carry on with their lives."

"But I can't create a calm atmosphere! I'm anything but calm. And I don't have strength either. My energy is gone, completely gone."

"Create some energy then," Reut said. "You were always strong, Efrat. Remember how much happiness and hope you brought into this home after Shemaryahu—" She stopped upon seeing the expression on Efrat's face. What else would her daughter need to go through? "Don't break down now, Efrati...go for a walk, breathe new air into this house. Eyal and Elitzafun need a happy home to come back to."

"*If* they come back."

"They'll come back! They'll come back to a house of happiness and joy."

"Amen."

Galit, Efrat's friend, knocked at the door of the house and suggested that she come out for a walk. Efrat suspected that her mother was behind the invitation, but she nonetheless chose to respond to the voice of reason in her head and accept the invitation.

Water bottles in hand, the two women left Efrat's home for the road around the *yishuv*. They walked together in silence, breathing in the scents around them: the crocus, the meadow saffron, and the cool, refreshing air after the dense summer heat. Galit knew exactly what was on Efrat's mind, yet she was mindful of her friend's right to remain silent. There was a great healing power in silence between friends, and the quiet walk was like a balm to Efrat's soul.

After parting from Galit, Efrat made her way through the vineyards that Shemaryahu had planted in order to reach her home.

Eyal had tried, unsuccessfully, to maintain those vineyards, but his shortcomings in that area had brought him back to the field of intelligence.

Nonsense. He had returned to intelligence work because of the passion for danger and battle that flowed through his veins. People like him couldn't sit quietly and work at any job that was free of tension and risk. The fact that he had come as far as he had in his career was proof that he was simply good at what he did.

She was so torn in her feelings toward Eyal. On the one hand she pitied him. She had pitied him even before overhearing that conversation between his friend and her father, but she pitied him even more afterward. And yet, she was very, very angry. Had he not returned to intelligence work, she wouldn't have been made to suffer in this way. Her son would have remained at her side, and Eyal wouldn't have been arrested for murder and forced to carry out who-knows-what in order to be allowed to return home.

Slowly, Efrat trod through the vineyard, looking down at the tracks her feet left in the earth. The Mossad agents had said that this was the route that Elitzafun's kidnappers had taken. Who would bring him back?

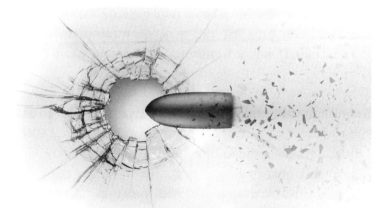

CHAPTER NINE

Ukraine

E litzafun." Eyal settled his son down beside him and whispered into his ear. "I need you to help me." He had to proceed on the assumption that the message that he had threaded into his phone conversation had not been understood. Or maybe it had been understood but the Fraternity members had been uncooperative. Either way, he would have to act independently and plan his escape alone.

"How?" Elitzafun asked.

"Soon X will come by and ask you if you want anything," Eyal began. Engaging his son's assistance was extremely risky, but making no attempt to escape was even riskier.

"I want to go to the zoo," Elitzafun said quickly.

"I know, but he's not going to let you do that. Instead, I want you to ask X for a remote-control car."

"But I don't want a remote-control car. I want a gigantic Playmobil castle with soldiers," Elitzafun said. "I already told him that's what I want. Do you think he's going to get it for me soon?"

Eyal picked up the little boy and hugged him, overcome by both love and despair. "Tell him that you want a remote-control car anyway, okay?" he said, murmuring the words softly, his lips barely moving.

"Why?"

"Because if you want to go home to Ima, you need to ask for that."

"I do want to go home to Ima," Elitzafun said quickly. "I don't need Playmobil, only Ima."

"Right." Eyal looked deeply into his son's eyes. "And when you ask for the car, you won't say that I told you to ask for it, okay? It was your idea."

"Okay."

"And if X says you can't have it, then you have to ask again," Eyal insisted, knowing that once Elitzafun was fixated on being given something he wanted, there wasn't much hope of getting him to back down. It was this aspect of his character that Eyal was counting on.

"Yes, sure." Elitzafun nodded his enthusiastic agreement.

"Okay, so now, let's daven like you do in preschool," Eyal said. Together, they started to daven. Elitzafun warbled an off-key version of *Adon Olam*, with Eyal none the wiser. The tune that every chareidi three-year-old could trill even in his sleep was completely unfamiliar to him. *Shema Yisrael… Ve'ahavta… Ani maamin.*

X entered the room, stopping in the doorway to watch the scene of Elitzafun sitting and chanting on his father's lap, neither of them paying any attention to his arrival. When Elitzafun finally fell silent, X turned to him with a smile. "You were praying?" he asked, his tone friendly.

Elitzafun nodded.

"I too used to pray with my son." A shadow passed over X's otherwise iron expression, but then the man shook himself as if to get rid of the memory. "Do you want some new toys to play with?" he asked Elitzafun.

"Yes. I want a remote-control car."

"Specifically remote control?" X looked from Elitzafun to his father, who simply shrugged.

X turned back to the boy. "Elitzafun, there's not much room here to drive a car. How about something else instead?"

As Eyal had predicted, the suggestion went down extremely badly. Right on cue, the boy started up a high-pitched wail. "No! I want a car! I don't want anything else! You told me I can have what I want! I want a car!"

"Okay, okay – calm down!" X appeared taken aback at the intensity of the child's reaction. "I'll send someone to buy one for you. Do you want anything else?"

"Yes. Chocolate milk." Elitzafun voice instantly dropped ten decibels.

"Coming right up." X smiled, but Eyal had the distinct feeling that he would rather have slapped him. Turning to Eyal, X continued: "And what do you want?"

"Nothing," Eyal said.

"We're not interested in having you play the part of the suffering martyr, Eyal."

"Fine." Eyal spoke slowly, as though convinced. "In that case, get me an electric kettle, a cup, a spoon, Brazilian coffee beans, and a coffee grinder produced by the German company Graef or the Japanese company Hario."

"Brazilian coffee beans! And a German coffee grinder! Only the best for you Eyal, eh?"

"I can't drink coffee without a kosher symbol on it any other way."

X grimaced. "I don't like it."

Eyal shrugged. "You asked me what I wanted," he said, "but

if you can't provide me with something as simple as coffee, then I can drink water or juice instead."

"I'll try and get you coffee beans and a simple coffee grinder. As for making the coffee though, how about my men take care of that? We'd prefer to avoid giving you access to wires from an electric kettle. There's too much you can do with those, as I'm sure I don't need to remind you."

"A Jew is forbidden to eat food that was prepared by a non-Jew," Eyal said, hoping that X wasn't well-versed in the intricacies of kashrus observance. "In any case, you monitor my every move, twenty-four hours a day, so what exactly do you think I can do while you're watching me? Why the paranoia?"

X's eyes narrowed. "You'll get your electric kettle," he said brusquely. He turned to Elitzafun and smiled. "And your father will make you a cup of chocolate milk just the way you like it."

"Make sure the milk is kosher," Eyal reminded him.

"Fine." X left the room. It took an hour, but eventually a knock at the door revealed John with a tray in his hands. Wordlessly, he handed it over and left. Eyal placed the tray on the table. So far, just the kettle, a cup, and a spoon, but when he saw that the spoon he had asked for was made of metal, his heart soared.

Eyal went over to the small fridge and removed a can of Coke. "Elitzafun," Eyal said. Elitzafun was in the middle of building a Clics tower. Toys, Eyal had noticed, were X's strong point – aside from blackmail, weaponry, and technology, that is. "Do you want to drink some Coke?"

"Why Coke? I thought you were going to make me a drink of chocolate milk."

"I'll make you that too, soon, but maybe you'd like to drink some Coke in the meantime?" Eyal bent down and took a can of peach juice out of the fridge. "Or maybe you'd like this instead?"

Elitzafun shook his head. "I like Coke better."

"Fine. And now let's have a race to see who finishes the drink in his can first."

"Yay!" Elitzafun said with excitement. "Ima never lets us play games with food. But if it's a race, then I want the juice. Because you can't drink Coke fast."

Eyal pulled open both cans, placed them on the table, and chanted out loud, playfully: "On your mark, get ready, get set, go!"

Elitzafun and Eyal both recited *brachos* and then quickly started to drink from their cans. Eyal slowed his pace to match his son's, and then to allow him to win. Elitzafun kept on spluttering over his drink, which spurted onto the floor with Eyal clapping him on the back every time he choked. By the time they finished, both of them were laughing so hard that they had tears in their eyes.

"Wow!" Elitzafun said, after his breathing had returned to normal and he saw the juice that he had sprayed all over the floor, table, and chair. "Look at this mess."

"Don't worry about it. Ima isn't here to tell you to clean up afterward..." Eyal shook himself, but when he spoke again, it was in that same offhanded tone of voice. "Elitzafun, how about we start a can collection? Look at all of these cans with funny Ukrainian letters on them. None of your friends have cans like these."

"Great idea!" Elitzafun agreed. "Chagelet will be really jealous. Cans are much better than her stupid sticker collection."

"We can look for stickers for Chagelet too," Eyal said. "But these cans will be yours."

There was a knock at the door, and Colin appeared. "X wants you."

Eyal got to his feet. "Elitzafun, soon they'll bring you the toy you asked for, and in the meantime, stay here and build a tower with your Clics, okay? I'll be back soon."

Elitzafun nodded, but a cloud appeared on his face. "When will you be back?"

"As quickly as I can."

Eyal and Colin left the room and headed toward the elevator. Eyal's trained eyes roamed over the walls and ceiling, creating a precise mental sketch of the house. That information could one day save his life and the life of his son.

When Eyal returned to his room he found Elitzafun dancing around a medium-sized box, a gleeful expression on his face. "Look at what a big car they bought me!" Elitzafun called out. "It's the biggest I ever saw."

Eyal pinched Elitzafun's cheek lightly. "Let's open the box and see if it's only the box that's big, or if the car's big too." He hoped it wasn't too big – ideally, it would be something he could hide on his body.

Elitzafun started to pull at the cardboard and eventually managed to get it open. Inside, the car was a beautiful shade of metallic maroon. It was bigger than Eyal had been hoping, but as he examined it he saw that the entire roof of the car could be removed so as to dramatically decrease its size. The remote control itself was a new and sophisticated model, and Eyal wondered how X had failed to foresee all the options he had provided him with.

"What are you looking at?" Elitzafun grumbled. "Let's play already."

Eyal inserted the batteries – thoughtfully included in the package – and soon Elitzafun had figured out how to maneuver the car around the room. Eyal opened the trundle bed beneath the main bed, creating a step of sorts. He picked up the car and placed it on his bed. "Let's see if it can go down," he told Elitzafun, taking the remote control from him and jerking the lever.

To Elitzafun's excitement and Eyal's relief, the car flipped over on the makeshift step and then turned over again before continuing onward.

"Let me play with the car, Abba," Elitzafun said. "You're playing with it too much."

Eyal handed the remote control back to Elitzafun, and the boy started to guide it around in a circle. They played together until they were interrupted by knocks on the door.

"X told me to give you this." Ahmed handed Eyal a simple coffee grinder and a bag of intoxicating-smelling coffee beans. He was about to place them on the table when he turned to look at Elitzafun. "It looks like you're having a good time," he said.

"I like playing with Abba," Elitzafun said, his eyes shining. Eyal hoped that his plans for the following evening would not cause the flicker in his son's eyes to dim forever. *Hashem*, he prayed, *please don't allow this incident to leave a lifelong mark of trauma on him. Don't let him realize that our lives are on the line – and let this be the last time that such things ever happen to him...*

"Do you want to play hide-and-seek?" Eyal asked Elitzafun after Ahmed had left the room.

Elitzafun nodded, though his eyes expressed his doubt. "There aren't too many places to hide in this room."

"Of course there are." Eyal lifted up the trundle bed, revealing a storage compartment beneath it. "Here. You can hide in here. Or you can sit behind the curtains, or maybe lie down in the bath."

"But you know all the hiding places already!"

"Let's play anyway. It can still be fun. You count and I'll hide."

Elitzafun closed his eyes, and Eyal took out the package of coffee beans and set it on the bed. From under his shirt he pulled out an empty peach-juice can and managed to maneuver things so that the camera he knew was in the wall opposite saw nothing more than a man putting coffee beans into a grinder. The noise was approximately the same – most of the noise of an electric grinder came from the motor, not the substance being ground. Within seconds the can was reduced to tiny shards, and he tipped them into the second empty can before refilling the grinder with coffee beans.

He tucked the can of aluminum shreds under the bed covers and then turned off the machine. Elitzafun had reached fifty. "Are you ready?" he called out.

Eyal ducked under the table. "Yeah."

"I found you," Elitzafun trilled a moment later. "Under the table."

"Now it's your turn." Eyal got up, stretched, and started to count. Elitzafun hid behind the bed, and after conducting a long and drawn-out pretend search, Eyal eventually found him. Then it was again Eyal's turn to hide, and he clambered onto the window and closed the curtains behind him. Out of sight of the surveillance cameras, Eyal opened the window and used the metal spoon to scratch away at the rust on the bars. By the time Elitzafun found him, Eyal had an impressive amount of corroded iron in his pocket. Later he would add it to the aluminum in the can, giving him the ingredients for a thermite grenade. It was a dismal sort of bomb compared to the grenades he had assembled in the army, but it would probably be good enough to blow open the door to his room.

When the time came.

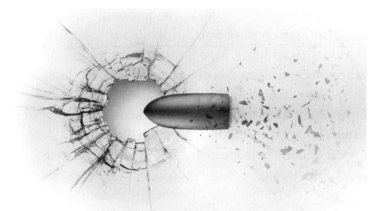

CHAPTER TEN

Ukraine

I 'm going to have to leave you by yourself for a long time today," Eyal said, sipping the coffee he had prepared by grinding coffee granules and mixing them with boiling water. "A really long time," he added, watching for the boy's reaction.

As he had expected, Elitzafun teared up. "I don't want to stay here by myself. I'm…"

"Scared?"

Elitzafun nodded. "Take me with you! Don't leave me here again. I don't like it by myself."

"Well, I'll see what I can do," Eyal said, drawing the boy close to him in a hug. "Don't worry."

X arrived several moments after Eyal and Elitzafun had finished davening. "We need you," he told Eyal.

Elitzafun paled. "I want to go with my father."

"Your father will be back soon. In the meantime, play with the nice car that we bought you."

"No! I want to go with my father to wherever he's going."

"That's impossible, Elitzafun," X said with a patient smile. "Your father is a very busy man."

Elitzafun began to sob, and Eyal quietly intervened. "It's not like he'll understand anything he sees anyway, and he's scared to stay here alone. You can understand that."

X was silent for a moment. "Okay," he said finally. "You can come with your father, Elitzafun."

They left the room together. "What about weapons?" Eyal asked as they walked down the corridor. "A bomb has to have ingredients."

"It's not your business," X said evenly. "You'll be provided with whatever you'll need at the time. And not a moment earlier," he added ominously.

"All the same, I'd like to see what you have, so I can make sure that my plans tally with what you have in mind."

X fixed him with a curious gaze. "I guess this is what comes of hiring staff with superior intelligence," he said. "In any case, it's not like you have freedom of movement... I was planning on showing it to you later, but now's a good time too. Come." X started to lead the way to what turned out to be the building's ammunition storage room.

"I'm going to have to tie your hands before we go in," X said, unapologetically. "As I'm sure you'll appreciate, I need to ensure against your appropriating any of my belongings."

"Obviously," Eyal said, adding quietly, "but of course you realize that if you do so, Elitzafun is going to panic. Until now we've been pretending to be good friends, and tying my hands will destroy that pretense."

"So what do you suggest?"

"Send him in before me, and tell him to count the number of guns that he sees there, or something like that. That way he won't notice you tying my hands."

"You tell him what to do, then."

"With pleasure." Eyal raised his voice slightly. "Elitzafun, this room is full of interesting stuff. Want to have a look? Go inside and count how many guns you can see, okay? Make sure not to touch anything, though – it might be dangerous."

Elitzafun grinned and nodded, and Eyal offered a tiny nod of his own as well. That was their sign.

X waited for Elitzafun to move away and then called out to his men: "John, Colin, come and stand on either side of Eyal."

The two men approached, and X addressed them in a low voice: "Each of you, tie a hand to one of Eyal's hands and then stand closely beside him so that the boy can't see that his father has been bound."

X's men quickly did as asked, entering the closely guarded space with Eyal between them. Eyal began to examine the state-of-the-art wave detectors, surveillance cameras, and weaponry that X had assembled for his militia.

The display was indeed impressive, but Eyal's expression was impassive as he examined the rifles, telescopes, and tripods, bullets, machine guns, sniper rifles, bombs, submachine guns, and heavy artillery guns.

"Well, what do you say?" X asked, his eyes sparkling.

"You've done a fine job here," Eyal said generously. "I take off my hat to you – metaphorically, of course."

"Let's go, then," X said. "We'll talk shop outside, and I'll have you released."

No one seemed to have paid any attention to the fact that Elitzafun had remained alone in the room for a full ten seconds.

Sixteen men sat around the long table. Most of them were new to Eyal, and he scanned their faces with interest. Elitzafun had been bought off with a large packet of Bissli and the long-awaited Playmobil castle, on condition that Eyal would return within the hour. Fortunately, he hadn't yet learned to tell time.

X lit a cigar and opened the meeting. "You all heard most of the details before Eyal arrived, but now that he's here he will clarify his position."

The men's eyes bored into Eyal, and he looked at them all intently, one by one, etching the memory of their features into his mind. Strangely enough, he felt almost at home. He was sitting at the head of the table with computers, maps, papers, and various pieces of equipment scattered about as he prepared to direct them on an important intelligence mission.

The difference was that here, unlike on his home territory, he was training everyone with the intention of foiling their plans when the time came. He needed to employ tremendous ingenuity this time.

"Begin," X instructed.

"First, I want to know your men's names," Eyal said, forcing a smile onto his face. "Identify yourselves – your names and cities of origin." The men glanced back and forth between Eyal and X. The authority that Eyal commanded was palpable. After years of directing complicated missions for the Mossad, Eyal was accustomed to being obeyed.

X regarded this statement with suspicion. A suspicious person by nature, this trait had grown progressively stronger following his abduction of Eyal. What was the man saying now? "Why?" he asked.

"I don't feel comfortable addressing people when I don't know their names."

A long moment of hesitation. "Give your names – and only your first names," X said at last. "No need for cities of origin."

The men stated their first names, each one in turn, and Eyal memorized the faces attached to the names. "As you all know," he began when they were done, "my principal task is to embed several of you in the president's security unit. And once I've accomplished that, it's up to you to maintain proper deportment."

"But—"

"Questions at the end, Ahmed." Eyal didn't glance at Ahmed as he spoke, and he continued where he left off. "It's an old Trojan horse that we'll be using, with new stripes. I will be in charge of sifting those wishing to enter the building, but I'm not going to be the only person on site. Other security officers will be around to ask questions if you create suspicion. For the first half hour, therefore, you need to pass muster as genuine guests at the event."

"But it won't take even…"

"Questions at the end, Leon. We're not children."

X watched Eyal with mounting incredulity. The man had learned the names of his men within minutes, and he was now prodding them forward like a herd of sheep.

"Soon, three of you will receive the map of bombs that I have drawn up. You will need to memorize the location of each explosive device." Eyal paused. "I'm assuming you are already familiar with the layout of the conference room and its relationship to the rest of the building's hot spots."

A quick exchange of glances.

"Are questions allowed now?" someone asked hesitantly, and when Eyal answered a reluctant "Yes," the man forged on. "Will you remain on site after we enter?"

"I'll be there for the first twenty-nine minutes after you arrive. The president will arrive thirty minutes after you do, and that's when I leave." *I won't though*, Eyal thought. *I'm not going to abandon the president like that. But they don't need to know that.* "You'll be on your own after that, if you can stomach such a thought."

"We were on our own before you came," Ahmed said, protesting at this slight to his honor.

"Oh, really?" A cynical smile. Eyal had already deduced just how closely X supervised his men.

"Who will be stationed around the hall?"

"I'll decide that after we conduct some field exercises."

"You're the one doing the deciding?" There was a defiant edge to Bruce's voice.

"Yes." Eyal tossed his pen from one hand to the other. "Do you have a problem with that?"

"Yeah, I do. We already answer to someone, in case you hadn't figured that out. Let's hear what he has to say on that."

"X." Eyal turned around to his abductor and kept his voice even-keeled yet also perfectly authoritative.

"Yes?"

"Bruce isn't coming with us. He can stay here and make the coffee or take care of the dog if you have one. He's not going to be part of the mission."

"Who put you in charge of appointing team members?" Bruce's eyes were shooting daggers now.

"The same person who put me in charge of the mission itself," Eyal said calmly. "I will not take anyone I suspect of insubordination."

"Eyal," X said, his voice betraying his own faltering confidence. "Let's push this quarrel off for later."

"This isn't a quarrel. It's a fact. You can't lead an operation using agents who have ideas of their own. This mission is perilous enough as it is, and I won't allow anyone to introduce unnecessary risks. I'm not prepared to endanger the success of the mission just to save Bruce from being insulted."

"Who do you think you are?" Bruce's voice rose with fury. Eyal folded his arms and eyed him much as a leopard might peruse a troublesome rabbit.

X looked at Eyal with an imploring expression on his face. "I will discuss the issue with both of you privately, later this afternoon," he said, looking at both Eyal and Bruce.

Bruce unclenched his fist and slumped into his seat. He glared at Eyal, but Eyal was unmoved. He had gone through similar experiences plenty of times, and he knew better than to back down. Insubordination was one of the worst crimes on the battlefield – nothing imperiled the success of a mission like the refusal of an agent to obey the commander unquestioningly, when necessary. Many of Eyal's operatives had complained about his strictness, to which Eyal invariably responded: "I will give up my life for your sake, take risks for you, give you a pep talk before a mission, and invite you for a celebratory picnic afterward. But during the mission itself I am the commander, responsible for my fighters' well-being and the success of the mission. And that means that during the mission, nothing exists aside from getting the job done and getting out in one piece."

"Any more questions?" Eyal asked, returning his thoughts to the present. "Soon we'll be going on a training mission, and following that I'll be telling X who I believe should belong on the team."

X nodded and held out a packet of cigars. "May I offer you one?"

A moment of hesitation, and Eyal took the packet along with the proffered box of matches, a faraway look in his eyes. He lit a cigar and, with seeming absentmindedness, placed the packet in his pocket.

The incident passed without a glitch. Thank G-d. "Should we leave now?" he asked.

X stood up. "Of course."

Despite his still overwhelming exhaustion, Eyal didn't go to sleep that night. The training he had overseen that afternoon had been complicated and grueling, but he needed to remain awake and supremely alert in order to put his escape plan into action.

An awful sense of dread overtook him. He had planned dozens of escapes before, and he had successfully executed most of them, but never before had there been a child involved. With a precious five-year-old in his hands, he needed to avoid the line of fire at all costs.

The time had come. It was now or never. By tomorrow X would have noticed the remote-control car in his ammunition warehouse. Had he taken a dangerous risk? Reached faulty conclusions? But the truth was that he had no choice. He had been given no guarantee that he would be released after he concluded this mission – that is, if he even remained at liberty and somehow eluded the clutches of the Americans themselves. X's word was worthless, and with a bargaining chip like Elitzafun in his pocket, next time he could up the stakes immeasurably.

Decision made, Eyal lifted his son's pillow to reveal the remote control to Elitzafun's car. He switched it on.

In the warehouse downstairs the car began to drive. It activated the motion detectors, which in turn sounded the alarm, which Eyal was confident would bring X's men running.

Without turning on the room's light, Eyal woke up Elitzafun and whispered, "Elitzafun, there's going to be a bit of noise and mess, but don't be scared, because Hashem is watching you and I'm watching you too. Just do what I tell you to do, and keep saying, 'Hashem, help me go home to Ima,' very quietly, okay?"

With terrified eyes, Elitzafun nodded quickly and wordlessly.

Moving at lightning speed, Eyal took the electric kettle and cut through the cord. With nimble fingers, he removed the copper wiring from inside the plastic casing and threaded it through the can containing the aluminum shards and rust shavings. He had removed the car's batteries that turned on the light and sirens that morning and placed them under his mattress. Now he smashed them with the foot of the bed, again and again, until the electrolyte gel was exposed. Then he inserted the open batteries into the can.

Of course it would have been better to have prepared all this in advance, but since he hadn't been able to conceal his activities from the surveillance cameras for long enough without raising suspicion, he had been forced to wait until the last moment. Quickly,

Eyal finished his preparations. He pulled out the box of matches that he had taken from X earlier that day and removed all of the red phosphorous heads, save for three, pouring them into the aluminum can. Next, he lit one of the three remaining matches, placed it carefully into the can next to the wire, and hung the home-grown bomb on the door handle.

Leaping across the room, Eyal huddled in the corner, shielding Elitzafun's small frame with his body.

The wire began to burn.

Eyal counted for a mere six seconds, waiting for the fire to take hold of the phosphorous-aluminum-rust combination that he was counting on.

A medium-sized explosion rent the air. The shock waves of Eyal's improvised bomb centered around the door lock, which morphed into a grossly distorted shape. Eyal utilized the moments of softening metal to kick the door and successfully conclude the break.

Eyal lifted his son into his arms and raced out of the now-open door and down the steps. He knew that the parking lot was situated one floor below ground level, and he also knew that within moments X's men would be at his heels, once they discovered that the alarm in the ammunition warehouse had been set off by a toy car. His image had certainly been captured on the security cameras on his way down. There was no time to lose.

The next few moments would seal his – and Elitzafun's – fate.

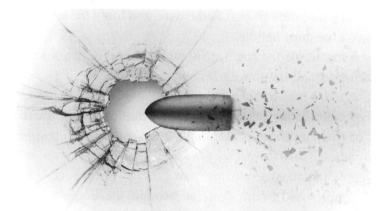

CHAPTER ELEVEN

Ukraine

Eyal set his son on the floor and headed out into the parking lot, after warning the boy not to make a sound. He sprint- ed over to the booth at the entrance, catching the guard unaware and knocking him down to the ground, unconscious. After slinging the man's submachine gun over his shoulder and removing his gun from his holster, Eyal raced back to Elitzafun, pulling him out of the building.

There was a heavy steel door between the building and the park- ing lot, and Eyal locked it with a key hanging on the wall and then smashed the key into the lock. Then he ordered Elitzafun to lie down on the ground. The boy's eyes were round with fear, but Eyal had no time to consider the psychological effects this adventure would have on the child's life. Right now he was fighting precisely for that life.

Quickly, Eyal selected a small Isuzu truck, the largest vehicle in the lot, and jumped into the cabin. Driving in reverse, he backed the truck right up to the metal door of the building, effectively blocking it off with the heavy vehicle. That would buy him some precious time.

And not a moment too soon. The first of X's men had reached the other side of the door and were now firing at it with tungsten-filled bullets that could breach an armor plate.

"Elitzafun," Eyal said, making every effort to speak calmly. "Don't move, okay? We're going home soon, *b'ezrat Hashem*." He raced over to another vehicle and started to rip the upholstery off the seats and then tear the fabric into roughly square-shaped pieces.

"What's that noise?"

"Never mind. You just do what I tell you and everything will be okay. And keep talking to Hashem," Eyal reminded the boy before starting to make his way around the parking lot, opening the caps to all the gas tanks of the cars as he went, save for one small truck near the entrance. Then he went to retrieve Elitzafun and placed him in the back seat of the truck.

Ready for the final stage. Eyal lit the second of his three matches, set the torn pieces of fabric on fire one by one, and tossed them into the cars. When he reached the last car, he placed the flaming fabric as close to the open mouth of the gas tank as he dared, and then raced over to "his" truck. He jumped into the driver's seat, told Elitzafun to lie down on the floor, and then grasped the shift stick.

A second later, the final car's gas tank ignited.

Eyal was almost certain that X had men stationed at the parking lot exit. They weren't shooting yet, in order not to give away their presence, but Eyal knew that the moment he emerged, he was a moving target. He had planned on taking that risk, but then he noticed that the parking lot had a second exit, closed off with a locked gate. Could the truck break through? It seemed possible…

Eyal drove over to the far end of the lot and then switched gears, driving in reverse straight into the locked gate. He shattered the rear bumper of the car, but that was immaterial at this point in time. Turning the car around, he drove straight out of the parking lot via the hole he had made in the gate.

The road beyond was deserted. Elitzafun's startled cry as the vehicle lurched forward was the only human sound.

Two minutes later X's men finally succeeded in breaking through to the parking lot, which was by then a raging inferno. They retreated quickly back into the building, peering through the smoke.

Eyal was nowhere to be found.

X cursed him fluently in three languages, then hissed at his men to stop talking and start thinking.

"First, close off the emergency doors to the ammunition stores. If that goes up, we'll all be sky-high," he barked. "Colin, get the sprinklers activated. You'll have to deal with the blaze yourselves – we can't afford to involve the fire department. And you, Teddy, and John, and Ahmed, chase after Eyal while we deal with everything here."

"Chase?" Ahmed gestured toward the remains of their vehicles. "I don't think so."

"There's a motorcycle parked outside the front of the building," John reported. "I'll go with Ahmed."

"No. Teddy, you go with Ahmed. Take submachine guns and rifles, and don't forget spare cartridges."

Teddy caught X's eye. "What's the plan once we catch him?"

"You will bring him back here," X said, his voice hard as steel. "I haven't finished with him yet."

Eyal drove swiftly down the highway. He had no idea where he was, nor did he know where to head to. The truck's built-in Waze system was malfunctioning, and he couldn't slow down to read the road signs – not that it would have helped when he had no clear destination.

He gave a quick glance around the truck to see if there was anything of interest. On the floor near his feet was a leather satchel. Keeping his left hand on the wheel, he opened the satchel with his right hand and rummaged through it. A few seconds later he withdrew a real treasure – a cell phone. Now he could call Eli and then immediately destroy the phone, to stop them from tracking him down; though at this stage of the game that was not a major consideration, given that his was the only vehicle on the road. He hoped to remedy that soon.

He dialed the familiar number, and Eli picked up on the second ring. "Eli?"

Eli's shriek almost burst his eardrum. "Eyal??" If Eyal hadn't been so tense he would have smiled.

"I can't talk for long. Elitzafun is with me in a truck I stole after breaking out of their compound, which is now going up in flames. I have no idea where I am, so I need you to pinpoint my location as quickly as you can and let me know where I am and where to go from here."

"Don't you see any landmarks at all?"

Eyal glanced to his left. "There's a forest. Not so helpful. There's nothing else to go by. And I need to smash this phone within a few minutes or they'll track me from it, so get me the information as quickly as you can."

It took the Mossad technicians precisely one minute and forty seconds to locate Eyal. Eli gave the information to his friend, and told him how to reach the new safe house. Eyal memorized the instructions and then tossed the cell phone out of the window, reversing onto it and grinding it with the wheels of the truck.

Elitzafun, still in the back seat, stared with wide eyes. "Why did you throw out the phone, Abba? Now you won't be able to speak to Eli."

Eyal turned to him and offered him the most reassuring smile that he could muster. "Come and sit next to me in front, Elitzafun. You did great, and now we have to do even better."

"It's not dangerous anymore?"

"I hope not."

"The men with the guns won't chase after us?"

"Not now, not after I threw out the phone," Eyal said. Suddenly, his attention was distracted by something moving fast in the wing mirror. He turned a fraction, and saw a motorcycle coming up behind, gaining on him with every second. There was a bang, and he realized one of its passengers was shooting at him, likely aiming for the tires. If they got even just one good shot...

"Elitzafun!" Eyal's voice was taut with fear – not so much for himself, but for his son. "Get down here, by my feet. Yes, that's right. Do you see the big pedal that my foot is pressing down on? Great. So, now you're going to push down hard right where I'm pressing and make sure that the pedal doesn't move back up again. Can you do that?"

"Sure I can!" Elitzafun was already crouched at Eyal's feet, and now he placed both hands on the pedal and pushed down with all his strength. For a brief second Eyal reflected on the fact that the boy was more like his stepfather than like his biological father.

"Good," he said. "Okay, so now, I want you to lift one of your hands – no, forget it." The steering wheel would have to take care of itself. There was no choice. Elitzafun couldn't press both the gas and manage the steering wheel at the same time. "Hold the pedal down tight, okay?"

"I'll make sure it doesn't move even a bit," Elitzafun called up reassuringly.

Shifting over in the seat, Eyal looped a piece of string he found around the steering wheel so he could keep the truck on a reasonably straight course. Then he hefted the submachine gun and leaned out of the window. He took aim and fired a volley of bullets.

The truck wasn't holding so steady by then, its course wobbling with the movements of the string in his hand, and most of his bullets went wide off the mark, but one of them did graze the hand of the man sitting at the front of the motorcycle, and he shouted and momentarily loosened his grip. The man behind him reached out and regained control over the vehicle with superhuman effort. Eyal then shot another volley of bullets, and the motorcycle began to veer from one side of the street to the other in order to avoid being hit, accelerating as it went. The man in front seemed to have recovered his equilibrium now, and the man riding behind resumed his rapid fire. A second later a horrific sound rent the air, and Eyal's face paled. The gas tank had been hit.

The needle of the gas gauge started to jerk backward with amazing rapidity, but that wasn't Eyal's greatest concern. All it would take was a single spark to send both him and Elitzafun flying...

At that moment, he noticed a tall building with a low metal fence around it, just a short distance ahead. Eyal shifted back to the driver's seat and told Elitzafun to crawl away from the pedal, replacing the boy's pressure with his own foot. Pressing down hard, Eyal knew that he had no choice but to reach the building and abandon the truck as fast as he could. Escaping into the forest with a five-year-old boy was a disaster in the making. At least in this building, whatever it was, there might possibly be a means of communicating with Eli.

Eyal drove madly toward the building, crashing right through the metal gate and continuing on into the parking lot. Something started beeping, and the truck's lights went out. A moment later the engine spluttered and died.

Eyal lifted his son into his arms. "Let's go, Elitzafun. You were wonderful. And now we're going inside."

"Why?"

"I'll explain it to you later."

Eyal slung the submachine gun over his shoulder, checked that the pistol was still in his pocket, and raced toward the building with his son. Three bullets whizzed past him, but holding Elitzafun tightly to his chest, Eyal reached the door safely, kicked it open, and then slammed it shut behind him.

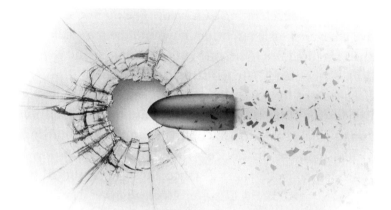

CHAPTER TWELVE

A clock hanging on the wall opposite the entrance told Eyal that it was ten minutes past three – reason enough for the building to appear deserted with not a single light burning. Eyal groped around for the light switch and turned it on, and a faint light filled the front lobby.

"What are we going to do here?" Elitzafun asked, shivering slightly. It was cold, bitterly cold.

"I'm going to call Eli," Eyal said, casting a look of concern at the boy. On the other side of the lobby a wide desk probably served as a reception of sorts. There were two phones on the desk, and he lifted one and quickly dialed the number. Meanwhile, he started opening drawers in search of useful objects – just in case? No, he would certainly need them.

Three plastic cables, a pair of scissors, and a small pliers. Eyal shoved the objects into his pockets as Eli's voice came over the line. "Eyal, I'm on the way."

"The plan's gone awry. My gas tank was shot at by motorcyclists, and I escaped into a nearby building, which is where I'm calling you from."

"Let me trace your location." Eli fell silent, and several moments passed before he was able to report his findings. "Rug factory."

"How far are you from here?"

"I'm about an hour or maybe an hour and fifteen minutes away, without traffic." Eli glanced at his speedometer. "I don't want to get into trouble with the traffic police. What are your plans?"

"I'm going to use what I can find here to stave them off when they come after me. The trouble is that the backup you have access to won't be enough this time. My captors are fully armed and extremely angry. And there are about twenty-five or thirty of them."

"So what do you suggest?"

"I need you to arrange for backup from the entire Mossad network in Ukraine." Eyal thought for a moment. "Of course, the problem with this is that such a confrontation may lead to a bloodbath."

"Our agents would all be delighted to play a part in rescuing a kidnapped child, despite the risk."

Eyal shook his head. "I can't. And it will take them too long to get here in any case. Those who are in the vicinity can't number more than one or two. Versus thirty armed and dangerous men? I don't think so."

"Do you have any other knights in shining armor you can turn to?" Eli asked.

An idea quickly flashed across Eyal's mind. "The police."

"What?" There was no end to the ideas that this man could come up with!

"Yes. Let me tell you what I'm going to do. I'm going to hang up and call your other phone. The police are listening in to all incoming calls on that phone, and the minute they hear my voice, they'll be here with about a hundred officers, machine guns, helicopters – the works. Despite its many shortcomings, the Ukrainian police force does actually have more manpower and ammunition than this gang I'm up against. So it seems that this plan is the only one that's going to save our skin right now."

"I don't like it," Eli said. "You're going to be thrown straight into prison. And what will happen to your son?"

Eyal shook his head. "They won't harm him. They can't afford to. As for me...I'll have to take whatever's coming to me. This is the best I can come up with right now, and I'm not going to risk my son's life in order to stay out of prison."

"I hear you." Eli sighed. "Okay, Eyal. I'll be waiting for your call."

"Eliohr Hadar's phone is lighting up," chief communications officer Nikita reported. "In just a minute we're going to track the call – and the caller." His voice was tinged with excitement.

"I don't believe it," Colonel Tadiev said. "They wouldn't be that dumb." The police were still licking their wounds from their most recent encounter with Eyal, and, unaware of X's network, they were still operating under the assumption that Eyal had some powerful accomplices in Ukraine.

"I'll put it on loudspeaker," the communications officer said, his eyes shining with anticipation.

"Turn on the loudspeaker connection to the next room and call Yanek. And set up the translating program. It's not perfect, but it's better than nothing."

Yanek was duly summoned, and he arrived within seconds. "Call Tomkin," Tadiev told him. "I don't like to involve the Secret Service, but we've been collaborating on this mission, and I don't want them to accuse us of withholding important information from them."

"We haven't been withholding anything," Yanek said. "Let's see them manage to trail Eyal on their own."

"Quiet!" Nikita said "Eliohr is answering."

Yanek and Tadiev listened in disbelief as none other than Eyal's voice came on the line – Eyal, the man whom they wanted to see locked away in their prison's dingiest cell forever.

"Eli, I need you to create a distraction at this factory. My life is being threatened by an armed group of men."

"What do you need?"

"Thirty or forty men with automatic rifles and submachine guns. I'm waiting."

The phone line was disconnected.

"Did you pick up his location?" Tadiev thundered.

"He's in a rug factory in the industrial zone in Pavlograd in the Dnipro district," Nikita said, frowning at the screen in front of him. "If we send out a team now, they should be able to get there within the hour."

"That's exactly what we'll do," Tadiev shouted, enthusiasm buoying him onward. "Yanek, gather our men. We'll need heavy ammunition for this capture."

"Captain," Yanek said, his voice hesitant. "I think it's a trap."

"A trap for who? He ran away. He was desperate to get out of our clutches. Besides, what kind of a trap can he lay for us? We have access to far more sophisticated weaponry than even the largest mafia clan."

"I hear you, but, all the same… Hadar's phone line has been dead for four days. Why has it suddenly come alive only to report on a group of armed gangsters heading to some remote factory? Something seems off."

"Report to Tomkin," Tadiev said, shrugging off the warning. "This may be a trap, but we still can't afford to ignore it. The stakes are too high. We'll arm our men to the gills and head out."

※

Eyal hung up the phone with mixed feelings. His hope that in this way he would rescue his son was mingled with fear over the bloodbath that might easily result once the police were involved. On the night that the militia had attacked the police convoy that had come to take him to prison, X's men had showed that they had no compunctions about murdering for the sake of achieving their personal goals.

Elitzafun disturbed his thoughts, tugging at his sleeve. "Abba," he said, "those bad people can't come in here, right?"

The truth would become blindingly obvious in only a few minutes, and Eyal decided to opt for candidness. "They can try. I'm going to do some things to stop them, but first I need to find a good place for you to hide until the police get here."

"What are the police going to do? Will they take me home?"

"Yes." Eyal bit his lip. Luckily for him, Elitzafun hadn't asked what they would do to his father. His thoughts flew ahead, seeing his son as a bar mitzvah boy coming for his biannual visit to prison, asking Eyal for his blessing and giving a blessing of his own that Eyal would make it out of prison before his wedding…

Eyal pushed the unpleasant image away. "*Im yirtzeh Hashem*," he added.

Eyal lifted his son in his arms and headed up the staircase. On the third floor he found what he was looking for: woven mats, rolled and ready for export. He unrolled one and told Elitzafun to lie down quietly inside. Then he rolled the carpet around his small body, lifted it, and placed it on a pile of rugs. Reminding his son to remain quiet and promising he wouldn't have to stay there for long, he headed back down to the lobby. He wanted to find a way to block both of the factory's entrances.

Eyal entered the packaging room and climbed onto a heavy forklift, driving it straight into the front entrance. The forklift probably weighed at least several tons and would be extremely difficult to move. Having blocked off one entrance, he returned to the packaging room, clambered onto a second forklift, and drove it over to the second entrance. Hopefully that would suffice to hold off X's men until the police got there.

With the doors blocked off, Eyal climbed the stairs again and headed toward the roof. With nothing at hand to enable night-time vision it was impossible to know if the motorcyclists were approaching. There were probably spotlights around the factory grounds that he could turn on, but he needed to find those switches first.

Heading back into the building, Eyal located the switches and bathed the outside of the building in light. He peered outside, and fear pinched at him. The motorcyclists were nowhere to be seen. They had obviously not retreated, and the question was where they had gone and what their plans were.

"Hands up," a cold, triumphant voice from behind him called out.

Instinctively, Eyal's hand reached for his gun. If he turned around and shot, then…

"Do not shoot as your turn. My finger is on the trigger of this gun. Throw your weapon to the ground so I don't feel compelled to shoot you. We will only have a reason to keep your child alive if you remain alive."

Eyal slackened his grip on his gun, then tossed it to the floor and bowed his head in submission.

"Turn around slowly," the man instructed.

Eyal turned around and saw Teddy, X's right-hand man, with a gloating look on his face.

"Walk ahead of me," Teddy said.

Eyal began to walk. "Where's Ahmed?" he asked.

"You are in no position to ask questions," Teddy said angrily. "I wouldn't want to be in your place when you next meet up with X."

"Regardless, he still needs me," Eyal said, making every effort to maintain a calm tone of voice.

"Yes, but I don't know what state he needs you in. Could be in a stretcher is also good. So walk downstairs slowly, so I don't get tempted to shoot you in the legs and carry you out. And keep your hands up."

Eyal walked deliberately down the stairs. His slow gait was meant both to satisfy the man with the gun and to gain time. His eyes darted from side to side, looking for any hint that the second motorcyclist was nearby. Eyal feared that he was searching the factory for Elitzafun. The factory was huge, but if the police didn't arrive quickly the man was liable to find his son.

Eyal's fears dissolved the moment Ahmed came into view. One of his hands had been hastily and incompetently bandaged, and his other hand was holding a gun. "Where's your son?" he barked.

"You didn't find him?" Eyal adopted an expression of feigned sympathy. "Too bad."

"Where is he? I'm going to count to five, and then I will shoot."

"No problem," Eyal said, scorn mingling with disgust. "Go right ahead."

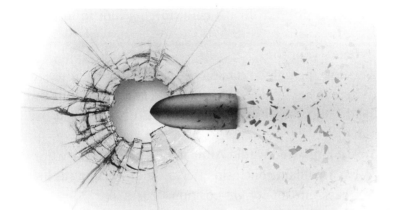

CHAPTER THIRTEEN

Ukraine

Eli sped down the highway, mindless of the speed limits. He had decided that it was too late at night for the traffic police to pay any attention to him and that just in case they were interested in pursuing him he would simply shoot their tires and drive on. He needed to reach that rug factory immediately. It wasn't just a priority – there was no other option.

When he still had about half the distance left to cover, Eli saw flashing police vehicles ahead and his heart filled with hope. It had to be Tadiev on his way. Eyal was right – it was the only workable solution – but he still wanted to get there before the police did. Even if it meant risking his own arrest.

"Relieve him of his weapons," Teddy told Ahmed. "Because I believe he has more than just that one gun."

Teddy kept his gun trained on Eyal as Ahmed groped around, removing Eyal's other weapons from him. Then he knocked the butt of the pistol into Eyal's chin, forcing him to look into his eyes.

"Where's your son?"

"I reserve the right to remain silent," Eyal said with a smile.

"Where is he?" Ahmed shrieked. He edged closer to Eyal and punched him straight in the diaphragm. Eyal doubled over and gasped.

"Leave him," Teddy told Ahmed. "He's not going to answer."

"What a brilliant conclusion," Eyal said, whistling as he pulled himself back into an upright position.

A kick and a bullet to his arm. As blood started spurting, Eyal automatically wrapped the fingers of his uninjured hand around his wounded arm.

"Where is the boy?" Ahmed shouted.

Eyal shook his head. A pool of blood started to form at his feet as he whispered through pursed lips, "You can shoot me to pieces but I still won't tell you where he is."

"I will shoot then." Ahmed cocked his weapon, but Teddy held a hand out.

"X needs him alive. If you shoot the arm with the microchip in it he will die." Teddy pushed Eyal forward. "Get moving. Quickly."

Ahmed fixed him with a murderous gaze. "Wait a minute. First I want to chain him to something and then search the building." He tucked his gun into his belt. "We can always burn the building down and force him to hand over his son that way."

"That would be a last resort. But tie him up in the meantime. X will be here in ten minutes."

Eyal glanced at Ahmed's watch. Twenty-five to four. He had spoken to Eli at ten past three, which meant that the police were unlikely to arrive before four. If X really did arrive within ten minutes, he would have at least a quarter of an hour to do whatever he wanted – which was a quarter of an hour too much.

The real question was Elitzafun. Would they leave without him? He doubted it. And twenty-five minutes was plenty of time to find him.

"He's not going to tell us where his son is," Teddy told X over the phone. "You've researched his professional history. He was interrogated under torture several times and he never once revealed a thing. And here we're talking about his son's life. Ahmed even shot him in the arm and he said nothing. I can understand why."

"The police will be here in forty minutes or less," X said. Eyal, listening in, felt his heart sink to his shoes. They knew. He had no idea how, but they knew. His guess was that they had an informer in the upper echelons of the police force, which would explain many things. And his guess was right.

"Forty minutes?" Teddy said. "I hope we find the kid before then. There are hundreds of places a boy can hide in this factory. It could take us hours to find him."

"Hours to find a little boy? Just go through the rooms calling out that you have a huge lollypop or an expensive game for him and that he should come out. He's only five years old!"

"Yeah, but he's his father's son," said Teddy, unaware that Eyal was only the stepfather.

X stared at the road ahead of him, thinking hard. "Then do as you suggested earlier."

"Burn down the building?" Despite realizing that this was the only feasible solution, Teddy didn't like the idea.

"Yes. That will certainly force him to betray his son's hiding place."

"Fine."

Eyal, listening to the conversation with an impassive expression, felt as though a knife had sliced through his heart. The blood drained from his face as he tried desperately to think of a solution.

"Eyal," Teddy said, his tone almost friendly, "we're going to set the building on fire. Should be fun. Do you want to tell us where your son is before we get going?"

Eyal shrugged and remained silent. The police could still arrive before the fire took hold, but if he capitulated to his enemy's demand and told them where to find Elitzafun, both of them would be whisked away within minutes. He needed to find a way to buy time.

"No response?" Teddy asked quietly, ominously. "In that case, I will be generous and give you ten seconds to change your mind, even though my boss didn't give me permission to do so."

Eyal shut his eyes and exhaled slowly. Meanwhile, Ahmed grabbed one of his hands and cuffed it to a nearby hook screwed into the wall.

"Okay, Teddy, let's do this."

Eyal's free hand was still bleeding. Sharp pains shot through him as he watched the two men tossing a match at a pile of rugs. The fabric caught fire immediately. It would be a matter of minutes before the entire first floor went up in smoke. The place was literally stuffed with flammable items.

Teddy smiled at the expression on Eyal's face. "A fire to rival yours. We'll burn your cover."

"Let me go upstairs," Eyal said weakly.

"So, he's not on the first floor. Ahmed, let's go up."

"Release me and let me go upstairs," Eyal repeated. His voice was dangerously stable. A small blood clot had formed around the wound on his arm, but the center hadn't dried yet and the blood flowed out unchecked. The wound wasn't a deep one, but if he didn't stanch it quickly he was liable to collapse, and collapsing at this point was the last thing Eyal could afford to do.

The fire blazed on. Ahmed left the building, and Teddy waited another minute before freeing Eyal from the hook on the wall. "Onward," he said. "Go and get him."

Before complying with Teddy's order, Eyal searched around to find what he was looking for – a rag that he could use as a face mask. Soaking it in water from a nearby tap, he wrapped it around his head and then started to race toward the steps. He ran upward at a speed he didn't know he was capable of, reaching the third floor within a minute. To his relief, Teddy hadn't followed him, relying on the fact that they would have to emerge straight into X's waiting arms.

The smoke hadn't reached the third floor yet, and Eyal unwound the rag and took several deep breaths. Then he hunted around for a suitable piece of material and found something on the floor. An unhygienic solution, but a solution nonetheless. He tied the woven material tightly around his bleeding arm, his face distorting with pain as he pressed the makeshift bandage over his wound.

"Elitzafun," he called out. "Come out. We have to go now."

"Abba?" Elitzafun said. "I can't get out of here by myself."

Eyal raced over to the rugs and quickly located the boy. At breakneck speed he unrolled the rug Elitzafun was hidden in. Incredibly, Elitzafun's eyes shone from the adventure.

"I didn't move or say anything, even when that man came in here and looked all around and talked very loud," he said proudly.

"You were great, Elitzafun. Really amazing. And now, let's go."

"You know," Elitzafun began, but then he stopped at the sight of his father's arm. "What's that? Are you bleeding?"

"It's nothing. I just fell and cut myself. Don't worry. I'll clean it up soon."

"The bad people left?"

"Not yet, but we're going now."

"The police came?"

"No, not yet. But we need to go right now, Elitzafun. There's a fire downstairs, so we have to get out of the building."

For the first time, the boy looked scared. "How will we get out?"

Elitzafun's honey-colored eyes looked deep into Eyal's green eyes, and Eyal felt as though his heart might explode from tension. Until then he had thought only of the urgency of reaching the top of the steps before they were overtaken by fire, but now there was no way back down. Rug samples hanging near the stairwell had drawn the fire upward, and the air was already smoky.

Eyal dug his nails into the palms of his hands. Their exit was blocked.

"His mission has become rather complicated, shall we say," the man reported laconically. "Right now he's trapped inside a burning building, with armed men waiting outside for him, and in less than twenty minutes they will kill him."

"They won't kill him," the man on the other end of the phone said calmly. "They still want him alive to execute his mission."

"His child is in danger."

"Yes, the child." The man cleared his throat uncomfortably. "We weren't expecting that to happen."

"You weren't expecting it, but it happened. You can't just abandon him to his fate now."

"I know."

"What are you going to do?"

Silence.

"I want to know what your plans are."

"We don't have any plans. We're simply going to have to rely on Eyal to manage somehow on his own."

"How very nice," the man fumed.

"I'm sorry. Once we have him under our jurisdiction we'll be able to help him, but not a moment earlier."

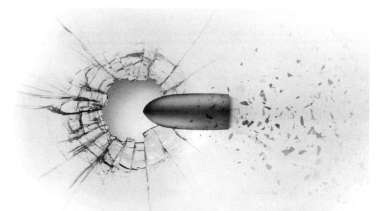

CHAPTER FOURTEEN

Ukraine

Eyal stood frozen in place, staring at the swiftly encroaching fire for a long moment. It was only when Elitzafun began coughing that he gathered his wits about him, grabbed his son's hand, and started to run with him toward the upper floor, accessible, he knew from his earlier tour of the factory, via another staircase at the far end of the huge hall.

"Elitzafun, we have to get up to the roof, as quickly as you can," he gasped, picking the boy up and tucking him under his arm when he realized that Elitzafun was too overwhelmed to run as fast as he needed to. "We'll find a way down from there."

Elitzafun nodded, his eyes wide with fear. Eyal, seeing his fear, forced himself to smile. "It will be okay. Don't worry. Keep talking to Hashem and asking Him to help, okay?"

They reached the fourth floor of the building, and from there they headed up to the roof. As Elitzafun breathed the cool, clear air he began to tremble. "Are you cold?" Eyal asked, looking at him with concern.

"Yes."

"Okay, so we're going down now," Eyal said, his voice restored to its usual calm and practical tone. He began to circle the roof, looking around for a rope or other object that would enable them to make it down to the ground safely. Soon enough he found a fire closet with a rubber hose wrapped around a rusty drum inside. Eyal poked a metal prong into the swiveling knob to prevent it from spinning too rapidly, and then took the hose and dragged it with him to the edge of the roof, on the side of the building farthest from the fire.

"Elitzafun." Eyal hugged his son close to him. "You need to hold on to me as tightly as you can while I climb, because one of my hands is...cut, so I won't be able to hold on to you as I climb down. Do you think that you can do that?"

Elitzafun nodded, and the fear in his eyes seemed to dissolve into a renewed sense of adventure. All the same, Eyal was concerned that his son wouldn't be able to hold tight for long enough. He took one of the plastic cables he had found in the drawer of the desk in the lobby and showed it to Elitzafun.

"Elitzafun, this will make it easier for you to hold on. I'm going to tie your hands with it, and then you'll hold on round my neck, okay? It might hurt a bit, but not for long. I'm sorry..."

He knew the cable would hurt, but there was no better option. Elitzafun held his arms out, and Eyal tied the plastic cable around his hands, wedging the sleeves of his thick sweater in between his arms and the plastic so that the cable wouldn't cut in too deeply as he pulled. "Slip your hands over my head and around my neck," he told Elitzafun when he was done. "And hang on tight so you don't fall, okay?"

Elitzafun did exactly as he was told. "This is how I used to hang onto you when you took me home from preschool," he said, smiling.

Merciless words. Would the day come when Eyal would once again pick his son up from school? Even if Elitzafun returned home safely, would he?

Despite his turbulent thoughts, Eyal's expression remained placid. "This might hurt a bit," he repeated. "But it's easier for you this way." Cautiously, Eyal began to lower himself from the roof, pulling the hose out of the pulley, foot by foot. "We're almost down, Elitzafun. Keep on holding on tight. Does it hurt?"

"It hurts...but stop asking me that every minute, Abba! I'm a big boy."

"I will ask you, another hundred times," Eyal said. They had descended ten feet already, and he began to relax. Everything seemed to be proceeding according to plan.

And then Elitzafun sneezed. His grip slackened and Eyal felt his hands slip down from his neck. Apparently, in his attempt not to cause Elitzafun too much pain, he hadn't pulled the plastic tie tightly enough. "Abba!" Elitzafun screamed. "I'm falling!"

Eyal quickly wrapped his injured hand around his son, and his breathing grew shallow as they remained suspended between heaven and earth.

"Abba!"

"Calm down, Elitzafun." The calm in Eyal's voice was inauthentic. There was no way they could remain in that position for more than a moment or two. His injured hand was throbbing with pain. "Look at me, Elitzafun."

"What?" Elitzafun's eyes were brimming with tears, and Eyal's heart clenched with pain. Why was this child being made to suffer?

"Calm down, Elitzafun. I'm here with you, holding you. And now I'm giving you a big hug." Somehow, he overcame his pain for long enough to extend his injured hand to pull Elitzafun up, and then he enveloped him in a loving embrace. "You're okay, right?"

"Yes." Elitzafun took a deep breath and swallowed back his tears.

"Good. Now hold the sleeve of your sweater and put your hand into the plastic tie again." Eyal could hardly breathe. He bit his lower lip until it bled. Pain obscured his vision and threatened to overwhelm him. He was fighting for his son's life. He couldn't afford to faint.

Elitzafun did as he was asked and managed, with great effort, to wrap his arms around his father's neck again.

"You did it!" Eyal exhaled deeply. The drag of Elitzafun's weight around his neck made it difficult to breathe. "Now hold on even tighter. Tighter! Pull the plastic tie as tightly as you can, using your teeth."

"Like the plastic ties for our sukkah," Elitzafun said.

"Exactly." What a great time for comparisons. "Just pull it quickly, Elitzafun. Please."

Elitzafun pulled, but there was no clicking sound to signal that the tie had locked properly into place. "You can't manage to pull all the way?" Eyal asked.

"No, Abba. Does that mean that I'm going to fall again?"

"With Hashem's help, we'll be okay." Eyal held on tightly to Elitzafun with his injured arm, feeling around for the plastic tie. With great effort he managed to pull it tighter until it locked into place, and then he loosened his grip and exhaled. "Elitzafun, you're doing a great job. Let's continue to climb down." Eyal grasped a nearby window frame, released still more of the coiled hose, and resumed his climb down. His forehead was beaded with sweat despite the cold. "Are you holding on tightly?"

"Yes."

With superhuman strength Eyal continued to progress down the side of the building. When they were about six feet above the ground Eyal jumped, landing crouched down and then rolling slightly to one side to break the fall.

"We made it!" Elitzafun was jubilant as he unwound himself from his father's shoulders. Eyal sank to the ground, incapable of moving. His bullet wound felt awful, and he had no idea how he had just survived that downward climb with his son. He had clearly received Heavenly assistance in his time of need.

"Abba." Despite the relief, Elitzafun's voice was trembling slightly.

"Yes." Eyal said in a whisper. "Give me a minute to breathe – just a minute."

Elitzafun fell silent. His arms were still bound together, and he rubbed them back and forth. "Just a minute and I'll cut the tie," Eyal said. "Then I'll see if I can find a car that we can use to get away from here." He rummaged in his pockets, finding nothing more suitable than a bottle opener, but it served the purpose. Then he grasped his son's hand and started to walk around the building. Maybe, just maybe, X had been unaccountably delayed…

His hopes were dashed as six familiar men in bulletproof vests approached with machine guns in their hands. Another two men appeared from a doorway and handcuffed Eyal's hands and shackled his feet. X walked behind them with measured steps. He was clearly livid, and his men stepped back in awe as he approached his captive. X studied Eyal, looking him up and down, taking note of his ragged, dusty clothing, scraped hands, bloodied makeshift bandage, and soot-coated face. Despite his appearance, a fire burned in the intelligence agent's eyes.

"So you thought you'd be a hero," he said finally.

"I still think so." Eyal clasped his handcuffed hands around Elitzafun, turning his son around toward him to prevent him from witnessing the scene.

"Don't think I will allow this to pass in silence." X's eyes were blazing fury. He turned to his men. "Take him, and the boy too."

"He's coming with me," Eyal said. His attempt to exude his normal aura of authority failed him, however, and his breathing grew labored as a result of the pain that he was biting back.

"No, he's not. I was a fool to trust you earlier. Right now I'm having you both sleep in separate houses."

"I won't cooperate with you."

"Really, now?" X's eyes were as hard as flint. "In that case, you'll find out that there are worse things in life than being separated from your son for a week."

"Let me at least tell him one last thing."

X summoned all his patience and cold logic so as not to turn down the request. Above all else he wanted to punish Eyal for his escape, but he knew that it was important to avoid a dramatic scene with the child. With great effort he nodded.

"Elitzafun." Eyal crouched down so that he was the same height as his son. "I need to go to the hospital now to take care of my injured arm. You go with these people and be good. They'll take care of you until I'm better."

Elitzafun released his tight grasp of his father's neck. "But…I'll miss you. And you told me we were going home."

"I know, and we will, soon. But first I have to take care of my hand. In a week we'll meet again, and Ima will come and get you." *You're a professional liar, you intelligence agent,* Eyal thought. *Didn't you promise yourself that you would never lie to your children?*

"Okay," Elitzafun said, fighting back tears. Somehow, he knew that there was no use in protesting.

X bent over and removed one of Elitzafun's hands from beneath Eyal's handcuffs. Eyal ignored him and hugged his son tightly. He held him close to his heart and only let go when he was ready. His eyes filled with tears as Leon and Mark led Elitzafun into one of the vehicles. His eyes continued to follow the vehicle until it disappeared after a bend in the road.

"Come," X said. "Quickly."

Eyal's feet had a hard time obeying, and X's men weren't as gentle with him as they had been with Elitzafun. They failed to account for the fact that his legs were bound, and only after he was bundled into the vehicle did X give him a sidelong glance.

A lone tear dripped from the intelligence agent's eye. His heart was being ripped to shreds.

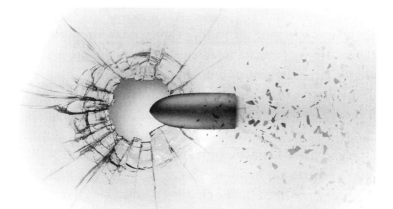

CHAPTER FIFTEEN

Ukraine

Flashing red and blue lights mingled with the flickering light of the flames as firefighters struggled to tame the blaze and dozens of police officers milled about.

Tadiev watched the firefighters blast water at the fire, and his eyes reflected his confusion.

"Do you think he set the building on fire in order to escape it?"

"No," Yanek replied. "And there's proof of that right here, at the back of the building." Yanek led Tadiev toward the backyard of the factory. The flames hadn't reached that part of the building, and Yanek pointed at a red pool of blood on the ground.

"Blood," Tadiev said shortly.

"And a hose," Yanek added, indicating the hose still hanging down the side of the building.

"Multiple footprints," Tadiev added. The courtyard projectors and dying flames precluded the need for a flashlight. The firefighters sprayed water relentlessly at the flames as the cold, damp air and wind that howled from the opposite direction enabled them to extinguish the fire quickly.

"So he was speaking the truth," Tadiev murmured. He fingered the hose. "He was indeed threatened by armed men, and he was apparently either injured or murdered."

"Either that, or he committed the murder."

"I don't think so," Tadiev said. "There isn't enough blood for that."

"The forensics team will be arriving shortly, and we'll hear what they have to say about this."

"You may not need their opinion," a voice called out from behind them. Tadiev and Yanek spun around, brandishing their guns in unison.

Eli stood opposite them, a tortured expression on his face.

"So it's you," Tadiev said. Yanek said nothing – for him, Eli represented the prisoner he had been sent to arrest several days earlier. Tadiev, on the other hand, had met Eli under friendlier circumstances.

"Yes. It's me."

"According to the rules, we need to arrest you and bring you in for questioning," Yanek said.

"You can arrest me if you really want to, but I would like you to know that I came here voluntarily so as to try and brainstorm with you. Like you, I would prefer to find a solution that will bring this story to a conclusion."

Yanek and Tadiev looked at Eli with an expression that combined anger and hatred with hope and curiosity.

"What do you know that we don't?" Tadiev finally asked.

"I don't profess to know everything, but I do know a lot."

Tadiev and Yanek exchanged glances. "Let's go," Tadiev said at last. "Get into the police car and we'll talk."

Eli and the officers headed to a parked police van. The expression on the police officers' faces was far from content. Tadiev was exhausted after a long day at work and a curtailed night's sleep, and Yanek was only slightly more refreshed, having gone home earlier and slept a few more hours, but he was still severely sleep deprived.

Eli realized that the two policemen were exhausted and angry at the man who kept eluding their clutches and making them appear like fools. He also knew that it would take all of his skill and agent's training to get them to cooperate with him.

"Let's start with what happened when the police convoy came under fire," Eli began. As an agent, he had learned how to piece incidents together in order to form a larger, coherent picture. With the few bits of information at his disposal and several words that Eyal had thrown his way, he felt he had a handle on most of what had transpired.

"So you're responsible for that?" Tadiev said coldly. "Six men were killed in that attack."

"No. I'm not the one behind that attack. The attack was led by terrorists who had selected Eyal as their target. They tried to coerce him to execute a complicated mission, although I don't know what that mission is." Eli didn't mention Elitzafun's kidnapping. He feared that the story would only cause further damage.

"Why do they need specifically your friend for this mission?" Yanek asked.

Eli smiled sadly. "I believe you know the answer to that question."

Tadiev nodded slowly and Yanek joined in. They had seen ample evidence of Eyal's ingenious cunning during the few days that he had been their prisoner, and it was obvious that many terrorists would be happy to exploit him for their purposes.

"Are these the same people who sent him to kill Rubinov?"

"No. And, once again I repeat, Eyal did not murder Rubinov, regardless of how much you would like to prove things otherwise.

But that's not what's important right now. What matters is that these people are blackmailing him to force him to do something for them, and that's why he ran away. He managed to escape, but from what I see here, he was captured again."

"And either injured or murdered," Yanek said drily.

"I don't think he was murdered. They wouldn't kill him before he completes their mission. It does seem that he was injured though." A shiver raced down Eli's spine as he thought of the puddle of blood beside the building.

"What is it that you want?" Tadiev asked.

"You want to close the case of Rubinov's murder, and I want to see my friend alive."

"So you want us to send a team to figure out where the people who captured your friend might be located?"

Eli nodded and pointed to the truck that Eyal had used to escape toward the factory. It stood bullet ridden and empty. "Eyal escaped from their compound in this truck. Presumably it belongs to one of the terrorists. Eyal told me that he set fire to the compound before escaping, so you might be able to identify it that way. He came from the southwest, driving for around half an hour before he reached here." Eli studied the policemen's faces to gauge their reaction. "If you hurry you'll probably still be able to find plenty of useful information there about the people you're going to be dealing with."

"And just what is it that you want in exchange for this all?" Tadiev demanded. Eli clearly wasn't collaborating out of feelings of fondness for the men who had arrested and tortured his friend.

"Freedom of movement, and your sharing the information that you find."

When Eyal came to after having been put to sleep on his way out of the factory, he found himself in what looked like a tiny cell with bars instead of walls. The cell was ice-cold and so dark he could only barely distinguish the bars. The next thing he noticed was that his hand had been crudely bandaged and that his wound was still causing him terrible pain.

Eyal attempted to stand up, and a wave of dizziness overcame him. He had clearly lost a lot of blood due to his injury, but his dizziness wasn't the only reason he couldn't get to his feet. His uninjured hand had been handcuffed to one of the bars of the cell. Apparently, the tugging of his hand activated something, for at that moment a light switched on, illuminating the cell. Now he could see that the tiny cell was situated in the center of what looked like a basement. Beyond the bars were four chairs, each one occupied by an armed guard. Other than that, there was nothing in the room.

Seeing him move, one of the guards whispered something into his radio and then resumed his silent vigil.

I'm in a bird cage, Eyal thought, his mind traveling back home to the bird cage on the enclosed porch, which housed Elishama's parrot. Eyal hadn't liked the fact that the bird was kept in a cage, and he had told Elishama to let the bird fly freely around the house during the day and only place it in its cage at night.

"And what if it flies out of a window and never comes back?" Elishama had protested.

"The bird is used to us – it's used to being fed by us, at the very least. If you close the windows I don't think it will find its way out, but I will not let a bird that is used to flying free be imprisoned in a cage that's barely larger than the bird itself."

"But…the cage isn't so small, and either way, my father bought me the bird and the cage!"

At this point Eyal considered relenting but then reconsidered. In a calm but firm voice, he told Elishama, "When you bought the bird it was still small and the cage was big enough for it, but now it's fully grown. The cage is too small, and I'm the father here."

In the next room, Efrat had drawn a deep breath upon hearing

Elishama's words, but now she exhaled with relief as she listened to Eyal's calm response. They discussed the conversation later that evening, and Efrat told him how amazed she was by how quickly Elishama had capitulated to Eyal's demands.

"A child can sense when the adults in his life are sure of themselves," Eyal had replied. "I am at peace with the fact that I am his father right now and that I have the right to tell him what to do."

Eyal recalled that conversation now, and bitterness filled him. The cell that he was trapped inside now was probably proportionally smaller than Elishama's cage had been for its occupant.

The basement door opened and X appeared, clearly still furious at the events of the previous day. "There has been a worsening of your terms of captivity. And I'm not apologizing for that."

"That's fine."

"You can blame yourself for my being forced to chain you and treat you in this manner."

"For some reason I'm having a hard time accepting the blame," Eyal said, trying to take his mind off the cold and the throbbing pain in his arm. "How strange."

"We tried to make things pleasant for you. We offered you generous and comfortable conditions. Life could have been much easier for all of us, but you insisted on trying to act smart."

"Interesting why a person whose son has been kidnapped, and who is being coerced into executing a mission that will probably lead to his death, might try to run away. Certainly a topic for psychological debate."

X looked at Eyal with loathing. Eyal returned his stare with equanimity.

"John, remove the handcuff from the bar, bind his hands, and bring him upstairs to my office." X spun around and then paused at the entrance to the basement. "I'll be waiting for you."

Eyal was uncuffed from the cell, and John used a plastic zip tie to bind his hands together. Then he led him upstairs and into a small office. Armed guards occupied two of the room's corners, and in the center of the room X sat at a desk, another chair opposite him. John pushed Eyal into the empty seat and then left.

There were a bottle of Coke and some plastic cups on the desk, but X did not offer Eyal a drink. He drank alone, and Eyal said nothing. His captors were probably waiting for him to ask for food and drink, but he wouldn't grant them the satisfaction of hearing him beg. X clearly needed him and wouldn't starve him to death. He wanted to cause him a bit of discomfort? That was something he could deal with.

"The plan hasn't changed," X said, a purposeful look replacing the previously furious expression on his face. "We will proceed with our plan, and I consider it only fair to warn you that if we spot anyone who resembles a police officer or detective in the vicinity, I will murder you son."

Eyal's eyes narrowed. "I'm sure you're aware that I don't control the movements of the Ukrainian police force."

"If you don't pull any fast ones and radio for help, then we won't see any police officers in the area."

"I want to speak to my son." Eyal said, changing tack.

"Out of the question," X said.

"How do I know he's even alive? Maybe you got rid of him already." X would never know how much it hurt him to even utter those words, Eyal thought.

"He's alive. You'll have to trust me on that one. You and only you are to blame for this situation. You could have remained with him, but you blew the chance to do this nicely. Then you endangered his life, which is more than we did, so I'd say you lost the moral right to come to me now with complaints. Subject closed."

"I still want to speak to him," Eyal said stubbornly.

"No." X poured himself another cup of Coke, and Eyal watched the fizz bubble up and then subside. He felt overwhelmed by dizziness, and now nausea. Eyal shook his head in an effort to try to clear his mind. He tried a different approach: "You want me at my best, don't you?"

"You *will* be at your best – either that, or you will not see your child again. Ever."

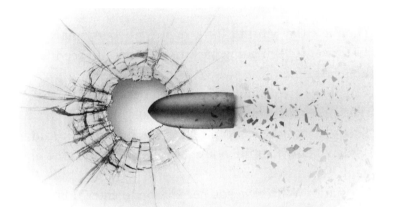

CHAPTER SIXTEEN

Ukraine

We can try to locate him via the weapons dealers."
Vitali, one of the Mossad's agents in the Ukraine
gulped down his drink and shrugged. "It shouldn't be
too hard. I have contacts."

Eli looked at the man, curious as to his inner workings. Who
was this Vitali? Had he ever lived in Israel? When had he begun
working for the Mossad? They were meeting in a bar on an obscure side street, and Vitali hadn't hesitated before ordering a
drink for himself, which probably meant that he wasn't bothered
about kashrus. What was certain, however, was the fact that he
could be depended upon for this mission absolutely. The Mossad
did not hire anyone unless the person was beyond suspicion.

"It definitely makes sense that your friends in the mafia will have some information to provide," Eli said. He held out a thick envelope. "Take this. Twenty thousand dollars to open mouths. If you need any more, just say the word."

"I already need more," Vitali chuckled. "I've got a mortgage to pay."

"Then ask the Mossad for a raise," Eli said, unamused. He leaned forward. "I'm going back to the house to see if I missed anything last time."

"The police are claiming it was an illegal arms factory," Vitali said. "Arms, explosives, maybe drugs too."

"That's what they've been telling the media," Eli said. "But the insiders know that the house belonged to a terrorist or criminal gang."

"No matter. Who gave you permission to enter? I know someone – never mind who – who tried to get in. Forget it! Police swarming everywhere you look."

Eli smiled. "That's not an issue for me. Colonel Tadiev is my good friend."

"Tadiev?" Vitali stared. "I thought he wanted you behind bars. He's still convinced that you were behind the attack in which six of his men were killed."

"No, no – I disabused him of that belief," Eli said. "And we met only yesterday, after they almost caught up with Eyal again. We came to a certain understanding, made possible by the fact that we currently share an enemy."

Vitali raised his eyebrows. "You impress me, Eli. Okay, so go and speak to him." The bartender approached and Vitali ordered another drink. He was clearly in no hurry to leave. "I will speak to my friends," he said quietly. "They'll be excited at the prospect of locating Rubinov's murderer. I imagine you've heard that there's a twenty-million-dollar bounty for whoever brings in Eyal's head."

Eli thought of the disappointment Tadiev must be feeling over Eyal's escape. "Vitali, Eyal is not the murderer," he said.

"Really? You could have fooled me."

Eli had to restrain himself from landing a well-aimed blow on Vitali's face. If even the intelligence world didn't believe in Eyal's innocence, how could he expect the police force to believe it? "You have my word on this."

Vitali put down his glass. "A bullet from Eyal's gun was in Rubinov's body, Eli. Eyal was the only person in the safe with him when he died. How can you proclaim him to be innocent?"

"Eyal told me that he didn't murder Rubinov." Eli watched Vitali shrug and resume drinking. Ordinarily, he would have ordered a drink of his own. He only kept kosher when Eyal was around, but religious reasons had nothing to do with his lack of desire to drink right now. It was the conversation that had killed it.

"And you believe him?" Vitali downed the remains of his glass in one gulp. "What a wonderful friend."

"You're right," Eli said. "You're a fellow agent, and I wouldn't lie to you. Eyal is my best friend, and if he told me he didn't commit this murder, then I believe him. He wouldn't lie to me."

"A true friend is a rare commodity for an intelligence agent," Vitali noted. "I only hope that in the future Eyal will have the opportunity to reciprocate your loyalty to him."

"Why?"

"Because I don't know if you will ever see him alive again."

Eyal was led back to his cell, and his injured arm was locked once more to the bars. The same four men with guns were there, lolling on their chairs, chatting among themselves and throwing him the occasional glance. There was no need for them to pay close attention to him – they knew he was trapped. Eyal's thoughts turned to Elitzafun, in his own strange, bewildering prison, and he fought back his tears.

Had he made a mistake by trying to escape? No. He refused to believe that. There had been a good chance that he could pull it off – he had been obligated to make that attempt.

Now too, he had to make some kind of attempt to escape. Giving up was a totally foreign notion to him. In this case it was tantamount to suicide, as there was no way X would leave him at liberty even if he did, by some miracle, survive the mission they had in mind for him.

The thought jolted him suddenly out of his semi-stupor. For all his desperate desire to protect Elitzafun, he was obligated to do what he could to save his own life if there was a good chance that both of them could emerge in one piece. And maybe, just maybe, there was a way…

At any rate, he had to make some kind of move, without involving the police – which he believed really would cause X to make good on his promise to kill his son if he managed to contact them. But there were other options.

His arm throbbed painfully and he shifted his position, trying to find a way to make himself more comfortable – and failing. Maybe the wound would be the ticket to his freedom?

He looked down at it now. If he lost consciousness, X would have to take him to the hospital, and there he would have infinitely more freedom than he had in his current location.

Slowly, Eyal reached along his arm until he felt the bandage. In the semidarkness the guards didn't notice his movements, and he continued to burrow beneath the layers of gauze. Although he couldn't see the wound, it was obvious from just a cursory examination by fingertip that whoever had treated him had done a clumsy job with the stitches.

A guard turned toward him and Eyal quickly feigned sleep. His thoughts surged forward. What would he have to do in order to get to the hospital?

He could try to get his wound infected, a task that would be fairly simple to accomplish. It would also be impossible to prove that Eyal was the one who had brought about his own infection. The trouble with that plan was that it would take time for the infection to set in, and he needed to reach the hospital by the next day at the latest. Worse still, if the Ukrainians didn't treat the infection properly, Efrat could end up becoming a widow a second time.

What else? He could cause himself to lose more blood so that a blood transfusion would become necessary. As it was, there was no telling that he didn't need a transfusion already. His symptoms certainly indicated that treatment of some sort was in order, but as long as his injury didn't seem life-threatening, X was determined to ignore it.

Failing to come up with a better option, Eyal decided that he would have to engineer copious loss of blood. He was counting on the fact that X still wanted him alive and in reasonably good health. But it would have to be convincing.

A glance in the guards' direction told him that none of them was focused too intently on him just then. Two of the guards were dozing off, one was smoking a cigarette, and the fourth was engrossed in his phone.

Eyal continued to prod his wound, paying attention to the method that had been used to stitch it up. Visions of a primitive Ukrainian doctor with a paper stapler flashed through his mind. The stitches were in fact metal staples, not closely spaced. That would make things easier.

Gritting his teeth, Eyal grasped the first of the staples and pulled hard. He had to clamp his mouth shut in order to stop himself from yelling from the agonizing tearing of his flesh. The wound began to bleed again, but the flow of blood wasn't as fast as he had been hoping.

Black stars danced wildly before his eyes and there was a terrible throbbing pressure in his temples. With his remaining strength he started to tug at the second staple, but he couldn't take the pain.

Three seconds later, blood started to spurt out in quantities and Eyal sank to the floor of his cell, unconscious.

CHAPTER SEVENTEEN

Ukraine

C olin pushed open the door to X's room and announced without fanfare, "Eyal is unconscious."

"What?" X jumped out of his chair, eyes staring. "It's impossible. He's just playing games with us. I won't fall for it, and I'm surprised that you did."

Colin's eyes narrowed. "I didn't fall for anything," he said coldly. "I know an unconscious person when I see one. Eyal's bullet wound has reopened, and it seems that he lost consciousness from the blood loss."

X bit back the string of curses threatening to burst from his mouth. "Call Dr. Bogdan," he ordered. "He's the only person I can trust right now."

Colin shook his head. "I don't think you can rely on him this time," he said. He knew Dr. Bogdan – a competent general practitioner but not accustomed to dealing with true medical emergencies. However, X misunderstood his intent.

"There's no choice. Eyal needs medical attention or I'll lose him before he accomplishes his mission, and that is something I'm not prepared to let happen."

"That's not what I mean," Colin said. "Of course Bogdan is reliable, but he's an amateur when it comes to cases like this one. We need to get Eyal to a hospital or you really will lose him."

"Bogdan is not an amateur, and Eyal is not going to any hospital," X said furiously. "If he could escape from the compound, then escaping from a hospital will be child's play for him."

"But he won't try it," Colin said. "Remember – we have his son."

"So he'll manage it another way – he'll get a doctor to pass on a message to his friends," X said. "I won't risk it."

"There's no risk. We'll sit at his side twenty-four seven. He won't be able to raise a finger without our knowing about it."

"Colin, I am not allowing Eyal to leave this house," X said. "That's final! I don't care whether his condition right now is faked or real. If he's taken to hospital, he'll find some way to exploit every opportunity given to him – or to create an opportunity if need be. I won't do it."

Colin went over to the window and looked out. "How large is the yard around this house, X? It looks a lot smaller than the yard of the compound."

"I'm sure it is smaller," X said, eyebrows raised. "Why are you asking?"

"I should probably get started digging a plot large enough to bury Eyal's body."

"His situation isn't that bad!" X protested.

"He's bleeding, his blood pressure is way down, his pulse is erratic, he's sweating, and his skin is clammy. Those are the classic signs of shock, which means that he needs an IV and a blood transfusion or else he will die."

This time X did curse, before getting up and heading toward the door. "I'm going to take a look at him myself," he said.

"You're not a doctor," Colin pointed out.

X fixed him with a cold, reproachful stare. "Call Bogdan," he said. "I'll stay with Eyal in the meantime."

X opened the door to the basement where Eyal's barred cell had been placed. The room was dimly lit, and X turned on the ceiling light in order to see better. Eyal was lying on the floor of his cell, sweating profusely, his face pale. Someone had apparently released his hand from the cuff linking him to the bar. His lips were white, and X recoiled at the sight of the blood pooling beneath him. After a moment he bent over and touched Eyal's wrist. No reaction. The Israeli agent really was unconscious.

X felt for a heartbeat and frowned. Too fast. Way too fast. There was truly no choice now, and he hated the man for forcing his hand.

X looked around the cell for anything suggestive of Eyal's having deliberately brought about a worsening of his injury. There was no evidence to back up his theory, but Eyal was too good an agent to leave any clues.

"We'll have to transfer him to another room," X said with a sigh. "John, have him taken upstairs to the third room on the left. Move the bed to the window, and handcuff his hands to the bars with a long chain or something."

"He's unconscious, X," John said. "He's not in any condition to be able to run away."

"Tell me about it."

"You want permission to search the compound?" Tadiev said, his eyebrows shooting up in surprise. "What can you possibly find there that my men didn't find already?"

"I won't know until I take a look for myself," Eli said. "A couple of hours should do it. What difference does it make to you?"

Tadiev shrugged. "None, I suppose. Okay. I'll give you permission, so long as you agree to share your findings – if there are any – with me."

"How about you share your findings with me first?" Eli suggested. Tadiev hadn't given him so much as a clue as to what the forensics team had found at the gutted site of the compound, and he assumed that the senior police officer's hands were tied on the issue. He wasn't about to risk his job by passing on classified information to a foreign agent who had insinuated himself into his good graces.

Tadiev fixed Eli with a piercing look. "I'm serious."

"So am I," Eli said. Maybe he would ask the Mossad to pressure the Ukrainian police into releasing details of their findings. Not that the evidence would be earth-shattering. Eyal's abductors were clearly smart enough to know how to cover their tracks, but there was always the off-chance that something of value might have been overlooked.

Tadiev exhaled slowly, and then scribbled something on a piece of paper. "Take this."

Eli glanced at the note and smiled. "Thank you."

"Wow, impressive fireworks here," Eli commented as he approached the red-and-white plastic roping off the area around the compound's perimeter fence. Even two days later, the strong odor of smoke and smolder in the air threatened to choke him.

Two police officers approached. "Who are you? A journalist? No one's allowed in."

"I'm not a journalist," Eli said. Calmly, he pulled out the pass that Tadiev had given him. "I need to go in."

The police officers grumbled. "We've had more than enough

people coming here to sift the earth and comb the dust. It's like they think they might find gold or something."

"Well, they say they were manufacturing drugs here," Eli said casually. "So even a small find could be worth big bucks." He removed a pack of American cigarettes from his pocket, took out two, and held them out to the police officers. "Did anyone find anything?"

"Whatever they found they took away with them. Whatever's still left here is of no interest to anyone."

Eli nodded. A friendly expression on his face, he pulled out a lighter and lit the two officers' cigarettes.

"Want to take a look around?" one of the officers now suggested.

"Of course." If only there was even the slightest of clues as to Eyal's whereabouts. Something that would give away his abductors' country of origin, their current location, or even just the identity of their weapons provider.

Anything.

Only once he was inside did he realize how gargantuan the task was. The building resembled a garbage dump. There was no order, no rhyme or reason to the places where he found items. There were dismembered wall hangings, plants, faucets, and random articles of clothing, but nothing with a useful mark, no names, no numbers, no concrete information. There were also a few books, a wooden closet that had been reduced to a charred lump, and the remains of food and drinks that had obviously been purchased at a local store.

Taking into account the number of people who must have lived in the building, Eli had to admit that they had done a great job covering their tracks.

Broken Coke bottles.

The oval-shaped kashrus symbol of Harav Landau of Bnei Brak caught his eye. Quickly Eli dialed Vitali's phone number. "Vitali," he whispered excitedly into his phone. "They bought Eyal, or perhaps Elitzafun, kosher Coke."

"So?"

"From what I understood from Eyal, there are plenty of religious Jews who drink Coke without a kosher symbol on it, thinking it's okay, but really it's not. But here, Eyal's abductors went all out in order to cater to his kashrut stringencies."

"So what?" Vitali repeated. His other phone was ringing, and he couldn't afford to waste time on stupid conversations like this one.

"In that case, we can assume they're going to continue to purchase kosher food for Eyal and Elitzafun," Eli said.

"What are you trying to say? That we should call all of the Fara and Silfo supermarkets because they have kosher sections – oh, and then of course there are also all the Chabad houses that have in-house kosher groceries. You must be out of your mind."

"Kosher food can be used as a means of tracking Eyal down," Eli said, his voice reproachful. "We can send a message to the Chabad houses telling them what we need them to keep an eye out for. We can also keep tabs on the main supermarkets, though maybe that would be better done by the police. If they put the word out that it's Eyal himself that they're after and that he can be identified by purchases of kosher food, we'll get plenty of co-operation. After all, there's a bounty on his head."

Vitali laughed. "Eli, please don't tell me you're serious. If we do as you suggest, we'll be sifting through thousands of reports, and trying to follow up on them will occupy half of the Ukrainian police force. They're not going to play along."

"We're not looking for people who just come into a store, buy what they need, and leave," Eli persisted. "We're only looking for someone who asks questions, who doesn't seem to know what kosher means."

Vitali shrugged. "If it was up to me I'd tell you to forget it. But as it is…well, I'll humor you. The *shluchim* at the Chabad houses will play along, though I doubt that the kidnappers would approach them. The stores – well, that's a different story. But we can try. Though I will do my best to ensure that the job of sifting through the thousands of callers reporting suspicious activity is given to you."

"No problem," Eli said. "If that's what it takes, that's what I'll do."

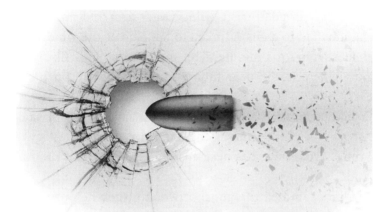

CHAPTER EIGHTEEN

Ukraine

A knock, and Colin and Dr. Bogdan entered the room.

"So, what do we have here?" Bogdan was Ukrainian, but his value system was that of radical Islam. He wasn't officially a member of any of the terror organizations, but he was a generous supporter of all of them.

"A gunshot wound," X said briefly. "He was shot yesterday, and his situation seemed stable at first but then it began to deteriorate toward evening."

Bogdan placed his bag on the table beside Eyal's bed. "Who tended to the gunshot wound?" Removing an IV line from his bag, Bogdan injected the needle into his patient's vein and then hung the drip from a protruding nail in the wall overhead.

"I did," Colin said. "I know it looks awful now, but when I

stitched it up I managed to get the blood flow to stop."

"I have good reason to believe that the patient made a deliberate attempt to reopen the wound," X said. "He's not exactly here voluntarily, as you can see."

"I do see." Bogdan tried lifting Eyal's arm and noticed that it was handcuffed to a chain linked to the bars of the window. "Can you release him for a minute? This man doesn't look like he's running anywhere in the near future. Do you know what his blood type is?"

"You'd be amazed at what this man is capable of," X said, but he instructed Colin to unlock the handcuff around Eyal's wounded hand. "We'll have to check his blood type. I don't remember offhand."

Bogdan examined the gunshot wound, then he opened Eyal's eyelids and shone a flashlight at the pupils. "You could be wrong in your assumption. Staples like these can open if they're rubbed or if there is an additional injury. If all of the stitches were torn open, then I'd agree with you that the patient was trying to cause his situation to decline, but since only one of the staples has opened, I don't believe he did this to himself."

X didn't respond. Instead, he turned toward Colin. "Find out what his blood type is," he said.

Colin left the room, and Dr. Bogdan took Eyal's temperature, blood pressure, and pulse. Next he conducted a quick check of his reflexes, and when he was done he turned to X.

"This man looks like he was tossed from a truck or subjected to torture. Are you responsible for his injuries?"

"No."

"Look, I really don't care either way," the doctor said. "You know I'm not going to report this. But if you want me to get this man back on his feet, it would help to know exactly what I'm dealing with. This is more than a gunshot wound that isn't healing properly. This man's body is simply too weak to address all of its issues."

"He went through a rough round of interrogations before he came here," X said. "You don't need to know more than that."

Dr. Bogdan pursed his lips. "I see." He looked around. "This man is in urgent need of a blood transfusion. He's going to need several pints of blood."

Colin entered the room. "I can't find his blood type noted in any of the documents we have here. The document with that information may have been lost in the fire, of course." He turned to Bogdan. "Now what?"

"It's not the end of the world. We can give him type O – that's suitable for all types. But getting hold of it is definitely going to cost you."

"That's not a problem," X said, turning to Colin. "Go take care of arranging the cash."

Colin left the room again, leaving X alone with the doctor. "How bad is he?" he asked.

"He needs good medical care in order for his body to be able to heal. Frankly, I'd say he needs to be hospitalized."

"Under no circumstances will I have this man admitted to a hospital. You'll do whatever needs to be done right here and we'll pay whatever you ask."

"Well, I'll need equipment to perform surgery. Call this number." Bogdan hastily scribbled a phone number onto a sheet of paper. "Tell whoever answers the phone that I need sterile operating equipment because I'm operating on a bullet wound. If you don't want to disclose your location, then arrange for one of your men to meet this person at a place of your choosing. I am not leaving this patient alone."

X nodded and left the room. Bogdan examined Eyal again, and when his fingers touched the bullet wound, he sensed that someone was looking at him.

With a tortured expression on his face and teeth clenched against the pain, Eyal stared up at the doctor. Apparently, the IV was already having a positive effect.

The doctor released Eyal's arm. "You're up?" The words were half-question, half-statement.

Eyal smiled weakly.

"How are you feeling?"

"Who are you?" Eyal asked soundlessly, moving his lips.

"I'm a friend of X. Who are you?"

"It doesn't matter." Eyal's voice was slowly coming back to him, but it was low and hoarse. "What happened to me?"

"You lost consciousness due to blood loss, and X called me to take care of you." Dr. Bogdan pointed to the wound in Eyal's arm. "Who did that to you?"

"Who shot the bullet, you mean?"

"Yes, but not just that, actually. Who's responsible for all the rest of it?" Bogdan's expression was a combination of pity and curiosity.

"Not X," Eyal said shortly.

"That's what he told me," Bogdan said. "But whoever it was did a solid job. You look as though you fell out of a third story window. Or maybe you were dragged down an entire block by a truck."

Eyal managed another smile. "I guess you can say that I feel that way."

"What did they do to you?"

"I was whipped."

"It looks like more than that."

"Electric shocks, whippings with a rubber pole, things like that." Speech demanded tremendous effort, and Eyal had no interest in wasting his precious energy on this doctor.

"And then you were shot?"

"Yes."

"I'm assuming that was due to an attempt to run away from jail."

"No."

"You're Eyal Gilboa, aren't you?"

"How do you know?"

"Your picture's all over the media. It's not hard to piece the facts together."

"So you know who I am," Eyal said. "Now what are you going to do about it?"

"First of all, I'm going to make sure you get a blood transfusion, and then I will operate on you under field conditions in the hope that it will suffice. I expect that it will indeed stabilize things."

Eyal tried to sit up, but the doctor placed a hand on his shoulder.

"Don't. You need to rest up in order to fight."

"Who says that's what I want to do?" Eyal's eyes smarted – but not due to his physical pain.

"I don't know," Bogdan said. "But if you're here against your will, I'm assuming there's a reason for that. I trust X and believe in his cause."

My redemption is not going to come from this direction, Eyal thought. He was certainly weak, but apparently he had not lost a consequential quantity of blood, given that he had not managed to land himself in hospital. He had taken a risk, and it was a risk that he had taken of his own free will, for the perils of remaining under X's jurisdiction were that much greater.

"So, what do you have?" Eli had returned to his rental apartment toward evening, and he had invited Vitali to join him there for a meeting and to impress him with a display of the sophisticated equipment the Mossad had graciously supplied him with over the past few days.

"Nothing you didn't know already. There are the obvious channels for bringing in goods without going through security checks or customs. There are the known bars and restaurants where orders and taken and details given for supply. There are the money launderers who take care of many additional things. The question is, where you want to start."

"I want to start with the arms dealers," Eli said.

"Okay...but they tend to have their specialties," Vitali noted. "What did these people have? It must have been good stuff if they were willing to take on the police."

"It was. They had heavy machine guns, snipers' rifles, and more. I'm not exactly sure what else, to be honest, but that's enough to start with." Eli opened the fridge in search of something to eat and then closed it with disappointment at the paltry offerings inside. "I'm still hoping to get access to the evidence the forensics teams managed to uncover at the burnt-out compound. I think some of our higher-ups should be exerting pressure, but so far I'm the only one pushing that method of operation. Admittedly, the Ukrainians are furious with Israel right now and cooperation is the last thing on their minds. They insist on viewing the terrorist group as a front for our own guys, and nothing I say makes a dent in their assumptions."

"Okay, so we know who we can't rely on, then." Vitali looked around the small apartment, taking in the impressive array of technology. "But they've provided you with state-of-the-art equipment all the same."

"This is something that the Ukrainians will never find out about." Eli smiled. "The Mossad has given us a day or two to try and come up with something through unofficial channels. They've also sent us a lot of meaningless reports."

"That say what?"

"That they've succeeded in tracing the kidnappers' route out of the country, but that it hasn't helped them to discover their identities. These are professionals who know what they're doing. They still haven't found their safe house, or figured out where exactly they came from."

"Well, what have *you* managed to find out?" Vitali asked. "I hope the information you've come up with is more useful than that report."

"I plan to call every kosher distributer in the area."

"That's crazy! You'll be opening two hundred mouths instead of remaining invisible. The kidnappers warned the child's mother not to involve anyone."

"I believe it's a necessary risk to take."

Vitali sighed, and his eyes seemed to be saying, "Don't try and convince the idiot; he won't understand you anyway." Aloud, though, he said: "Before getting citizens involved in this, let's visit some of the bars I mentioned." He stood up. "We'll stop off at my house first so that you can get dressed for the part. Right now you look no more like a mafia gangster than I look a Chabad chassid."

The door opened, and X and Colin entered Eyal's room. Colin held a bulky suitcase.

"The supplies you requested," X told the doctor.

"That was quick," Bogdan commented. "You must want him to survive."

"Most definitely," X agreed. "But your contact didn't have enough units of blood."

The doctor thought for a moment. "You can try this number instead," he said, writing a number on a piece of paper. "Ask him to deliver the blood to a meeting place just as you did with the supplies. You'll need to pay up on the spot – no funny tricks. In the meantime I'm going to sterilize the area, and I'll need an assistant."

"That would be me," Colin said.

"Wonderful." Dr. Bogdan opened the suitcase, removed a syringe, and filled it with a clear liquid.

Eyal watched the doctor work. "What are you doing?" he asked quietly.

X and Colin, noticing that the patient had awakened, approached his bed.

"I'm putting you to sleep," Dr. Bogdan said.

"You will survive this," X said.

"I don't need your platitudes." Eyal's tongue was sharp as ever. "If you're truly concerned about me, then concern yourself with my family."

"I'm not concerned about you," X said coldly.

"Of course – you're not." A powerful spasm of pain shot through his arm, and Eyal shut his eyes momentarily. "You're only concerned about your war machine."

"Of course. And about finding the button that makes escape and rebellion an option."

Eyal smiled. "You have no idea how many people have searched for that button before you." He bit down on his lips as the doctor touched his wound again. Then he drew a deep breath and tried to regain his equilibrium and restore the smug expression to his face. "Searched, tried, and failed," he added.

"You may have thought that you'd land up in a hospital," X said, ignoring the jibe. "You're staying here, however, to make sure you have no opportunity to contact any of your friends, wherever they may be."

Eyal was silent.

"You are under our constant supervision, and there is, and will be, no way for you to communicate with anyone other than the people we want you to communicate with. Don't even bother to think about escaping. There is no way out for you, Eyal. Remember what is hanging in the balance."

Eyal looked straight into X's eyes. "I won't forget."

"Put him under," X said, turning abruptly to the doctor.

A gray cloud seemed to wrap itself around Eyal's body. His plan to contact someone from the outside world had failed. And he had no other plan.

Yet.

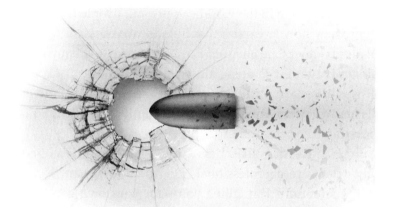

CHAPTER NINETEEN

Ukraine

T hey spent eight hours trekking between five different bars, going through them with a fine-tooth comb. Vitali was an expert at using his personal charm and wit to extract information, and in this particular case, that was exactly what was needed. Technology would achieve nothing. There are places where nothing is computerized and deals are made with a quiet handshake and cash. Information is memorized, and the few details that need to be recorded are written down with ink on paper. No credit cards, no bank accounts, no digital databases.

Nothing, however, can entirely obviate the need for the human element. Someone can place his money in an offshore account in the Seychelles Islands, but there will still be a person deciding whether to open that account or not, and then another person dealing with the actual deposits. Someone can bribe the airport security personnel in an Eastern European country to conceal all data referring to his flight departure times, yet all it takes is for one flight attendant to see too much, and his information will no longer be safe. No force in the world can prevent people from talking.

Vitali knew how to exploit that human weakness.

"You stay quiet," he had told Eli. "Your accent when you speak Ukrainian is awful. I'm doing all the talking, and that's final."

Eli was affronted. "Nobody looks at me twice here," he insisted. "Usually I speak Russian – which I do like a native. So I can be a Russian."

"You're a Russian like I'm a musician," Vitali scoffed. "I thought you were a professional. Do you really want to attract unwanted attention? I'm telling you – for your own good, let me do the talking. It's not just the language. It's the mentality."

That had been hours ago, and Vitali had done a lot of talking since, without a single tangible result. Now they entered their sixth bar, and Vitali looked around, attempting to identify the type of person he was looking for. Suddenly his eyes came to rest on a man sitting near the window, and he smiled.

"Look at that man," Vitali whispered, his lips barely moving.

Eli followed his gaze and saw a middle-aged man with hair that had obviously been dyed in an unsuccessful attempt to appear younger. There were several heavy rings on the man's fingers, and a thick chain around his neck. He looked like a hybrid of a mafia gangster and a businessman.

"Who is he?" Eli asked.

"Vladimir Kumshitz. A gold mine when it comes to weapons deals, and one of the best money launderers out there. He's exactly what we need right now."

"If you knew all this already," Eli said caustically, "you could have saved us eight hours of misery and just met him at his home."

"He doesn't do meetings. You have to know how to approach him. Don't worry – our eight-hour trek was worth every minute.

The truth is that there are other people like him, maybe even better than him, but he'll be good enough for what we need. He's a risk-taker, which isn't always the best thing, but it'll work to our advantage. He won't conduct a week-long background check before deciding whether or not to close on the deal."

Vitali stopped talking to Eli and sauntered over to Kumshitz, sitting down beside him seemingly by chance. "A bottle of Irish whiskey, and keep the change," he told the waiter as he walked past, handing him a hundred-dollar bill.

Then he turned around suddenly, as if to glance out of the window, knocking his elbow into his quarry. Kumshitz looked up, startled.

"You're Kumshitz, aren't you?" Vitali murmured, his eyes distant.

Kumshitz glanced at his three companions, who didn't seem to be paying any attention to this strange encounter, before replying, "What's it to you?"

"I'm a customer."

Kumshitz smirked. "Ah, you're interested in real estate? I have some beautiful apartments available. What neighborhood are you looking in?"

"You're a real estate agent like I'm a cucumber importer. Skip the word games. We both know you laundered Molrov's weapons deal."

"Excuse me." Kumshitz stood up and apologized to his friends. "I need to leave. Farewell."

The men nodded and turned back to their drinks.

Vitali got up and walked fast after a furious Kumshitz. "Wait a minute."

"I don't know who you are and what you think you're doing. But you are never to speak of such things near strangers."

"I'm sorry," Vitali said, and his tone of voice was so contrite that even Eli, close on his heels, believed in his sincerity. "I apologize, but it could not be avoided. I am in urgent need of your services."

"I don't do business with people who appear out of nowhere. You could be a police officer, a detective, a foreign intelligence agent, or anything else, for all I know."

"I could be, but I'm not. I'm a member of Rubinov's mafia. You can easily verify that if you want." Vitali slipped Kumshitz a business card. Underneath the name Vitali Lemberg was written "Security Adviser."

Kumshitz barely gave the card a glance. "I'll look into the matter," he said, turning to go.

"It can't wait," Vitali pressed. "This concerns Rubinov's murder. I'm striking out on my own for this one, and I need help." He handed Kumshitz an envelope. "We'll be in touch."

The men parted ways, and Vitali and Eli watched Kumshitz enter his car and drive off.

"He won't be back," Eli told Vitali in a disappointed tone. "He's going to suspect a rival mafia of approaching him with harmful intentions."

"Oh yes, he will be back," Vitali said, his voice brimming with confidence. "He's known to be immensely greedy for money, and he's often lax when it comes to taking precautionary security measures."

Vitali's phone rang suddenly, and he winked. "See that?" He answered the phone quickly.

"I'll be there."

Vitali gave a victorious smile. "He's in. Too bad I didn't bet on this."

"What did you put into that envelope?"

"Ninety thousand dollars and a note telling him to meet us in an hour at a certain location." Vitali turned toward his car.

"Your whiskey, Vitali. Isn't it a shame?"

"Me and whiskey? I drink only vodka."

Eli chuckled. "Tell me about it. But – what about the other ten thousand in the envelope that I gave you?"

Vitali smiled. "I set that aside to cover my mortgage."

❧

"So all you're interested in purchasing is information," Kumshitz said. His voice was laced with disappointment. He had been hoping for a weapons order.

"Yes. We're trying to trace the people who murdered our boss, and we have enough money to grease whatever information wheels need to be greased." Vitali opened a bottle of whiskey and poured some of the liquid into Kumshitz's glass.

"I see. So what is it that you want from me?"

"We have reason to believe that the gang purchased various pieces of equipment and some heavy weapons. Brownings, MAGs, grenade launchers, shoulder-fired missiles, and maybe also ground missiles and air missiles." Vitali finished speaking and poured himself a shot of vodka, downing it in a single gulp.

Eli, watching Vitali, wondered if the man's drinking style was a show that he put on in order to be accepted as a typical Ukrainian, or if that was simply who he was. His perfect accent told of genuine Ukrainian origins, but that said nothing about his past or present, how or why the Mossad had recruited him, and if he had been raised in Israel or not.

"An impressive list," Kumshitz said, swirling the liquid in his glass appreciatively.

"We don't know what they're planning, but we are clearly not going to remain silent on this." Vitali poured himself another shot of vodka. "We have more money at our disposal than they do, and we're after information. We need to know exactly who we're up against."

"I didn't take care of the money laundering for any such deal," Kumshitz said, shrugging as he drained his glass.

Only Eli drank nothing.

"They may have divided the money between several launderers to avoid suspicion," Vitali said. "I'm estimating that they spent about twenty to thirty million dollars obtaining their equipment." Vitali gestured to his attaché case. "It'll pay for you to help us find them."

"Fine." Kumshitz stood up. "My fee is ten percent of whatever the amount turns out to have been."

Vitali nodded his consent. "Agreed."

The answer arrived faster than they had expected. Kumshitz was apparently proud of having uncovered the information so quickly.

Kumshitz sent his handwritten response in a simple-looking envelope. "Your purchasers have no name – that is, it's not a recognized organization. Their leader goes by the name X, and he has purchased enough weapons for a war. He bought four different safe houses in four different parts of Ukraine and paid for them in cash. One of those houses recently burned down in what was likely an attempt to escape a police investigation. Many documents and dangerous substances were destroyed in the blaze. Two of the remaining houses are in Kiev; the third is in Odessa."

Vitali sent a note back with a courier: "I need the addresses of the other safe houses."

A few days later Kumshitz sent the information, and Vitali let Kumshitz know that the money transfer would be made shortly. He handed him an advance of five hundred thousand dollars in cash, and the men parted ways.

Eli, aghast, confronted Vitali with what seemed like an obscene use of funds, but Vitali was unrepentant.

"We'll bargain with him later," he replied. "You can't be stingy in the mafia. If Rubinov could spend two million dollars on a pretty picture frame, I can't destroy my cover story by offering less."

Kumshitz didn't return home that evening, and his body was never found.

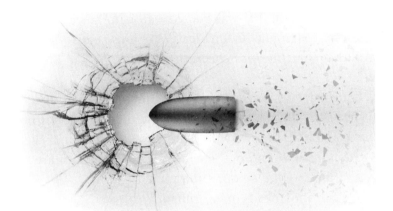

CHAPTER TWENTY

Ukraine

"H e died," Vitali told Eli the next morning, undoing the knot of his tie as he spoke. "Ties are intolerable! The worst part of being a businessman!"

"Who died?" Eli said.

"Kumshitz." Vitali calmly removed a pack of cigarettes from his pocket, lighting one and offering Eli another.

"How do you know?" Eli asked, refusing the cigarette.

"What are friends for? The last people Kumshitz saw are you and me."

"So they were onto him." Eli pursed his lips, and his thoughts galloped onward. "Which means that they'll probably abandon their safe house, and they may harm Eyal and his son in the process."

Vitali shook his head. "I don't think so. From the scanty bits of information I received from my informant, Kumshitz was killed because he expressed a general interest in X, and nothing more than that." Vitali puffed rings of smoke into the air, clearly taking pleasure in the smog that was being created in the close confines of the room. "Men like X don't leave any loose ends. As soon as X heard that someone was checking into him, he had him eliminated."

Eli coughed. "So long as this has nothing to do with Eyal, I'm okay," he said. "I'll pause momentarily, though, in honor of the deceased, and after that we will begin our examination of this X's three safe houses to find out where Eyal and Elitzafun are being held – and then we'll plan our infiltration."

"The infiltration needs to be brilliant."

"Correct," Eli said. "Because if it's not, we will both die too."

Eli eyed the three men who had flown hastily into Ukraine with interest: Danny, from the Mossad's Kidon unit, and Avi and Shuki from GSS Special Operations. Eli wasn't overjoyed at the prospect of working with agents from both the GSS and the Mossad in the same mission, but no one had asked his opinion on the matter. This particular operation needed the best manpower available – and Eli had asked for the best and had been given precisely that.

He couldn't complain.

Eli cleared his throat. "We have satellite support from the Mossad, the most up-to-date technology for the infiltration, and anything else that we might need."

"Their safe houses will be monitored around the clock."

"They're not houses," Vitali said. "They're fortresses, and they're virtually hermetically sealed."

"That's what these guys are here for," Eli said impatiently. "We didn't call them here to meet arms dealers in bars and get them killed." He bent to look more closely at the papers in front of him, and a gloomy expression settled on his face. The photos had been taken using the Mossad's satellite cameras as well as Arrowlite, an unmanned drone outfitted with both electro-optic and FLIR C2 thermal cameras. "I can't see this happening," he muttered.

Avi took the top paper from the table. "Security cameras, motion detectors, field-of-vision decoders, robots, alarms, and various other equipment." He sighed. "There's even a robotic security guard."

"Which means that we don't want numbers," Shuki observed. "That will just spark a war, which is not quite what we're interested in. No – we need silence, total silence."

"Great idea," Eli said acidly. "Now just tell me how to achieve that, given that they have all the possible access routes under constant observation. The slightest unexpected movement will be checked out within seconds."

"So maybe we can cause the gas or electricity to stop working, and one of us can get hired as a technician to sort it out." That was Vitali's contribution.

"These guys weren't born yesterday. If what I've heard is accurate, this X is supremely suspicious of anything and everything, and they never hire anyone from the outside to take care of things."

"So let's have him removed from the equation," Danny said.

"Great idea," Shuki said sarcastically. "Especially since we have no idea who he is."

"In that case, we need to find that out," Danny countered.

"A wonderful idea. Only, as things stand right now, none of us has ever seen him, spoken to him, or heard from him."

"Aside from Eyal."

Eli started. "Wait a minute...yes – that's it!" He opened his laptop computer as he continued, "Eyal's wife spoke to him, once. Just after the kidnapping. Wait a minute..." Eli pecked at his keyboard, and a few minutes later he found the conversation he was after. He pressed *play*, and suddenly a man's voice filled the room.

"I'm sorry to have to hurt you, Mrs. Gilboa. But you need to understand us. I am also a father, and I understand what a father's concern means. My children, my six-year-old, my four-year-old, and my one-year-old, were killed a little over three years ago. In November of 2014 Assad's army wiped out my home, my children, and my life. Your child will return, I hope, but my children never will. My country is going through a holocaust, and no one cares."

"He doesn't give his name."

"He says that he has three children who were killed, and he says when the attack took place. How many people had children of those ages who all died in a single attack on that date?"

"Oh, only about twenty thousand, I guess," Shuki said.

"No, no…it's narrower than that. I think we have something to start from," Eli insisted. "Let's give it a shot."

"I want my father." Elitzafun's light-brown eyes were filled with grief and loneliness as he looked up at Leon. "I want my father. I want my father. I want my father!"

Leon was in a quandary. X had ordered them to be patient with the child, but he didn't see how it was possible to remain patient with a child who repeated the exact same sentence in the same tone of voice again and again, until he thought he would go crazy.

"No," Leon said shortly. "Enough. I said no, and that's it. Stop driving me up the wall!"

Elitzafun screwed up his face. "But I want my father."

"I said, *enough*!!"

Elitzafun screwed his face up tighter in an unsuccessful attempt to fight the tears that were threatening to gush from his eyes. Bitter wails escaped from the boy's throat.

"Enough!" Leon shouted. "I told you to stop!"

Elitzafun wailed louder.

Mark, watching the scene, was amused. "For some reason I'm getting the feeling that this isn't the way to get a child to stop crying."

"In that case, genius, maybe you want to get him to stop crying yourself?" Leon was at the end of his tether. He was an expert at improvising explosive devices, and he was a first-class sniper, but when it came to children…he hadn't the faintest clue how to go about dealing with such a task.

Mark bent over Elitzafun and addressed him softly. "Hey."

"Ima!" Elitzafun cried. "Abba! Ima!"

"Enough, Elitzafun. Enough." Mark tried a well-worn tactic. "Tell me what you want, and I'll get it for you."

"I want my mother," Elitzafun said, tears still streaming down his cheeks. "I want my mother, or my father."

A moment of bewilderment passed before Mark came up with a response to this request. "Your father is very busy right now, and your mother is far away, in Israel."

"Where am I?" Elitzafun was angry and lonely, and Mark's evasive answer just wasn't working.

"You're abroad," Mark said, hoping that this response would give the child something to think about.

The attempt failed. "I want to go back to Israel. I don't like it here. Abba said that he would take me to the zoo, but then he didn't have time. I want to go back to my mother." Elitzafun picked up a box of Playmobil and threw it angrily to the floor. "I don't need this. I don't want anything." He started tossing random items from the shelves. "I don't want to be here!"

"Your father is working on very important things," Mark said, hoping for inspiration.

"I don't care," Elitzafun shouted, tears streaming down his face. "I don't care what he's doing and how busy he is. I want him to come here right this minute. He always says that he'll make time for me even if he's very busy." Elitzafun reached for a pile of books on the desk and started flinging them to the floor.

Leon and Mark exchanged glances. They knew that X would never approve another meeting between Eyal and his son. Eyal was too dangerous and needed to be kept on a short leash. X had tried to treat him gently but Eyal had been uncooperative. Both Mark and Leon knew that it was only Eyal's stubbornness that had led him to be jailed in freezing temperatures, starved of food and drink, chained to the bars of his cell. It was a good thing his child couldn't see him just then.

"Maybe you want a special snack that you never tried before? Or a toy?"

"No!" Elitzafun suddenly grew silent as his cries petered out. His anger fizzled out too, leaving him simply sad and deflated, sitting amid a pile of toys, books, and assorted food items.

"What do you want, then?" Mark asked, confused by all the whirling emotions in the air.

"Nothing." Elitzafun got up, sat down again, and picked up a book at random. He flicked through the pages, and his eyes suddenly lit up as an idea came to mind. "I want to speak to my mother."

"That's not possible," Leon said.

"Why?" The five-year-old's honey-colored eyes demanded a cogent and plausible response, but the adults in the room had none to provide.

"Because her phone isn't working," Mark said at last, hoping that his response would be something the child would accept as unshakeable fact without flying into another tantrum.

"So, then I want to speak to my father. Or my grandfather."

"Impos—"

Mark hushed him. "The phone isn't working, but maybe I'll still be able to find someone for you to call." He pulled a small bottle of Sprite out of a bag. "Have a drink in the meantime." He placed the bottle on the desk and gestured to Leon that they ought to leave. "We'll take care of the phone, and we'll be back."

"Are you crazy?" Leon told Mark as soon as they left the room.

"Why did you promise that he'd be able to call someone? X will never sanction this."

Mark pointed to the closed door. "X might not sanction this, but think about the boy for a minute. He's alone, scared, and confused... I think we need to let him speak to someone."

"Who? Eyal?"

"I didn't say that he needs to speak to Eyal, or to his mother, but we need to find a way to calm him down or he'll cry here all day and all night."

"So he'll cry," Leon said. "How long can he keep it up? Eventually he'll stop."

"X said to keep him calm and happy," Mark reminded him.

"That was when Eyal was around. Eyal would have gone crazy if he'd heard his son crying, and that wouldn't have advanced our goals any. Now that he can't hear anything, it makes no difference."

Mark grimaced. "Why be cruel to a child?"

"Because we have no choice in the matter!"

"So we'll create a choice."

Leon shook his head. "Mark, forget it. Heads will roll if you mess this up over some misplaced sympathy."

Mark looked back and forth between his friend and the door to Elitzafun's room. "It's quiet inside," he said. "He must have fallen asleep." Despite his own words, he didn't sound convinced.

Leon eyed him reproachfully. "You're too taken in by him."

Mark didn't respond.

"The number of databases the Mossad has access to is something you can never get used to," Vitali said. He plunked a pile of papers onto the desk, alongside maps, pens, papers, and laptops. "These are the printouts here from Echelon, courtesy of Uncle Sam."

"What have they come up with?"

"The man's name is Bashar Hobeir. He's not Muslim by birth. He's American, and he converted to Islam after September 11, claiming to have seen the light."

"Right," Danny said. "The fire when the Twin Towers went down switched on lots and lots of lights."

"So what does that give us right now?" Eli asked. His current mood gave him little patience for jokes or sarcasm.

"For our current operation, nothing. But knowing his identity might help us to create a psychological profile. We'll be able to pinpoint his weaknesses. Right now we know that he moved to Syria with his family and self-identifies as a Syrian. We know of his personal grievance against Assad, as is to be expected of a man who lost his entire family. This leads us to conclude that he wants Eyal to accomplish something related to Syria. He views himself as a freedom fighter, and his men believe in their cause. Most likely he truly believes that he's using Eyal for the world's greater good."

"How very decent of him."

"There's another point we need to keep in mind," Danny said quietly, switching topics. "Eyal and Elitzafun are probably being held separately. They may not even be in the same safe house. That means that they have to be freed simultaneously – otherwise, whoever is still in their custody when the other one is freed will be – well, you know."

Eli shook his head. "We're going to need the help of someone – at least one person – on the inside. There's no other way that we're going to be able to pull this off. We need inside information."

"How do you propose to buy an ideological freedom fighter?"

"I have no idea."

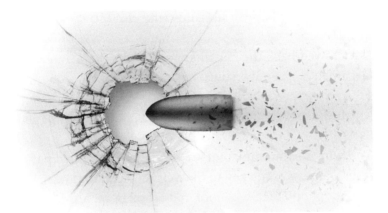

CHAPTER TWENTY-ONE

Ukraine

I think you need to replace Mark," Leon told X over the phone. "The child is causing him to crumble."

"There's something to what you are saying," X said. "I'll send a replacement soon, and in the meantime, I want you to keep a close eye on him."

"It's not as if he's about to release him or anything even vaguely like that," Leon hurried to clarify. "But we'll be better off with him keeping his distance from the kid. If Mark is with Eyal he'll be fine. He hasn't shown any special sentiments toward Eyal."

"Thanks for the tip." X hung up, and another call appeared on his screen. "Hello."

"X, it's Mark." Mark's voice sounded hesitant, and X immediately concluded that Leon's assessment had been correct.

How bizarre that hardened men could totally break down when it came to children.

"Is everything okay?" His tone of voice was businesslike.

The timidity in Mark's voice grew more pronounced. "Tell me...will anything happen if I allow the child to speak to someone?"

X swallowed back the instantaneous retort that came to mind and assumed a friendly voice instead. "Who do you have in mind?"

"Maybe he can call one of his friends..." Mark's voice petered out.

"And why do you think that's a good idea?" X asked patiently. His forbearance was the key to the magical spell that he managed to cast over people. He was cool and aloof in regard to his tactical maneuvers, but when it came to his men, he treated them with warmth and exceptional understanding.

"Because he's really in a bad way. He cries all the time, and he keeps demanding to see his parents." Mark's hesitation disappeared, and heated emotion replaced it. "I explained to him that he can't speak to his parents, but I thought that maybe there's no harm in his calling up a friend or something. I mean...someone whose phone isn't tapped. The call won't be traced, and probably the kid won't even tell anyone that he got a call. Just once..."

X paused, as if to consider. "I'm with you on the idea of treating this child humanely. As you know, I tried to exercise consideration and even allowed Eyal and his son to share a room, but you saw what the result of that was."

"A five-year-old child can't be compared to Eyal," Mark protested. "What can the boy achieve with a simple phone call?"

"This isn't only about the child. It's about us. Sometimes information can be conveyed without intent – a simple word, an intimation. We can't take the risk. We've invested too much in this mission to jeopardize it with a single phone call intended to placate a crying child."

"Fine." Mark hung up the phone with a heavy heart. He passed Elitzafun's room and heard him whimpering. His heart contracted in pain, but his leader's orders carried more weight.

"What's going on with Elitzafun?" Eyal asked quietly. He had been given a few hours to recover from the surgery on his gunshot wound. Food and drink were once again part of the equation, as was a potent vitamin complex. Dr. Bogdan had warned that it was vital to strengthen the body after so much blood loss. X had also removed Eyal's hands from their handcuffs so that his wounded arm could rest.

For his part, all Eyal asked was to talk to his son.

X's expression was furious. "Don't even think of meeting up with him again."

A pained expression appeared on Eyal's face. "He's only five," he said, wincing as he spoke.

"I know how old he is," X said caustically. "And you have only yourself to blame for what happened. You were together in the same house and even in the same room. Had you not pulled a fast one, you'd still be together with him."

"Are you waiting for an apology?" Eyal twirled a pen between his index finger and thumb. After a moment he stopped, placed the pen on the table, and looked blearily at X. "If I apologize, will you allow me to see him?"

"No. You should have thought of the repercussions of your actions before."

Ten responses crammed into Eyal's brain at once but he chose to remain silent.

"Within a week all this will be behind you."

"A week is a very long time for a child." Eyal looked down at the pen on the table so that X would not see the look of longing and anguish in his eyes. "A long time to be locked up with strangers in a strange country."

"I'm *so* sorry. But this was your choice."

Eyal bit his lip. X, who was careful to pay close attention to everyone's body language, especially the body language of his captives, grew thoughtfully silent for a moment. "He isn't suffering," he said finally. His voice was chilling. "Act as you have been ordered, and you won't suffer either."

Eyal looked up and turned toward X. Instead of the burning longing that had filled his eyes seconds earlier, a fire of fury filled them instead. "You will not touch him, X, because that will be more than I can bear."

"That will be the case as long as you do what I ask."

"I am trying to do what you want, but you will not touch him in *any* case. Because if you do, I will use all of my power to harm you and everyone you hold dear."

"Oh, really?" X sounded amused. He removed his gun from its holster and stroked the trigger gently. "I don't believe a corpse has the power to inflict harm. Don't you realize that if you fail at this mission, I will kill you?"

"I have enough friends to take over for me even after I die," Eyal said coldly. "So save your threats. My life has been threatened plenty of times. If you really know as much about me as you claim to, then you surely know that you're not the first person who has threatened to eliminate me. And, should I survive this mission, you won't be the last either."

X silently returned his gun to its holster and stood up. "Back to work," he ordered.

"I want to speak to Elitzafun."

"That's not going to happen."

Elitzafun woke up suddenly. He hadn't even realized that he'd fallen asleep. Someone had brought in food for him as he slept: chocolate milk, pudding, and a roll. He was vaguely hungry, but he had no desire to eat. He knew that it was nighttime because the large house was dark. The sun couldn't be seen from the window in his room during the daytime either, but a glance at the slit under the door told him that the corridor outside his room was dark too, and that meant that everyone was asleep.

Elitzafun thought for a minute, trying to decide whether to turn on the light in his room. If he turned it on, those two men might come in, and he really didn't want to see them right then. But staying in the dark was scary.

So, it would be scary. That was better than Leon and Mark coming into his room – maybe. He got up, walked over to the door, and tried to open it.

Locked.

True terror wrapped itself around him. If the door to his room was locked, then what would happen if there was a fire in the house? How would he be able to run away in time? And what if a robber came? Or if there was an earthquake? He began pounding at the door. "Mark! Mark!" Mark was a lot nicer than Leon. "*Maaaark!*"

Less than a minute passed before Mark opened the door in alarm, clearly roused out of his sleep. "Elitzafun! What happened?"

"Why did you lock the door?" Elitzafun asked, shaking. "What if there's a fire?"

"If there's a fire, I'll run in quickly to get you," Mark said, trying to quell the sympathy he felt for the child, and failing. "Why aren't you asleep?"

"Because I miss my mother." Elitzafun's lips trembled and his eyes filled with tears.

Mark ran his tongue over his lips, indecision tugging at his heartstrings. "Do you want to speak to someone?" he finally asked.

"To my mother?" Elitzafun's eyes sparkled with hope.

"No, you can't speak to your mother." Mark thought of the family in Israel tensely awaiting the tiniest shred of information.

"But maybe you'd like to speak to a friend instead?"

"A friend?" Elitzafun looked at Mark in surprise. "Which friend?"

"A friend from school."

"I'm not in school yet. I'm in preschool. But I have lots of friends."

"Tell me their names."

"Yotam Zucker, Neria Meir, Yossi Tal." Elitzafun thought for a minute, and a shadow crossed his face. "Yossi's not my friend so much, because I won a game of ball with him."

"Do you know your friends' phone numbers?"

Elitzafun shook his head. "No. It's hard to remember numbers. Oh, actually I know Yotam's number. Abba once played a game with me and he taught me how to remember lots of things by heart. Especially numbers. So I know Yotam's number by heart."

"Perfect." Mark removed an old cell phone from his pocket. He had purchased the device fifth- or sixth-hand with his own money. "Tell me the number." He had been thinking that he might have to browse the web in order to find Elitzafun's friend's number, but things had just grown simpler. Thanks to the spy games that Eyal played with his children in his free time, he wouldn't have to leave digital footprints anywhere. Absorbing details by heart was an integral element of espionage.

"But it's the middle of the night! I can't call him and wake him up."

"It's almost seven o'clock. It's the same time here as there. You can call." In the worst case, they really would wake someone up, but there was no real harm in that. Probably...

"Okay." Elitzafun looked up at Mark, who was waiting expectantly. "It's 8825783," he said, smiling at his ability to recall.

It took several tries before Mark realized that he needed an area code after the country code, but eventually he got through and passed the phone to the child, his heart pounding. Was he making a mistake? The last thing he wanted was to jeopardize the safety of the mission, but what harm could this do? He wouldn't let Elitzafun say anything that might give information away.

One ring. Two. Three. They waited tensely.

"Hello." An older child's voice came over the line.

"Hi, Yochai," Elitzafun said, excited to hear the familiar voice. "I want to speak to Yotam."

"Who's this?" *Children are a curious and tactless people*, Mark thought, his ear close to the phone as he listened in. *Let the kid on the other end of the line be quiet already and stop asking so many questions.* The involvement of an older child could completely mess things up.

"Elitzafun Gilboa."

"Just a minute." Mark heard the boy yell, "Yotam!!"

The sound of running and someone lifting the phone receiver. "Who's this?" This time it was the voice of a young child.

"Hi, Yotam, it's me."

"Who's me?" the voice asked.

"Elitzafun!" Eltizafun said.

"Oh, Elitzafun. What do you want?"

"Um..." Elitzafun moved the phone away from his mouth and whispered. "What should I say I want?"

Mark smiled. "Tell him that you want to know how he's doing."

"Oh, okay. How...how are you, Yotam?"

"I'm okay. What about you? Why didn't you come to *gan*?"

"Because...?" Elitzafun turned to Mark again in a whisper. "He asked me why I'm not coming to *gan*. What should I tell him?"

"Tell him that you're on vacation." He had definitely taken an unnecessary risk, endangering things for no good reason. He hadn't expected things to proceed in such a manner, but it was too late now.

"Because I'm not in Israel, Yotam. I'm on vacation!"

"You're on vacation?! Wow! Where are you?"

Elitzafun looked at Mark again. "Where am I?" he asked.

"America." Mark said quickly.

"America." Elitzafun told Yotam.

"Wow!" Yotam repeated. "When are you coming back?"

"I...I don't know," Elitzafun said.

"You're so lucky." There was a note of jealousy in the child's voice. "You went to America with your whole family?"

"No. Only with my father. But now I'm by myself, because he needed to go to work."

"Okay. Do you want something else? Because I'm coloring here."

"No. Bye."

"Bye."

Elitzafun hung up, clearly happy about the call, and Mark smiled. "Things are better now?"

"Yes." Elitzafun lay down on his bed and closed his eyes. "Tell Abba to come," he mumbled before drifting off to sleep, a relaxed expression on his face.

Mark gazed at Elitzafun for another moment and then left the room, locking the door silently behind him. He would flush the SIM card down the toilet and destroy his phone, and no one would be the wiser.

Israel

"Who calls a house before seven in the morning?" Galit, Yotam's mother and Efrat's good friend, said. "Who was that on the phone, Yochai?"

"Yotam's friend."

"What was so important that he needed to call so early?" Galit said. "Yotam, what did he want?"

"I don't know. He wanted to ask me how I was doing."

"Really?" Galit raised her eyebrows. "Which friend was it?"

"Elitzafun Gilboa," Yotam said casually, flipping through his coloring book as he spoke. "He asked how I was, and that's all. Did you know that he went to America on vacation?"

"Elitzafun? Are you sure?"

"Yes," Yotam said. "He's so lucky. Why don't we ever go to America?"

Galit hurried over to the phone to check, and she saw a lengthy and unfamiliar string of numbers on the screen. An international phone number. She stood without moving for a long moment before she finally said in alarm: "Yochai, please watch Yotam and Avigayil for a few minutes. I need to go out."

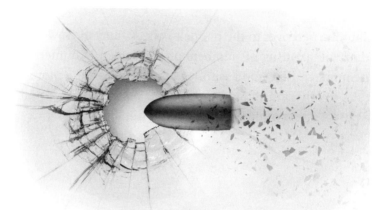

CHAPTER TWENTY-TWO

Israel

"Elitzafun called?" Efrat asked incredulously. "It can't be."

"He spoke to Yotam," Galit insisted.

"How could it be? It's impossible," Efrat said. "Where are you getting this from?"

"Yotam told me," Galit said. "Yochai picked up the phone." She looked at her friend expectantly, hoping that the news would be of some help.

"Maybe...maybe it was someone playing a prank on Yotam," Efrat said. She was afraid to be hopeful and to begin believing. "Someone who was pretending to be Elitzafun."

"That doesn't make much sense," Galit said. "This seems to be real. Elitzafun somehow managed to get hold of a phone, and he called. And he told Yotam that he's in America. Why would another boy do such a thing?"

"But...if he got a phone, then...then why didn't he call me?" Efrat's voice shook. "I could have heard his voice." Emotions overwhelmed her, and Galit dropped her gaze in discomfort. Her child could answer the phone, color, go to school, come home, shout, play, and fight – and meanwhile, Elitzafun was...where was he? Was he really in America? When would he come home?

Efrat was the first to recover. "I'll pass on the information. Thanks for coming by, Galit."

Galit didn't know what to say to the tormented mother. A comment like, "It was nothing," or, "I was glad to be of assistance," would sound trite. She chose the open truth instead. "I'm davening that he comes home in peace."

Israel-Ukrainian Phone Line

"What do you make of this?" Uri asked, after briefing Eli on the surprising news that Elitzafun had somehow managed to contact his friend in Israel just before seven o'clock that morning.

"There's no record of the conversation?" Eli asked with disappointment.

"Nothing," Uri said. "The call was made using a prepaid cellphone SIM card, which won't be easy to trace. Depending on the circumstances of the call, it's also possible that the SIM card was destroyed immediately after the call was made, which means that there isn't much for us to learn from all of this."

"There is one thing," Eli said quietly. "Someone on the inside is acting out of sympathy for the child."

"What do you mean?" Uri asked.

"Elitzafun obviously couldn't put that call through by himself. Even if he somehow managed to get hold of a cell phone, there's no way that he could have known what the code for Israel is, and so forth. Someone dialed the number for him, and I highly doubt that X authorized the call. Not after Eyal's bitter escape attempt."

"So you think we've found the weak link."

"Yes. That's exactly what I think."

Israel

Two cigars and a cigarette were contributing to the haze in the room. Mossad chief Zev Avshalom, GSS head Shaul Lerner, and Uri Shabtai, head of the Mossad's special operations, were meeting to discuss the latest developments. Lerner had wanted someone else from his staff to be invited, but Avshalom was against the idea. "The more people who find out about this kidnapping, the greater the chances of the abductors finding out our plans."

They were gathered around a table in one of the meeting rooms at Mossad headquarters. The paraphernalia on the table was minimal: three laptops, two maps, and a few other gadgets. The screens on the walls showed various images – one featured a street map of Kiev, another displayed several pictures of buildings that had been photographed from various different angles, and the rest were as yet blank.

"This is the house that Eyal was previously held in." Avshalom moved the cursor and clicked open a picture on one of the blank screens. "We received this information, along with various other details, from a local who paid with his life for doing us the favor – an expensive favor, I might add. The rest of our information is derived from photos taken by our satellites, online images from our security cameras, and via human trackers and confirmed by local presence."

"Let's move on," Lerner said, characteristically impatient. "What plans do we have, and what stage are we up to?"

"Getting there," Avshalom said briefly. "Our team is based

here," he added, indicating the spot on the map, "and these are the basic routes they're currently considering. They're looking into sophisticated, as opposed to sensational, means of infiltration."

Avshalom's cell phone buzzed, and he whipped it out of his pocket. "Sorry," he apologized, glancing at the screen. When he saw the number displayed there, the expression on his face transformed. He leaned over toward Shaul Lerner, turning the screen to face him, and asked him if he recognized the number.

Shaul shook his head. An incoming call from an unfamiliar number on the Mossad chief's personal phone did not herald good news.

Uri pulled out a cable and used it to connect Avshalom's cell phone to one of the computers on the desk. The call would now be recorded in the Mossad's main database. "Now answer," he said curtly, and, as Zev took the call, Uri pressed a button, summoning Eran, the communications technician, to the room. Eran would be able to locate the caller quickly and precisely.

The map of Israel on the screen zoomed in as the computer picked up a location. Northern Israel.

"Hello." The voice was young and awkward with an undertone of confidence. The three men in the room exchanged quick glances.

Avshalom gestured almost imperceptibly with his finger, and Lerner took the hint. Avshalom wanted him to answer, just in case the anonymous caller was counting on recognizing his voice.

"Yes," Lerner said shortly.

A moment of hesitation on the phone line, and then, "Am I... speaking to Zev Avshalom?"

"You're speaking to his secretary," Lerner said. He ignored the smirk on Avshalom's face. The man would have been willing to go through a whole lot in order to hear that sentence again.

"Okay..." It sounded as if the young man was slightly disappointed. His voice was definitely not that of a secret agent or potential terrorist. "But I do need to speak to Zev Avshalom."

"Who are you?"

"I..." The young voice hesitated again. "My name is Giddi Frisher. I'm Eyal Gilboa's brother-in-law."

"Yes, Giddi," Zev's authoritative voice interjected as he retrieved his phone from Lerner. "Shalom."

"Is this the Mossad chief speaking?" Giddi asked. How he hated himself for feeling so awkward.

"Yes," Zev said shortly. "Speak up, Giddi. We're listening." The use of the collective pronoun was intentional.

"I...this...it's just..." Giddi stuttered. He hadn't thought that he would actually manage to contact the Mossad chief. At the very most, he assumed he would be put through to some clerk who might or might not pass on the message to the chief. To his bewilderment, the number saved in Efrat's phone as "Zev from work" was actually the Mossad chief's personal number. He cringed as he imagined the consequences for his impetuous act. Efrat would not look good, though they would probably save the reprimand for later. Worse still, for him personally, Efrat would find out that he had sneaked away her phone, the one nobody was allowed access to. He gulped.

"Speak, Giddi," Avshalom's voice softened. Uri Shabtai was gesturing with his finger. "What news do you have for us?"

"First of all, this can't go to the media. My father and sister don't know that I'm calling," Giddi said, beginning from the end. "This is...classified."

A narrow smile unwittingly appeared on the men's faces. Eran had made an appearance by this point, and he too smiled at the boy's naivete. Most conversations conducted by the Mossad chief were classified. And they were usually classified for reasons other than family intrigue.

"No need to worry, Giddi. Your call is safe. You can speak freely."

Uri motioned to Eran to leave the room. His services were unnecessary, as the caller was making no effort to conceal either his identity or his location.

"I called from my own phone, not my sister's, because…well, I had my reasons. I guess it doesn't matter so much to you," Giddi said. His listener's patience and apparent empathy reinstated his feelings of confidence.

"This call is being recorded by us, but you did well to call from another number, as it's impossible to know who else might be listening in," Zev said, although he had no idea why he did. "How can we help you, Giddi? Is there something we can do for you?"

"I'm not calling for myself. I'm calling for my nephew and my brother-in-law. For my entire family. I know that you're dealing with the situation, but you need to understand that even though we're their family, we have no idea what's going on. I decided that the situation can't go on like this. You tell us that you're working on getting them released, but in the meantime, we're going out of our minds with worry. No one is giving us any details, and all we can do is wait. It's not…it's not good this way."

Uri removed his pen from his pocket and scribbled a note onto a nearby sheet of paper. He thrust the note under Zev's nose, and Zev looked at the scrawl there, trying to formulate a response to the question posed to him by the young man on the other end of the line. His caller did deserve some kind of answer, after all.

Uri's handwriting was awful, but Uri could just about make out what he had written on the note: "How old is this kid?"

"Please try to understand, Giddi," Zev said, extricating a pen of his own and scribbling a response to Uri as he spoke. "We're doing everything we can, but we cannot share the details of the mission with ordinary citizens. If we did that, not only would we be endangering your nephew and brother-in-law, we would also be imperiling our agents and damaging the chances of the mission succeeding. Can you accept that?"

"Not really." Giddi's voice was a lot steadier now, but Avshalom had to exert a good deal of effort to refrain from exploding at the boy. First of all, who was to blame for the security breach by giving him his private number? Now it would have to be changed – added aggravation. Second of all, didn't he realize that minor functionaries existed precisely for this purpose – to deal with side issues that any dumb clerk could handle? Why was the kid wasting his time?

Uri took the piece of paper that Zev Avshalom pushed toward him as Giddi's voice sounded again. "I'm not asking you to give me details of names or places. All we want is something concrete to reassure us that action really is being taken."

Avshalom fell silent for a moment, and Lerner wondered if it would be considered correct protocol for the Mossad chief's secretary to pick up the phone in the middle of a private conversation. He decided that he didn't care much about the laws of etiquette and took the phone. "From what I understand, you are after a bit of news from the chief, Giddi," he said.

"Correct."

Uri read Avshalom's scribbled response to his query regarding the young man's age: seventeen. He grimaced. Just a kid.

"I'm sure you realize that we can't provide ordinary civilians with updates, Giddi. Even if we'd like to, and even if it's relatives asking." Avshalom toyed with a pen on the table. "We're doing everything we can. Okay?"

"Look," Giddi said after considering this for a moment. "Of course I know I can't expect a full report, but what you just said means nothing." He swallowed hard, knowing it sounded terrible, but there was no point in calling otherwise.

Avshalom took the phone back. "I understand you, Giddi." Another note thrust beneath his nose forced him to pause. He looked at Lerner's message: "Give him what he wants. He deserves it, and the request is legitimate. Tell him something, and we'll deal with the consequences."

Avshalom nodded. "Your brother-in-law's good friend is involved in this mission. His name is Eli Hadar. He has recruited a team of agents to locate your nephew and to try to find a way to get him out of there. Is that enough?"

"Well...I guess so," Giddi said. The words had gone some way toward reassuring him. Action really was being taken – they hadn't just abandoned Elitzafun. Giddi tried to overlook the fact that Eyal hadn't been mentioned. That could mean any number of things, but he was grateful for the information he had been given. "Is there anything we can do?" he ventured.

Avshalom was about to dismiss the offer, but then a picture of Elitzafun in one of the files on the table caught his attention, and he felt as though his heart were being painfully squeezed. The boy looked so much like his own young grandson. "There is something that you can do," he said quietly.

"At your service," Giddi said. A spark of vitality immediately filled his voice.

Avshalom sighed. They needed to bring this young man's nephew and brother-in-law home. "Pray," he said. "We need your prayers."

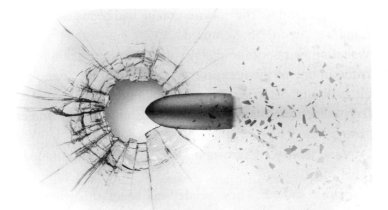

CHAPTER TWENTY-THREE

Ukraine

Mark?" Leon entered the room where Mark was sitting and playing tic-tac-toe with Elitzafun. "X wants to see you."

"He's here?" Mark's heart skipped a beat. Why would X have left Eyal? Had he discovered what Mark had done? Had someone overheard the conversation? Maybe the boy had let something slip?

"No. He's not here, but he sent John over, and he wants you to change places with him."

"Did he say why?"

"No." What Leon didn't tell Mark was that he had been the one to initiate the exchange. Mark left the room and went down the stairs with a heavy heart. His limbs were almost numb with fear. If it became known that not only had he taken a risk but that he had done so against the express command of their leader, things would be very bad for him.

But maybe no one knew anything and he was simply worried for nothing. Mark opened the door and slowly walked outside. John, serious and in a rush, was waiting for him in the car.

"Get over there fast," he said, climbing out of the driver's seat and handing Mark the keys. "We don't have much time. We're starting training in just a few hours."

"Who's we?"

"You'll see. Bye." John headed into the building, and Mark took over at the wheel.

He turned out of the narrow street, following the route indicated on a note taped to the dashboard. It was a circuitous route, with several loops back, crossing the river three times. Mark didn't notice the scenery, though. His thoughts were with the kid. John would be looking after Elitzafun from now on, and Mark was worried about how he would handle it. John was an even tougher nut to crack than Leon, and the combination of an overwrought child and an impatient handler was unlikely to turn out well.

He hoped Elitzafun would survive the week.

"Something's going on here," Avi called to Eli. He was watching the grainy images produced by the satellite camera trained on one of the safe houses, his brow furrowed in concentration. "Someone just pulled up in a car...wait a minute...someone just left the building." Eli came to stand behind him, his eyes also following the moving figures.

"They're swapping places," Eli said, his voice excited. "The guy who just arrived is going inside and the other one's driving away."

"If only that meant something," Avi said glumly. "It didn't look like there was anyone in the car other than the driver, and neither of those two guys was Eyal."

"Of course it means something," Eli said, refusing to let Avi's mood affect him. "We just have to figure out what. I think I have an idea, but I don't have the facts to corroborate it."

"Let's hear," said Shuki, bored after hours of watching screens.

"I'm assuming they're not holding Eyal and Elitzafun in the same safe house. Given the fact that Eyal escaped with the boy before, they were being held together, but I doubt that's the case now."

The other agents nodded. "They underestimated Eyal, big time," Avi noted.

"We've been keeping tabs on the safe houses for several hours," Eli continued. "No movement. Nothing. Nobody coming, nobody going. Then suddenly, right after this call is put through by Elitzafun, things start moving."

"They figured it out?" Shuki asked. "It doesn't seem that way to me. There would have been more dramatic action if that was the case."

"No," Eli countered. "They can't afford anything dramatic, anything that could draw attention to them. So what I reckon is that the person responsible for the phone call is being recalled to HQ, to be reprimanded, or punished, by X himself. And his place guarding Elitzafun has been handed over to someone else."

"Meaning that the house we're watching is where they're holding the boy," Avi deduced. "And the guy who drove away—"

"Is the guy we want. The terrorist who had second thoughts. Sounds like the title of a spy novel," Eli said with a smile.

"He was lucky to get out of there in one piece." Vitali's voice came over the loudspeaker. "If what you're saying is right, then I should be able to spot him on his way over." Vitali was stationed in a top-floor apartment a few blocks away from the second safe house. The third one, in Odessa, appeared to be empty. All the thermal imaging had come up cold.

"Let me know the minute you see him," Eli said, his voice tense. "It's our job to make sure he doesn't make it back to X, and that means intercepting him neatly, not too close to home."

The five agents fell silent as they watched the screens, alert to any suspicious movement. Now that they knew what they were looking for – a gray Lada – it was much simpler.

"Got him!" Vitali crowed. In his telescopic sight, he had the clearest view of them all.

"Pictures," Eli said curtly. "Take a few good shots of him and send them straight to Mossad headquarters. They may have something on him." He turned to the other men in the room. "Shuki? Danny? Are you ready?"

"Ready as ever," they replied.

"Eli, you're not going," Vitali interjected quickly. "Your face is too well known. If this man knows Eyal by sight, then he probably knows who you are too. Your face was all over the media after that stunt you both pulled at that clinic. We can't take the risk of having you come along."

Eli opened his mouth and then closed it again. "Okay," he said finally. "In any case, someone needs to keep watch here, to keep an eye on everyone. Where is he now, Vitali?"

"Coming down Pushkina Street," Vitali said. "Turning left... turning left again onto Shevchenka."

A satellite picture appeared on Eli's computer screen within seconds. "Okay, guys. On your way," he said to Shuki and Danny, who raced down the stairs and out of the building.

Shuki was on a motorcycle and Danny was in an old Lada. Directed by Vitali, they set off on parallel courses, converging just in front of Mark's car. Shuki executed a perfect skid and slammed straight into Danny's car, jumping off in time to avoid serious injury. The motorcycle was totaled, but that was part of the plan.

Mark, still lost in thought, only just managed to brake in time to avoid joining the mass of twisted metal. He watched as the two agents confronted each other, hoping they would sort out the mess quickly so he could get going, but it didn't appear likely.

"Where do you think you are – Honolulu?" Danny yelled at Shuki. "This isn't the Third World! Didn't you ever hear of traffic laws?"

Shuki, pretending to nurse a twisted ankle, hobbled forward, eyes narrowed and fists balled. "What did you say, mister?" he said coldly.

Mark groaned. The wreck was blocking his way forward; behind, a line of honking cars prevented him from making a U-turn and getting away. Resignedly, he got out of his car and approached the two men.

"Listen, just move your car to the side, will you?" he addressed Danny. "Look how many people you're holding up."

Danny turned to glare at him. "Who asked for your opinion?"

"Yeah, right, who asked you?" Shuki added, closing in on Mark from behind. A sharp prick from a taser dart, and Mark would have crumpled if Danny hadn't caught him. The two of them quickly bundled him into Danny's car, and before any of the shocked motorists behind them could react, they were gone.

"Nice work, Shuki," said Danny appreciatively, as he swerved onto the highway and sped away. "He's out cold? Okay. Keep him on ice for now."

"You want me to betray my boss?" Mark said in disbelief after the taser darts had been cautiously removed from him and he had regained consciousness. "You must be out of your mind."

"You'd be amazed at how many people just as stubborn as you collaborated with us in the end." Danny smiled. "No need to make such premature declarations.'

"Nothing in the world can get me to collaborate with you," Mark said.

"That's interesting," Shuki said, entering the room with a dossier with the Mossad's symbol in his hand. "Based on what it says here, you've been selling us secrets for weeks already."

"What?" Mark said in alarm. "What kind of nonsense is that?"

"Nonsense? I don't think so. Take a look at what we have here. Here's your photograph, your signature, your bank account details... You're being paid very nicely, I can see. I wish I was paid as well as that."

Mark fell silent, struggling to think of something to reply to this fabrication. He knew they were lying, and they knew he knew, but that wasn't the issue. If they sent this dossier to X, it was curtains for him. With the mission at an advanced stage, there was no time to check things out. As a matter of caution, he would be eliminated.

"I can even send your boss a picture of us speaking to you right now, if you like. I'm sure he'd appreciate that."

"I'll tell him exactly what happened," Mark said. But he knew that X would not accept his explanations, and his tone lacked conviction.

"What will you tell him?" Danny feigned a sympathetic tone. "That we kidnapped you and forced you to play ball?"

"I'll tell him that I refused!"

"You can try that, yes," Danny said, and then suddenly lost patience. "It won't work, and you know it. When we release you, with no signs of violence suggesting the pressure you want to pretend was applied, he's going to smell a rat. And when he finds out the precise details of the boy's phone call to Israel, he's going to smell a whole nest of them. You know that, don't you?"

Mark paled. "Regardless of what you say, I won't do it."

Shuki shrugged. "Mister, you don't have a choice. You won't leave the country intact unless you pick sides. What I mean to say is, unless you pick our side. We won't let you go back to your boss in peace. And if you try to get back home under your own steam – well, I don't fancy your chances."

Mark was silent for a long while. "What do you want?" he said finally.

"Ah, just the question we've been waiting for," Danny said, grinning. "It always comes in the end. What we want, Mark, is very simple. You go back to your boss, just like you were going to do before our little traffic accident, and do whatever he wants you to do."

"And then I betray him to you, I suppose." Mark's voice was bitter.

"Why do you have to use such dramatic language? Things are so much more pleasant when we dress them up prettily. All you do is tell a story. A story about a man who was abducted, a child who was kidnapped...you wanted to help the child, didn't you? So now you're helping to get him back home to his parents. There are plenty of other people who can take care of revolutions, wars, and uprisings. You focus on the kid, okay?"

Mark didn't reply.

"So, I take it we have your agreement."

Mark still said nothing.

"Mark, are you with us?"

Mark looked up, an expression of anguish on his face. "How will I explain my delay to X? I should have arrived at his safe house almost an hour ago."

"Don't worry. We'll take care of the details. All you have to do is follow our orders. If your boss calls the police station to find out what's going on, he'll receive a report about an oil truck that turned over on the road, obstructing all traffic until the spill was cleared up. One of our men is in your car as we speak, already at the scene of the accident. Security cameras in the area will have footage of your car sitting in the pileup."

"You think of everything."

Danny smiled. "We try," he said. "And it's obviously superfluous for me to warn you that if you ever try to sell us even the tiniest of lies, we will hand over the details of this conversation to X. He'll finish you off a lot more efficiently than we would."

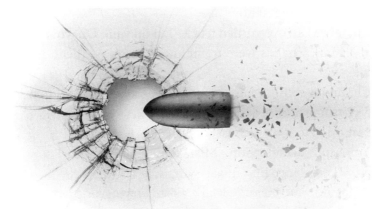

CHAPTER TWENTY-FOUR

Ukraine

Mark left his car in the parking lot of the safe house where Eyal was being held. He got out of his vehicle and drew a deep breath. X was an expert in reading body language, and he needed to make sure that he exuded an aura of calm and innocence when they met. If X deduced that he had something to hide, he would certainly take action.

Never in his life had it occurred to him to disobey an order from X, but now, following one stupid mistake, he was being forced into his second act of disobedience. No – not his second act. The second phase of his actions. He had no way of knowing how long his handlers would want to use him. The thought sent a shiver down his spine.

He was trapped between a hammer and a block of wood, and

he could see no way of emerging unscathed.

Mark quietly entered the house. He hung his coat on a hook near the entrance and walked into one of the rooms.

X approached, a strange smile on his face. "Where have you been?" he asked pleasantly.

"There was an overturned truck…an oil spill. Unavoidable, I'm afraid." Mark's hands were trembling – he thrust them deep into his pockets.

"Ah, an oil spill…what about the other spill?" X said, his tone of voice still pleasant.

Mark tried to look bemused. "Spill?"

"Your spill of sympathy. Mistaken sympathy, but I suppose I should acknowledge that it was sympathy nonetheless."

"What do you mean?" Mark asked, trying unsuccessfully to steady his voice as he spoke.

"The child spoke to his friend, I hear," X said.

"What makes you think that?" Mark asked. He wasn't sure if he should confirm or deny X's words. If he admitted his crime, he might end up paying the price. But denial could be worse, for that would imply a conscious decision made to flout X's rules. The noose felt like it was tightening around his neck.

"I don't think it. I know it. The boy told Leon about it," X said. His voice was soft and forgiving, and it produced the results its owner had anticipated.

"I admit it." Mark lowered his eyes. "I just couldn't stop my-self…the child broke my heart with his misery and loneliness. I really didn't think it would do any harm. It didn't do any harm!"

"It's really fine," X said softly. "I can understand this aspect of your personality. But it's not necessarily something that suits us here, and so I decided that you would serve me here instead."

Mark tried to figure out if he was being reprimanded or en-couraged. Either way, he still had no way of knowing what the ramifications of the episode would be – from X's point of view.

"Go upstairs, Mark. We're having a briefing with Eyal in an hour.

I hope you feel no sentiments of sympathy toward him as well."

"Most certainly not," Mark said passionately. Eyal was perfectly capable of taking care of himself, and his actions had already resulted in a lot of trouble for them.

"Good. In that case, go and get ready, because we need you to be in shape."

Mark walked cautiously past X, and immediately he felt the butt of a pistol being wedged into his back. A Ruger SP101. X's favorite pistol. Mark stiffened with fear.

"I don't have any sentiments regarding individuals either." X spoke the words through clenched teeth, and suddenly Mark felt a bullet whizz right past his ear. It embedded itself in a sandbag in the corner of the room. "Go."

"We're going outside for our last round of field practice in ten minutes," X told Eyal.

Eyal kept his eyes focused on the computer screen and the words that he was rapidly typing. "I know that," he said. "Print this."

"No problem." X eyed the chart, and his heart swelled with pride. Immediately, however, he suppressed his feelings. He mustn't allow his optimism to affect him like this. So many things could still go wrong. Oblivious to X's train of thought, Eyal continued to record various pieces of information, backup plans, locations of shooting ranges, snipers' positions…

Just like in days gone by, Eyal thought sadly as he looked over his plans. *Only this time I'm giving my talent to the Syrians.*

X had selected a small enclosure surrounded by a barbed-wire fence and adorned with a "Do Not Photograph" sign for field practice. Eyal suspected that the location had once served as a boot camp and that X had somehow managed to acquire the plot of land. There were tall ladders, ropes strung from one tree to the next, iron poles of various heights, a bit of marshland that they needed to walk through, mannequins for target practice, old buses with clearly marked targets, buildings that served no particular purpose, and a pile of tires with bullet holes pocking them like Swiss cheese. Everything a boot camp might require.

After several hours of practice and tests, with Eyal observing the men in action, the session was over. On the way back, X turned to Eyal and asked him with a bland expression that barely concealed his curiosity: "So, after all that you saw, what do you have to say about our chances?"

"I want to speak to Elitzafun." Eyal automatically uttered his mantra.

"Answer the question," X said.

"First let me speak to him."

"Enough." X lifted his voice threateningly.

Eyal was unmoved. "I won't stop. I need to speak to my son. If you want you can listen in on every word, but I want to be able to reassure him and tell him that everything is okay."

"It's a shame that you don't seem to be able to absorb the fact that you are simply not going to be speaking to him."

"Look," Eyal adopted the decisively convincing tone that he so often used. "You want me to perform at my best and to offer advice on this mission. I can do what you are asking under duress, because you are using my child as collateral. Or you can fulfill my request and I'll perform far better."

"I can use other forms of pressure as well."

"There is no way you can force someone to be at his best. The only way to do that is by earning his consent and cooperation."

"Consent and cooperation!" X repeated the words derisively. "Sorry, but I'm not buying those words. Definitely not, not when it comes to you."

Eyal was taken back to his freezing-cold cell. He was

handcuffed to one of the bars but he did not protest. He sat down on the concrete floor and hugged his knees. The chair had been removed.

X watched Eyal, and a shadow crossed his face. At first Eyal didn't notice that he was being observed, but when he turned and saw X looking at him he said again, "I want to speak to Elitzafun."

"Enough!" X shouted. "Stop the pestering. You're an expert at annoying people."

Eyal smiled. "You're not the first person to have told me that." A bolt of pain shot through his injured arm, but he quickly stifled the feeling. "Soon you'll say that I'm stubborn too, but it is those very same character traits that have brought me to my current position. I need to know that my son is okay. I will not relent until I achieve that goal."

"You know what?" X asked, bending suddenly. Perhaps the change in attitude was due to the fact that he knew that Eyal was talking in all seriousness and that he would certainly continue to make himself a nuisance until he succeeded in getting what he wanted. "I can't allow you to speak to your son in person, but I have another suggestion. I can take a video of you speaking to him, and I'll allow Elitzafun's guards to show him the video."

"The beginnings of a good idea," Eyal complimented his captor. "But I am going to take it a step further and ask that a video be taken of Elitzafun responding to me. Is it a deal?"

"Only if we drop the matter of your having a face-to-face conversation with Elitzafun."

"We can drop it for a week," Eyal said, giving voice to his fear that in a week's time, after the president's capture had been achieved, additional missions would be demanded of him.

"Fine." X's statement was neither a denial nor a confirmation. He turned to Colin. "Remove his handcuffs and take him out of his cell. Let's stage a performance. Get your cell phone so that we can video him." John had returned to the safe house where Eyal was being held.

As the preparations for the video took place all around him, Eyal carefully considered the words that he would say. He knew that he needed to give Elitzafun the impression that he was doing well, that he was happy and relaxed. Elitzafun would probably watch the video over and over – he would certainly notice if Eyal appeared stressed or unhappy. Briefly, he considered weaving a hidden message into the film, in case Eli or another agent managed to obtain it, but in the end he decided against taking that risk. If anyone did get access to the video, it would almost certainly mean that they had released Elitzafun as well. And if that was the case, then Eyal would do his utmost to run away.

The light was turned on in the cellar, and Eyal was told to sit at a table upon which were a few pens and sheets of paper. Aside from the props that would be visible in the video, the rest of the backdrop was spine-chilling: six armed men with machine guns trained directly at him. The brightly lit room was in reality a freezing-cold basement, devoid of even minimal comforts, and his bandaged forearm had to be kept out of sight, under the table. All that Elitzafun would see would be a smiling Eyal, speaking calmly and reassuringly. But then again, that was what Eyal too wanted.

X motioned from the side. "You have sixty seconds. Make sure it's good."

Eyal didn't grace him with so much as a sideways glance.

"Start," John instructed.

"Elitzafun, my dear son," Eyal said steadily, gripping one of the pens on the table. "I can't speak to you on the phone because I'm in the hospital, and I'm not allowed to call from here. But I want you to know that I'm okay. My injured arm is getting better. I think about you all the time, and I hope and pray that you're doing fine and that the people who are looking after you in the meantime are treating you well. In another few days I'll be out of the hospital and we'll be together again. I love you very, very much, and I'm sending you hugs and kisses. Goodbye, Elitzafun!"

John was now told to go back with the video and tell Abdul, who had replaced him, to report back to X. He turned off his phone and glanced up at Eyal. "Satisfied?"

"That's a ridiculous word to use under the circumstances," Eyal spat, refusing to credit X or his men with a single generous gesture.

"Okay. Achmad and Teddy, take him back to his cell and put the props back in order," X ordered, ignoring Eyal's response. "John, you will take this video to the child and tell Abdul and Leon to film him using a different media card." X glanced at Eyal to make sure that he was listening before adding, almost as though it were an afterthought: "The exchange of cards will take place manually. Nothing goes online. Not even offline, in fact."

"A video from my father for me?" Elitzafun was overwhelmed with emotion.

Leon, for his part, was brimming with impatience for the child and his moods. "Yes. A video from your father. We've filmed him. Do you want to see it?"

"Of course!" Elitzafun's eyes shone. Something good was finally happening at the end of a long and difficult day, when the only one of his guards whom he liked a bit, and who used to play games with him, had left. His guards were bad people. He was sure of that. Why else would his father have tried to run away from them? And now, all that the guards did was bring him boring games and tell him to be quiet.

"Take this." Leon placed a device in the child's hands, and Elitzafun's eyes filled with tears as he stared at his father's image, even before pressing play.

"Why are you crying?" Leon asked with impatience. "Aren't you happy?"

"I am," Elitzafun said, his voice choked with tears. He knew Leon hated it when he cried, but he couldn't stop himself.

He watched his father speak softly and lovingly to him. For days he had been deprived of all affection, and now it was being offered to him via a phone. When his father finished speaking, the floodgates of his tears opened up, and he burst into bitter wailing.

"Abba!" he cried. "Abba! Come and get me! Abba! Come!"

Leon stared at Abdul in confusion. He hadn't anticipated such a reaction.

"Enough," Leon began, but Abdul placed a hand on his shoulder.

"Let him cry. He misses his father, and it's normal for him to cry."

"But why's he crying now, after he saw him? He should be relieved!"

"Don't be a fool." As a father himself, Abdul understood, somewhat. "He's cut off from everything familiar, and he's lonely and afraid. His mother isn't here, and he's only being permitted to see his father via a recording. I don't pity him, but I do understand him."

Leon fell silent and allowed the child to sink onto his bed and cry. He pressed the button on the device over and over again to replay his father's message to him.

"Elitzafun," Abdul said after about ten minutes had passed. "Your father wants us to video you and to send the video to him so that he can see you. Do you think he'll be happy if he sees you crying?"

"No." Bravely, Elitzafun conquered his tears. "I don't want him to think that I'm sad."

"That's great. So go wash your face, and then I'll take a nice video of you speaking to your father. Okay?"

"Okay." Elitzafun got up and went to wash his face at the sink with all of the determination that a five-year-old could muster.

Leon eyed Abdul in astonishment. "Your psychology worked like a charm."

"Learn to see things beyond the telescopic sight of your sniper rifle."

An hour later X entered the basement where Eyal was being held, cell phone in hand. "As I promised, we have a video from your son for you," he said coolly.

Eyal's eyes gleamed with happiness. "Let me see." He sat up as straight as he could and gazed at the device with longing. X pushed the phone through the bars of the cell, and Eyal's eyes shone as he took it. For a moment X thought of the irony of it all. Here was a man who conducted top-secret international missions, he was a hardened intelligence agent, a commander of all mediums of war, he withstood tortures, spoke of death with equanimity, yet melted with emotion at the prospect of a video from his son. Perhaps such was human nature.

"You have twenty seconds to look at this video," X said. "And even that is far more than what you deserve."

Eyal took the device and turned on the video.

But he didn't look at it.

Instead, Eyal overcame his desire to see his son. He pressed the tiny button on the screen, and as Elitzafun's voice echoed through the basement, Eyal's fingers worked at lightning speed to key in a message blindly, without even seeing the letters.

He had but one goal.

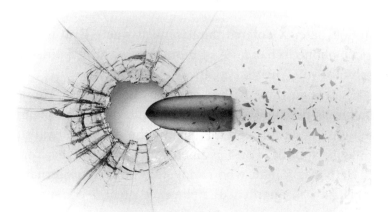

CHAPTER TWENTY-FIVE

Ukraine

"T hese are the floor plans of the houses," Eli said, sweeping everything that had been on the table onto the floor with an impatient motion. Mark had come through, and the first batch of information had been transmitted just an hour ago. Unable to leave the building without arousing suspicion, he had been forced to take the considerable risk of using his own phone to send penciled sketches of the two safe houses. The papers he had burned; the messages he had erased. But X was nothing if not a technological whizz. Mark knew that if he suspected him, he would find a way to retrieve those messages.

Eli, who had been waiting impatiently for Mark's communications, had printed them off as soon as they came in, and now he was eager to get started on the next phase of their mission. Accordingly, pens, records of the tabs they had been keeping, pencils, rulers, remnants of food, disposable dishes, cups, partially filled bottles – everything was pushed aside to make room for the floor plans that were so crucial to the success of their mission. Just in time, Shuki removed an empty bottle of Nemiroff vodka and placed it on the kitchen counter.

"You're getting carried away," Danny said. "Who's going to clean this mess?"

"You – who else?" Eli sighed. His disregard for the importance of tidying up was nothing new. "Don't you think such things are rather inconsequential at this point?"

"No, actually I don't. Oops." Danny caught an almost-empty cup of coffee that Eli tossed in his direction. Droplets were now sprinkled liberally across the carpet. "Cool it, Eli, will you?"

"Well, I need this table now," Eli grumbled.

"*Chevreh*, you need to stop leaving your food all over the place. If you don't, I'm just going to throw everything out." Danny's voice rose in annoyance. "I don't understand why you can't eat at the kitchen table like human beings. And Shuki, in case you're wondering, your sandwich leftovers are in the garbage."

"I don't believe it." Shuki shot over to the bin to rescue his poor sandwich.

"When a normal person finishes a meal, he either takes the plate over to the garbage or he washes it. Instead, you guys have left traces all over – on the dining room table, under the beds, on the night tables, in the front closet, on the bookshelves, next to the computers. I keep on seeing plates, forks, and leftovers all over."

"That's because we don't stop work to sit down and eat," Vitali said, shrugging. He was holding a smoked sausage in one hand and a cup of borscht in his other hand as he spoke. He had taught Avi how to make the borscht, and it hadn't come out too bad. "Calm down, Danny, okay? Shall we get down to business, or is food more important to you?"

"Not to me. To you!" Danny exploded. "I don't eat all day long. But...okay," he consented, letting his anger fizzle out. "Enough."

"That smells great," Eli interjected, eyeing Vitali's sausage. "I hope it's not *treif*, because Eyal wouldn't like that. Definitely not in his house."

"If only he were here to say what he liked," Vitali said. "That would save us a whole lot of trouble."

For a moment Eli couldn't think of a suitable retort. All five of them were totally dedicated to the success of the mission and full of determination to see it through to a triumphant conclusion. But only Eli felt personally involved in the situation. Only he had seen Eyal in prison; only he knew, not just imagined, something of what Eyal was currently going through. The other agents were cold-blooded professionals in this case, whereas Eyal was Eli's friend. His best friend.

He – and only he – had wanted to ask Mark about how Eyal was doing and how they were treating him. But Vitali had vetoed any such idea. "It will only waste precious time," he had insisted.

Now Eli brought his thoughts back firmly to the present. With the table cleared, he spread out the pages he had printed off from Mark's messages. They all crowded around – all except for Danny, who was busy sweeping the floor and missed Eli's description of the basement, planning to catch up later.

"This is the parking lot, and here is where—" The beep of an incoming call interrupted Eli, and he reached for his phone in surprise. Not too many people knew the number. He looked down at the screen and saw that a text message had been sent from an unfamiliar number.

leaving few hours zhuliany 3 buick cars somianska / me in car 3 with x / shoot out car 1 kill all / dont try to get son no police / eyal

As the recording of Elitzafun ended, Eyal's mind raced to try and think of a way to erase the incriminating message. It was Colin's phone, and it wasn't hard to imagine what would happen if he saw that Eyal had used it.

Eyal sighed, looked up, and caught X's eye. "Can I watch the video again?" he asked quietly, a pleading quality to his voice.

X nodded and Eyal set to work swiftly deleting the message from all of the places where it was stored. He knew it would still be possible to retrieve it, but he was counting on the fact that Colin wouldn't suspect anything like what he had just done and wouldn't go to the considerable trouble of recovering lost data.

Elitzafun's voice once again rang through the cell, and Eyal bit his lips as he listened to the boy's lonely, broken message, even though he was clearly trying to sound upbeat.

"Abba, I'm okay. I'm not sad. The people here are giving me nosh, and toys and I'm very..." A whoosh of air. "I miss you, but it's not so bad because we'll meet soon. I love you very much and miss you a lot."

Eyal just had time for a quick glimpse of Elitzafun's face after deleting his message and before he had to return the phone. The image brought tears to his eyes. Would they ever meet again?

Eli looked down at the phone in confusion. "Vitali, what do you make of this?" he said, pushing the phone over the table to the other agent.

Vitali read the message and looked up in disbelief. "Eyal sent a message? *Eyal* did? That guy is superman, I'm telling you."

He proceeded to read it aloud for the benefit of the others, adding detail to make it intelligible. "We're leaving in a few hours for Zhuliany airport, via Solomianska. We'll be in three cars, Buicks. I'll be in the third car, together with X. Shoot at the first car and kill the driver and all the passengers. Don't try to get Elitzafun and don't call the police. Eyal."

"Well, that kind of alters all our plans," Danny said. "And just imagine if he hadn't sent that text. We wouldn't have made it over there in time – they would have already left."

Eli was already opening a map of the area indicated. "The route passes the Solomianska Park," he noted. "I'm assuming you know the area, Vitali?"

Vitali nodded. "Excellent place for an ambush. Plenty of tree cover. But we'll have to get moving quickly."

Eli got to his feet; the others followed suit. "Let's get the two cars loaded up with gear. No time to waste."

Shuki went over to a crate in the corner and removed the various sections of a Tango 51 sniper rifle and started to piece it together: telescopic sights with laser marker, tripod, and silencer. He replaced the short barrel with a twenty-four-inch one and added a pair of binoculars to complete the outfit.

"You really think you're going to use all that?" Vitali said. "Try this instead." He dragged another crate to the middle of the room and handed each of them a machine gun. Shuki groaned at the unexpected weight, but Vitali was unrepentant. "This is what we're going to use: a 7.62 millimeter MAG with a metal ammunition belt."

Eli raised his eyebrows. "Shuki's a sniper, not an amateur militia man," he said.

"Eli, shut up. I know what I'm doing, okay? I'm the local expert." Eli stared, but he remained silent. "We're five men against who knows how many. What we lack in manpower we have to compensate for in firepower. We won't get a second chance at this, as you should have figured out for yourself."

"Where did you get this stuff?" Eli asked curiously.

"The mafia," Vitali said shortly. "The Mossad picked up the tab."

The five men donned bulletproof jackets and took their weaponry. Then they headed out to their cars, carrying the gear in backpacks. Eli lingered behind.

"I'm reporting to Uri," he said. "We don't want this story to take the Mossad by surprise. Wait for me downstairs – I won't be long."

Eli hooked the phone up to the computer and punched in the codes. "Eyal contacted me. We're on our way to capture X and release the captives." He deliberately didn't mention Eyal's order not to attempt the rescue of Elitzafun. This was no time to get into arguments with HQ.

Uri's response was short and to the point: "What's the risk factor?"

"High. Wish us luck."

"Your time has come." X entered the basement and approached Eyal's cell. His eyes shone with anticipation.

"We're leaving?" Eyal asked.

"Yes. Put this on." X opened the door to the cell, released Eyal's left hand from the bar, and handed him a new suit. "Put on make-up. No one is about to let Eyal Gilboa cross the Ukrainian border."

"How are you planning on achieving that?" Eyal asked.

"Forged passports. Don't worry. No one will pay you special attention."

Eyal smiled bitterly. "I'm not worried," he said. "But it might be a good idea to let me see who I should be trying to look like."

X handed him his passport. "So," he said. "Would you really prefer to go back to jail?"

"Why are you asking?"

"Why am I asking? Because we're giving you a free ticket out of the country. If not for us, you would be locked up here for life, condemned as Rubinov's murderer. They would have gotten that confession out of you one way or another – and failing that, they would have beaten you so badly that you wouldn't be able to say another word to anyone, ever. So I think some gratitude is in order. Not that I expect you to be so gracious."

"You're quite right not to expect it. In any case, I'm not in the mood to get into an ideological debate. Let me finish my mission, give you what you want, and then forget about you forever."

"I won't take that personally."

"Danny and Shuki – have you reached your posts?" Eli was conducting this mission the way he had conducted many other Mossad missions in the past – with professionalism, precision, and cool nerves. Eyal was his friend, but now was no time for emotions. As the danger mounted, all considerations other than the success of the mission fell away.

"Give us another two minutes." The dense copse of trees provided them with excellent cover, and their positions would give them a perfect view of the route that X's convoy would be taking.

"Okay. Great. Vitali, are you ready?"

"In another minute." Vitali found himself a perch and took up his sniper position. He was the last of the agents in the line, and if his contribution was needed, that would mean the situation wasn't good. In which case he would shoot to kill, without distinguishing, without compunction.

"I'm going to start the countdown as soon as I identify the cars," Eli continued. "Avi and I will focus on the first car. Danny and Shuki – nothing until you see my signal. Is that clear?" Eli's hands moved as he spoke. He was placing the first of three bombs camouflaged in a hollow piece of stone-shaped Styrofoam along the road.

"If the bomb doesn't go off," he said, "then you, Danny, will focus on the first car along with Avi and I. If it does detonate and the first car is taken care of, you and Shuki will shoot out the tires of the other cars. That's what you're doing either way, Shuki – okay?"

"Fine."

"Vitali?"

"Yes, boss."

"You're not in the mafia now. Are you at your post?"

"Yes."

"If the convoy reaches you unharmed, you know what to do." Eli's eyes narrowed. "Nobody's getting out of here until we do what we came for."

"Mafia style," Vitali said. It wasn't for nothing that he had been given that role.

Eli placed the last of the three bombs in its place on the road and then hurried back to his post. He could feel the tension in his entire body, all the way down to his toes. Adrenaline was coursing through his blood, and he knew why. This wasn't just any mission. The life of his friend was at stake – the friend who had been at his side for so many missions in the past. Without Eyal, could he really pull this off without a hitch? And if there were hitches, what would they cost them?

He glanced at his watch. Five minutes had passed since they'd arrived there. An hour since Eyal's text message. "A few hours" might mean two; it might also mean six, and unexpected delays could mean even longer. Just as long as X didn't change their plans entirely. They would wait.

"How much longer is this supposed to take?" Danny said over the radio.

"As long as it's supposed to. One hour or six. Or more."

"Great. Why didn't you remind me to bring chocolate?" Danny quipped.

Eli was in no mood for joking. "I need your eyes and your head to be in the right place, Danny," he warned. "Don't rely on me to spot the convoy. They might not be bunched together. We need to be sharp for this one – no wisecracks."

Danny fell silent. They all did. This was no time for joking and they knew it.

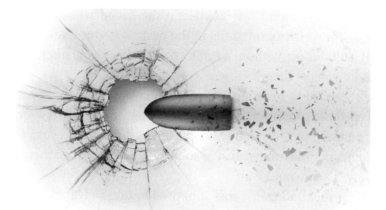

CHAPTER TWENTY-SIX

Ukraine

T he men filed down the stairs and entered the parking lot. Eyal forced himself to remain calm, no easy task considering the stakes. He had no way of knowing if Eli had the ability to respond to his plea. One man with a few guns was obviously powerless to overcome a well-trained band of terrorists. On the other hand, if Eli had received reinforcements, the attack might appear too professional, leading X to suspect that Eyal was somehow behind it – and that would undoubtedly have undesired consequences for Elitzafun, not to mention himself. His only hope was that X would attribute the attack to one of Ukraine's many mafias, which wasn't so preposterous. If anyone at Zhuliany had leaked information related to their flight and the unusually large amount of luggage they had checked in advance, that could certainly arouse mafia interest.

Three Buick Rendezvous models were glinting in the sun, like monsters preparing to descend on their prey. Their luxurious interiors seemed totally incongruent with the mission they were being used for. Eyal realized for the first time the extent of the resources X could draw upon. He had barely suffered a dent in his finances even after the loss of an entire safe house stocked with ammunition and a parking lot full of vehicles.

X walked toward the last car of the convoy, motioning for Ahmed, Daud, and Teddy to enter the vehicle with him. Then he told Jamil, Yusef, Mark, and Colin to enter the second car and Abed, Jamie and Raoul to enter the first car.

"Jamie, you'll be driving. Abed and Raoul, handcuff Eyal's hands to each of your own. He's riding together with you in the back."

Eyal's heart plummeted. For some unknown reason, X had changed the plans they had drawn up and in doing so he had just signed Eyal's death warrant. There was absolutely nothing he could do at this late stage to save himself from a probable death by friendly fire. He had done what he could, but the outcome was in Hashem's Hands.

On so many occasions in the past, this realization had proved a source of comfort. Before he had returned to his roots, he had been wracked by anxiety regarding the outcome of a mission; now, he knew that he only had to do what he could and then stop worrying.

As a young, secular Mossad commander, Eyal had always viewed himself as entirely responsible for the success of any mission that he was involved with. His feelings of guilt whenever one of his men was killed were sometimes crippling, even if his senior officers absolved him of all culpability.

"You take too much upon yourself," Buki, his handler, had once said. "We don't mean that you should dump the responsibility on someone else, or act carelessly, but not everything is contingent on you. You cannot control everything."

After returning to his heritage, new and intoxicating vistas had opened before him. Had Eyal not been in his thirties, and a hardened intelligence agent, he would have cried tears of relief. His responsibilities as an agent were crushing. Not because his missions were difficult, but because it was tough to face the results. Upon realizing that he was not responsible for everything turning out right, a huge weight was lifted from his shoulders. Ironically, Eyal was fired from the Mossad precisely when he was beginning to understand such things.

And then he had been forced to wage war on the Angels of Peace…

You're not in charge of the results, Eyal. The words reverberated in his mind, a voiceless prayer. He was praying for his salvation and the salvation of his son. Only Hashem could save him now.

A sudden thought came to mind. Eli might kill him…but it was his only way to remain alive…

X drove in distracted silence. John had insisted on riding with him, leaving Elitzafun alone with Leon and Abdul. X had berated him for this, but John hadn't been willing to back down.

"Abdul and Leon are with him, and that's enough," John had insisted. "I need to come with you. You aren't taking enough manpower to the United States, and that's an extremely bad idea."

"It's an even worse idea to leave Elitzafun without enough protection. He's our most important playing chip in this game."

John's face had soured. "And your toy is getting you the results that you're after, isn't it?"

"In the meantime, it's getting me far more than I counted on," X had said. "But I'd like to make sure things stay this way."

"So I'll ask Bruce to go and stay with them."

"Leave Bruce out of things. I'll send Muhammad over instead. He'll do a good job." X had always been proud that his militia was comprised of fair-haired, blue-eyed men fighting alongside born-and-bred Arab Muslims. Leon and Achmed, Jamil and Colin... It was like the fulfillment of the prophecy of the End of Days.

"There's a car coming," Danny reported, zooming in with his telescopic lens. "A driver; two, maybe three men in the back. And two cars just behind, full of men. All Buicks. Eyal knew his stuff."

"Ten seconds," Eli said in a low, clear voice. "The moment the car hits the bomb we open fire." He loaded a round of bullets into the chamber of his machine gun and listened to the sound of his heart thumping as he counted down. "Ten. Nine. Eight." Eli quietly spoke the numbers aloud, and the men counted along with him soundlessly.

"Seven. Six. Five. Four," Eli whispered.

A car approached.

Danny and Shuki tensed. Their weapons were loaded and ready to shoot.

"Three. Two."

Eyal, in the center of the back seat of the first car, was sitting up straight and staring out of the front windshield. Looking out for what? He wasn't sure. His tense, strained posture might have set off alarm bells in Colin or John, who knew him somewhat and were accustomed to seeing him apathetic and listless. But Abed and Raoul hardly knew him and failed to detect anything out of the ordinary.

Suddenly, he saw it. It was too far away to know exactly what it was, but he could guess. And knowing Eli, he was sure that his guess was right.

"Stop!" he called out, his tone of voice urgent. "Right now!"

The driver maintained a steady grip on the steering wheel. He had no intention of obeying his captive. X, however, heard the alarm in Eyal's voice over the radio, and he realized that something had to be up. "Did something happen?" he called out over the radio.

"We're headed straight into a trap," Eyal said, injecting just the right tone of panic into his voice which had the desired effect on X.

"Stop," X ordered.

The three vehicles swerved abruptly onto the hard shoulder and came to a halt.

"What did you see?" X called out to Eyal over the radio. "I don't see anything."

"I have been trained to recognize bombs even when camouflaged," Eyal said. His tone of voice was cutting. "There's a bomb beneath that stone, three meters away from our car."

"It can't be." X got out of his car and approached the first vehicle, the one with Eyal inside.

"Release me from the handcuffs and I'll show you that I'm right," Eyal said.

"No. Raoul and Abed, step out of the car with Eyal. Daud and Teddy, keep an eye on him."

A hundred yards away, Eli and Avi inhaled sharply. "Something's wrong," Avi whispered. "They aren't continuing."

Danny and Shuki, a little further away, exchanged glances. Someone had discovered their plan...

"They're close enough," Danny whispered. "I can kill some of them."

"No," Shuki whispered back. "From this distance, at this angle, it's too risky."

Danny reached into his knapsack and pulled out a rope "I'm moving over to the next tree. If they notice me, you'll open fire to distract them. If not, so much the better. You'll give me a minute or two to get organized and then I'll fire a missile. I'll be less than a hundred yards away, which is good enough."

"You won't be able to pull off such a maneuver with a machine gun on your shoulder," Shuki cautioned. "It's too rash. They'll fire back, and we won't achieve a thing."

"The gun weighs only seven kilograms, and the missiles weigh another five. My youngest daughter weighs more than that. I'm not missing this opportunity to wipe these guys out." Danny tucked another submachine gun into his belt, an IWI Tavor X95. Next, he looped the rope and tossed it to the next tree, tightening the loop around the thick branch it snagged.

Shuki wound the rope around his hand and shoulder, bracing himself, and Danny swiftly slid across the length of the improvised zip line. From atop the next tree, closer to the parked cars, he could see that X's men were involved in a heated debate. He motioned toward Shuki and slowly began counting to ten.

"Someone betrayed the details of our plan, and he will pay for this with his life." Eli's eyes were aflame as he whispered the words.

"Mark?" Vitali said. "You suspect him?" He too could feel the searing disappointment. It was terrifying to think that a five-year-old would remain in hostile hands, after all their efforts and preparation. He had gone to extraordinary lengths to obtain the weapons they needed for this mission, and he was furious at the thought that it would all have been for nothing.

"Who else?" Eli was trembling with rage. "We shouldn't have let him go."

"Don't be ridiculous," Avi said. "We didn't let him go for humanitarian reasons. We let him go because we needed one of X's men to collaborate with us."

"Well, apparently, he told his boss that we contacted him, and they took more precautions than we anticipated," Vitali said. "In the end, of course, we didn't make any use of the information he provided. It seems there was a good reason for that."

"Okay, guys," Eli said, trying to shake off his feelings of anger and despair. "I'm going to make my way through the trees, sneak up on the cars, and eliminate him, before we pick off the rest of them, one by one. I'll start with Mark, though – not because I want revenge, but because he knows too much about us."

"Eli – one minute," Vitali said. "Think this through first, slowly." He was worried that Eli was letting his emotions overshadow his better judgment. Having observed him carefully over the past few days, he had come to understand what Eli had told him at their first meeting: Eyal and Eli were too close for Eyal to lie to him. The sadness, pressure, tension, and pain… Eli's words clearly showed that he was deathly afraid of losing Eyal.

"I've thought enough. More than enough. He doesn't deserve another thought of mine. Maybe it was even him who sent that text message, supposedly from Eyal? So if we don't strike quickly, they're going to hit us first. Back me up, Avi. I'm closing in on them."

"No unnecessary risks," Vitali said quietly.

"Why? Mark deserves to die for revealing our plans to X. And who knows what else he told him? First things first – self-preservation."

"You're right," Avi said. "Just a minute, Eli. I'm heading over to the next tree to provide better backup for you."

"I'm waiting fifty-five seconds. After that I'm throwing my grenade and firing the detonator. Both the grenade and our foul agent will explode together."

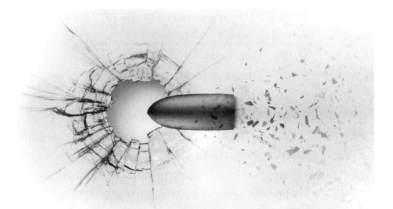

CHAPTER TWENTY-SEVEN

Ukraine

X frowned. "Remove Eyal's handcuffs," he told Abed and Raoul reluctantly. "Teddy and Daud, keep an eye on him to make sure he doesn't try any nonsense."

Eyal's handcuffs were released, and he advanced toward the suspicious-looking rock at the side of the road. He knew Eli's style when it came to designing bombs, and it certainly looked like this was one of his...

X watched his prisoner through narrowed eyes as Colin exited the second vehicle and trained his gun on Eyal, following his every move.

Eyal bent down and crawled forward on the ground just as a bullet whistled through the air. Without a second's thought, he followed the protocol for what to do in case of attack – roll over and take cover in the thick foliage.

Eyal's swift movements saved his life as the bullet hit the bomb that he had been heading for, detonating it and sending shrapnel flying in all directions. The sound of thunder filled the air as the burning metal landed in the trees and on the grass. Some of the shards hit X's men, and their confused and pain-filled shouts rent the previously serene and quiet forest scene.

Time to open fire, Danny decided. He slid a missile into place, checked the wind direction, and launched. The recoil wasn't too great, although it did shake Danny, precariously balanced on a tree branch. The growling sound produced by its flight was followed by a tremendous blast as the missile hit the second car of the convoy, which went up in flames. Danny's expression was grim and forbidding as he got ready to launch a second and final missile. It was the last one he had with him, and he hoped it would be enough.

The second rocket hit the first car, transforming it into a blazing inferno. It was safe to assume that the occupants of both cars were now no longer in the world. But the fire was spreading rapidly and had already reached the tree nearest the first car and threatened to put the entire forest at risk.

Meanwhile, the third car, the only one left unscathed, reversed cautiously from the scene. One of the passengers fired at the spot that Danny had occupied just seconds before, but by then he had moved on, swinging back to the first tree with the help of the zip line that he had rigged up.

Now Danny raised his submachine gun and fired at the last car. He wanted to intimidate the passengers, not to harm them, for fear that he might injure Eyal. As yet, none of the agents had figured out that the man disguised to resemble the photo in his forged passport was Eyal – he could easily have been killed by Eli's fire.

The passengers in the last car responded by opening their own line of fire, and bullets whistled back and forth through the air.

"I don't see that we're making any progress here," Eli said over the radio. "Danny and Shuki, try to disengage and put some space between you and them."

It wasn't so simple, of course, to retreat under fire. But there was no way of knowing whose ammunition would be the first to run out, and if Eyal wasn't planning on making his presence felt, it was hard to know what they were achieving.

Danny looked around. "We're going to need to find a way to get out of here," he observed. A bullet whizzed past his ear, missing him by just a centimeter, before he could complete his sentence. "And fast."

Eyal crawled slowly out of the brambles where he had taken cover and looked cautiously around at the scene. He was unharmed, but two of X's cars had gone up in flames, presumably killing all their occupants. Flames were now also licking at the trees, making this an extremely good time to get out of the forest and back on the road.

For a brief moment, Eyal allowed himself to feel grim satisfaction at the damage his friends had wreaked. A moment later he sobered, considering what could happen if X were to discover that he was behind the ambush.

"Eyal!" X called, as soon as he noticed his prisoner stepping out from between the trees. "Don't move, or you might get hit. I'm radioing in for backup."

"Don't call anyone," Eyal called back. "It's better that we just leave. What do you want to achieve by summoning more men to a gun battle with the mafia? I thought your mission was more important than petty street fighting."

X paused for a moment to consider.

"Hold your fire," he told his men eventually.

Complete silence followed his command.

"What's going on there?" The open radio connection allowed Vitali to listen to the battle as it unfolded. He strapped his sub-machine gun to his bulletproof jacket. "He just acted on his own there. I thought I could rely on Eli..."

Eli remained frozen in his spot, several feet from X's vehicle.

Avi whispered quietly into the radio: "What's going on? Looks like Danny and Shuki have been caught in heavy fire."

"Who issued the first shot and got us exposed like this?" Vitali grumbled.

"Me," Eli said heavily. "And I'm worried that it was actually Eyal – the man I nearly hit when I fired. I didn't really look at his face, but it makes sense that he spotted the bomb."

"Was he injured?" Avi asked anxiously.

In the same breath, Vitali asked: "What happened to him?"

"Nothing. He wasn't harmed," Eli said woodenly. "But as you said, I gave my position away."

Eli fell silent, but shooting could still be heard in the background. Finally, Shuki's voice came over the radio. "Eli, calm down and take control here. Danny hit the first and second cars with an RPG missile. He aimed from a distance of less than a hundred yards, and I can't imagine that anyone inside the vehicles is still alive. Only the men from the last car are firing at us."

Eli gathered his wits. "Do you have a way of getting out, or do you need backup?" Despite the shock that he felt upon realizing that his bomb had nearly murdered his friend, he couldn't allow himself to fall apart.

"I think we can go out on our own," Danny said. "It's going to be a bit difficult, but it'll be fine in the end. What about you?"

"We're okay too, in the meantime. Danny, stop shooting and start to retreat. Vitali, be on the lookout. I'm assuming they're going to turn back now, so the other bombs are redundant at this point, and you're not going to see any action after all. But just in case they do still try to make a run for the airport, be ready."

Vitali stroked the barrel of his sniper rifle. "I have the

ammunition necessary to stop them," he said. "But I agree with your assessment – I really doubt that they'll continue with their original plan after losing so many of their men and two of their vehicles."

"What did you mean when you told Eli that we'd be able to get out of here, after you set this whole forest on fire with your mad shooting?" Shuki asked.

"Setting the forest on fire is actually a great idea," Danny said, still careful to keep his head down. "It'll give them something else to deal with."

"No," Shuki said. "You're insane!"

"Correct," Danny said calmly, hopping from one tree to the next. "Tie the rope to the next group of trees," he said. "Quickly."

"If I understand your plans correctly, who do you think will throw the match into the beautiful bonfire down below?"

"I won't throw a match. I'm going to shoot from a distance of several hundred yards. But it's not just insanity. I want to give Eyal a chance to make a run for it. We don't really know what he intended with that message of his – if it was his message, that is. But surely he meant something!"

Shuki thought for a moment. "Right. Eli should have been onto that, but he lost his cool after he almost killed Eyal. I'm not totally sure that he should have been commanding this mission, you know?"

"I know. But this is our last shot to make something of it. Okay?"

"Okay."

The two men skipped, agile as monkeys, from one tree to the next. The shooting had ceased, but they didn't stop to consider what that might mean.

A hundred yards away from the third car, Danny bent down

and fired a lengthy volley of bullets, aiming in the direction of the tree that he had been sitting in seconds earlier.

The ammunition belts he had left there exploded, just as he had hoped, and the clump of trees quickly caught fire.

"Now run!" Shuki yelled. "We don't have long..."

"Do you see that?" X said. "I gave the shooters a moment of respite, and look at what they did..."

"Get everyone back into the car and get away from here as quickly as possible," Eyal said, repeating his earlier instructions in a firm tone of voice. X gazed hard at him, as if to gauge his dependability. After a moment, he decided to follow his instructions.

"Everyone in. Colin – stop shooting. We're getting out of here."

The surviving terrorists ran for the remaining vehicle, slamming the doors behind them. The driver reversed swiftly, making his way around the burning vehicles and speeding away in the direction of Kiev.

Seizing the opportunity, Shuki and Danny ran back through the woods to their car and headed back to base.

Without Eyal.

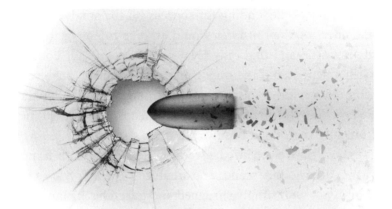

CHAPTER TWENTY-EIGHT

Ukraine

X entered Eyal's room later that evening, after some semblance of order had been restored. The loss of so many of his men had been crushing, but the core members of his team had survived and the mission had only been postponed.

Eyal was now housed in an upper floor, in a room next to that of X himself, in comparatively comfortable conditions, but with one arm still handcuffed to the bars of the window. He looked up as X entered the room, but then went back to staring listlessly at the wall, even though he was consumed by anxiety over the possibility that X would suspect that he was behind the ambush.

"I'd like to tell you about something very strange, very odd," X said.

Eyal looked up again with assumed indifference. "Really?" he asked, his tone expressing no interest whatsoever. In his mind, he was still going over the ambush, wondering whether it could have ended differently. It had been a long shot – that he had known from the outset – depending for success on the small chance that the members of the third car would emerge to engage the Israeli agents in battle and that only Eyal would escape. Of course that hadn't happened, and the only thing that had been achieved was the elimination of a number of evil men. Considering that he didn't even know if his friends had all escaped unscathed, he was far from sure that it had been worth it.

"Yes, really. We retrieved several bullets and bomb fragments from this afternoon's scene, and analyzed them." X's gaze was fixed on Eyal, who simply shrugged and gazed back blankly. "The bomb, disguised as a stone, was built according to the precise pattern used by Hezbollah agents in Lebanon."

"Ah, so I was right about that stone," Eyal said, his voice betraying his satisfaction.

X narrowed his eyes. "Yes…interesting you should put it that way, especially as it is known that the Israelis soon started to copy that method. What do you have to say to that?"

"Me? Nothing."

"No kidding. From where I'm standing, it looks like you should be pleading for your life. Or perhaps the life of your son." X was clearly livid, and even more upset at his failure to provoke Eyal into some kind of reaction.

Eyal laughed. "Pleading for my life? If it wasn't for my superior powers of observation, you wouldn't even have a life to plead for. Is this how you show your gratitude?"

"Eight of my men died. I don't see that I have to thank you for anything when you were clearly the one to provoke the ambush."

Eyal felt his body flood with relief. At least X didn't suspect that he had actually divulged the details of the convoy.

"Provoke? What did I do? Surely you realize that I don't control the Mossad via telepathy? I can't actually make their operative decisions for them. If they try to rescue me, there's really nothing I can do about it."

"There is. I want you to remove your friends from this equation."

"So let me speak to them, and they'll leave. I guarantee it."

"You're going to drop them some kind of hint."

"A hint about what?" Eyal's eyes were red from lack of sleep and never-ending tension. "You see that they figured out on their own where I am. I'll tell them to leave the country now and they'll listen to me."

A guarded expression came over X's face. "You wouldn't want me to harm your child," he said. He handed his phone over to Eyal.

Eyal made a move to take the phone, but X stopped him. "One minute. This conversation needs to take place in Hebrew, so that Eli doesn't realize that anyone is listening in. I'm going to summon Ahmed."

Ahmed duly arrived, and Eyal dialed Eli's number, his heart thumping wildly.

Eli picked up the phone after a single ring.

"Eli, it's me. I managed to slip out of my room and get to a phone. We don't have much time. He who silences even a fool…"

Ahmed frantically gestured that he didn't understand the words, and X fixed Eyal with a furious expression. Eyal hurriedly scribbled onto a piece of paper: "A code I used to speak to Eli."

"Enough," X whispered.

"Eyal, why did you do all of that?" Eli was wounded and hurt. He had been so hopeful and he had risked so much, only to have his plan completely implode. The shock of almost killing his friend had been almost too much to bear.

"I had no choice. I saw that you had made a bomb and that the car that I was in might get blown up." Eyal's heart pounded with fear. Eli was familiar with the *passuk* that he had just quoted and he knew the continuation: "is considered a wise man..." Eli would surely understand from those words that the conversation was being monitored, and he would take care not to reveal Eyal's part in the ambush.

Swiftly, Eyal changed the subject, getting straight to the reason for his call. "Eli, I need you and all of your crew to leave the country."

"Are you insane?" Eli said. His voice was filled with disappointment and hurt. "You want us to leave you and Elitzafun like this? Never!"

"Do you want to help me or cause more harm? Please, Eli, I'm begging you: Leave Ukraine and make no attempt to rescue me. Every additional moment that you are here will only make more trouble."

"Eyal, is someone listening in on this conversation?" Eli asked. His voice trembled as he spoke.

"No. I already told you that I managed to slip away for this phone call." Eyal was a veteran liar, but the act of deceiving his best friend left him with a bitter flavor in his mouth. "This is urgent, Eli. Do not attempt to rescue me, because it will be me, and not you, who will pay the price for your attempts."

Eli balled his fingers up into a fist. "Have they done something to you?"

"Nine millimeters at point blank, in the arm." Eyal didn't mention when the shot had been fired. "But for my sake, Eli, forget about it."

"What about Elitzafun? How can you surrender him so easily?"

"I'm doing everything that I can for him." Eyal swallowed with great effort. "Trust me."

"You need backup!"

"That is true, Eli. But the backup that I need cannot come from a human source. Be the friend that I know you are and leave out the egotistical: 'How could I have left him alone in this mess?' Just make sure that your name is listed on the next list of tourists departing from Ukraine for Israel."

"I'd never leave you, but…"

"This is the best thing you can do for me." Eyal sounded exhausted, and Eli's heart contracted with pain. What else would this man have to go through?

"I'll go."

"Thank you, Eli. And make sure that all of your friends leave together with you. I'm trusting you."

"Fine, but Eyal, what will be with you?"

"I'll be okay."

"What do they want of you?"

"They want another Rubinov."

"Good luck, Eyal."

"Thanks, Eli."

Eyal hung up the phone, and he looked at X. "Are you satisfied now?"

X looked at Ahmed, and Ahmed nodded. "Fine," he told his boss.

X looked back at Eyal. "I'll be satisfied when I see your friends' names on the next list of departures."

Eyal collapsed onto his bed, fully clothed and exhausted. The conversation had drained him completely. He had, of sound mind and soul, given up on his friend's help, and he had never felt more alone. Throughout his years as an agent, no matter how secret the mission, he had always had a friend or two together with him. At the Mossad, too, there had been another dozen or more people who had known what he was doing, and he had known that they were rooting for his success. There were always people working behind the scenes for him, gathering information for him.

But now he was on his own.

X entered the room an hour later. He had come by to say something, and he stopped when he saw the sleeping man on his bed.

He wondered how much longer he would be able to continue to prod him before he fell apart. X remained in his place, immobile. He looked at the sleeping Eyal and noticed how his appearance was completely different from his waking image. The steely green eyes and war-veteran expression was gone, replaced by drooping eyelids. The look of determination, resoluteness, and ferocity was gone as well, along with the smug complacency that so often graced his features. In its place was a silent, sad, and very human figure.

X continued to examine the exhausted man's face, and finally he nodded his head with approval. The Mossad definitely knew how to do a good job.

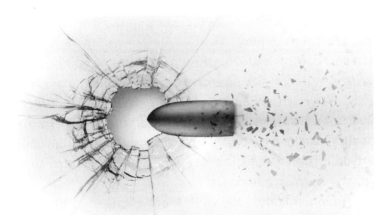

CHAPTER TWENTY-NINE

En route to the United States

Border inspection passed without a hitch. Eyal glanced at the men accompanying him and admitted, albeit only privately, that he would never have gotten through the inspection more smoothly on his own. X had procured perfectly forged passports. Presumably, various members of the group were wanted by Interpol, and Eyal himself was certainly a highly sought-after figure in Ukraine, but none of the computer scans picked up on the fact that the men were anything other than who they were claiming to be.

They had decided to travel in two separate groups: X, Eyal, and Colin made up one group, and Teddy, John, and Ahmed made up the second group. Leon was conspicuous by his absence, and whenever Eyal was reminded of that fact, his heart constricted in pain. Leon had remained behind in the Ukraine to watch Elitzafun, and he was hardly known as a figure sympathetic to children. Eyal highly doubted that X would let him send another video message to his son, especially as he would have to send it electronically. Now there was nothing he could do for Elitzafun other than pray.

Passport control and departure passed too smoothly. Eyal felt a searing sense of disappointment each time their passports were returned by yet another bored-looking clerk. He so desperately wanted to be detained...but in Kiev everything went smoothly; when they reached Frankfurt and changed planes, nothing untoward interrupted their journey; and now they were about to disembark in Washington, DC.

In the United States, one clerk spent a long time studying the tourists and comparing their faces to the images that appeared in the passport. Perhaps his hesitation stemmed from the nervous, taut expression on Eyal's face. Eyal's heart leaped with hope when he saw the clerk waver, but then X whispered, "If he suspects anything, your son's life will be worth less than a garlic peel. All it will take is a single word to Leon and the whole thing will be over."

Shaken, Eyal pasted a calm, self-assured expression on his face once again. The clerk returned his passport to him, and he wished them all a pleasant stay in the United States. The men then entered two cabs and traveled to the hotel where X had booked them rooms.

As he had requested, their rooms were on separate floors, with Eyal and X in a room on the third floor, Colin and Teddy in a room on the second floor, and John and Ahmed in a room on the first floor.

"Zero hour is approaching," X told Eyal as he looked around their room. "Tomorrow you will meet with the president as was originally planned. Be on your best behavior, and stay away from trouble. You have a real knack for that sort of thing."

Eyal peered out of the window at the urban view below.

Hundreds, perhaps even thousands, of people passed below, hurrying to and fro, each one absorbed in his own life, his own issues. Eyal gazed out for a long moment, wondering if a single one of the people below felt as lonely as he did.

"You'll be starting tomorrow."

"I know."

Washington, DC, USA

The architectural beauty, clean streets, elegant city squares, and historic buildings greeted Eyal on his first visit to this city. The cool breeze brushed his cheeks as he strolled through the streets like a tourist, X at his side. The Lincoln Memorial, Capitol Hill, the Peace Monument...all famous sites with a fairly recent history. Nothing here dated back more than three hundred years, Eyal thought. It was a far cry from home...

"You know," X said pensively, "I too can say 'I have a dream,' just as Martin Luther King said while standing not far from here. My dream is similar to his, although it isn't a dream of equality, but rather a dream of life."

Eyal didn't respond.

"Let's go," X said. His tone changed and grew purposeful once more. "Let's go."

Eyal began to walk once again, and X continued to talk. "One thing I will caution you in advance of the next stage of our mission. Do not forget that we are listening in to your every word. You are not carrying any obvious monitoring device, as you are going to be thoroughly searched for such things, but there are more sophisticated listening devices that will permit us to listen in from great distances. So I feel it's only fair to warn you that we will not tolerate any double games, hints, or suspicious behavior of any sort. And if anything happens that seems to threaten the success of the mission, regardless of concrete proof or the absence of it, we will consider you responsible, and your son will pay the price."

Again, Eyal remained silent.

"My men will be following you like shadows wherever you go. You may be entering the White House on your own, but we will know exactly what is taking place there. We have our people infiltrated on every level, and they will report back to me on your every move. If anything seems strange or unexpected, I will harm your son. Do I make myself clear?"

Eyal nodded.

"Take this." X held out a watch. "I noticed that you don't have a watch, and it occurred to me that you will probably need one."

Eyal fixed X with a derisive look. "I hope you didn't hide a listening device in your extremely generous gift, because the counterespionage team will certainly examine it, and if they find something, it will be you, not me, who will suffer as a consequence."

X shook his head, a smile on his face. "I can promise you that the thought never so much as entered my mind. I have no need to resort to outdated technology in order to monitor your words and deeds. This is a simple watch – a timepiece, if you will. If the model is not to your liking, feel free to exchange it for another – I saved the receipt."

"Your taste truly is awful. I might just take you up on your offer. Where did you buy it?"

"Don't insult my taste. I chose you, too."

"You used that line on me already, and I reminded you that it was the president who made the choice, not you."

X said nothing, and his smile remained in place despite his annoyance at Eyal's quicker wit. Perhaps it merely reassured him that he had acted wisely in "adopting" him.

Eyal kept walking, this time unaccompanied, though he was sure he could feel X's eyes on his back. He had every reason to believe that his men were strategically placed, keeping tabs on him, and that a single word, glance, or movement that was not to their liking could prove fatal for Elitzafun.

Twenty minutes later he reached the gates of the White House.

A man approached. "Eyal Gilboa?"

An ebony-skinned man held out a hand. "I'm Michael Morris, chief of security at the White House. Please come with me. We have been waiting for you." The man was tall and almost entirely bald. The few hairs that had survived the fifty-seven years of his life were entirely white, and the expression in his piercing eyes was sharp, albeit friendly.

Eyal haltingly extended his own hand in favor of clinging to his role as the aloof and accomplished Israeli security officer. Modesty almost never hurt.

"Follow me," Michael instructed.

They walked along a broad path, and Eyal took in his surroundings with keen interest. He passed through a metal detector before entering the building and walking down a long corridor lined with doors. Near the end of the corridor, Michael lifted his hand and knocked purposefully on a door, which was immediately opened.

"Come in," someone inside said.

Eyal flashed Michael a questioning look, and Michael smiled. "Security procedures," he said apologetically.

Eyal was led into an average-sized room. He had been personally invited to the White House by the president, and Bentzy had informed the president of his coming, but that didn't mean that he had security clearance privileges. He was examined thoroughly, with the security guard probing his entire body.

The guard's hands automatically paused when they reached his bandage. "What's this?" the guard asked. "Roll up your sleeve, please."

Eyal rolled up his shirt sleeve, revealing the bandage that Dr. Bogdan had wrapped around his arm.

The guard's eyes glinted with suspicion. "What is this?" he said. Nothing could be simpler than smuggling a weapon in a bandage...

"A gunshot wound," Eyal said drily.

"May I see?"

"If you must." Eyal gently unwrapped the bandage, looking away when the wound was exposed. He had dealt with his fair share of gunshot wounds, including under battlefield conditions, but he had forgotten how bad injuries could look. This particular wound was already several days old, but the gash still looked raw and deep. Of course, having ripped out one of the staples himself hadn't helped matters.

The guard looked at the wound, clearly suspicious. Anyone could fake a wound for all sorts of purposes. After a long time, the guard finally nodded. "You can replace the bandage yourself," he said.

Eyal did so, and then he pulled his sleeve back down. Michael watched with evident interest. The wound looked like a very painful one, but the Israeli agent had shown no sign of pain when the security guard handled it none too gently. Eyal's face was a sealed mask, and had the president not trusted him implicitly, Michael would certainly have been afraid of him.

"How did you get that?" Michael asked him curiously.

"While cleaning my gun," Eyal replied briefly. "No big deal."

Michael nodded, not believing the agent's words for a moment. "Follow me," he told Eyal once again.

Eyal followed the security chief with silent self-assurance, looking all around and impressing the images of his surroundings upon his memory. Every so often, Michael turned around to check on him, and Eyal felt a surge of bitterness. Why was he being given such a cold welcome here? He was reasonably confident that the Americans knew better than to accept the Ukrainian account of

Rubinov's murder without making investigations of their own, but perhaps suspicion had been attached to him nonetheless?

They ascended a set of stairs and then turned and entered an elevator. Eyal absorbed every detail: the locations of the mirrors, the thickness of the carpets, the distance between each of the tightly clustered security cameras. Nothing escaped his notice.

They reached a door and Michael rapped his knuckles against the polished wood. A thunderous voice, half-ironic, half-angry, called out: "Enough of the etiquette, Michael; just come on in."

With a smile Michael pushed open the door, and the two men entered. The president was already making his way over to the door, and now he stood opposite them, taking stock of the new arrival.

Eyal's breath caught in his throat. It was similar to how he had felt when he first met up with Rubinov. After so many long and difficult moments, he had finally reached his goal. He had been through a long and traumatic week. Never before had he faced such a complex assignment with such agonizing decisions to make. He was also exhausted, physically and emotionally – he felt drained, his thoughts and feelings torn in so many different directions. It was hardly the right frame of mind with which to approach this new mission.

The president watched Eyal, studying him closely, and Eyal made his own study of the president. Their eyes met, and the president was the first to smile.

"Welcome." The president extended his hand. "I've been waiting for you."

"I'm happy to hear it," Eyal said simply.

"Come, let's sit down." The president gestured toward an armchair. "I want to speak to you. Michael, give us a few minutes, please."

"But..." Michael began.

"It's okay. I have a sixth sense about these things." The president smiled broadly. "He's okay. If he had wanted to kill me I'd be dead by now. This man is dangerous. We're just lucky that he's on the right side of the law."

Eyal felt himself growing rattled by the president's sense of humor. He responded to the expression of gaiety in the president's eyes with a small smile of his own.

Michael left the room, and the president opened a drawer, took out a large sheet of paper and a pen, and handed the items to Eyal. "Draw a picture of the White House," he said.

"What?"

"Draw everything you saw from the moment you entered the gates until you got here. Take your time. I can be patient."

"Do you have a ruler?"

The president opened his drawer again and removed a simple metal ruler, the type used by schoolchildren. Eyal began to sketch the route that he had taken, down the path that Michael had led him, and all the way up to the Oval Office. He had made a mental note of the number of steps that he had taken, and he was now able to accurately depict the length of the hallway. He marked every turn, drew every security camera, and noted many other pertinent details, just as he had done so many times in the past.

Five minutes. Ten. Sixteen minutes, and Eyal completed his drawing. The sketch of the White House was vivid, accurate, and precise, down to the very last detail.

The president's mouth dropped upon viewing the completed drawing. "This is amazing," he said with disbelief. "You can become an architect."

Eyal offered a modest smile. "I learned this while working for the Mossad," he said. "Whenever I enter a building of significance, I automatically absorb the details of my surroundings. All I need is to take several steps along the length and breadth of the place, and I'm able to gauge the exact measurements, give or take."

"So, you have enough information to deter a novice terrorist."

"A novice terrorist isn't going to try to blast his way into the White House."

The president looked pointedly into Eyal's eyes. "And an experienced terrorist?"

Eyal returned the president's stare with a steely green stare of his own. "He can try."

"Do you know of any such plan?"

Eyal's face didn't pale and his heart didn't skip a single beat. Not a single muscle moved on his face. As an intelligence agent he had learned to have complete control over his facial expressions, heart rate, and body language. Skilled agents, and skilled criminals too, were experts at beating the polygraph.

"Like any former Mossad agent, and any upstanding citizen really, I know that there are plenty of terrorists who would like to lay their hands on the most powerful man in the world."

The president kept his gaze fixed on Eyal, and Eyal returned the look with an expression of calm equilibrium. His gaze was unwavering, and the president was the first to look away. "This," said the president, pointing at Eyal's sketch, "is the reason I need you here with me."

Eyal smiled and didn't reply.

"Take a look at this room." The president made an expansive gesture that took in the entire Oval Office. "I want you to locate all of the security cameras and listening devices here."

Eyal stood up. "Do you have a pair of pliers and a screwdriver?"

The president shook his head, but he murmured something into the intercom system, and immediately the two items were brought into the room.

Eyal got up, walking slowly along the perimeter of the room, tapping at intervals with the screwdriver. For thirty minutes he patiently took apart outlets and perused the contents of the room. His search turned up six security cameras and two listening devices.

The president eyed him with satisfaction. "I want you on my team."

"You told me that already." As per the Mossad's indoctrination, Eyal was unimpressed by the heady scent of power.

"Let's go down to the shooting range," the president said, rising from his chair. "I'm interested in seeing how you fare."

Eyal raised an eyebrow. "Surely there's no need for that. As I believe you've already heard, I am willing to provide you with security while you are in Ukraine, but that's as far as it goes. What are all these tests for?"

"Nevertheless, please join me." The president was unaccustomed to having his requests refused by anyone.

"Okay."

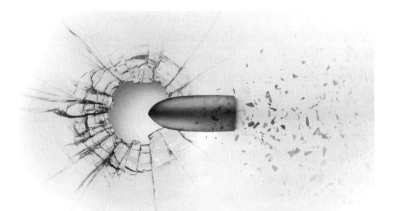

CHAPTER THIRTY

Washington, DC, USA

They left the room together – an older man with white hair, blue eyes, and the weight of the world on his shoulders, but with a quick and enthusiastic gait; and a young man in his thirties, with dozens of intelligence missions under his belt. The younger man was tall with an athletic build, but despite the scale that seemed to be tipped in his favor, his gait was slower and more lethargic than that of the older man at his side.

Michael approached them, a concerned expression on his face.

"Mr. President, I hope the interview was to your satisfaction. Nonetheless, I have to inform you that the alarm went off in the security room several times."

"He's to blame for that." The president clapped Eyal on the back affectionately, and Eyal winced just slightly as a searing pain shot down his arm. The wound pounded all day long, and even the slightest touch caused his muscles to grow taut.

The president noticed the expression on Eyal's face. "What happened?" he asked.

"Nothing." Eyal resumed his usual poker face.

"Perhaps you'll clue me in nonetheless?" The president was too curious to let a riddle go unsolved.

"He has a gunshot wound in his arm," Michael said. "You'd be thrashing in pain if you were in his place."

"My apologies." The president's expression grew inquisitive once more. "How did you receive your wound?"

Eyal shrugged. "I told Mr. Morris here that I shot myself while cleaning my gun, a none-too-infrequent occurrence."

"And what will you tell me?"

Eyal smiled. "Why shouldn't I tell you the same thing?"

Michael emitted a strange gargling noise from his throat and the president laughed. "You're a man after my own heart, Eyal. And because I'm sick and tired of everyone tiptoeing around me, I will leave you alone. I called you here, and I want to host you well." The president's eyes suddenly narrowed. "On the other hand, there's another matter on which I do want your full transparency. I want to know what happened with this Rubinov guy. The last thing I need is a hired assassin on my staff."

Eyal shrugged. "He was an obvious candidate for murder. I can't go into more detail than that."

"In that case, I'll have to check with the CIA. They must have been briefed by the Mossad."

"This was an unofficial operation."

"So? They have their ways of knowing things. I'll get the answers I want – you'll see."

The president resumed his brisk walk, with Michael and Eyal following closely behind. They reached the shooting range, and the president took out a gun and handed it to Eyal. "I want to see your shooting skills," he said.

"You can find out about them in my file from the Mossad," Eyal protested. "They surely won't refuse you my file if you ask for it. Why do you need to see a live performance?"

"I like to see things for myself. I don't rely on anyone until I have firsthand proof."

"How sweet," Eyal said.

Michael once again emitted his strange form of chuckle, and when Eyal turned around to stare at him, Michael whispered, "You really have no respect for anyone."

A sliver of a smile appeared on Eyal's otherwise granite features. "Comes with the territory," he said.

"How was it?" X greeted Eyal. His voice had all the excited qualities of a child who had just been to a birthday party.

"Okay." Eyal released his tie. "Except for the part where I had to explain my gunshot wound to the president."

"So sorry about that," X said. His voice was devoid of shame or remorse. "And what did you tell him?"

"I didn't mention the role that your man had to play in it, if that's what you mean," Eyal said tersely.

"Thanks." X eyed him eagerly. "So, what's going on?"

"Tomorrow I'm going to meet the members of the security staff who are traveling with the president to Ukraine. I'm supposed to train them, and then we'll see how I can weave my…plans into it all."

"You are the head of the president's security team during his trip to Ukraine?"

"Yes. Isn't that the reason you had me abducted?"

X nodded, clearly pleased. "You were there for a while."

"I walked around the White House with the president." Eyal fell onto his bed, exhausted. "He checked me out, asked lots of questions, interrogated me about my past, and so forth."

"Okay." X turned out the lights. "It's been a long flight, and a long way until we got to this stage. Go to sleep."

Eyal didn't respond. He was already fast asleep.

Eyal met the Israeli team first. When he saw Bentzy and Yonatan a surge of happiness filled him, and he shook Bentzy's hand for a moment too long. "Where were you for so long?" Bentzy whispered.

"In lots of places," Eyal said sadly.

"You're not with them anymore," Bentzy said. He too had once worked for the Mossad – with Eyal as his commander. "What's going on, Eyal?"

"Do you want to hear my autobiography?" Eyal offered a smile, but Bentzy knew him too well to believe that the smile could be real.

"Definitely." Bentzy's voice shook slightly as he took in the strongest person he knew, crumbling before his eyes. After fifteen years of joint missions he was familiar with Eyal's emotional and physical capabilities, and he couldn't figure out what had happened to him. "We're dying to know. Let's meet over coffee somewhere. You certainly don't look like the person I remember so well."

"There's something to that." Eyal looked at his watch. "I'm meeting with Michael and Bernie Hammer, head of the Secret Service, for a briefing soon, and I can't be late. After that meeting I'm going to meet the guards at the unit's training camp, so today's a busy day."

"I'll come to the camp," Bentzy said.

"I wish, Bentzy. I'm going to be too busy putting the guards through their paces."

"I'll wait until you're done and we'll leave together."

"That won't be possible. I have to return immediately after

that to my hotel." Eyal's smile faltered. "Debriefings for a secret meeting...maybe we'll meet after that."

"Of course. The meal's on me."

"Look for someplace kosher."

"At your service, Rabbi."

"Chief, you mean." Eyal whacked Bentzy on the shoulder.

"Still a snob, aren't you?" But his former chief's humorous line encouraged him slightly and returned the sparkle to his eye.

"You already know the Israelis in the group, right?" Michael asked Eyal as they met up prior to a debriefing with the Secret Service members slated to guard the president during his trip to Ukraine. The unit members were, unsurprisingly, not happy at the news that their debriefing would be conducted by a young Israeli. Eyal had known that he would have to deal with the discontent, but he wasn't too concerned about it.

"Yes." Eyal fell silent, and after a moment's thought, he added: "I don't know how smart it is to mix the Israelis with the Americans."

"There's someone else who shares your opinion." They reached an office, and Michael swiped his card and motioned for Eyal to enter before him. A man with a cold, detached expression on his face was leaning against a wall in the office. "Bernie Hammer," Michael said. "Head of the Secret Service."

Eyal stepped forward and extended his hand. "I've heard a lot about you and I'm happy to be meeting you."

Bernie kept his arms crossed in silent demonstration and didn't proffer his own hand. "So," he said. "You're the new toy around here, I see."

"I don't like to think of myself as anyone's toy." Eyal flashed a friendly smile and returned his hands to his pants pockets. His demeanor reflected no sign of feeling insulted, and he truly was not affronted. "I prefer to think of myself as simply someone who provides assistance."

"Call it whatever you like," Bernie growled. "The president is crazy and I told him as much."

"Not crazy." Eyal selected a more nuanced description. "How about *peculiar*."

"You don't know him like I do." Bernie looked like a lion whose prey had just been snatched from his jaws – furious, ferocious, and longing for revenge.

"True," Eyal admitted.

"Inviting a stranger to oversee your security in a strange country is beyond weird."

Eyal was silent for a long moment. "What do you want me to say?" he said. "The president asked me to come and I'm here. If you can't accept that, I can leave, but you will have to provide an explanation to the president regarding my departure."

The man narrowed his eyes, clearly frustrated. "We've never had a president like him before." Bernie spoke as though Eyal were somehow responsible for that fact. "And I don't understand how the most wanted person in Ukraine managed to get out of the country in one piece – or at all, for that matter. Most importantly, I don't understand how a murderer can be hired to provide security."

Eyal chose to ignore Bernie's aggressive approach and the unspoken message that came through loud and clear – namely, "I want you out of here as quickly as possible." Instead, he offered a diplomatic suggestion. "I understand you, Bernie. If you'd like me to go back home to Israel, I will, but you're going to have to be the one to let the president know about it."

"You know that isn't possible." Bernie sat down at his desk and gestured to the seat beside him. "Sit," he said shortly. "Let's talk about our plans."

Eyal sat down, summoning all of his personal charm to soothe the other man's battered ego. "Tell me what your thoughts are."

"Eyal isn't in favor of Israelis being part of this mission either," Michael suddenly interjected.

"He'll have to remove himself from the equation in that case, because if I remember correctly, that is the country of origin that appears in his passport."

Eyal fell silent. This was the policy that the Mossad adopted at times, and it was a policy that worked when it came to international scandals generated by the different intelligence bodies. The policy worked, with partially successful results, in his relationship with his father-in-law, and he hoped it would work with Bernie as well.

Eyal forged on. "I am very much opposed to the idea of having Israelis on this mission," he said. "It's only natural for tension to develop between the two different staffs, and with such a tight level of security that needs to be maintained, the tension won't help any."

"So, what do you suggest?"

"I suggest removing the Israelis from the picture," Eyal said calmly. Neither Michael nor Bernie could possibly have guessed that the reason he didn't want the Israelis to join the mission was that he had good reason to believe that the attempt to capture the president was liable to cost lives – perhaps a good many of them. "There are only ten Israelis. They can be easily replaced – I'm sure you have plenty of good men who are more than capable of being part of this mission."

"We'll have to ask the president what he thinks of the idea." Bernie grimaced. "He's like a child, insisting on getting his way in matters that he doesn't even begin to understand."

Eyal decided to once again ignore Bernie's uncomplimentary remark. "You know what? I'll ask him myself. Is there anything else you would like to bring to my attention?"

"Yes." Bernie leaned over, a hint of a threat in his otherwise level tone. "I don't know why the president has decided to place his trust in a murderer. And it makes no difference if that murderer has the Mossad's back—"

"He left the Mossad," Michael interrupted.

"So they say," Bernie said. "And I say: What can be simpler than the Mossad's hiring an agent and stating that he's quit? But that's not my business. My business is the counterespionage team. The president may trust you, but I do not. Rest assured, we will be keeping an eye on you."

Eyal's smile widened. "The pleasure is all mine."

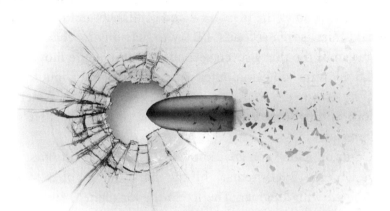

CHAPTER THIRTY-ONE

Near Washington, DC, USA

The training camp was huge, Eyal thought with admiration. The field was larger than any Israel could ever permit itself, due to the country's tiny size. It was sprawled out over an area the size of a medium-sized town, and it contained everything necessary for whatever sort of training a field commander could dream up.

The group of soldiers did not disappoint Eyal with their capabilities. Bernie had handpicked the forty men, and Bernie was someone who had a personal interest in impressing him.

"Hi, guys." Eyal's English was impeccable, and he had a perfect New York accent. If Bernie had been hoping that Eyal would aggravate his men with a strong Israeli accent, those hopes were about to be dashed. "I'm Eyal Gilboa. My job is to make sure that anyone interested in harming our president will regret the moment that he dared to entertain such a notion. Now, I know that some of you are less than thrilled to see me, an Israeli, here. Those feelings are completely legitimate, but I need anyone feeling such sentiments to step up to the plate now and state them out loud within the next thirty-seven seconds. I'll try to help any troubled fellows out, but once the thirty-seven seconds are over, we're moving on, and I don't want to hear another word of complaint about this."

"Why do you say 'our' president?" a young African American shot out, wiping some sweat from his brow as he spoke. "He's not your president."

"Come on. Don't you guys know that Israel is the fifty-first state of the Union?" Eyal's remark hit the mark, and all of the young men roared with laughter. The ice in the air melted, and a smile replaced Eyal's formerly stern expression.

"We need to make a careful study of anything and everything that could pose a danger to the president. We are going to clearly coordinate our positions. Our positions en route from Washington to Kiev will obviously change every day, but the change is one of location only. Our relative positions will not change in any way. And one more thing needs to be absolutely clear: You are to take orders from no one except me. Not even from your direct superior. We will synchronize each soldier's position very clearly, and those positions will not change unless I say so. You will take orders from no one else. I don't care if the Ukrainian prime minister has a word to say on the subject. You will relate to his orders just as you would relate to clear air, because only my word on this issue carries any weight."

"What if, for some reason, you can't issue commands once we're out in the field?" a tall blond soldier called out.

"I have a second in command, in case the need arises, but pray very hard that it won't come to that. For your sakes." Eyal smiled again. "And for mine too, of course…"

The men laughed once again. Several moments later, though, as Eyal started barking out orders in the training area, their smiles faded. Eyal was a harsh, unforgiving trainer. He demanded only the best of his young charges, and he left them gasping for breath. He demonstrated the most difficult tasks himself, and Bentzy, watching from the side, couldn't get his head around the fact that Eyal was still capable of so much with his injured arm. To Eyal, however, the injury was immaterial, as he climbed and weaved his way over obstacles, shot with perfect aim, and merited whistles of amazement from young men who had witnessed plenty of talent before.

During a short break, while Eyal was drinking from a bottle of mineral water, Bentzy approached. "My congratulations."

"For what?"

"For once again reaching great heights while everyone watches with admiration."

"I'd give it all up in a second, with the greatest pleasure, believe me."

"So why are you doing this?" Bentzy genuinely wanted to know. "You're not telling me how you got out of Ukraine, but why didn't you just go home?"

"Right now this is not up for discussion," Eyal said coldly. "All I'm focusing on now is protecting the president." He poured water from the bottle over his head, rubbing at the dirt on his face and chin. "There are many things you don't know about me, Bentzy, and trust me that it's better that way."

"Should I trust you?" Bentzy said, scanning the face of his former officer closely as he spoke. "This is exactly why I want to talk."

"I can't talk in this condition." Eyal's body, from the top of his head down to the tips of his shoes, was caked in mud. "No normal restaurant will allow me inside looking like this."

"Any normal restaurant should be told not to allow you in regardless, even when you're looking more decent," Bentzy commented. "There's no way of knowing what you could be hiding under your jacket."

"There's a guard at the entrance," Eyal deadpanned. His usual unruly glint appeared in his eyes, making him once more resemble the old familiar Eyal.

"Don't make me laugh."

"I've heard they're very excited about you at the White House," X said. He had returned to their hotel room to see Eyal sitting and staring listlessly out the window. This was a change from Eyal's standard position at his computer, where he could usually be found scrutinizing the various options, intelligence warnings, upcoming operations, and all sorts of other data that hadn't even occurred to X to examine, despite the fact that he thought of himself as someone who considered everything.

Eyal turned around to look at X. "What?" he said. His voice made it clear that he wasn't focused. He was exhausted. After returning to the hotel earlier he had taken a shower, changed his clothing, and collapsed onto an armchair to stare out of the window and try to figure out what to tell his friends. Or, more to the point, what not to tell them.

"I heard they're very excited about you at the White House," X repeated. "Has anything changed between us?" He looked at his watch. "Aside from the fact that you made up to meet with two of your best friends in another hour and a half?"

"I already know that you're keeping tabs on me all the time. You don't need to prove that to me now. You can stop those games." Eyal's expression betrayed his scorn. He had already figured out that X could hear him as long as he remained within a half mile of one of his men. The question was if there was a way for him to somehow put a greater distance between them. Should he make his plans in the White House or in some other building related to intelligence, where eavesdroppers wouldn't be able to listen in?

"I am the one who will decide whether to stop or not," X said. His voice was as supercilious and patronizing as ever. "Allow me to consider whether I want you to meet your friends, or whether I prefer to keep you safely locked in this room until your next meeting with the president."

Eyal's face suddenly lit up with a thin smile that stretched and stretched until it turned into genuine laughter.

"What's so funny?" X asked, even as he realized that this was the first time he was hearing his captive laugh out loud.

"You're reminding me of my schoolteachers." Eyal was pensive for a moment. "And of one teacher in particular, who always tried to detain me after class when everyone else had left. He had plenty of reasons to issue those detentions, but somehow he never managed to go through with them."

"Why not?" X asked. His curiosity was authentic, for it was always interesting to hear another person bare their soul.

"Because I always managed to escape. Once I escaped down the drainpipe, another time I escaped using a rope that I tied to the bars of the window. And once, when I was locked into the principal's office for the umpteenth time, I did what I do these days – I blew the door open."

"Really?" X's tone was laced with disbelief. "How?"

"I combined cleaning agents with some other basic substances." Eyal smiled at the memory. "You can imagine what the principal and teachers had to say about that."

X laughed, and for a moment there was a surrealistic bond between them. "You mean to tell me that if I don't allow you to meet your friends, you'll blast your way out of here?"

Eyal was still smiling. "That's just one of many options."

"Okay. I won't chance things with the hotel doors... You're free to go. But, I must say, a moment ago you seemed too exhausted to go anywhere."

"Oh, I have an inexhaustible supply of energy." Eyal got up, put on his jacket, and stuck his tie into a pocket as X looked on.

"I've noticed that." X jerked his head in the direction of Eyal's pocket. "Why did you put that tie there?"

"Don't worry, I'm not going to use it to strangle anyone. I just don't like the look of a tie. But there are some restaurants where one must wear a tie in order to be admitted, so I decided to bring mine along, in case there's a need for it."

"How did you manage practice today with your wounded arm?"

"My arm is the least of my worries," Eyal said. He shifted with impatience toward the door to the room. "Bye."

"Summon Colin on your way out."

Eyal offered a half nod and left the room. His arm was still painfully reminding him of its existence. He had finished his supply of antibiotics and creams, and he needed more. He also needed his bandage to be replaced, as the bandage that he had hastily and unprofessionally wrapped that morning had torn completely during his frenzied bout of training exercises. X had either forgotten about tending to those matters or he was waiting for Eyal to ask for help.

Eyal wasn't going to ask for medicines or bandages. And he wasn't going to summon Colin either.

Why not? Because.

So X would get upset. Big deal.

So now Eyal needed to make his way to the restaurant on foot, as X hadn't given him a credit card or cash. Perhaps he was waiting for him to ask for that as well.

Forget about it.

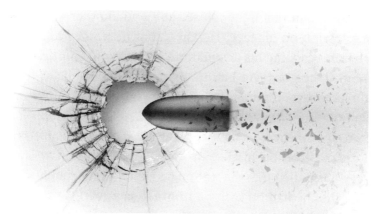

CHAPTER THIRTY-TWO

Washington, DC, USA

You need to shake off your trackers, Eyal thought, stepping outside into the cool air of the capital city. His breath created visible ringlets of steam in the air, and he smiled as his thoughts took him to Elishama and Elitzafun. Like all young children, they would pretend that they were smoking cigarettes on cold days when the warm breath from their mouths created a mist in the air.

Eyal looked around, expecting to find the usual two of X's men shadowing him. This time he spotted two unfamiliar faces, but it was obvious that they had been assigned to follow him. Briefly, Eyal considered the implications of the fact that X clearly had many of his agents in America, embedded in society, possibly in positions of influence.

Eyal walked hurriedly away from the hotel, his eyes roaming from side to side, taking in his surroundings. Yes, there was no doubt about it. He had been trained to spot people tracking him, and it didn't take him long to ascertain that he was being followed by a man in a light-colored suit and another man with an icy expression on his face. He knew that he needed to shake his tails before reaching his destination. X knew what his destination was, but if he got there before his men, then maybe at least he would have several minutes during which to transfer information to Bentzy.

Eyal approached a bus stop, staring at the timetable with a bland expression on his face as he waited for a bus to appear. When a bus pulled into the station he got on immediately, despite the fact that he had no cash on him. He saw Icy Eyes dart into a taxi and Light Suit board the bus together with him.

Eyal pushed himself up against the rear doors of the bus and waited for the bus to pull into the left lane just before reaching a traffic light. He was assuming that the driver of the cab following the bus would turn on its left blinker in order to continue the chase, and he knew that the rear doors of most buses could be manipulated by hand.

The scene played out as planned. The bus pulled into the left lane before a traffic light, and as the light changed to green and the driver prepared to move on, Eyal quickly shoved open the bus door and shot outside, as the passengers shouted in alarm.

Icy Eyes, in the taxi behind the bus, was forced to turn left, thanks to the angry honks of the drivers in the cars behind him. Light Suit continued on the bus to the next stop. In the meantime, Eyal hurried to the nearest subway station, where he was swallowed up by the dozens of passengers there. Instead of passing through the turnstile, however, he swung round and headed out via a different exit, onto a main thoroughfare. Only then did he start walking quickly to the restaurant, hoping he had achieved something of value.

He had lost half an hour in his attempt to shake his trackers. He wondered if X had managed to send someone over to the restaurant in the meantime, or if the first set of trackers were still trying to track him down, suspecting that he had changed his destination.

"So you've stopped trying to find out who really killed Rubinov?" Bentzy asked Eyal at the entrance to the café, the moment he arrived. Eyal's gaze automatically took in his surroundings, searching, as usual, for the perfect spot in which to sit. He needed somewhere that gave him a good view of the rest of the tables, and somewhere that didn't leave him vulnerable to anyone passing by on the street. Then he noticed Yonatan already waiting at a table and saw that he and Bentzy had already selected such a spot, and that all he needed to do now was join them.

Eyal placed a finger to his lips. "Just a minute. Just a minute. Let's sit down first." He offered a tired smile.

Bentzy was restlessly energetic. The man he admired most in the world was displaying signs of cracking, and he refused to accept it. Perhaps it was due to the overwhelming stresses of his work, which, after years on the job, certainly challenged one's emotional strength. But it might also be due to his facing a threat that was greater than he was capable of dealing with. "I haven't given up yet," Bentzy continued.

"Are you sure you're not being tracked?" Yonatan asked, a concerned expression on his face.

Eyal fixed him with a long stare. "Why would you think so?"

"From a security standpoint, you're in an extremely sensitive position," Yonatan said quickly. "And certain people believe that you have a criminal background. Let's just say that the combination makes you a good candidate for keeping tabs on."

Eyal didn't respond. Instead, he tested his friend's reaction.

"Bernie admitted that they'd be keeping tabs on me. In fact, he was quite insistent on letting me know that. But that's not what I'm concerned about."

Eyal sat down. Bentzy stirred his espresso with disinterest as Yonatan sipped beer from a bottle. Eyal hadn't ordered anything yet. His eyes were still roaming, suspicious, nervous.

A waiter approached their table. "Can I take your order?"

"A beer," Bentzy said, seeing Eyal wasn't about to reply.

"I don't drink while I'm on the job," Eyal protested, although his tone was light.

Yonatan dismissed his worries. "How much alcohol is there in beer anyway?"

Bentzy was impatient. "Nu? What's going on, bro?"

"I…" Eyal was almost stuttering, and had Bentzy not known better, he would have said that the man before him was a stand-in for Eyal. Bentzy's former Mossad commander had never been unsure of himself, and he had certainly never stuttered. The Eyal he had seen conducting the training at the camp earlier was an entirely different Eyal from the man now before him. "I don't know what to tell you or where to start."

"Start from when you were arrested," Bentzy suggested impatiently, draining the last of his coffee. "That's when I lost touch with you."

"Okay. I was arrested, interrogated, and refused to cooperate. They were furious."

"Did they act on their fury?" Bentzy asked. He hoped that it was this, and nothing else, that was responsible for the recent injury on Eyal's left temple.

"Something to that effect." Eyal flashed a wan smile, blinked, and looked down at his beer. He stared at the words on the bottle without processing them. "For two days they applied moderate pressure, beating me, starving me…all of the usual means used to extract information from a prisoner. After that I escaped from prison, and then I was captured again." Eyal stopped talking. A man in a light-green shirt seemed to be too engrossed in reading his menu.

"And then?" Bentzy didn't bother asking for the details of Eyal's escape from prison, or how he had been captured afterward. Curiosity was a luxury that an intelligence officer couldn't always afford. Bentzy needed to focus on the necessary elements of the story and forget the fluff.

"What happened afterward is classified." Eyal smiled again, this time in an attempt to soften the blow of his words. "I'm sorry, Bentzy and Yonatan, but I can't share those details with you. Thank you for listening to everything until this point."

"What?" Bentzy began. "But you—"

Eyal stretched out his hand. "See you both tomorrow."

Bentzy grasped Eyal's hand, and a tiny scrap of paper passed from Eyal's hand to his own. Bentzy showed no sign of having noticed anything. "I hope that one day you'll be allowed to tell me what this is all about."

"Me too." Eyal flashed his familiar smile, a smile that took extraordinary effort for him to summon out of the depths of the deep chasm into which he had fallen.

Eyal left the restaurant, and Yonatan watched his receding image in confusion. "Do you understand what's going on over there?"

"No," Bentzy said. He would tell his friend about the note he had been given later.

"What do you think?" Yonatan's expression revealed his concern, and Bentzy guessed that the expression on his own face was very similar. Even so, Bentzy was surprised that Yonatan was seemingly so emotionally involved in the story when he wasn't such a close friend of Eyal's.

"He looks like a man who's up against something he doesn't know how to deal with." The note was burning a hole in Bentzy's hand, but to read it in public was out of the question.

"Since this is Eyal that we're talking about, I'm going to assume that the threat is of nuclear proportions. He wouldn't be this concerned even if it was a question of breaking into the Bank of America and stealing gold bullion."

"True." A shiver ran down Bentzy's spine. The menace looming over his friend's head was scaring him. "Let's pay and leave."

"Yeah. It's not like we got what we came for."

"No. But I've got some great ice cream at home. How about joining me for a cone?"

Yonatan raised his eyebrows a millimeter as his eyes met those of his friend. "Great idea," was all he said.

Bentzy opened the note as soon as they entered his apartment. Yonatan waited expectantly and then took the note from his friend's hand. The two men exchanged glances.

"What do you make of this?" Bentzy asked, his brow furrowed with concern.

"There's something going on that is way beyond the words written here." Yonatan fingered the scrap of paper as though he were hoping to find a fold in it that, when opened, revealed a hidden message.

Bentzy considered this as he picked up his phone and passed it absentmindedly from one hand to the other. "One call to Mossad headquarters and the missing details will be filled in."

Bentzy dialed the familiar number as Yonatan reread the note, biting his lip. Something was about to go wrong, and there was no way of knowing who would have to pay the price – he, Eyal, or the president.

One of the most difficult skills to cultivate when becoming an agent is the ability to alter one's demeanor at a moment's notice – from cool haughtiness to cheerful exuberance to apparent recklessness and then back again to an icy exterior – all in a day's work. After years in the field, Eyal adapted effortlessly to the demands of his surroundings, as he did now on his way back to the White House. As he entered the Oval Office he automatically switched from Eyal the friend to Eyal the hardened security officer, and a seasoned and arrogant Israeli security officer at that.

"Eyal, step inside," the president called out, even though someone had already ushered him in. "Take a seat. What's going on? What do you think of my men?"

"They make an extremely favorable impression," Eyal said.

"You were probably expecting to meet raw, untrained recruits – like all Israelis who look down on the rest of the world," the president said, a broad smile on his face. "That's one thing I don't like about your countrymen, I must admit. You all think you're the only ones who are any good."

Eyal shrugged and chose not to take the bait.

"Anyway, let's get straight down to business," the president continued. "You wanted to talk to me about something – at least, that's what Bernie told me."

"Yes." Eyal absentmindedly shifted his weight from one foot to the other. "It's about the trip to Ukraine next week. I think Bernie actually agrees with me on this one. Neither of us is happy about the team dynamics when the team is made up of two different nationalities. I've been giving this a lot of thought, and I'm really not sure that the combination of security officers is going to work. My assessment is that you're best off taking the Israelis out of the equation."

The president frowned. "That's no small matter." There was a glint in the his eye, and his fist closed around his coffee mug. "What are you plotting, Eyal? There's a reason you want to give up on your Israelis, and I want to know what it is."

Eyal smiled, and his heart rate didn't speed up in the slightest as he replied, "I thought it was only the Mossad that teaches its students to automatically adopt the criminal mindset." A slight undertone of mockery accompanied his words. "But, on the subject of the Mossad, they also taught me to decide on which way to go and then to keep going unswervingly in that direction. It doesn't serve your purposes to set up a situation that almost begs for a competition to erupt between the Americans and the Israelis. The Americans on your team have pride, Mr. President, and there's no use denying it."

"If our team members are proud of themselves, they surely have good reason to feel that way." The smile on the president's face broadened. "But, dear Eyal, graduate of the Israeli Mossad, tell me: Does the Mossad teach you to be total snobs?"

Eyal was finding the president's manner of speech highly disturbing, but he didn't show it. If the president was so confident in the accuracy of his deductions and in his understanding of human psychology, and those two elements also worked to his advantage, he was better off letting matters lie.

"Our team is even more efficient than you can imagine, but it is comprised of over twenty-five men who view the entire world as beneath them. Now contrast that with your twenty personal guards. Snobs, as you say. I won't deny it. The combination is liable to cause, at the very least, some unpleasantness. I estimate that it won't stop there. And therefore I consider it my responsibility to apprise you of this, Mr. President. We can't run the risk of letting ego warfare wreck our security arrangements. It would be bad enough here, on friendly turf, but in a foreign country it would be exponentially worse."

"Don't they teach you how to take an insult or two at the Mossad?" the president asked. A serious expression replaced his former amusement – finally, long overdue. "From the sound of things, you're definitely trained to calculate every eventuality in advance and to take every possible detail into account."

"We're taught to be patriots," Eyal said flatly. "And if we hadn't been taught to consider everything in advance, I could have been killed fifty times over by now."

"I don't know." An expression of uncertainty appeared on the president's face, and, not for the first, time, Eyal wondered at the wisdom of allowing so many easily swayed people to vote when the result was someone with an admittedly shiny exterior but exceedingly dull inner content. "I haven't gone through Mossad training, and I haven't died even once yet."

The president had yet to overcome his obsession with having the last word, but Eyal wasn't about to permit him that pleasure. "If not for my presence here and the professional training that made me who I am, you would soon be dying for the first and last time in your life. Because the people meant to protect you would all be engaged in contests of ego and bravado."

The president shook his head. "You have your own way of seeing things," he said. "But logic is on your side. Tell Bernie to find replacements for the Israelis."

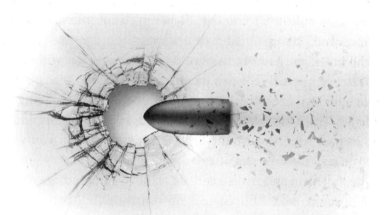

CHAPTER THIRTY-THREE

Washington, DC, USA

"Eyal met up with your two Israeli guards, Mr. President," Bernie Hammer said. This was an opportunity that he was unwilling to pass up – incriminating the arrogant Israeli agent who had been foisted upon him and who, it seemed, was slated to replace Bernie in the top spot for the immediate future.

The president eyed Bernie. "Which tells us what?"

"That he, and they, are not to be trusted," Bernie said.

"That's a stretch of the facts," the president snapped. "It's not what I pay you to do."

"True," Bernie said, "but you do pay me to analyze threats, and I see one here. If you prefer to shut your eyes to it, that's not my business." *Or maybe it is*, he thought to himself, but there was no use telling that to this particular president.

"Besides, those two are his friends," the president added. "Isn't it natural for him to want to meet up with them, after he hasn't seen them for so long?"

Bernie took a step forward and fixed the president with a penetrating gaze. "What's the story here, Jack? When it comes to these Israeli agents, all sense seems to fly out of the window. You trust them blindly, and now you've hired a paid gun to protect you—"

"The members of my private guard are paid guns too, to a certain degree, no?" the president said in a scathing tone of voice. "A soldier is, essentially, a hired assassin. He kills the enemy, and his fellow countrymen applaud."

"You can't compare the two." Bernie's voice was angry and insulted. "Eyal murdered Rubinov for his own reasons, not for the good of mankind."

"Really?" The president fixed Bernie with a long stare. "And how do you know that?"

Bernie fell silent. He bit his lip and flushed in embarrassment, but then quickly regained his equilibrium. "Your being secured by these Israelis still seems ridiculous to me."

"Bernie, you were there when Israel prevented that attack on the boulevard," the president said quietly. "If not for the Mossad agents' incredible attention to detail, you and I would have been booted out of office. Hundreds, or perhaps thousands, of wounded and dead Americans wouldn't have made for a very pretty picture in the media. It was that incident that showed me just how capable Mossad agents are."

I would have been kicked out of office, not you, Bernie thought. "So what? There's no shortage of attacks prevented by the CIA. With all due respect to the Mossad's agents, I don't think they can do anything that we are incapable of doing ourselves. It was more luck than brains on that boulevard."

"Bernie," the president said tiredly, "it's not that I don't trust you, but there are certain things that can be seen from this side of the desk that others don't see."

Bernie's eyes glinted. "That's exactly what I mean. You seem to know about something I am unaware of."

"That's enough." The president raised his head sharply. "From now on, there are no questions asked."

Bernie flinched. The president didn't usually shut down all dialogue – and they were on quite friendly terms. Bernie paused as he deliberated whether to say something more. In the end he decided to remain silent, and the president fixed him with a long, cold stare. "You are free to go."

Bernie was affronted, but he left. What he wanted right then was to confront that braggart Israeli officer who concealed the pride that he felt in his mission beneath a veneer of pleasantry. For some reason his angry feelings were directed above all toward Eyal. His pride had been wounded, and it would have to be avenged. Bernie clenched the fists, which he had thrust into his pants pockets. He needed to vent his fury, but there was no one around. Instead, as he drove back home, his mind filled with thoughts of revenge.

Phone call between Washington and Israel

"I want to know something," Bentzy told Uri over a secure phone line.

"Yes, Bentzy, how can I help you?" Uri sounded totally exhausted, and hearing him, Bentzy wondered why so many of the people he had been speaking to lately sounded wiped out. Were they all going through some sort of difficult crisis that he was unaware of?

"I want to know what the story is with Eyal."

"What?" Uri said sharply. "You spoke to him? Did he tell you something?"

"No. He didn't tell me anything, which is why I want to know, without him having to say anything, what on earth is going on."

"You mean you met him?" Uri had lost nights of sleep since Elitzafun's capture. He hadn't left the Mossad building since, other than to attend a very few select meetings. He had vowed to return the child safely home, and it was a vow he intended to deliver on.

"I'm the one who started with the questions," Bentzy protested. But he answered Uri's query nonetheless. "Yes, I met him. What's going on?"

"Was he on his own?" Uri asked with evident excitement.

"Wait," Bentzy said, annoyed. "First answer me!"

"We're working on the case here in Israel," Uri said. He drew a deep breath. "And there's obviously no need for me to inform you that this is classified."

"Obviously," Bentzy said with impatience. He wasn't a teenager anymore, thrilled to be party to his country's secrets. His memory held plenty of such secrets already.

"Bentzy," Uri said, his voice measured and deliberate, "Eyal's son was kidnapped."

A long moment of silence passed as Bentzy's fingers froze over his phone.

"Bentzy?" Uri said loudly. "Are you still there?"

"I'm here." Bentzy's voice was disjointed. "How… I… Who?" Eyal didn't have a child of his own, Bentzy thought. His wife's three children filled his entire world. He had raised and cared for them, and he loved those children as if they were his own. "Which…which child was kidnapped?"

"Elitzafun, the youngest. Do you know him?"

"Of course. But how could such a thing happen? Eyal had his entire house outfitted with the very latest in security gadgets. Did they take him from school?"

"It doesn't matter to you. Or at all, right now. But…Bentzy, as far as I know you're the only one who's been in touch with Eyal since he left Ukraine. Honestly, I didn't even know that he had been in touch with you, but what I can tell you is that we're thinking of sending in a team, and—"

"You don't need to send anyone over," Bentzy said sharply. "I have men here, and we can deal with this without involving the authorities. But why didn't anyone tell me anything of this before? When did this happen?"

"A week ago," Uri said, and Bentzy could hear the exhaustion in his voice. Which probably meant that he was wearing himself out completely with this case.

"I'm going to stop myself from saying the obvious," Bentzy said angrily.

"With all due respect, we didn't know at the outset that he was planning on traveling to the United States. He arrived there only yesterday, right?"

"Twenty-four hours have passed since yesterday! Twenty-four wasted hours! What do his kidnappers want from him?"

"They want him to carry out a certain mission. We have no idea what that mission is, and you'd better not dream of asking him, as he is under constant surveillance. If they even guess that someone knows that his son has been kidnapped, they won't hesitate to kill the boy. Is that clear?"

"Of course. I wasn't born yesterday. I've been on a few missions in the past few years. In any case, Eyal himself hasn't told me a thing." Bentzy was clearly agitated, but he was choosing his words carefully. "He passed on a certain message to me, which now, based on what you told me, shows just how much he fears for his son's life, although he wrote nothing about the kidnapping. I'm going to get moving right away. We have to track down the kidnappers and then figure out what it is that they want. I have ten men here. It should be enough."

"Ten men?" Uri said sharply. "Are you crazy? You are not to tell a soul about this! You're playing with the life of a child, Bentzy! You're on your own, and no one may know anything about this, no matter what. Not even Yonatan. Our plan was to send a team of men who would be told absolutely nothing about the true nature of their mission. We would compartmentalize them completely so that only the commander would know what this was all about."

"Got it." Bentzy ended the call and remained standing in place, lost in thought. Elitzafun in the hands of kidnappers; Eyal forced to play their game...

"Oh, no, no, no!" The realization hit Bentzy so suddenly that his phone fell from his hand to the floor, smashing into pieces. "You idiot! You mindless maniac! You brought this tragedy upon him!!"

Ashen-faced, Bentzy ran a trembling hand through his hair, and he drew in a deep breath, trying to calm himself. It was suddenly crystal clear to him what it was that Eyal's captors were after. They had clearly given him a choice: either the president, or Elitzafun. Eyal, unlike the other men in the security unit, wasn't under the CIA's constant surveillance. He was a citizen of a foreign country with a certain level of diplomatic immunity, owing to the sensitive nature of his mission, and he was therefore free to come and go as he pleased. There was no one keep track of where he spent his downtime, and this made him a perfect candidate for manipulation toward a nefarious end.

And you, Eyal's dear friend, have brought this mission of death upon him. If he succeeds he will sit in an American jail for the rest of his life – in a best-case scenario. In a worst-case scenario, he will sit in the electric chair for minutes. But if he fails at his mission of death, his son will be murdered.

Unless you find a third option.

Washington, DC, USA

"How was your meeting?"

"Let's drop the pretense, X. I know you sent your men after me and that you know exactly how it went."

"That's just it. I *don't* know how this meeting went, and I have a bad feeling about it. Why bolt from my men just to tell your friends hello and how you fared in a prison in Ukraine?" X stared hard at

Eyal, his eyes narrow slits of suspicion. "Something doesn't add up."

"You heard everything I said." Eyal knew that he had given over no substantial information and that nothing he had said could possibly incriminate him.

"True. But written words aren't going to appear on the audio record." X clenched and opened his fists repeatedly.

"What about the man in the green shirt who was two tables away from where I was sitting? Didn't he bother to reassure you that I didn't write anything down either?"

"He did tell me that no writing took place, but that doesn't mean you didn't hand your friends a note."

"A secret note? Wow! And without your man noticing anything?" Eyal's eyes were almost shooting sparks. "I see you don't think much of your agents. Or maybe you're just a sick and suspicious man."

"Maybe so, but I know better than to trust you. How about we call one of your dear friends and see what he knows." X kept his gaze focused on Eyal, as though trying to peer into his brain.

"Sure." Eyal shrugged, seemingly apathetic to X's declaration. "You can try. Go right ahead."

"Which friend would you like me to speak to first?"

"I'll let you choose." Eyal returned X's piercing stare with a calm gaze of his own.

"I'll have you call Bentzy then, since his name starts with a B." X handed Eyal the phone. "Dial. And do not mention a word, or drop a hint, about the fact that I'm listening in. Is that clear? Speak a regular Hebrew, and I will pass on the transcription to Ahmed."

Eyal dialed his friend's number, praying silently as he did. Bentzy was no fool, but one needed to have a very warped mindset in order to anticipate X's train of thought.

"Eyal?" Bentzy said in surprise upon hearing his friend's voice. "Either I don't hear from you at all, or I hear from you twice in an hour…What's going on?"

"I need something from you," Eyal said easily. He knew that there was no way to weave a message or code into his conversation with Bentzy without X realizing.

For his part, Bentzy was trying desperately to make out what lay behind this phone call from his friend and former commander. There was clearly something going on, but he had no idea what that something was.

"I need antibiotics."

"Really? What for? What happened?"

"I'm serious," Eyal said frankly. "I was injured by a stray bullet, and I need antibiotic ointment so the wound doesn't get infected."

"You need to see a doctor," Bentzy said, appalled. "You know what can happen to an infected gunshot wound if it's not properly tended to."

"Let's just say I don't have time for doctors."

"I'll have a doctor come over within half an hour. Just tell me what your address is."

"Bentzy, I told you I need something, you asked me what I needed, and I told you. I didn't mention anything about a doctor."

Bentzy relented. "Fine. I'll bring the antibiotics over."

"Thanks."

Eyal hung up and looked at his captor. "Satisfied now?"

"Satisfaction would be a preposterous description, as someone once told me. For some reason, I have a feeling your friend knows more than he should."

"So interrogate him and ask him whatever you want. But keep in mind that he has a senior position, and lots of questions will be asked by the president's security team if he disappears."

X didn't respond. Eyal was a far more slippery character than he had realized; it was proving impossible to anticipate his next moves. *Perhaps*, he thought with unease, *this man is willing to take more risks than I was counting on.*

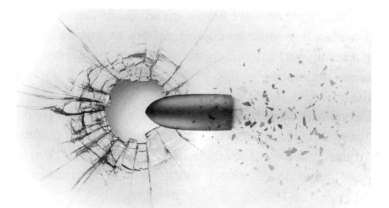

CHAPTER THIRTY-FOUR

Washington, DC, USA

E yal left the house the next morning together with Teddy.
X had decided to minimize the risks and enhance his surveillance. Up to that point his men had been trailing Eyal
in secret, making it possible for him to escape their pursuit under
the pretense that he knew nothing about their existence. But now
things had changed.

Eyal wondered if X had taken into account the probable reaction of the counterespionage team assigned to keep tabs on the
Israeli agents. What would they think when they saw Eyal being
chaperoned by unknown persons? But Teddy was just one man,
and in his guise as Eyal's driver there was no great reason for
anyone to suspect him. All the same, there was something about
the counterespionage team that disturbed Eyal, but he hadn't yet

managed to figure out what it was. No matter – he would deal with it when the time came.

Over the course of the day, more complicated issues would arise.

They were on their way up the street leading to the White House when a man dressed in ordinary citizen's clothing approached them. "Excuse me?" he said. Something about his expression and demeanor offered more than a hint that he was less innocuous than he appeared.

Eyal's heart skipped a beat.

"Yes?" Teddy turned toward the stranger. "What do you want?"

"I'd like to see some identification or a passport." The man's voice was polite and friendly.

"And just who are you?" Teddy asked.

"Private Detective Bob Milo," the man said drily. He turned toward Eyal. "And you are Eyal Gilboa if I'm not mistaken."

Eyal nodded. "Correct."

"You are under arrest, and I am legally obligated to warn you that everything that you say can and will be used against you in a court of law."

"Just a minute," Teddy said. "Why are you arresting him? What's he being charged with?"

The detective fixed Teddy with a disdainful look. "The murder of Dimitry Rubinov."

At the detective's signal, two men, also dressed as regular citizens, approached from the side. They handcuffed Eyal as Teddy looked on in frustration.

Quietly, Eyal addressed him, "Tell him not to worry. Certain people in high places will deal with this. I expect I'll be back before the evening."

The detective had been blessed with a sharp sense of hearing. "I wouldn't be so sure if I were you," he said grimly. "The Ukrainians have applied pressure on the White House, and the president has unenthusiastically agreed to cave in to their request for your arrest."

Teddy and Eyal exchanged glances. They both knew that he was certainly capable of escaping.

The detective noted their glances and interpreted them correctly. "Entertain no notions of escape," he said coldly. "There are ten plainclothes officers in the immediate vicinity and three police cars waiting on the other side of the street." The detective pulled out his radio, whispered something into it, and three squad cars with flashing lights immediately headed over from the other end of the street.

Eyal made a tiny, imperceptible gesture with his head, and Teddy nodded back. Eyal was apparently still insistent that he would, in fact, be released by evening, and he had a hard time controlling the smile that almost spread across his face upon considering the bizarre fact that both he and Teddy were on the same team now.

Two police officers took hold of Eyal, and he was led into the detective's car. The police cars switched on their sirens as they cleared a path for the detective's car to make its way down the road.

Eyal looked out of the car window as they drove away – and then, suddenly, the driver stopped the car, and they all tensed in anticipation as another car approached and came to a stop beside them.

A short, stout man exited the second car and approached. The detective who had arrested Eyal jumped out of his car and strode toward him with a respectful expression on his face.

The short man ignored him, bent down to the window of the car, and addressed Eyal. "You're Eyal Gilboa, correct?"

Eyal nodded. "Guilty as charged."

"Very good." The man turned toward the detective. "Release him, Bobby," he said.

"But he might—"

The short man, apparently a senior officer, stared at the detective with a benign expression on his face. "He's fine. Let him go."

Bobby was visibly reluctant as he pulled out the keys and opened Eyal's handcuffs. His expression was one of real fury as he watched Eyal hand over the handcuffs, which had been clamped shut just a tad too tightly, to one of the police officers.

"We'll continue on our own from this point on," the short man said. He looked at Eyal, and the Israeli agent nodded. "Good. We'll dispense with the warnings of what will happen if you escape, because we won't be giving you that opportunity." He turned back to Bobby. "Take your men, Bobby; and thanks for your exemplary service on behalf of the security of the United States."

"You're going to take him on your own?" Bobby asked the short man.

"Yes."

"But...you don't know..."

"I know more than you think." The man smiled with confidence. "Eyal, get into the car. Into the passenger seat, please. No games."

Eyal did as he was requested and a measure of relief filled his heart. These people seemed to respect him. There might still be a long road ahead, but the trust that these men displayed filled him with a renewed sense of hope.

The man drove along in silence, his sharp, wise eyes wholly focused on the road ahead. Upon reaching Dolley Madison Boulevard he suddenly asked, "Familiar with the area?"

"Looks like we're in Virginia."

"Do you have any idea where we're headed?"

"I might have a clue or two."

"You're probably on the right track then."

The car entered a huge, congested parking lot, and they drove all the way up to the entrance of the large, impressive building of the CIA headquarters in Langley.

"Get out," the man instructed. "They're waiting for you."

Eyal slowly opened the car door, and the man handed him a badge. "This will allow you to enter the gate and elevator. You need to go up to the fourth floor. You'll be called in. Don't even think about trying to escape."

Eyal didn't respond. Instead, he took the badge and left the car in silence. It seemed as though there wasn't a person on the planet who hadn't mentioned that line to him over the past two weeks. Some of them had backed up their words with all sorts of convincing-sounding stories.

Eyal's gaze took in the scene as he slowly approached the entrance. People were coming and going, most of them dressed in business suits, but some in jeans and T-shirts. Everyone seemed focused, busy, and tense, and most were visibly armed, with expressions of distrust in their eyes. Eyal approached the door to the building and presented his badge to the guard standing there. The guard stepped respectfully aside for him, and Eyal held his badge against the clear doors so that they opened for him. He entered the building, held up his badge again, and another set of doors opened for him. Four sets of doors opened at the presentation of his badge before he entered a large lobby with impressive chess-style floor tiles adorned with the CIA's gigantic emblem in the center. Instead of walking straight through the lobby, Eyal took care to avoid stepping on the symbol so revered by millions of Americans. A sign directed him to a row of elevators, and after holding his badge against the operating panel he was directed to elevator K44.

The elevator arrived, and Eyal was beset by a sense of discomfort bordering on claustrophobia. As an agent he preferred not to ride in elevators, yet he had also trained himself not to automatically defer to his instincts. If there was any safe place for him in the world, it was this building in Langley.

The elevator ascended to the fourth floor and Eyal was thrust outside by the human tide. Without even looking for his shadows, he guessed that he was being watched at all moments and that invisible eyes were tracking his every move.

Eyal paced back and forth in the corridor of the fourth floor. He knew that he would soon be called in to one of the offices, and he chose to spend his waiting time taking in his surroundings. All he could see were offices painted in subtle hues, and the usual office furniture. Everything seemed so normal, it was hard to believe what went on in the building. Here, information was gathered that people would have a hard time believing; highly trained agents were sent out on complex missions based on that information; plans were laid to preserve America's standing in the world; and, occasionally, the order went out to eliminate people deemed to be threats to state security.

In some strange manner Eyal felt as though he had come home. The Mossad wasn't the CIA, but the two establishments had much in common. Both organizations expected their members to perform above and beyond and scorned the possibility of failure.

"Eyal Gilboa?" A door opened, and Eyal turned toward the man standing in the entrance.

"Yes."

"Come inside."

Eyal walked in, past his host, feeling a mixture of trepidation and confidence. The door was closed gently behind him, and the man returned to his seat. The office was like the others on that floor – painted in light colors, with attractive furnishings. But it was a prison nonetheless. Not a prison like in Kiev, a dank dungeon with the threat of torture hanging over him. But he was not a free man here.

How very naïve for him to have once thought that he could be his own boss. He felt like a plaything, manipulated by human hands that insisted on tossing him back and forth because they knew he would agree to perform whatever tasks they asked of him, no matter how difficult those tasks were.

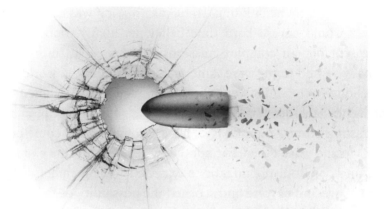

CHAPTER THIRTY-FIVE

CIA Headquarters, Langley, Virginia, USA

S it down, please." The man hadn't introduced himself yet, but he offered Eyal a comfortable upholstered seat directly across from the wall unit, which was blasting out a fair amount of steam. The radiator, Eyal reasoned, was probably broken. "Would you like some coffee?"

"No, thanks." What a difference between this interrogation, if that was what this meeting could be called, and the one that had taken place in the Ukrainian prison... But even though things were friendlier in Langley, Eyal wasn't anticipating any sympathy here. The man across the desk was certainly no novice at interrogations, and if there were no electric shockers or rubber poles, that was only because they didn't think they would need them – this time.

"I'm Paul. Paul Ferguson," the man introduced himself, while jabbing a button on the air conditioner remote. When the appliance refused to cooperate he climbed onto a chair, straightened the vents, and wiped off the accumulated dust with his fingers.

Eyal couldn't help smiling. The man clearly held a senior position at the CIA, but he wasn't above doing such jobs himself. He liked that.

"Let's not waste time describing my role in this place," the man said, jumping down from his chair to the floor and pushing the chair back over to his desk. "That's really inconsequential right now. All you need to know is that I am your contact person here at the CIA, and from what I understand, you have some extremely significant things to tell us."

"Correct." So, Bentzy had taken care of Eyal's request on the note that he had slipped into his hand, whispering the right words into the right ears.

"The fact that you will be in charge of security for the president's overseas trip next week despite your shady history is something we are already aware of," Paul said. "What else can you tell us?"

Eyal didn't answer. Instead, he gathered his thoughts while Paul poured him a cup of coffee, despite his earlier refusal.

"I don't know what you know about me," Eyal said at last. He made no move toward the coffee mug. Instead he kept his eyes trained on a pen on the desk, avoiding Paul's gaze.

"I know a lot more than you think," Paul said.

"Then you surely know about this." Eyal stretched out his arm on the desk, displaying the scar several inches below his elbow.

"So, you've been tagged by the Fraternity." Paul leaned backward and rocked his chair gently. "From what I understand, that means they're keeping tabs on you at all times."

"Exactly."

"Why don't you have the microchip removed?" Paul asked.

"Because it's connected to vital organs in my body," Eyal said flatly. "As soon as I have it removed, some of my systems will shut down, and I honestly have no idea just which systems those are."

"So you're being monitored at all times and you have no way of avoiding that," Paul said, pouring some coffee for himself. "What now?"

Eyal leaned forward. "They wanted to force me to eliminate Rubinov, but he was murdered by someone else before I managed to do anything. Of course that didn't stop them from accusing me of his murder, as I was very effectively framed. But I'm sure you already know about my subsequent arrest, and how I was then forcibly released from police custody." Eyal smiled bitterly as he recalled the shootout leading up to his "release." "I'm in captivity right now, and I'm being watched at every moment of the day, even without my current captors using a microchip."

"If that's the case, they're surely wondering what you're doing here in Langley."

"That's the reason I asked my friend to have the Washington police department arrest me and not you guys."

Paul's eyes widened. "Nice touch, that, I have to admit. Assuming they fell for it."

"Oh, I think they did. At least, it will definitely take time for them to tumble onto anything, if they start getting suspicious. In the meantime, I can speak without fear of being heard."

Paul shook his head, impressed despite himself. "What do they want from you?"

"They want me to capture the president, on Tuesday of next week, at the World Peace Conference in Kiev." Eyal almost added the words "with G-d's help," but he caught himself in time.

A stunned expression appeared on Paul's face. A moment later, though, the expression changed to one of amusement. "You really think you can succeed?"

"Absolutely."

Paul's lips remained curved into a smile, but when he saw the serious expression on Eyal's face he sobered up. "You're serious," he said in disbelief.

"Completely."

"The fact that you're the head of the president's security team doesn't give you a free hand in all security manners."

"I know that."

"So how will you, the president's trusted bodyguard, morph to become a kidnapper?"

"All in a day's work for someone with my background," Eyal said dryly. "The plan I devised is perfect. If everything goes according to that plan, by next Wednesday morning the president will find himself in Syria."

"I'm assuming you haven't come here in order to be arrested." Paul tapped his desk with his pen. "Kidnapping the president will earn you several terms of life imprisonment. And that's only if you get an excellent lawyer on the case. Otherwise it'll be far worse."

Eyal shook his head. "If you want to stop the president from being captured, then please go right ahead and make your preparations. As far as I'm concerned, I need to work with the terrorists on this one."

"Why?" Paul put his pen down and leaned forward. "Why don't you consider killing them or escaping? I've read enough about you to know that you are an expert in both of those fields."

"I can't. They have my son, and if I don't go through with this," the words caught in Eyal's throat, "they'll kill him…"

"Whoa." Finally a flash of sympathetic understanding lit up the CIA agent's eyes. "So, you want us to somehow overcome them, release your son, and make sure the president remains unharmed? In that case, why not make things easier by telling me exactly what your plans are? Once we know them, we'll figure out a way to stop them."

"That's exactly what I'm afraid of," Eyal said. "If you operate in such a manner, the terrorists will realize that I tipped you off and my son will pay the price. I already tried escaping together with my son, and..." Eyal displayed his other arm, "this was the result. A bullet at point-blank range. Which is really not a big deal, because the main thing is that they didn't harm my son. But following that, they made sure to promise me that if they ever see anyone suspicious in the vicinity of my son, they will kill him."

"So, you want us to become invisible."

"No. I want you to act like you know nothing. And in order for you to act that way I need you to *really* know nothing."

"With all due respect, Eyal, we can't allow you to leave this building without knowing the full plan."

"So then don't allow me to leave," Eyal began, but he instantly regretted his words. There was no reason for him to exercise his muscle when he ought to be acting like a comrade. He decided to switch gears and leaned forward, a firm look in his steel green eyes. "Look," he said, "I have never given up information involuntarily. You can ask my Ukrainian interrogators to back me up on that, and believe me, that interrogation was only one of a long series of interrogations, some far worse, that I've been through. I'm not willing to jeopardize my son's safety."

"So why have you come here?" Paul asked. He appreciated Eyal's determination, but his expression revealed his frustration.

"In order to give you clear instructions. Act accordingly, and you will save the president. Be off by a single millimeter and he won't make it back to the White House."

Paul considered this. Had he been more arrogant and less focused, he would probably have given in to his anger and told Eyal exactly where to get off. After all, Eyal was a foreign agent, and here he was presenting himself as the president's bodyguard, threatening his life, refusing to cooperate with the CIA, and loaded down with his own requests to boot.

But Paul was an astute, intelligent man, and he acted according to the well-known maxim, *Don't be right, be smart.* "Fine," he said, after a long pause. "Let's hear you out."

A tremendous sense of relief flooded Eyal's body. "Thank you," he said simply. "Because my conscience is far from tranquil these days. By helping me you'll be helping us both."

"So, what's your plan?"

Eyal told him.

They were on the road from Langley back to Washington. It was late, and Eyal kept checking the digital Waze clock.

"Nervous?" Paul asked. He clearly had a senior position at the CIA, and perhaps he even served as the deputy director, but he was still the one driving the car.

"You could say that," Eyal said. "I'm supposed to be in a Washington police cell right now, and I need to present proof that I was indeed there."

"No problem. We'll send a nice couple of mug shots to the local police's security cameras, and we'll put together a nice file for you."

Eyal nodded, lips pursed into a tight line. His gaze moved from the digital clock to the road map on Waze, but it was X's face that he was seeing and X that he had to convince.

"We'll pass through the precinct's office, put together a file for you, snap a few nice pictures, and make sure it all reaches the correct hands."

"I need to come up with a good reason for my release," Eyal said thoughtfully. "I can say that the president demanded that I be released despite his earlier capitulation to the Ukrainians, but I'll have to hope that X accepts my story without verifying it."

"Eyal, don't worry. We'll fix all that for you. We can do letters, letterheads, even presidential signatures…in fact, maybe we're even on a par with the Mossad when it comes to getting things done." Paul smiled, though his eyes were serious. "I'm not taking this lightly."

Eyal fingered his seat belt, thinking of all of the fingerprints that he was leaving behind. "I appreciate that, but I can't stress enough how important it is to pay attention to every single detail. I have no idea where X will have posted his men. You have to get me into the precinct without being spotted, and you haven't told me yet how you plan on doing that."

Paul drummed with his fingers on the steering wheel. "I don't have to reveal all our state secrets to you, actually," he noted. "But there are ways and means. Above ground and below." He swung the car around left and stopped abruptly. "We're getting out here and taking what I'll call an elevator," he said. "Come."

Eyal got out of the car and followed Paul into a narrow alleyway and then into a side entrance of a building that opened to a punched code. Long corridors were punctuated with doors, and eventually they reached a locked gate. Paul called someone on his phone, and a moment later they were buzzed in.

"Okay, here we are," he announced festively. "Into the office, Eyal. I'm going to get someone to take some snapshots. I'll be right back."

He was as good as his word. "Now, let's give you a close-up look at an interrogation room, just in case your friend wants details." They entered another room, and Eyal sat down and stared at the walls. Just then a police officer walked in.

"Do you want me to interrogate him now?" he asked Paul. His request seemed so completely serious that Eyal wasn't sure whether or not he had been briefed.

"With men like him you ought to get straight down to the physical pressure." Paul chuckled. "But I think he had enough of that already."

Eyal smiled weakly. "I think we're good. I just need all those documents that you talked about, and then you can escort me out the front door, like the VIP I am."

The documents were handed to Eyal, and Paul asked a young officer to process his release. This police officer was quite obviously unaware of the fact that Eyal was no regular prisoner, and this was evident in the manner in which he treated him. He was rough and degrading, and Eyal silently blessed him. The less people who knew about his backstory, the better.

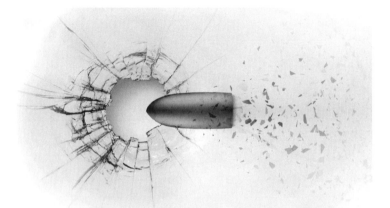

CHAPTER THIRTY-SIX

Washington, DC, USA

I see him."

X sprang from his seat, pressing the button on his radio. "Where?"

"Exiting the police station on Idaho Avenue."

X drew a deep breath. The American government worked quickly. "Follow him," he said shortly. "And make sure he doesn't get up to any nonsense."

"He's going to be up to nonsense no matter what," Ahmed said. It wasn't clear whether he was trying to be sarcastic or not. "It really doesn't matter if I follow him or not."

"Offer him a ride. He is not to walk around alone. Men like him can reach any location around the globe within hours."

"You think he's going to accept a ride from me?" Ahmed

laughed. "We don't exactly enjoy the most cordial of relationships."

"He'll accept your ride, because it's either that or a long walk back to the hotel, and I doubt he has much energy left after today."

"As you wish." Ahmed revved up his engine and drove slowly in Eyal's direction. The Israeli agent's lethargic footsteps reflected his exhaustion as he walked slowly down the sidewalk. "As you said, he really doesn't seem up to the walk," Ahmed commented. "He'll probably appreciate a ride, even if it's from me."

Eyal looked up in surprise at the sound of a car's honking. One o'clock in the morning wasn't usually the time for honks of recognition, and besides, honking was illegal. He peered closely at the approaching vehicle with the blinking headlights, and his sixth sense went into high gear.

"Good morning, sir. Would you like a ride?" Ahmed asked, holding back a smirk.

The sight of the man's face infuriated Eyal, although he acknowledged the reprieve that the ride would offer him. He was utterly exhausted, and cold. The Hilton was only about an hour's walk away, but it was one hour too long as far as he was concerned at that point in time.

"How very kind of you," Eyal said, opening the front door and slipping into the seat beside the driver. "So nice of you to be concerned for a poor man walking all alone. I'd love a ride to the Canary Islands, please. Anywhere warmer than here."

Ahmed hid his smile. "At your service," he said, driving along. "How's the heat? Do you need me to adjust it? Would you like classical musical or jazz?"

"Stop." Eyal leaned against the headrest of his seat. "Quiet already. Just take me to the hotel."

"That's not very polite," Ahmed said, adopting an injured air. "Is that any way to greet an old friend?"

"What a sentimental description. Friends don't shoot at each other."

"Sorry about that, but don't you think friends need to exchange gifts of equal value? I owed you a gunshot, so I was a good friend and gave you one." Ahmed rolled up his sleeve, showing the mark from the bullet Eyal had shot in his direction. "I'm still not at peace with the fact that you fired a submachine gun while I just used a regular weapon."

Eyal's lips curved upward into a thin smile, and he lowered the volume on the stereo so that the music faded completely. "Don't feel so bad," he said. "It was an unequal contest. Next time, don't take on someone out of your league."

X opened the door at the very first knock and dragged Eyal inside. "How did you manage your release?" he asked. "I've been extremely worried about you."

"I'm happy to be the subject of your concern," Eyal said, slumping onto his bed and closing his eyes.

X was unimpressed by his captor's display of exhaustion. "How did you get out of there?" he asked again.

"I told Teddy that you shouldn't worry," Eyal muttered. "Like I said, I pulled all the right strings, and here I am."

"I hope you didn't reveal anything you weren't supposed to," X said. There was an evil glint in his eyes. His prisoner's latest escapades had given him cause for alarm, and although none of their plans had been disrupted as a consequence, he was forever on the alert. And Eyal's seeming innocence rattled him even more. Innocent was the last word one would use to describe Eyal.

"Do you think I'd play games with my child's life? Drop it." Eyal handed over the documents he had received in the precinct. "Read these and enjoy."

"I can see that you're tired," X said, ignoring the papers in his hands.

"Correct. Let's see you answer questions, none too gently asked, over the course of ten hours."

"Go to sleep. You need to be up again in two hours." X stared at the president's curved signature authorizing Eyal's release and contemplated the irony of the president freeing the very man who would be ousting him from his position.

"I know."

"Take this." X handed Eyal a cell phone, the first phone he had been given since his capture.

"What's this?" Eyal asked in surprise.

"It's a lot easier to hear someone with one of these."

"I already told you that you can't put a listening device into any object on my person. The counterespionage team will pull apart every object that I bring in to the president."

"Calm down; there's no listening device inside. I just want you to have a cell phone so I can speak to you whenever I want. This isn't for outgoing calls or for you to speak to all of your friends and listen to their outlandish ideas. Is that clear?"

"Clear as day."

Teddy watched as the gate to the training camp swung open as Eyal approached. Eyal stepped inside and Teddy remained in the car, watching, several feet away from the gate.

A man in plain clothes approached, a cold expression in his eyes. "This isn't a parking lot," the man said.

"I'm waiting for him," Teddy pointed to Eyal. "I'm his driver."

"Your identification, please."

Teddy pulled out his forged passport, and the man examined it. "You have no permit to be here," he said. "You'll have to find somewhere else to park."

Teddy decided not to argue despite the fact that the device he was using to listen in to Eyal could pick up on signals only within a half-mile radius. "Okay. So tell Eyal that you told me to leave," he said, before revving his engine and driving off. "I'll be back later to pick him up."

It was another strenuous day of training for Eyal, using a variety of weapons and a broad selection of targets. "Now I want you to switch over to pistols," Eyal said after the first hour. "Despite the shorter range and less precision, they're much more easily drawn, which makes them a lot more practical in certain situations." Eyal vacillated momentarily between the Glock 17s, austere pistols with a deviation divergence that allowed for greater accuracy, and the German Sig Sauer 230, imported by SIGARMS in New Hampshire. In the end he decided to try out both. "Half of you take a Glock," he told the soldiers, "and the other half take the Sigs. I want to see how you manage, and then we'll start to assign positions."

Three hours later Eyal arrived at the White House, tired but satisfied. It was always a pleasure to work with professionals, and the Americans were quality fighters. Now he stepped into his other role – that of security coordinator, meeting with Paul and the president. Together they would decide on which role each of them would play, ensuring a seamlessly executed mission, if everything went according to plan – and hopefully even if things didn't pan out as expected.

"The president will meet with you now, Eyal," Paul said, motioning toward the Oval Office. "And with your permission, I will sit in on this meeting."

Eyal nodded, and the three men entered the room.

"Welcome again, Eyal," the president said.

Eyal stepped forward and the president sighed. "I don't know why everything that concerns you has to be so complicated."

"It's because I'm a risk-taker," Eyal said. He sat down, his usual arrogant smile in place. Meeting his gaze, the president picked up the man's vibes of strength and capability. Eyal may have been a dangerous person, but that was precisely what the president so liked about him.

"I've been briefed on your plan. Two of my best men, Michael and Bernie, insist that it's a nutcase job and went as far as to call you a crazy megalomaniac and me a senseless lunatic."

Eyal laughed. "I'm in good company then."

"I just want to confirm a few important things." The president gestured toward the pictures of former presidents hanging on the wall. "I'm sure that the presidents who once sat in this very office are turning over in their graves right now. As you said of yourself, however, I'm a risk-taker too. Which puts me up there in the front lines, together with my venerable predecessors who fought for the stability of the Union and the wider stability of the global order." A serious expression came over his face.

"So you say that you'll fly me to Ukraine, get me into the World Peace Conference, and, despite the fact that there are people who want to abduct me, you will get me out of there in peace, and in one piece."

Eyal shook his head. "I will not bring you into the hall. But I will bring you to Ukraine, and I'll drive you to the hall."

"What is the point of that?"

"X is the head of a Syrian terror militia, Mr. President," Paul said. "We want to lay our hands on him, and preferably nab all his men too. We won't allow him to get anywhere near you, but we do want you to make your way to the peace conference, as that is the only way to lure him to Ukraine with his men."

"So, you're using me as bait." The president looked at Eyal. The agent's phone was ringing incessantly. "Who is that? If it's your wife, you have my permission to answer."

"If it was my wife I'd answer even without permission," Eyal said, with utter disrespect for the president and the presidency. "But it's X."

The president and Paul looked at the agent in surprise. "So then why don't you answer him?" Paul said.

"What for?"

"Don't you think there will be repercussions for snubbing him?"

"He can try what he likes." Eyal shrugged his shoulders with disdain.

"Why not answer him instead of risking a confrontation?" Paul asked. Eyal's behavior seemed bizarre to him.

"You need to understand something about the relationship between captor and captive, blackmailer and blackmailed," Eyal said, speaking more to the president than to Paul, for there was openly curious questioning in his eyes.

"I know the psychology," Paul said dismissively.

"And I'm living it. X knows that he hasn't kidnapped a teenager or a cadet. I need to show him that I have my own strength, in any manner possible. Even if it seems to work against me in the short term, in the long term he will subconsciously absorb the message that I am a fearless person, and that will give him the confidence that I will succeed." The president was clearly enraptured by Eyal's explanation, and seeing that, he forged on. "A powerful captive doesn't play by the usual rules. That's a fundamental principle." Eyal fell into a flustered silence as he noted the expressions on both the president and Paul's faces. "Should we move on?" he said.

"Look here, Eyal," the president said. "I'm willing to go through with this despite the admittedly considerable risk factor. I've decided that it's worth it if we enable the CIA to gain control over this new and dangerous militia, which is liable to develop into a significant terrorist organization. I don't want another ISIS, just when we finally broke that organization's back."

Paul nodded. "There are plenty more terrorist organizations still functional all over the world. If we can destroy this one while it's still small, then that is a risk that I am also willing to take. You are not to enter the conference hall at any point, Eyal, and I will see to the arrangements for making that seem natural."

"You're both free to go," the president said. "Rest assured that I will act according to your plan."

They rose from their seats and turned toward the door. The president's voice stopped them. "Eyal?"

Eyal turned around. "Yes, Mr. President?"

"Don't let me down."

"I'll do my best."

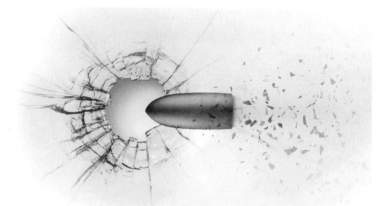

CHAPTER THIRTY-SEVEN

Washington, DC, USA

T hings have been arranged with the president," Eyal said as
he entered his hotel room.

X jumped up and came toward him, his expression one
of anger mingled with relief. "Finally, Eyal! You didn't answer
your cell phone, even though I must have tried you a hundred
times! I was just about to assume the worst."

"Then your instincts were right on target," Eyal said.

"What do you mean?" X stared.

"I mean that the worst of all has already happened. It's happening right now. I'm working for terrorists."

X ignored his comment. "Eyal, you'll tell me right now why
you refused to answer my calls," he insisted. He was clearly on
the brink of a major temper tantrum, and Eyal was enjoying the

show, despite knowing that he might end up paying the price.

"I'm sorry," he said. "I was busy." Slowly, Eyal withdrew a black radio device from his pocket and handed it to his captor.

"What's this?"

"The unit's radio device." Eyal took out an additional device and rolled the antenna between his thumb and index finger. "This one here is for me."

"Meaning that, with this device, I will be linked, as of now, to your security team's communications," X said.

Eyal nodded, and X eyed him with open admiration, all anger immediately forgotten. "How did you manage to get this out of there?" he asked.

"I'm in charge of the security team – or have you forgotten? I asked for three transmitters, just to be on the safe side. One for you, and one for me."

"And the third one?"

"For emergencies."

"You have no idea what I planned on doing to you while you were away," X said. "But the truth of the matter is that you've really proven yourself over here."

Eyal ignored X's words of praise and changed the subject. "And I spoke to the president."

"What for?" X's voice instantly reverted to its usual suspicious tones. Apprehension and paranoia were the fuels that powered his life.

"Because I'm responsible for his safekeeping, of course, and I needed to tie up some loose ends before heading to Ukraine."

"Why is it that I somehow suspect that your excursions to the White House will destroy my plans in some way?" X knew that Eyal was aware that his men couldn't listen in on any of his conversations that took place in the White House. Electronically, the White House was hermetically sealed so that no listening devices could transmit signals to outside the building.

"I don't know. I'm not a psychologist, and your suspicions are beyond the realm of the reasonable." Eyal sat down and placed his phone on the desk, next to the radio device. Quietly, he added, "I think you have a pretty good bargaining chip that you're using to blackmail me, so I don't understand the reason for your excessive caution."

"I hope you value the life of that chip more than you value the president's life," X said, examining the two-way radio carefully.

Eyal raised one eyebrow. "The president's *life*? I thought we were talking about his capture, and ultimately returning him in peace."

"That's what I mean." X set down the device he had been holding and calmly folded his arms. "So, what have you made up with the president?"

"The president is leaving for Ukraine tomorrow evening, which gives you at least thirty-six hours to get your men ready. If you'd like me to do something in the hall before the conference, you will need to provide me with various items in advance. I will be flying early tomorrow in order to get the hotel ready for the president's arrival. At night, after I finish up at the hotel, I will go to the conference hall to prepare the incendiary devices that you asked me to take care of."

"Your shopping list of equipment is ready and waiting in Ukraine. Everything is in sealed boxes, protected by armed guards."

Eyal nodded. As he turned to leave for the hotel's dining room, X called out, "Eyal, you forgot something."

Eyal's heart skipped a beat, and his knees felt as though they might buckle beneath him. Slowly, he turned around. If X had discovered his connection with the CIA, then it was curtains for him, and for Elitzafun. "What?" he asked, using great effort to steady his voice so that it sounded completely matter-of-fact.

X held out a package of medicine.

⚜

Eyal sat at the desk in his hotel room, pen in hand, deep in thought. X entered the room an hour later and watched him in silence. X began to go through the motions of getting ready for bed, but Eyal made no move to do the same.

"Is everything all right with you?" X asked.

"What?" Eyal shook himself, looking up from the paper on which he was sketching and writing. "Did you ask me something?"

"I asked you if everything is all right."

"I'm thinking about something."

"What?"

"Whatever I'm thinking about has nothing to do with you."

"Eyal," X said, "I've already told you that anything connected to you is connected to me as well."

"Which makes you a perfect example of a parasite." Eyal got up and removed a picture from the wall.

Stupefied, X watched as Eyal placed the picture on the desk and placed a sheet of paper on it. "What are you doing?" he asked.

"Using a glass surface to write on."

"What for?"

"So my pen doesn't make an imprint on the surface of the desk," Eyal said impatiently. "Are you going to sleep or not? Give me a break, will you?"

X, familiar with Eyal's mode of speech by now, was unimpressed. "How kind of you to explain."

"I meant what I said, okay?" Eyal's eyes clearly reflected his frustration with the interruption. "I'm busy, and you're disturbing me."

X remained standing in the same position, arms folded, watching Eyal's pen move over the paper, until Eyal finally stopped and looked up at X with a mocking expression in his green eyes. Imitating his captor, he folded his arms and waited.

"I want to see what you're writing," X said, though he knew

that Eyal would write nothing incriminating in his presence.

"Here you go." Eyal got up and tossed the page toward X. It was a series of doodles, nothing more.

X looked at the sheet of paper for a moment and then handed it back to Eyal. Then he got into bed and pulled the blanket up to his chin. "Wake me up if you figure anything out."

Eyal didn't write a single word on his paper that night. Instead, like the legendary detective Sherlock Holmes, he sat and analyzed the storehouse of facts in his mind. As an agent, he was used to the debriefings that followed every mission. He was accustomed to answering hundreds of questions related to the intelligence information at his disposal that made it possible for him to see beyond the confusion that had been a part of his life for the past two weeks. His expression grew wholly focused as he processed his thoughts, oblivious to everything going on around him.

Eyal was familiar with the method of room-by-room information retrieval. His mind was like a container of virtual rooms, and each room held a single memory, or several linked memories. By focusing on one room at a time Eyal could easily extract all the pertinent elements of information.

A door opened in his mind. His interrogation by Laduskin.

"You don't know who the Fraternity sent to murder Rubinov?"

"No."

Laduskin did everything in his power to get me to admit that the Fraternity sent me. But aside from Rubinov, who had died and who could no longer testify, only Yabrov knew about the Fraternity's role in the case.

In the virtual room an additional door suddenly swung open before him.

A meeting between Eyal, Rubinov, and Yabrov.

"You've heard of the Angels of Peace, I assume?" Eyal had said.

"Yes," Yabrov had answered. *"I have heard about them, and I have also heard that they hired someone to assassinate my boss."*

"All true. I am the assassin."

Eyal drew in a deep lungful of air as his heart danced about wildly in his chest.

Why wasn't Yabrov interrogated after the murder? He knew everything. Why didn't he tell the police what he knew?

Another door: the trip to Washington. The meeting with the president, and then the follow-up meeting with Bernie.

"The president may trust you, but I do not. Rest assured, we will be keeping an eye on you."

Where was the counterespionage team? Why didn't they realize that I was being followed? Why didn't they look into X's identity? What about the surveillance that Bernie had promised?

Another door opened up. A meeting with Paul.

"What now?"

"You said you know the answer to that."

"I know a bit." Eyal had seen the man blink. "But I want to hear what you have to say about this."

Did Paul know too much? He had agreed to everything I requested of him. Any surprise on his part was almost completely absent.

Suspicious behaviors were jumping out of every room in Eyal's mind, leaving him with the overwhelming impression that nothing was what it seemed.

The continuation of his conversation with Paul.

"Why don't you consider killing them or escaping? I've read enough about you to know that you are an expert in both of those fields."

What did Paul read about me, and why? Paul had known of me even before we met. How? And more importantly, why?

Suddenly, another door opened up in his mind. The meeting with his friends.

"Are you sure you're not being tracked?" Yonatan had asked, a concerned expression on his face.

Eyal had fixed him with a long stare. "Why would you think so?"

"From a security standpoint, you're in an extremely sensitive position," Yonatan had said quickly. "And certain people believe that you have a

criminal background. Let's just say that the combination makes you a good candidate for keeping tabs on."

Yonatan!

The conclusion set a lightbulb off in his mind. Had he not been in the presence of a lowly terrorist whom he had no desire to awaken, he would have shouted: "Eureka!"

He was still missing some details, and he was going to fish for them straight from the source. The conversation he needed to have would not be easy, Eyal knew. Someone would have to pay the price, but there was nothing that could be done about it. There were always some losses on the path to victory.

Dawn broke, and Eyal collapsed onto his bed, solely to show X that he had slept. His eyes were red from lack of sleep, and he was hoping that X wouldn't guess that he had been up all night. He would need to conduct an investigation of his own while managing the president's security team and putting together a stunning capture. He would have to stretch his capabilities, which were not so mediocre in the first place, to the limit. Hashem, Father of those who had been blackmailed and Judge of all kidnappers, would help him.

"You're headed to the airport?" X had decided not to have any of his men accompany Eyal this time, and Eyal understood why. The men of the special team traveling to the Ukraine would easily be able to pick out a stranger in their midst, and X trusted Eyal, for he knew that there was nothing he could do to sabotage his plans at this point in time. There were less than thirty-six hours left before the capture, but it was enough time for him to put together an effective plan.

"Yes." Eyal's expression was inscrutable and his voice toneless, making X wonder what he was really thinking.

"Do you need an escort?" X asked, his voice dripping with sarcasm.

"No, thank you." Eyal paid no attention to the barb. He had more important things on his mind.

Eyal headed down to the parking lot, pressed a button on his remote, and opened the door of the car X had arranged for him. His movements were instinctive, for an intelligence agent would never open his car door by hand. He needed to take care of a certain matter before leaving the country, and he hoped to be finished in under an hour, as he didn't have much time before his flight. There was a reason X was allowing him to travel unescorted. He knew that Eyal had no free time at his disposal.

He would have to create that time.

Eyal braked before the gates of a medium-size, unassuming building. The building seemed nondescript on the outside, but there were several bullet-proof vehicles in the parking lot, with barred windows. Eyal did not need to be told what went on in the building. Those who knew, knew, and those who didn't had no need to find out.

A guard approached his car. "No parking here."

Eyal rolled his window down halfway. "I need to speak to Paul Ferguson."

A note of ridicule wound its way into the guard's voice. "Really? Get away from here as quickly as possible."

"No problem." Eyal rolled his window down all the way and placed his arm, in typical, arrogant driver mode, into the open space. "Tell him that Eyal Gilboa is downstairs and that he wants to speak to him."

The name seemed to invoke some sort of memory. "Just a minute." The guard retreated, spoke hastily into his two-way radio, and turned back to face Eyal. "Mr. Ferguson says you can go up to his office."

"No. Tell him to come down to the minus-2 floor, to the shooting range. I'll be there waiting."

A momentary flash of hesitation. "I'll tell him," the guard said reluctantly.

Eyal got out of the car. Nervously, the guard looked at the pistol visible in Eyal's holster, and, with effort, he did what the security regulations required of him. "Leave your gun in the car," he instructed.

For a moment Eyal considered arguing, but then decided against it. He tossed his gun into the car and allowed the man to take over at the wheel and steer the car into the building's parking lot. Eyal entered the building via a side entrance Paul had shown him, which was accessible with a punchcode, and took the stairs down two flights. There he opened the heavy door and entered the shooting range. There was no one there at this early-morning hour. Paul had told Eyal that he always arrived at the building before his colleagues, and that he was usually one of the last to leave at night.

Never reveal too much about yourself to an intelligence agent, Eyal thought. *They're trained to file all information into invisible compartments within their brains.* Paul had apparently forgotten this important point.

Eyal removed a gun from the shooting range and aimed it toward a moving target.

"Eyal?"

Without thinking, Eyal spun around and locked the "intruder" in his gun's sights. Then, seeing who the person was, he lowered his weapon and smiled. All the same, the muscles in his shoulders stiffened. "Did you want something?" he asked.

Paul forced a broad, friendly smile onto his face, despite that being the last thing that he wanted to do. He was overcome by the strange feeling that Eyal had discovered a missing piece to the puzzle of unfolding events. "You asked me to come down here," he reminded him.

"You don't need to be a genius to figure out why," Eyal said coldly.

"Actually, I have no idea why. All I know is that you're supposed to be on your way to the airport as we speak."

"Obviously. Because I need to provide the president with

security." Eyal paused. "And I need to provide for his captors as well."

Paul frowned. "Has something gone wrong, Eyal?"

"You could say that." Eyal was still playing with his gun. "Is there any other way of describing the manipulation of a former intelligence agent of a foreign country for one's own interests?"

Paul's face paled. "What are you talking about?"

"I'll give you a clue." Eyal pursed his lips. "It's eight letters long."

Paul looked at Eyal, uncomprehending.

"Jonathan," Eyal said slowly. "The CIA's employee, whom they so brilliantly recruited. He's the man who will help you manipulate Eyal Gilboa all the way."

Paul exhaled slowly, keeping his eyes on Eyal. Denial would be of no use. This man knew too much. "How did you figure that out?" he asked quietly.

Eyal turned slowly and shot a bullet into the target's head before dropping his gun. "It doesn't matter. All that matters is that I became your toy. A sophisticated shooting machine, an advanced robot soldier – call it what you like. I was everything but a human being and the father of a child." Eyal's voice broke. "A child who is not mine. A child whom I undertook to shield and protect when I married his mother. I had no idea that by becoming his stepfather I would bring tragedy into his life."

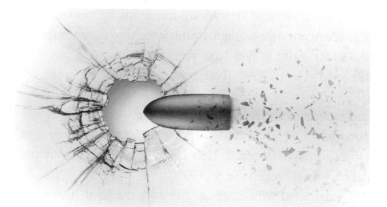

CHAPTER THIRTY-EIGHT

Washington, DC, USA

Paul fell silent – unusual for him, he had nothing to say.

"I didn't think that an intelligence agency of a supposedly friendly country would use my acquaintances to spy on me," Eyal continued, his unnaturally subdued tone of voice masking a deep well of emotions. "I didn't think that an American agency would ask my friends to bring calamity onto my head."

"I don't know what conclusions you've drawn," Paul said, finally collecting his thoughts. "I think you're exaggerating the danger, and drawing too many inferences from the little you know."

"Really?" Eyal raised his head and looked Paul straight in the eye. "So how about you tell me the rest of it, what you think I don't know yet? Because I saw Yonatan, extremely agitated, in that coffeehouse. He asked who was following me before I gave Bentzy that note, and he's not a prophet. He didn't *guess* that someone was following me – he *knew* it. Add that to the fact that I was asked to provide the president with security shortly before X abducted my son, and that virtually proves my theory that someone new on the American scene got the president to appoint me as his private bodyguard. Bentzy and Yonatan are the new men on the scene, and being that I suspected Yonatan already, the power of simple deduction led me to conclude that he is the one behind this."

Paul shifted his weight from one foot to the other. "I admit asking Yonatan to ask you, through Bentzy – who knows nothing – to provide the president with security. That way X would ask you to abduct—"

"*Ask* me! I like that term! Continue."

Paul continued, unmoved. "That way, we assumed X would ask you to abduct the president for him. We manipulated things in this manner in order to bring about the arrest of X, the head of a dangerous terrorist militia."

"Meaning, you wanted things to follow the script that you outlined at our meeting with the president. And the president didn't really seem so surprised at X's plan, and it didn't take much effort to get him to agree to your idea. That's what really set off the red lights in my mind, leading me to the conclusion that it was the CIA who had Yonatan offer the idea to X. By the way, how do Yonatan and X know each other?"

"X thinks that Yonatan is his mole within the president's security team. Apparently, they met in a field hospital that Israel set up at military post 105 in the Golan, during some battles there. Yonatan was the commander of the GSS debriefing team."

"Got it," Eyal said shortly, glancing at the clock and frowning. There wasn't much time left before his flight. "Let's move on to the rest of the story. The CIA asks Yonatan to convince me to head the president's security team for the peace conference. I take on the job as a favor for Bentzy, and once the ground has been laid, Yonatan suggests that X kidnap the president in order to bring him to the

Syrian battlefield, which is something that X is eager to do in any case. The CIA developed this plan in order to capture X and his men, but they needed something to really get the ball rolling. That something happens to be a five-year-old child. How will you like it if I let this story leak to the media?"

"You won't let it leak," Paul said quickly.

"Really? Why are you so sure of that?" Eyal was literally trembling with rage. These people had toyed with his child, and himself, like pawns on a chessboard.

"I can be cynical and tell you that you wouldn't dare let the story leak because the very first person to suffer would be your child, but I won't be quite so cruel as that. Instead, I'll tell you how much I respect your professionalism, and how much I admire your ability to continue to function at your very best despite your outrage – which is admittedly justified."

"Your respect and admiration are misplaced, then. I am not an intelligence agent now, but a father. A father who will do everything in his power to bring his child back home."

"I'm sorry, Eyal," Paul said, but his words sounded trite even to his own ears. "What happened to your son was not a part of our plan. We knew that X was a violent man, but we didn't think that he would stoop to kidnapping a child. This wasn't part of his psychological profile."

"So that's your answer, is it, Paul?" Eyal said, and his voice was dangerous. "You're sorry, and that's all you have to say?"

"Eyal, we truly didn't think this would happen. We will do everything we can to return your child to you safely. Just tell me what you need."

"What do I need? We've already spoken about bringing my child back home, and I wasn't satisfied then with what you had to say. I'm more terrified than I've ever been in my life, and I can envisage my son returning home in a coffin. Still, I think we've done what we can under impossible circumstances."

"So what do you want now?"

"For starters, I want to know who else is involved in this story. Bentzy? Zev Avshalom? Shaul Lerner? Take a look at what you've done, Paul! I can't trust even my closest friends anymore."

"It's good that you're here in this shooting range, then," Paul said, and Eyal wasn't sure if Paul was trying to change the subject or if he was goading him on. "Because you can release your pent-up emotions right here. No one besides Yonatan is involved in this. You have my word on that, Eyal."

Eyal looked at Paul for a moment, as if sizing him up. Then he went back to the firing range and retrieved the gun that he had put down there earlier. It had cooled off. When he spoke again, his voice was a dangerous whisper. "In my opinion, Paul, you're best off heading back to your office as fast as you can, because I cannot take any responsibility for my hands right now."

"You called me down here!" Paul protested, taking a step forward. "And I will take no responsibility for what I might do when faced with someone holding a weapon. I need to see you put that weapon down, Eyal."

"No problem." Eyal tossed the gun aside and slowly approached Paul. "Would you prefer hand-to-hand combat? The idea quite appeals to me at this moment."

In an instant the cool air was replaced by the passion of war, as Paul tossed his suit jacket onto a chair and unfastened his tie. "No problem," he said, releasing a Japanese war-shout. "*How!*"

"*Kiai!*" Eyal yelled back, and they were instantly locked in battle – Eyal, graduate of an elite army unit, former Mossad agent with seventeen years of successful missions under his belt; versus Paul, professional CIA agent but two decades older and having spent the past ten years behind an office desk. Even if Eyal had been determined to lose the battle he wouldn't have succeeded. The scales were unfairly tilted, and within three minutes a subdued and bleeding Paul was lying prone on the floor with Eyal's knee in his abdomen and the barrel of a gun wedged between his ribs.

"Very funny," Paul said with a dry smile.

Eyal gave him a long stare, free of every last vestige of friendly feeling. He lowered his face so that his eyes were just inches from the other man's and, in a voice dripping with venom, he whispered: "This gun is loaded and waiting, Paul."

The CIA agent's eyes darted to the sides, and the fact that he had told no one where he was going, due to the trust he had placed in Eyal, suddenly hit him.

"No one will be here for at least another hour," Eyal said quietly. "There are only clerks and guards in the building right now, and not one of them has any reason to step into the shooting range. There is nothing to prevent me from pulling the trigger and sending you to a place that is...well, I don't know if it really will be a better place for the likes of you."

Eyal's taut muscles relaxed slightly, even as he wedged the gun deeper into Paul's diaphragm. A full minute passed before Eyal withdrew the gun and got to his feet.

"This was just an exercise, Paul. A simple exercise to demonstrate how no one is to start up with Mossad agents, and certainly not if they are fathers."

Paul pulled himself up to a sitting position and breathed slowly and deeply, struggling to regain his equilibrium. He was embarrassed to realize that he was actually sweating with fear. When was the last time someone had managed to scare him like that? When he was ten? Fifteen?

Of all the possible reactions to his painful confrontation with Eyal, Paul chose the least professional and least relevant of all. "Is that gun really loaded?" he asked.

Slowly, Eyal turned away from Paul toward one of the targets on the wall. He shot a bullet into the bull's-eye, and a horrific boom resounded in the large hall. "But why were you so scared? You said you trusted me not to allow my rage to overcome me, and to act responsibly."

Paul blinked twice, and the staccato beat in his head began to slow. Drawing a deep breath, he urged himself not to allow Eyal to turn him into a failure. "Eyal," he said, getting up and walking toward the man, "you have just threatened the deputy director of the CIA."

"Really?" There was a cool smile on Eyal's lips, and as Paul looked into his eyes, he couldn't prevent a chill from running down his spine. "You know what, Paul? When I was a child, my parents taught me that certain boundaries are not to be crossed. But when I discovered that there are places in the world that completely disregard all human boundaries and treat humanity like lab rabbits in a research project, my own boundaries moved several meters forward."

Paul looked at Eyal, this man who was as close to invincible as he had encountered in all his years of working for the CIA. He was silent as he searched for a way to counter Eyal's statement, to protest that he was on the side of the moral and the good. He remained silent, unable to find the words, as Eyal turned on his heel and walked out, leaving the building without a backward glance.

Paul remained rooted to the spot, an indecipherable expression on his face.

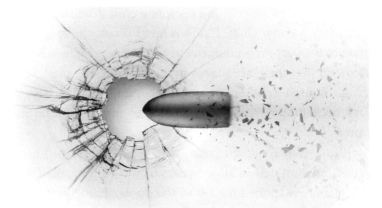

CHAPTER THIRTY-NINE

Ukraine

E yal landed in Kiev's Boryspil airport together with Louis, one of the security team's deputies, and Samuel, a young African American who had co-directed previous presidential security operations. Barry, the second deputy of the team, was still in the United States, where he was directing the remainder of the security team until they would fly to Ukraine together with the president.

The three men were met by a team of Ukrainian security guards, who escorted them to the Hyatt Regency Hotel, where the president and his entourage would be staying. The hotel had set aside a large, lavishly appointed conference room for them, and the Ukrainians ushered them inside and quickly reassured them that within, they could speak freely with no concern of wire-tapping devices.

One of them, who turned out to be the police chief of security for this particular mission, approached with a friendly smile on his face. "Ivan Jankowitz," he introduced himself, extending his hand.

Eyal took the man's hand and shook it firmly. "Eyal Gilboa."

A shadow crossed the man's face, and Eyal was reminded that the president himself had intervened to ensure that he would be permitted to enter the country and leave it again as a free man. It was certainly a strange world. His last encounter with the Ukrainian police was far from one he was keen to recall, and he had left the country with a bounty on his head. Yet here he was, returning as an honored guest.

For a moment Eyal entertained amused thoughts about what would happen if Colonel Gregory Tadiev, Kiev's police chief, were to arrive on the scene. As far as he knew, the man was still determined to extract from him an admission that he had murdered Rubinov. If they were to meet now, their conversation would undoubtedly be an interesting one.

Eyal shook himself from his thoughts, responding to Ivan's question about whether or not to leave the hotel's boutique stores open.

"There are two parking lots," Ivan continued, checking off an item on a list. "One of them will be placed at your disposal, and the other will be reserved for members of the hotel's staff. Do you have a preference regarding which parking lot you would like to use?"

"I'm sure we will have a preference, once we take a good look around," Eyal said noncommittally. "If you don't mind, I'd like to get going right away. We don't have time to lose. Louis? Samuel? You guys ready?"

"We can escort you," Ivan offered. He was clearly brimming with curiosity as well as the desire to learn from people who had earned names for themselves as some of the world's top security personnel.

"We prefer to conduct our tour on our own," Eyal said gently. "Thank you, all the same."

"It will take you hours," Ivan protested.

"That's what we're here for," Eyal said pleasantly. "We have twenty-four hours to finalize the preparations for the president's arrival."

Ivan shrugged, but he seemed insulted. "As you wish," he said. "Meals will be served when you ask for them."

Eyal smiled. "Thank you."

Ivan handed him a magnetic door pass. "If you need anything, I am at your service."

"Thank you once again," Eyal said. "Of course, we are proceeding on the assumption that you have already made excellent preparations. If we weren't confident that you had laid the groundwork for a flawless security mission, we would have had to arrive here a full week earlier. As it is, our president has the utmost faith in your professionalism. My compliments."

The man seemed somewhat mollified. "Okay, Eyal," he said with a smile. "You have my cell phone number, so call me whenever you need me."

Eyal returned the smile, and then the threesome headed out to the lobby. It was important to him that good relations be maintained with the Ukrainian security forces, in order to eliminate all possible sources of friction.

"We'll start from the bottom and work our way up," Eyal said as they entered an elevator. "The first parking lot is two floors down. Personally, I don't like being so far underground, so I think we'll take the other parking lot on the ground floor, but it still needs to be checked out."

Louis turned to him, a questioning look in his eyes. "I thought all this was settled already," he said. "You've had the plans of the hotel and the surrounding streets since last week."

"Sure I did," replied Eyal. "But there's only so much you can do without seeing the place with your own eyes. I don't anticipate making any major changes to our plans, and not even minor ones. But it could happen that we'll need to be flexible. We'll see."

For the rest of the day, they made their way methodically through the hotel, checking and double-checking their plans. They took only brief breaks for meals, and, as arranged in advance, Eyal's double-wrapped and sealed kosher meals from the Taki Da kosher restaurant were delivered to him from the hotel's kitchen. At ten o'clock that night they found themselves on the roof, checking out the hotel's helipad by the powerful light of several projectors on the balustrades. Below them Kiev glistened under a dark sky.

"Okay guys, let's call it a day." Samuel was spent – so were the others. They headed back down to their suite and quickly unpacked their few belongings before dropping into bed, exhausted. Except for Eyal.

Taking a laptop out of his travel bag, Eyal sat down at a desk and started typing.

"Aren't you going to sleep?" Louis mumbled. Samuel had already drifted off, and Louis saw no reason not to join him.

"Soon." Eyal closed his laptop and stood up. His body was crying out for sleep, but he didn't have the luxury of being able to provide it. "Go to sleep. You have a busy day tomorrow."

"So do you," Louis replied.

"That's right," Eyal muttered to himself. "I really do."

Three hours later Eyal left the hotel. He was dressed in simple dark clothing and rubber-soled shoes. He left the hotel's grounds, turned a corner, and found the motorcycle that had been stationed there at his request. Twenty minutes later he arrived at the conference hall.

Two dark figures stepped out of the shadows to greet him. "Eyal?"

"Yes." He forced his heart rate to slow down. There was no reason for him to be afraid of Louis and Samuel finding out about this excursion. Paul was backing him on this. The Secret Service unit might not be in on the plan, but the CIA was.

"Here are the packages that you asked for. Everything is inside." The man spoke quietly, in an accented English whose origin

Eyal could not place. "How long do you need to prepare the explosives?"

"Two or three hours. With assistance."

"That's what we're here for." The man bent down and lifted two of the suitcases. "Take the other two cases and follow me. We're obviously not going in through the front door. I will get everything ready for you, and when you're finished, no one will know that you were here."

"No one but my conscience."

"I left mine at home."

Eyal returned to the hotel at five o'clock that morning, exhausted beyond belief. He opened the door to his room without waking his two colleagues and collapsed onto his bed. In another three hours he needed to get up to meet the president.

The explosive devices that he had prepared were weighing on his mind. Paul had promised that everything would go according to plan, but they all knew that even in the best-laid plans there was a margin of error. What was more, X was unpredictable, as had already been shown with the kidnapping of Elitzafun. No one at the CIA had anticipated that, but it had happened, and it had, apparently, been accomplished flawlessly.

Furthermore, the Mossad was known for its sometimes excessive level of caution, especially when it came to civilian lives. The CIA, on the other hand, was not accustomed to calling off missions at the last minute just because someone's grandmother unexpectedly turned up on the scene. For the Americans, collateral damage was part of the equation. For Eyal, however, the collateral could end up being his own life – or, far worse, that of his son.

Eyal tossed and turned, tormented by his conscience and his worries and yearning. It would take a miracle for everything to go as planned, for the president's car to arrive just as Elitzafun was brought to the building, for everyone and everything to work in perfect synchronization, and for the explosives to detonate when only X and his men were in the hall...

In the end, despite Eyal's fears, his exhaustion won out and he drifted off to sleep.

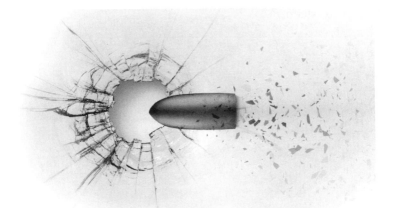

CHAPTER FORTY

Ukraine

A ir Force One sliced through the clouds with practiced ease, circling in the sky over Kiev one final time before swooping down for a landing.

Eyal, standing in the terminal and looking out of the huge window, felt his innards twist in tension and anxiety. Never before had he faced such a fraught and complex situation. Dangerous as his former missions may have been, they had always been legally, ethically, and politically sanctioned. This time, however, he was on his own. The CIA knew what was going on but the members of the security team with whom he was working had not been clued in to the background of the current operation. Paul had promised him that a team of top-notch CIA agents was on its way to Ukraine to lend their support, but Eyal didn't trust them in the same way that he had once trusted Mossad commanders and colleagues, especially after the crushing discovery he had made just before leaving the United States.

The president's airplane glinted in the pale rays of the sun that somehow managed to penetrate the Ukrainian sky, before swooping down onto the tarmac and decelerating toward the arrivals area.

A tense silence fell over the airport as the engine of the plane grew still. A set of steps was driven toward the aircraft and attached to the door, and a red carpet was rolled out to the foot of the steps. A moment later the president stood framed in the doorway of the plane, smiling down at the large crowd of people who had come to welcome him. It was only after the president had descended the stairs and finished greeting the various high government officials that Eyal approached him with a smile. "Welcome, Mr. President."

"Thank you. Is everything okay, Eyal? Everything going according to plan?"

A shadow crossed Eyal's face. "As okay as possible."

"Worried?" the president asked.

"If I wasn't worried, then you would have real cause to be."

The president laughed, and Eyal responded with a small smile of his own.

The security procedures went off without a hitch. Eyal maintained a steady line of communication between the airport security personnel and the Ukrainian government's security teams and made sure that all the necessary procedures were executed correctly, without a single glitch in the system. Every member of each team had a clearly defined task to complete, with one clear goal. Only Eyal was straddling two worlds. Somehow, he needed to bring both the president and Elitzafun to safety.

The first part of that equation was, of course, the easier one. When all the formalities were over, Eyal ushered the president into the car that was standing ready, and then took his place beside him. The motorcade started on its way toward the hotel through streets that had been cleared in advance. The president was in good spirits, laughing and joking, and Eyal responded with his own brand of humor, despite his tension.

After about half an hour of driving they crossed the Dnieper River, and Eyal turned to the president.

"We are staying at the Hyatt Regency," he said. "It's just a few minutes from here. As you know, I arrived here yesterday with Louis and Samuel, and we did a thorough check. The Ukrainians have done an impeccable job in preparing everything for your arrival. Everything is secured."

"What about the hotel staff?" True to type, the president chose not to rely on the judgment of his advisers and preferred to get firsthand answers to questions that concerned him.

Eyal nodded, already accustomed to this quirk in the president's character. "All vetted by Ukrainian security," he assured him.

A few minutes later they arrived at the hotel grounds and the gates were ceremoniously opened for the presidential motorcade, consisting of dozens of vehicles. They headed for the parking lot at the rear of the building, chosen by Eyal as the more practical in case of any necessity to evacuate speedily.

Eyal got out and stepped around the car to open the door for the president. "Thank you, Eyal," the president said. "Which way now?"

"This way, Mr. President." Dozens of Ukrainian security agents stood around the sides of the parking lot, and now they marched toward the president with Ivan leading them. The final member of the procession was flanked by Michael, the chief of security, on his right, and Jim, the secretary, on his left. Eyal walked behind the threesome, tense as a tightly coiled spring. He was doing his best to relax, for there was no danger lurking in the hotel grounds, but the choking responsibility made it difficult for him to breathe. They ascended the steps to the hotel lobby and then entered a conference room, where Eyal invited the president to sit and wait while he and Louis went up to the president's suite to give it one last check.

They ascended via the elevator in silence, and once in the suite they got to work quickly, checking and rechecking all points of access and making sure that all the electronic devices were accounted for. Then they returned to the conference room and accompanied the president along with three senior officers back up to the suite.

The three officers and the president entered the suite while Eyal waited outside, his weapon drawn and his finger on the trigger. His eyes scanned the area ceaselessly; his mouth was set in a taut line.

"First time overseeing the president's security team?" Louis asked with a wink.

Eyal's response was nothing more than a slight smile, aimed at concealing the overwhelming anxiety he was feeling.

"Are you okay?" Louis asked, a touch of anxiety evident in his own eyes.

Eyal nodded as his pulse raced. If someone could see beyond his steel exterior, that meant that he needed to polish his act.

"Everything's just fine," he said. In his line of business no one was allowed to know what he was thinking or feeling. But then again, never before had his son been captured by terrorists.

"We have to do our utmost to remain invisible," George told the agents accompanying him. "Not just because we're working on foreign territory that's not exactly on friendly terms with the States. There are two lives dependent on the success of our mission. And, unlike with other operations, if we are discovered, the CIA won't lift a finger to get us released."

"What's the background?" Richard, one of the agents, asked. "How much are you going to tell us?"

"Not much," George replied. "But I'll just warn you now that, on the record, America knows nothing of all of this. If anything goes wrong, the official line is that we were caught off guard. I don't like it – it makes us look totally inept – but that's the story."

Tony, practical as usual, changed the subject. "So, what's the plan?"

"First we head to one of our safe houses in Kiev," George said. "We'll go over the plans and maps there, I'll tell you all the framework I devised, and then we'll discuss our options and decide how to operate. The short time frame here is mostly working against us, but we haven't chosen you arbitrarily. Now's the time to prove yourselves."

"Is that a compliment or a warning?"

George smiled. "Both."

"We're picking up the vehicles," Ahmed told X over the radio. "A BMW and Chevrolet, and they should be reaching us in about ten minutes."

"Wonderful. Bruce, Teddy, Jibril – have you taken up your positions?"

"Yes." Teddy placed his sniper's rifle on the ground and stretched his limbs. They had been waiting for some time already, and they needed to be at their very best when the time came. He was only a backup in their scheme, but there were plenty of times when a backup was thrust into the role of main player. Each of them needed to be ready for every eventuality.

"Leon," X addressed the senior member of the team, "the direction of the wind has changed, so remember to account for that. None of you can afford to miss your targets on the first try. You will have exactly ten seconds to gain control over the group."

"Got it," the four men responded. Leon's eyes narrowed; as the first one in the line, the success of the plan depended primarily on him.

The minutes passed in agonizing slowness.

"One more minute," Ahmed reported.

Tension levels mounted. The two vehicles that they would be ambushing contained no less than six skilled American agents, and it was obvious that if Paul had sent these men, they were the best of the best. If the agents had time to realize what was going on and responded too quickly, the entire plan was liable to backfire.

"Leon, they're all yours."

Not a muscle moved on Leon's face as he pulled the trigger three times in quick succession. The bullets hit their target, one after another, ripping holes in the first car's motor with utmost precision. Within seconds the vehicle began to emit smoke.

This was the cue for the rest of the ground team to act. In total silence and with lightning speed, the four men exited the cars parked in the undergrowth on either side of the road and attacked the agents with electric shockers, pepper spray, and clubs. The battle was over before it began, as the six agents were caught completely unprepared. Within less than five minutes the men were shoved into the waiting vehicles and transported away from the scene. Paul, who was in touch with his agents every half hour, had yet to call. As X had predicted, the speedy execution of the operation had been crucial.

Eyal was still standing in front of the president's door on guard when his radio cackled to life. "Eyal?"

"Yes, Joseph. How can I help you?"

"Six men with photo IDs are at the entrance to the hotel. Should I allow them in?" There were ten American security officers patrolling the various access points to the hotel, as well as another five Ukrainians posted outside the main entrance. The division of tasks between the two teams was clear, due to close coordination between Eyal and the Ukrainian commander, and so far there had been no friction – which was nothing to be sneezed at.

Eyal looked at the pictures that had been sent to his cell phone. Six men were standing at the gate and a feeling of relief flooded his body. These were the men who were charged with attacking at the right moment in order to liquidate X and his gang. "Let them in," he instructed.

As angry as Eyal was at Paul, his assistance at this juncture in time was vital. His men would be on hand to rescue his son.

"They are armed," the guard reported.

"I know." Instead of presenting their CIA cards, the men had shown the guard at the door basic ID cards. That had been the arrangement with Paul. Neither the Ukrainian security guards nor the presidential security team knew of the involvement of the CIA, and so Eyal himself was charged with guaranteeing that the agency's operatives were granted access to the hotel based on a regular ID alone. It should have been foolproof – after all, no one attempting to infiltrate would have dreamed that a simple ID would be enough to get him in.

The six men nonchalantly entered the hotel.

Eyal turned to Louis. "You take over my post here for ten minutes or so," he said. "I'm going down for a debriefing with the new arrivals."

Louis nodded. "You've been here for three hours already. I was sure you'd fall asleep at the door," he joked.

Eyal didn't even smile. "I don't sleep when I'm on duty," he replied.

He headed down the corridor and started to make his way down the steps leading to the lobby. There was no need to tell the agents about X, who was presumably still listening to his every word, but Paul had briefed the men on what was going on, and he had told them which subtle nuances would be woven into the conversation.

Eyal left the stairwell and entered the lobby. The six men were standing in a group, facing different directions; at the sound of his approach, they all turned toward him.

"Good to see you here," Eyal greeted them, even as a strange uneasiness trickled down his spine.

Something clicked, and the third man from the left signaled to the others.

Automatic rifles were drawn, and someone shot the radio out of Eyal's hand. Another fraction of a second later the shooting began.

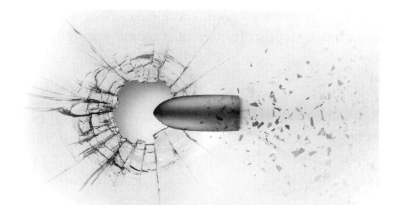

CHAPTER FORTY-ONE

Kiev, Ukraine

E yal's response was instinctive. At the first click of a rifle being readied to fire he was already tensed to spring, and a second later he was taking cover in the stairwell as the bullets started to fly. As he raced up the stairs he berated himself for his stupidity, for his failure to anticipate that X would be one step ahead, as always, never trusting him, never relying on anyone, suspicious to the last.

He reached the corridor outside the president's suite and gasped out to Louis, still standing guard outside: "Open the door! Right now!"

Hearing the urgency in Eyal's voice, Louis pushed the door open and dragged Eyal inside together with him before slamming the door behind them and bolting it.

"What happened?" Louis asked, gazing about fearfully.

Eyal didn't respond immediately. Instead, he took the radio from Louis's hand and shouted: "Calling all teams, calling all teams. Code red! The hotel has been overtaken by terrorists."

Eyal's announcement was greeted with silence, leading Louis to reach the obvious conclusion: "There's a frequency jammer in place."

"Clearly."

At that moment the president emerged from an inner room. He looked from his guards to Eyal, and his face turned pale. "What does this all mean? What's going on?"

"It is exactly as you heard," Eyal said tersely. "Six terrorists have taken over the building. I don't know what damage they've caused already, but it's obvious that more is yet to come. Most likely they'll admit the rest of their gang, and it will be all-out battle." Eyal put his ear to the door and listened to the noise of the terrorists' submachine guns firing again and again, and the Secret Service members retaliating with their own weapons.

"Our men will do their very best, but there's no telling who will gain the upper hand," Eyal continued. "In any case, their job is defense and then victory, while our job is to preserve your life and liberty."

"How?" Michael asked Eyal, and there was unspoken criticism in his tone of voice. Eyal should have foreseen this. He should have arranged for an additional layer of protection. They had been relying on him.

"It's not all lost," Eyal said grimly. "There's a reason I chose this particular suite. We can exit the building from a certain passageway leading from the president's bedroom straight to the upper parking lot. We will make sure that you make it to your car, Mr. President, and we will take you out of the hotel. Your car contains enough heavy weaponry to enable us to blast our way out of the hotel grounds even if the gates are locked."

A barrage of bullets interrupted their conversation as the door to the president's room came under fire. "12.7-centimeter hollow bullets," Eyal murmured. "It won't be long before the door looks like a sieve.'

"I thought the door was bulletproof," Michael said. "At least that's what the Ukrainians told me, and I had no reason to doubt them."

"This door really is bulletproof, but only against 9-millimeter bullets, not 12.7 millimeter bullets. And certainly not if they're hollow." Eyal looked around. "We don't want them following too closely on our heels. We have to buy some time – even just a few minutes." His voice took on a commanding tone. "Louis, help me grab this bed and prop it up against the door. It has a metal frame and will provide us with a bit of protection and a few minutes of breathing space."

Louis and Eyal lifted the bed together, standing it up against the door. On Eyal's instructions, Michael, along with Jim, the president's personal secretary, moved a heavy closet in front of the bed, although the task required much more effort than Eyal and Louis had exerted.

"We've just bought ourselves five minutes," Eyal said. "But we'll need to create a distraction in order to—"

A voice suddenly sounded from the radio. "Eyal?"

Eyal froze. The voice belonged to none other than X.

As he had guessed, the six men he had believed to be CIA agents had opened the hotel gates to allow in the terrorists and their leader.

"I hear you," he said.

"Do not attempt to escape to the parking lot. We've booby-trapped the entire area from wall to wall. If you turn up there with the president, we will blow the whole place sky-high." X's voice was smug and self-assured like someone who had just completed a difficult task to his satisfaction.

"Where are you?" It was a foolish question, Eyal thought, but he asked it nevertheless.

"Not far away at all," X said casually. "In fact, if you open the door you can have the pleasure of conversing with me face-to-face."

"Forget it," Eyal said, but he knew he was being foolish. If X threatened him with doing harm to Elitzafun and demanded that he step outside, he knew he would have to comply.

"Don't you want to meet an old friend?" X continued, and Eyal could picture the smirk on his face.

"What do you want?" Eyal asked, cutting straight to the heart of the matter.

"I thought that our friendship was deeper than that, and that you knew exactly what I most desire. We've had some long conversations about my plans, as I'm sure you'll recall when you're in a more stable state of mind."

"What do you want?" Eyal repeated. Despite the danger, his anger toward X was mounting by the moment.

"I want the president, just as we arranged." All of X's artificial cheer faded from his voice instantly, leaving only the clear threat of violence. "Open the door, Eyal. Let me take him, and we'll part as friends. Good friends even, I'd say."

Three men looked at Eyal in shock, while the fourth man in the room looked horrified but not surprised.

"How do you know Eyal, Mr. Terrorist?" Michael demanded, turning his attention furiously to the radio.

"Haven't you figured it out yet?" X asked. "Eyal is my best friend. Okay, maybe not my best friend exactly, but he is definitely one of the best. By now we've known each other for a long time, and he and I have been collaborating on a very important project. He has led the president straight into this trap. Don't even consider trying to contact the police or Ukrainian security, as the frequency jammer will not allow any such communications. I might like guests, but I don't like it when they take me by surprise. If I see a police officer or soldier anywhere in the hotel grounds, I will start killing the hostages in the lobby. One hostage for each officer, agent, or soldier who shows up."

Eyal was seething, yet he was also astounded by X's brilliance. He was manipulating the rift between him and his team members to perfection. How would anyone agree to follow his instructions now?

"You…" Michael began.

The president intervened. "Don't believe a word," he said quietly. "That man is a pathological liar; Eyal is faithful to me, and I know it. But what is our plan now?"

"We need to head upstairs," Eyal said, speaking so softly that the others could only understand by following his lips as he motioned for them to do the same. "It shouldn't be too hard, and there are two helicopters there that are ready for takeoff."

"How will you get us upstairs?" the president asked.

Eyal looked at Louis. "What do you have?"

"One sniper's rifle, two guns, a few cartridges. What do you have?" Louis's voice betrayed his hesitancy. Despite the president's declaration, his own faith in Eyal had begun to waver.

"One submachine gun and three other guns," Eyal said quickly.

"What's your plan?" Louis asked Eyal.

"There is a way to exit via the bathroom, through the plaster ceiling," Eyal replied. "You'll have to break through somehow."

"Who said it leads anywhere useful," Louis said tensely. He could already picture the trap closing in on the very man he had been entrusted to protect, although he wasn't yet thinking about the fact that he was in the same trap himself. "We could just run into concrete."

"Open the door," X commanded, his voice cutting through the door instead of the radio. "This is my final call before we resume shooting."

Eyal quickly directed Louis toward the bathroom. Louis climbed onto the marble counter around the sink and began to knock at the plaster ceiling, searching for a hollow sound that would indicate that he had located a concealed vent or other way out. After just a few seconds he started to break through into a wide chute and had soon created a hole large enough to enter.

Peering inside, he called down to Eyal: "I think this will do. Let's go."

Eyal shook his head. "You go, all of you. I have to stay here and deal with…this. There's no choice."

Louis and the others stared. "You'll be killed," Michael said, doubt in his eyes. But there was no time to waste. He started to help the president climb up, and then he and Jim followed suit. As they scrambled away, heading – though they didn't yet know it – to a small maintenance room on the floor above, Eyal stood guard near the door to the presidential suite, counting the seconds and waiting for as long as he dared.

"Okay, okay, I'm coming out," he said finally as a rivulet of cold sweat ran down his back.

"I don't need you. I need the president." X was unmoved by Eyal's gesture of surrender. "I need not warn you what will happen if I don't get him."

Eyal's whole body began to tremble. Exactly what he had feared was transpiring, and he was helpless to prevent it. With defeat in his voice, he said, "I'm moving the beds and closet away from the door. It will take a minute."

Eyal began to drag the objects away from the door, his heart pounding in fear – fear for his own life, but even more so for the life of his son. Would X's determination to seize the president prevail, or would he immediately exact his revenge on Eyal? There was still the slenderest of chances that X would keep him – and Elitzafun – alive in order to continue to serve him.

Eyal closed his eyes for a moment, drew a deep breath, and turned the key twice in the lock.

He now stood face-to-face with X.

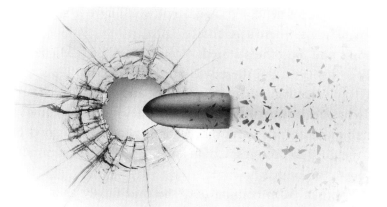

CHAPTER FORTY-TWO

Kiev, Ukraine

Eyal's and X's eyes met for a moment before X pushed Eyal aside and entered the room. Chaos and all the signs of a panicked retreat met his eyes, and for a moment X silently took it all in. Finally, he addressed Eyal in a furious rage: "Where is the president?"

"He escaped," Eyal said shortly.

"Where to?"

Eyal shrugged, and X quickly began to conduct his own investigation. Just twenty seconds passed before he found the hole in the bathroom ceiling.

"Teddy," X called out, and his assistant instantly appeared from the entrance of the suite. "Tell Leon to take his men up to the second floor. They went out through the ceiling."

Teddy pointed to Eyal. "What about him?"

"Tie his hands and take him down to the hall with the rest of the hostages." X turned to Eyal. "As with any battle, we've lost some men and so has the other side. But we had the upper hand all along. You're finished now, you and the rest of them in the dining room. Although we may yet find a use for some of you."

"How many people were killed?" Eyal asked, even as his throat constricted painfully in his effort to get the question out.

X shrugged. "Ask Bruce. He's in charge there."

"What about those who were wounded?"

"They're restrained." X made no attempt to camouflage the scorn in his voice. "Don't think I'm taking any chances. Those are well-trained men. But my men are better."

"Who's tending to their wounds?" Eyal asked.

X chuckled. "You sound like a lawyer, not a hostage. I don't see that it's of any concern to you. They'll recover – or they won't. It makes no difference to me."

"Allow me to tend to them," Eyal said. His voice was commanding, not pleading.

"You're the last person I'll permit such a thing." X turned away from Eyal to address Teddy instead: "Bind his hands and take him away. I'll be down in the hall soon."

Teddy twisted a plastic cable around Eyal's hands and shoved a pistol into the small of his back. With a kick in the shins he got him moving, out of the room and down the corridor to the stairs. Slowly, Eyal descended the steps, thinking hard. Could he salvage something from this disaster? Would the president somehow reach the roof before X's men caught up with him? Within minutes it would likely all be over.

Teddy opened the door to the dining room, shoving Eyal inside. A sad smile came to his lips as he set eyes upon the beautifully upholstered seats and the tables already set for supper – elegant silverware and crystal glasses, fine wines and silk napkins. It was almost surreal.

"Do not create a scene," Teddy said quietly. "Your son's life is hanging in the balance until we lay our hands on the president."

Eyal nodded, and with supreme control over his emotions, he remarked: "Thanks for the reminder, Teddy. I almost forgot about that for a moment."

The hostages were seated around the perimeter of the room, a few feet between each of them for added security. As they noticed Eyal entering, a notable aura of relief flooded through them, even though he was ostensibly in an identical predicament.

Bruce shoved Eyal into an empty space along one of the walls and forced him into a sitting position on the floor. Immediately, Eyal started to scan the room, taking stock of the situation. He called out to several of the men and addressed them in the calmest and most authoritative tone he could muster. "Who can report on the situation to me?'

"Three dead, five wounded," one young man at the end of a table said, his eyes bright with worry. "Two of the men are in critical condition, but they won't let us treat them." He jerked his head toward the three men patrolling the room with drawn submachine guns.

"Bruce," Eyal said, turning toward the light-haired man, "I ask for permission to treat the wounded."

"Permission denied," Bruce said. He was obviously intoxicated with the feeling of power and anticipation of total victory.

"Why the unnecessary bloodshed?" Eyal asked, purposely injecting a pleading note into his words.

"Who says it's unnecessary?" Bruce retorted. His words were intentionally designed to break the morale of the man for whom, in his opinion, X had shown far too much reverence.

"Do you really want all the negative publicity that will ensue if you let your hostages bleed to death?" Eyal asked bluntly. "I thought you wanted to portray yourselves as humanitarian freedom fighters."

Jibril turned to Bruce. "Let him take care of them," he muttered. "What do you care?"

Bruce looked at Eyal with open hostility for a moment before turning back to Jibril. "What do I care?" he said. "I care because the minute that we release him, he'll be sure to pull some stunt to take control of the situation, and that is obviously not something I can allow to happen."

"So, don't release me then," Eyal said. "My medical knowledge isn't too impressive in any case. All I know is how to stitch up gunshot wounds and apply a tourniquet. There are others in this room who are far more skilled than I am." He pointed at the young man who had reported on the wounded officers earlier. "That man's name is Dale Norman, and he's a combat medic."

"Fine." Jibril walked over to Dale and slit open the cable holding his hands together behind his back. "You have permission to deal with the wounded," he said. "And that's as far as it goes. One false move, and I'm not asking questions – I'm shooting."

Dale shrugged and didn't even bother to meet Jibril's gaze. Instead, he said, "I need an assistant."

"You're not going to get your commander's assistance," Jibril said.

"Did I say I was asking for it?" Dale retorted. "Choose whoever you like, as far as I'm concerned."

"So I'll release another hostage. Someone who's not a member of your security team."

Eyal suddenly noticed that there were about fifteen members of the hotel's staff in the dining room, ranging from a young waiter who looked like he was about sixteen years old to a valet he had seen the day before, who was probably close to seventy.

Jibril's eyes met those of the elderly valet. "You. You're going to help tend to the wounded."

The older man nodded, and Jibril slit the cable around his hands.

"Thank you for your assistance," Eyal said. "What's your name?"

"Volodymyr."

"What's the situation, Dale?"

"I'm going to create a tourniquet for Danny here. He's unconscious and has lost a lot of blood."

"What about the others?"

"Robby's unconscious too. I'll check on him after I finish here."

"Who else has been injured?" Eyal asked, pursuing his line of questioning as though his captors weren't anywhere in the area.

"I was." Tony's face was pale from blood loss, and he bit his lower lip to keep from yelping in pain. "Allen and Jeff were wounded too, but I think we'll be okay once someone stops the bleeding."

"What happened to you?" Eyal asked.

"Allen and I got in the way of a couple of bullets. My bullet managed to escape me but Allen kept his as a souvenir. And Jeff fell from a third floor balcony to the floor below. An armchair cushioned his fall, but it still wasn't so pretty."

"Jeff?" Eyal called out to the man who was lying sideways on the floor, snoring quietly. "How are you doing?"

The man opened his eyes and smiled weakly upon seeing his commander. "I'm sorry. Must be I'm allergic to heights."

"You should be thankful that you fell onto an armchair instead of a table." Eyal smiled. "How are you feeling?"

"Oh, like someone who fell off a balcony, I guess."

"That's enough!" Bruce had lost his patience. "Eyal, shut up. I'm getting sick of the sound of your voice. This paramedic here will take care of as many people as he can. There's no need for talking."

Eyal watched Dale run around and administer first aid with the few items he had in his pockets and around the room – gauze pads, pain relievers, tweezers, a scalpel, silk napkins...

Suddenly, Eyal sensed a pair of eyes fixed on him. He lifted his gaze and looked toward the man staring at him. It was Barry, his assistant. Their eyes met, and Barry silently mouthed the words: "What do we do?"

Eyal shrugged and shook his head. He saw no way of breaking free in their current situation. There was no reason to start a losing battle. He shifted his gaze toward the guards, and Barry sighed at the unspoken message. With their hands bound and the guards patrolling the room, any form of resistance on their part would be suicidal.

Eyal's eyes roved the hall. Their situation didn't look good – which was putting it mildly – but sitting quietly and waiting for events to unfold was not his nature. He had to try something.

They had reached the top floor and had managed to barricade themselves behind a door leading to a long corridor – at the end of which was the exit to the roof. So far, there had been no shooting as they escaped; Louis assumed that they wanted to capture the president alive rather than dead or wounded. But from outside on the roof, the sounds of a fierce gunfight reached them. It was encouraging to know that there were still some American agents holding out; on the other hand, it was clearly impossible to reach a helicopter until the terrorists on the roof were either eliminated or beaten back.

The president and his three companions exchanged glances.

"Do you have enough ammunition to hold them off, Louis?" Michael asked.

Louis shook his head, and then thought better of it and tried to muster a bit more confidence to show his companions. "It depends for how long," he said. "It depends on our men out there – let's see if they can get rid of those guys."

"X?" Leon called into his radio. "The president is on his way up to the helipad."

"As I figured."

"They still have about ten men defending the helipad, and

they're good ones, too. Four of our men are already dead and one other is wounded."

"Tell them to surrender," X fumed, "or we will shoot the president."

"The president isn't in our hands yet," Leon said.

X cursed. His assessment of Eyal's behavior had been off, and he couldn't forgive himself for not predicting this. The man had been cooperative while preparing for the operation, operating at top form due to the threat to his son's life, but now that it was the president's life that was in danger, he wasn't acting according to the script that X had written for him.

Perhaps it was time to bring the boy into the picture. Only through the manipulation of Eyal's son would they be able to convince Eyal to tell his men to drop their weapons and surrender. The minute things calmed down, he would send one of his men to bring Elitzafun to the hotel. In the meantime, he needed every last ounce of his warrior spirit.

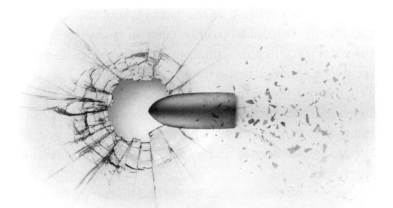

CHAPTER FORTY-THREE

Kiev, Ukraine

yal scanned the dining room. His precise knowledge of the hotel map told him that the terrorists had made a wise choice when selecting this room for the hostages. The room held a plentiful supply of food and drink for the captors, and Jibril was indeed helping himself to the cakes, but that wasn't the reason the choice was a wise one. The room had clearly been selected due to the fact that not one of its walls bordered on the hotel grounds, making any attempt at escape that much less likely to succeed.

"Eyal?" Samuel whispered. He was sitting about ten feet from Eyal, and the terrorists were just then at the other end of the room, keeping close tabs on Dale and his ministrations to the wounded. "Do you think there's any chance we can overcome them?"

Eyal nodded. "But we need to wait for the opportunity and not be overly hasty," he said. "At the right moment, I'll give you a signal."

"What are you planning?"

"There's a door leading to the kitchen, and the kitchen contains anything we could possibly need to make some kind of explosive device. Of course, that's just the first stage. Getting out of here doesn't guarantee anything."

"What about going through the underground parking lot?" Samuel suggested quietly.

"It's booby-trapped," Eyal whispered. "That is, they told me that the ground floor lot is, and somehow I doubt they overlooked the other one."

"Given enough time, we can locate and dismantle the bombs."

"Maybe, and maybe not. If they've done a good job, then we'll only manage to do so by using a controlled explosion." Eyal's voice was barely audible. "But I doubt we'll have time for any of that. What we need to do now is get rid of these three men. And we need to do it fast, before any of them has the opportunity to report to X – that is, their leader."

"Our hands are tied." Samuel said, stating the obvious, as well as indicating his doubt that any plan could possibly succeed.

"There is one man here whose hands aren't tied." Eyal jerked his head in Dale's direction. The medic was focused intently on the needs of the wounded, aided by the elderly Ukrainian.

"They're watching him too closely," Samuel said. "Nothing suspicious will escape their notice."

"I have to figure out a way," Eyal said, more to himself than to Samuel.

"After Dale, you're the next most scrutinized person in this room."

Eyal ignored the comment and instead tried to be practical. "Samuel, what do you have on you that can be of use?"

"Nothing. Our weapons were all taken from us. My pockets

are empty. Not even a tissue—"

"Shut up." Bruce headed toward Samuel and struck his head with his rifle butt. "Stop talking!"

Samuel grimaced in pain as blood started to trickle from his head. Bruce fixed Eyal with an expression of loathing. "You," he sneered. "Get over here."

Eyal struggled to his feet and faced Bruce. "What got you rattled? Why the fuss?"

"I don't like you sitting and plotting escape routes together with your friends. I'm going to isolate you. Come with me."

Eyal walked toward Bruce, and a feeling of impending doom settled into his stomach. Bruce's hand was stroking the trigger of his gun, and his eyes were narrowed with hatred. It wasn't too hard to imagine what he planned to do.

Samuel watched Eyal's eyes follow Bruce's hands, and he understood. Bruce was leading Eyal out of the room in order to kill him. He was isolating him from the others so that there would be no witnesses, and the silencer on his weapon would ensure that the sound was muffled. Presumably, Bruce intended to tell X that Eyal had been killed in an attempt to flee.

Samuel's thoughts churned at a frenzy. He needed to come to his commander's aid.

But Eyal was already in the kitchen, and the door was closed behind him.

"I have been waiting for this moment," Bruce said, his eyes full of loathing.

"You're going to kill me, right?" Eyal's green eyes were filled with calm indifference.

"Got it in one," Bruce said as he cocked his weapon. "Right from the outset, I didn't like X's plan to use you."

"The feeling is mutual."

"From the moment you got here, you were trying to rule over our men as if you were the tyrant of some third world African country. X certainly won't miss you after you're gone."

"He actually told me that he still needs me, but you're definitely free to think otherwise."

"In that case, I'm going to have to explain the circumstances surrounding your death," Bruce said thoughtfully. He pulled out a sharp knife. "Turn around, and I'll cut the cable from your hands."

"Why?"

"To make it look like you tried to escape. But don't even think about actually doing that. And now, take this explosive, *please*."

Eyal took the light-gray package from Bruce's hand.

"Here is the fuse." Bruce handed Eyal a small metal component. "Create one of your signature bombs right now."

Obediently, Eyal embedded the fuse into the center of the explosive. Bruce clearly intended for him to blow a hole in the kitchen wall and blow himself up in the process, but Eyal had other plans. All the same, he was following Bruce's orders, as their interests were mutual, and Eyal needed to break a path to the outside. But he was proficient enough to know how to blow up the wall and remain unharmed, even while standing nearby.

"Place the bomb near the wall," Bruce ordered.

Eyal did as he was told, attaching the explosive to the wall, then turning it so that the main thrust was directed toward the other man.

"Now activate the bomb," Bruce said, taking two steps backward as he spoke, and following Eyal's every move.

"This room is so small that the fire will immediately consume all the oxygen. Open the door so you don't suffocate." Eyal was counting on the fact that Bruce would do the exact opposite of what he told him, and he wasn't disappointed.

"I didn't ask for advice," Bruce said brusquely, remaining firmly planted in his spot, partially shielded behind a huge metal cupboard that Eyal knew would give him little protection.

"The shock waves are going to hit you straight on if you stay there," Eyal warned. All true, but Bruce wasn't about to believe him, which was exactly what Eyal wanted.

"Shut up. Just say goodbye to the world and detonate the bomb, or I'll shoot it now and detonate it myself."

"You're welcome to do exactly that."

"No problem." Bruce raised his weapon and fired a shot.

A horrific, sickening explosion rent the air as broken glass and countless flying objects whirled around the room.

And then there was silence.

"Mr. President?"

The president turned to his deputy security head. His normally calm eyes now darted wildly around, like a hunted animal. "Yes?"

"There are two helicopters on the roof." Louis was watching the president carefully to make sure he was absorbing what he was saying. "There's also a gunfight in progress on the roof, and a bunch of hoodlums are about to break through the door here. So we can't delay much longer. We'll have to be quick – super-quick, in fact. Do you think you can do it?"

The president stared at Louis with his piercing blue eyes. "Do I have a choice?" he asked quietly.

"No." Louis's eyes flickered for just a moment.

"So let's go," the president said.

The sound of gunfire seemed to be getting louder. Louis trembled, well aware of the immense significance of the decision he was making.

"Mr. President – just one more thing first, with your permission. About Eyal...is he a traitor?"

"No." The president uttered the word with complete resolution. "Eyal is loyal to me, and I know it intuitively. But it's not only that; there's more to this case than you realize, Louis. Eyal is not a traitor. And now let's move. We need to be fast. Do you feel up to that?"

The president's perfect imitation of Louis's voice had Louis, Michael, and Jim all smiling despite the gravity of the situation and the real threat of death hanging over their heads. The three men approached the door leading out to the helipad.

"There are crates stacked just outside this door," Louis said in a low voice. "There's a narrow opening leading between them, then the helicopters, and from the sound of it, the gunfight is going on mainly on the other side of the roof, the side that the elevator accesses. That means that although we'll be in range of their fire, we might just make it into the nearest helicopter without their noticing."

"What if they shot out the helicopters to prevent us from making a getaway?" Jim, the president's secretary asked.

Louis turned toward him and noted how pale the man's face was. Jim had been trained to deal with emergency situations, but that was years ago, and he had never come face-to-face with danger like this. Somehow, Louis had to calm him.

"Helicopters can take a lot of bullet holes before serious damage is done," Louis replied. "The fuel tanks are protected, and even if the metal is dented it won't make a difference to us. Only heavy submachine guns and mortar shells can cause real damage, but luckily, it seems that our enemies don't have those. And now it's time to get going, Jim and Michael. We're going to dive straight into the first helicopter and take off right away. Mr. President, you will make sure to stay low down at the back of the helicopter so that you aren't shot at. And we'll pray that everything goes well."

"X?" The radio cackled to life. "Our men are still trying to gain control of the helipad, but the enemy is employing all of its remaining resources to protect the site. They're not giving up so easily on the president's only escape route."

"I hear you," X said. "You sound like you're smack in the middle of a war zone."

"We're breaking into the helipad. We didn't want to bomb our way in, but now we have no choice. The question is if I should wait for you to get here before we break through."

X looked down toward the lobby and then upstairs. The situation in the dining room was under control, and they could always call him if he was needed. "I'm on my way," he said. "Wait for me."

The deafening explosion shook the floor of the helipad, momentarily paralyzing the four men heading toward the helicopter. A shard entered Louis's leg, but he had no time to check it out. Instead, he fumbled at the door to the helicopter and finally succeeded in opening it; the metal had been warped, but it was still functional. Thrusting the president forward, he pushed him inside, followed by the others.

"Michael and Jim, get down as low as you can. I'm going to take off."

Behind him, the three men huddled down on the floor of the chopper. Outside, the gunfight was still raging, and Louis tried not to think about the heavy price his compatriots were paying for this chance to get the president off the scene.

Settling into the pilot's seat, he switched on the lights. The last time he had piloted a helicopter had been several months ago, but he knew exactly what was involved in takeoff.

He pulled the trigger switch of the ignition.

Nothing.

Louis pursed his lips. They needed to take off immediately. It wouldn't be long before X's men called for reinforcements – including the kinds of weapons that could totally ground the chopper.

Louis realized he was trembling as he ran his gaze over the control panel. The fuel tank gauge was showing that it was full, and the speed indicators were all pointing in the correct direction.

So what was it? Then he noticed that one of the warning lights was blinking. "Got it," he whispered. It wasn't clear if he was talking to himself or to the others. Finally the engine revved to life, drowning out the sounds of the battle outside.

Like a herd of hungry lions, the motor of the helicopter growled. Louis waited impatiently for the blades to begin to whir...and waited, and waited. Nothing. Nothing but noise, heat, and vibration. No movement.

Louis's face paled as the blood drained from it. His already trembling hands shook with force.

Someone had sabotaged the helicopter. So simple. So brilliant.

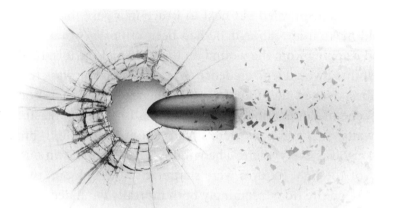

CHAPTER FORTY-FOUR

Kiev, Ukraine

Something was trickling down his forehead. Eyal reached up and was unsurprised to feel the sticky sensation of blood, oozing from a wound on his scalp. It wasn't the only wound, of course; the rest of his body was riddled with tiny shards. But the head wound seemed the worst, though not bad enough to cause him to lose consciousness, thankfully.

The moment he had seen Bruce raise his arm to fire he had ducked behind a cabinet nearby, hands over his head, body scrunched down for maximum protection. It still wasn't good, but it was good enough. He was alive, after all, and it could have turned out very differently.

He turned to Bruce, who lay motionless on the floor. He had refused to heed Eyal's warnings about his dangerous position, and he had suffered the consequences. Eyal bent over his body now and felt for his pulse.

There was none.

The sound of approaching footsteps. Eyal quickly dropped to the floor and sprawled out next to Bruce in a pose that he hoped would make it appear as if he had been critically wounded. The blood dripping from the wound on his scalp and the torn fabric of his clothing would lend credence to the sham that he was creating.

Jibril opened the door to the kitchen and froze in shock at the scene of devastation within. Cupboards had been blasted off the walls; pots and pans were strewn about like confetti; broken crockery was everywhere. The windows had been blown out and most of the light fixtures were shattered. In the gloom, two figures lay on the floor, seemingly both mortally wounded.

Jibril was nearest to Bruce, and he reached down to check for a pulse.

It was now or never.

In a movement as quick and sinuous as a snake's, Eyal shot out an arm toward Jibril and seized the gun from his leg holster. A click, aim, and Jibril crumpled to the floor, shot through the heart.

Eyal jumped to his feet and leaped over to the door, expecting the third of the guards from the dining hall to appear at any moment. This was Stefan, a quiet, morose character who seemed to be perpetually brooding about some perceived injustice or other. The moment his profile appeared in the doorway Eyal shot him at close range, again aiming for the heart.

Stefan collapsed to the floor, and Eyal ran experienced hands over his body, relieving him of all his weapons and ammunition. Then he gave the other two terrorists the same treatment and headed back into the dining room where the men, still bound (including Dale, who had presumably been restrained when Jibril went to see what had happened to Bruce), were waiting fearfully to see what would happen.

"Men, the road is all clear," Eyal said quickly. "The kitchen is bombed out, and now there's a hole leading to the outside. Their snipers are certainly prowling outside, and you'll have to deal with that, but the battle can still be yours."

Samuel was the first to recover his focus. "Where is everyone? And what happened to you?" he asked. The blood was still flowing down Eyal's forehead, and it made his condition seem far worse than it actually was.

"I'm fine. It's just surface wounds…or whatever. I'll get it all seen to later. That's not the issue now." Eyal drew a deep breath. "We need to move quickly, before they realize what's happened here."

Eyal started cutting cables, making his way around the room. As soon as a man's arms were released, he grabbed a knife from one of the tables and set to work freeing others, so that within twenty seconds everyone was free.

"What about the wounded soldiers?" Dale asked. "There's no way they can deal with an escape under fire."

Eyal frowned. He had no doubt that a furious X would murder whomever remained behind.

"We can't move the two who are still unconscious – they're in critical condition, and they won't make it. But we can take the other three with us. Dale and Samuel, knock the legs off this table and tie Jeff onto the board with plastic ties – courtesy of our erstwhile captors." He turned to another member of the security team. "Albert, you and Steve are in charge of Tony. Russo and Blake, take Allen. Bob, Terry, Mike, Ronald, and Richard, we have three submachine guns and three guns from the terrorists. That's not enough, but it's better than nothing, so take them. You'll have to move quickly, and I wish you the best of luck."

There was no need for Eyal to say anything else. The men had practiced evacuating hostile territory with wounded men, and under fire, dozens of times in the past. The exercise was simply becoming a reality now.

The men started to make their way out through the hole blasted by Bruce's bomb. Eyal counted the men as they left and murmured a prayer.

"What about you, Commander?" one of the men asked. "You're taking up the rear?"

"No. I'm staying here."

"What?" The man eyed Eyal with shock. "They'll kill you."

"They might. But...I can't just abandon the president. He needs me." Eyal looked around the destroyed kitchen and added quietly, "And my son needs me too..."

"Step outside with your hands in the air," X called into the megaphone that Omar had helped him hook up to the hotel's PA system. "One superfluous move and you will be shot."

Silence.

X's leadership traits included an extra measure of self-control and restraint. He was capable of extreme patience if it would help him to achieve his goals, but everything has its limit, and X's patience was about to give way. "We are giving you another minute," he said into the megaphone. "And then we start shooting."

Only then did Louis's voice ring out, chipper and clear. "This is Louis Moran," he said. "I am in charge of negotiations, and our goal is to reach a compromise."

"Wonderful. It's a great pleasure to meet you," X said coolly. "But, Mr. Moran, the president is in our hands and you have no bargaining chips. In such circumstances, it is irrelevant to speak of compromise. We have sabotaged the helicopter, and you are surrounded by our men on all sides. We do not wish to negotiate. All four of you are to step outside with your hands in the air. I give you another ninety seconds to surrender, Mr. President, or the United States will never forgive you."

Eyal listened to the sounds of gunfire for another minute, hoping, both for his sake and for the sake of the president's team, that the gates were open. It wasn't difficult to bust a gate, but with Eyal's injuries and an ongoing firefight, it would prove a complicated maneuver.

A minute passed. Eyal turned to Danny and Robby, still lying motionless on the floor. He pulled a few tables around them in a haphazard formation and covered them almost entirely with tablecloths. If no one went to check out that corner of the room, they probably wouldn't be found. Whether that was a good thing or not depended on who was doing the looking.

Next, Eyal went back to the kitchen and filled his pockets with useful kitchen items: a sharp knife, a lighter, a pair of pliers, and a few other things. Then he turned to the dead terrorists and relieved them of their cell phones; there was no telling how one of the devices might prove helpful to him in the future.

Bending over Stefan, he noticed a familiar tattoo on the dead man's arm. It was a tattoo of a seal. Had the man once been a member of the US Navy SEALs? Eyal filed the question away in his mind and hurried out of the kitchen and down a narrow flight of stairs toward the parking lot.

Entering the booby-trapped lot would be perilous. It was possible that the terrorists had fitted the place with thermal detectors or motion sensors and that his appearance – be it fast or slow, cautious or rash – would blow the whole place sky-high. But Eyal had no choice but to risk it.

He reached the bottom of the staircase and switched on a light. The door to the parking lot was locked. Drawing a deep breath, Eyal busied himself with the lock. Bombs were frequently set to detonate when a door was opened, but – again – he had no choice if he wanted to get out of the building.

Eyal focused intently for a full twenty seconds on picking the lock. When he finally succeeded, he slowly and cautiously pushed open the heavy iron door just a crack. Then he placed a finger into the doorframe and ran it along the top of the door, feeling for a thread connecting to a bomb's detonator.

Nothing.

With meticulous caution, Eyal swung the door open until the gap was wide enough for him to pass through. In the dim light he scanned the parking lot.

Parked there were ten vehicles belonging to the president's team, as well as six motorcycles. Four of the motorcycles belonged to men in the unit, and two, apparently, belonged to the terrorists. There were also three cars there that Eyal didn't recognize, and presumably they too had been brought there by X's men.

Eyal's experienced eyes scrutinized the walls of the parking lot, searching for any sign of the booby trap X had claimed was there. Nothing. X must have been bluffing.

Eyal switched on the flashlight on one of the terrorists' cell phones and began examining the vehicles in the lot. When he reached the third car, he froze. Under the driver's seat, in a small, nondescript box that belied its potential, was an incredibly powerful bomb. Not just powerful – it was oddly familiar, and a moment later he realized why. He had seen a similar bomb in the past.

Buried memories were dredged up and a powerful image came to mind: Afghanistan. Eyal had been there on a mission that had involved close contact with a team of American soldiers who had expertly concealed the bombs they had made in their efforts to subdue Islamic terror.

Eyal moved on from the vehicle he was examining and continued his inspection of the parking lot. A few moments later he spotted another explosive device beneath one of the cars that he knew did not belong to the president's team.

Bending down, Eyal peered more closely at the bomb. He had the expertise to be able to neutralize it, but that wasn't the issue. He continued to make his way through the lot, locating two more bombs constructed in a manner similar to those used by the Americans in Afghanistan. It made no sense at all. Or did it?

Eyal straightened up and ran his gaze over the parked cars, noting how each vehicle that housed an explosive device was placed strategically, either near a supporting wall or near one of the pillars in the center of the parking lot. There was no doubt that X's intention was to bring down the entire building with the detonation of these devices, and as far as Eyal could tell, he would very likely succeed.

But there was more to the picture than that.

The cogs of Eyal's mind whirled as he tried to assimilate the information. There were a number of puzzle pieces that didn't fit. They simply didn't correlate.

And then he saw it.

Someone has made a mistake and jumped to incorrect conclusions. And that someone is you.

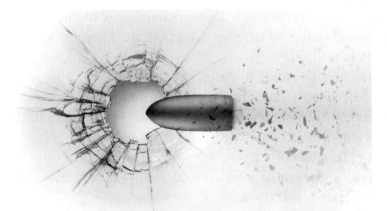

CHAPTER FORTY-FIVE

Kiev, Ukraine

E yal turned back and bent down to study once again one of
the bombs that so intrigued him. Using one of the terrorist's
cell phones, he snapped a picture of it. Perhaps if he could
identify the manufacturer, he would be that much closer to solving
the riddle of X and his merry men.

Fragmented sentences and half-remembered words swirled
through his mind. They were clues of sorts, but in the heat of the
moment, and under pressure, he couldn't figure it all out.

In any case, it wasn't a priority, but he knew what was. Dialing the
familiar number, he waited impatiently for the phone to be answered.

"Hello?" Finally, Eli's voice came through on the other end of
the line, calm and clueless as to the identity of his caller and the
situation he was in.

"Eli, it's me." Eyal's voice echoed his frenzied state.

"Eyal? Where are you calling from?"

"I'm trapped in the hotel. Last I knew of the president, he was trying to make his way up to the helipad on the roof, but I have no idea if he made it there. But you can't call in the police, or Uri either. There's Elitzafun to consider." Eyal's heart constricted in pain as he uttered the last sentence.

"Thanks for telling me what not to do. Now, how about a few words letting me know what you *would* like me to do?"

"I think it's likely that someone's going to leave the hotel grounds within the next few minutes. My estimation is that X is going to have Elitzafun brought here so that he can maximize his manipulation of me. Have whoever leaves the hotel followed, and try to rescue Elitzafun, because the original plan of having my son returned to me in peace isn't going to work out."

"We already know where you son is being held," Eli told his friend. "We had an informant."

"Okay, great. But…I'm sure I don't have to remind you that these guys are dangerous. Please be careful." His words were the essence of understatement, but Eli knew Eyal well enough to detect the emotion behind them.

"Got it."

As Eyal ended the call, he heard the unmistakable sound of a weapon being cocked from behind him. Instinctively, Eyal ducked, and the bullet hit the wall just above the place where he had been standing.

"Hey," the intruder said. "Fancy meeting you here."

"What a pleasant surprise," Eyal responded, getting to his feet. "You're a great shot, Ahmed. I can see you really enjoy your day job."

"You're right. I love it." Ahmed's voice held a triumphant note to it. "But X won't be too disturbed by your death, and in any case I only intended to injure you, not to kill you." Ahmed motioned toward the door. "Let's go back upstairs, shall we? Just do me a favor and lift your hands high into the air. Make sure not to annoy me along the way. I'm a bit trigger happy, as you've surely noticed."

They made their way out of the parking lot. Then Ahmed examined Eyal closely, taking in the bruising and dried blood. "Who were you speaking to when I found you, if I may ask?"

"Sure you can ask. We're good friends and I'm not about to hide the facts from you. I let the Mossad know that the president has been captured by a band of terrorists threatening his life."

Ahmed's face whitened with fury. "Are you serious?"

"Totally. You can check the number I dialed without too much difficulty."

"Are you crazy?" Ahmed's voice shook with fury. "X will murder the hostages."

"Good luck to him then," Eyal said. "But he'd probably prefer to hear what I have to say first, as it's quite a gripping revelation I have for him."

"Move along." Ahmed shoved Eyal back into the dining hall. "X is sure to be delighted to see you. I'm going to call him down, and then we'll see who'll have the last word."

"No one's come out yet, and I've been standing in this same spot for ten minutes," Bentzy reported to Eli.

"So wait some more." Eli's voice was tense. None of his Mossad training had prepared him for a situation in which his friend's son was at the mercy of a ruthless gang of terrorists who cared not the slightest about snuffing out precious life.

"I've been waiting plenty," Bentzy said. "At what point do we conclude that Eyal was wrong in his estimation?"

"Bentzy!" Eli shouted. "Just be quiet and do what I tell you to do!"

"Sure, Eli. No problem. You're here to teach me absolute faith in Eyal, no matter what. But the guy isn't omniscient, you know. It could just be that he made a mistake, you know. So don't…wait a minute. Someone's pulling out. I'm on my way."

"Bentzy, be careful." How Eli wished he could have been on site to be part of this mission.

"I know how to track a car," Bentzy said, weaving through the heavy Kiev traffic. "Stop acting like a child."

"I'm not a child," Eli whispered. "But Elitzafun is."

"This isn't the time for that," Bentzy said sharply, just as he was stopped by a red light and had to leave the other car to drive on without him. There was no sense in arousing suspicion by running a traffic light when he could get satellite support instead. "Listen, Eli, I need your help now. Get me that vehicle tracked. And quit the dramatics, okay?"

"Mr. President?"

The president's face was pale, but the expression in his eyes was one of fierce determination. His habitual calm and level-headedness hadn't abandoned him, despite the situation he was in. "Yes, Louis?"

"I think we're running out of options, to be honest." Louis pronounced the words with difficulty, devastated over the fact that he was the one who needed to be speaking to them.

"Maybe there's still another way." The president spoke calmly, and only an extra furrow in his brow betrayed the enormous pressure he was under. "Maybe we can think of—"

"Mr. President." X's voice came over the megaphone once more. "We are holding a large number of your men, and every moment that you delay your surrender will lead to the murder of another member of your team."

The president said nothing as he rose from his spot. Louis tugged at his sleeve. "They knew exactly what they were getting themselves into when they swore to defend you in all circumstances,

Mr. President," Louis whispered, even though he knew it was useless. "If we wait another few minutes…"

"What will happen then?" the president asked, shaking his head. "We've reached the end of the road and you know it. At least with my surrender I will prevent the senseless deaths of who knows how many young men. I couldn't live with that."

Louis didn't respond. He had no counterargument. As the president had said, they had truly reached the end of the road.

Louis opened the door of the helicopter and slowly climbed down onto the roof. Jim stepped out after him, and the two men stood stiffly at attention as the president followed behind.

X's lips turned upward in a triumphant and gloating smile.

Michael followed the president out of the helicopter, taking up the rear so that the president was surrounded on all sides. Nonetheless, the men were all painfully aware that they could offer him no real protection. X strode forward and, with an unmistakably authoritative gesture, motioned for Louis and Jim to move aside. The guards looked questioningly at the president, and he nodded, striding forward himself.

The president's gaze locked with X's. The president, who was responsible for the lives of millions of people, confronted X, who was perfectly willing to sacrifice those millions of lives, in order to achieve his goal.

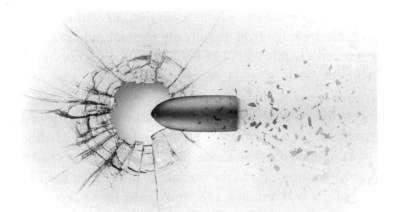

CHAPTER FORTY-SIX

Kiev, Ukraine

Neither man was willing to be the first to drop his gaze. Eventually, X broke the impasse. Extending his hand, he said, "Welcome, Mr. President," in a voice that oozed with triumphant glee. "I'm so happy to finally be meeting with you. We have invested a huge amount of time and resources so that this meeting would take place, and I confess that the superlative abilities of your men severely hampered our efforts. Ultimately, however, we prevailed."

The president looked at X with an expression of utter scorn. "Quit the flattery and get to the point. You're holding your gun in your hand. What are you waiting for?"

"Hasn't Eyal told you about my plan?" X asked, clearly surprised. "I thought he made it clear that your demise will be anything but immediate."

"X?" a voice called out from the radio.

"Yes, Ahmed."

"I've captured Eyal." Ahmed's tone of voice was one of smug satisfaction. "I'm taking him to the dining room."

X raised his eyebrows and shook his head in confusion. To the best of his knowledge Eyal had already been taken hostage, which made Ahmed's words seem like nonsense. "I'm on my way down now with the president and three of his guards. I think we're going to have a very interesting meeting."

It was clear to Eyal, listening to the exchange with foreboding, that neither of them knew that the hostages had escaped. Although they had undoubtedly been shot at as they fled, the shots had probably gone unnoticed, given the firefight that had then been raging on the roof. He was certain that X would react to the developments with rage; the question was what he would do as a result.

Ahmed opened the doors to the dining room and froze. Ten seconds, twenty, and still he stood frozen in place. Finally, he turned toward Eyal, who was standing just ahead of him, Ahmed's gun wedged into his back. "Where are the hostages?" he roared.

Eyal shrugged. 'I have no idea," he said quietly. The tiniest spark of merriment danced in his eyes.

"They escaped," Ahmed cried in disbelief.

"Certainly looks that way," Eyal said with assumed nonchalance. Out of the corner of his eye he saw the bodies of Danny and Robby, still unconscious – or maybe dead – lying in a corner. Abandoning men was never good, but sometimes it was unavoidable.

"And no doubt you are the one responsible for that." Ahmed was fairly seething with rage, and he was barely able to control himself. If not for his fear of X's retribution he would have shot the man on the spot.

"As it happens, you're correct in your assumption." A smile spread over Eyal's features. "But of course, that doesn't mean that I know where they are right now; although I assume that they are still somewhere in Kiev. I'm also assuming that they're smart enough not to tell anyone about what's taking place at the hotel, as they are well aware of the possible ramifications of their tale-telling."

"You...you..."Ahmed was incoherent in his fury. "Sit down," he said finally, pushing Eyal into a nearby chair. Eyal sank down, and Ahmed surveyed the area. "Where's Bruce? And Stefan? And Jibril?"

"Why don't you look for them?" Eyal suggested.

Ahmed brandished his gun. "Do you think X will just allow this to pass quietly?"

"Actually, I don't think anything of the sort." Eyal was still smiling, forcing his fears to the back of his mind. "I'm pretty certain that he won't."

Ahmed approached him and bent down so that his face was parallel to Eyal's. "You are going to pay for this. You and your child." He pulled out a plastic cable. "You're going to wish you were never born."

"You can tie me up – no problem – but try to think logically. If I had wanted to escape, I would have done so when the opportunity arose. I stayed around for a reason, and that reason is still keeping me here, doing much more than any plastic ties can achieve."

"I don't like your logic." Ahmed said. He bound Eyal's hands and feet to the chair. "I prefer to adopt my own way of thinking." With that, he left the room, heading to the floor above. Not for him the task of reporting to X on what had transpired...

Eyal looked around, his gaze completely sober. X would not give up the chance for a seething revenge, that much was clear. His only hope was that with the president in his hands he would be somewhat more inclined to a measured reaction. But there was no guarantee.

❧

"Yonatan?" Bentzy's voice rang out of the two-way radio. "We've located him."

Eyal had been correct about X's next move. Someone had left the hotel in an armored jeep, driven to the safe house that had been identified a few days earlier, and entered the enclosure. A garage door opened to admit the car and then closed behind it. Ten minutes later, the door opened once more and the car drove out, left the enclosure, and set off again. Although he was too far away to know for certain, it was safe to assume that the driver now had human cargo – Elitzafun.

"Are you sure it's them?"

"As sure as anyone can be. But we're going to have to lay a trap for him – or them – because they're sure to be armed to the gills. How far away are our boys?"

Yonatan quickly checked the locations. "Fifteen to thirty minutes," he said.

Bentzy frowned. "I hope they get there in time," he said. "And I'm going to be there too."

"Then I'll meet you," Yonatan said. He quickly looked around, trying to figure out which vehicle to take.

"Tell me where you are and I'll pick you up," Bentzy suggested. "We don't need a fancy car to advertise our presence. Just something serviceable."

"Okay, no problem. I'll be ready. Get here as fast as you can."

As Eyal had hoped, X's rage was somewhat tempered by the fact that he had secured his prime target – the president himself.

"I see," was all he said as he confronted his one remaining hostage – Eyal himself. Meanwhile, his men busied themselves restraining the American guards they had overpowered on the roof, along with the three who had accompanied the president. "I take it that this is your doing," he added, glancing briefly in Eyal's direction.

"Right."

"And where is Jibril? Bruce? Stefan?"

Eyal was impressed that X kept such close tabs on his men. "You might want to check in the kitchen," he said.

A few moments later X returned, not visibly affected by the sight of three of his men killed. "Who triggered that bomb?" he wanted to know.

"I did. But your man was responsible. In fact, he ordered me to detonate it."

"You...?" X stopped and looked at Eyal. The man's clothing was ripped in places and stained with dried blood. The wound in his head looked unpleasant if not serious, and the expression in his eyes was grave. By contrast, X was almost merry in his manner. He had achieved most of his goals, albeit at the cost of the lives of several of his operatives. But he had expected that, and like any terrorist, he had little regard for the individual. Sacrifice was the name of the game.

He could afford to be forgiving when total victory was so close.

"Yes." Eyal looked at the three men who were now sitting beside the president. Their hands were bound and their faces were pale. "What are your plans now?" he asked.

"If you're referring to my remaining hostages...I haven't entirely made up my mind," X replied. "Most likely I will simply dispose of them, unless I can think of something useful to do with them."

Eyal narrowed his eyes. "And the president?" he asked. The president seemed relatively calm, unlike his men. Perhaps he had come to terms with the prospect of his imminent death, or perhaps he was still holding out hope that he would be ransomed with negotiations. Certainly he must have known of the long-standing US policy ruling out negotiating with terrorists, but exceptions to the rule were not illegal. Eyal wondered if the rules would be changed when it was the life of the president himself hanging in the balance.

"The president still has a brief but vital role to play."

Eyal looked at X and realized that the time for secrecy was past. The end was in sight – there was no more need for concealment.

"Brief?" he questioned.

"Very brief. Thirty minutes to an hour." X smiled at the president, and the older man returned the look with a cool, proud gaze.

Eyal spoke slowly, his hatred evident in his voice. "You told me you were going to take him to Syria. I don't think you can reach Damascus in an hour, or even two."

"Oh, that? Well, I'm sorry to say that I have altered my plans." Not an ounce of apology was present in X's playful tone. "It turns out that I'm going to need the president for something else entirely. Something that won't take long at all."

"And then?" Eyal asked.

"And then we will leave the hotel via helicopter while everyone still inside will go up in smoke, together with the building," X said, smiling. "But don't worry, Eyal. I won't be leaving you behind. You are still useful to me, for various reasons. My mission is not yet complete, and I need to return home safe and sound."

"You're seriously expecting me to help you escape?" The bile rose in Eyal's throat. X was about to murder his team, and then he would coerce Eyal to cover his men's tracks. Oh, the price he was being forced to pay for his child's life…

"Of course." X was thoroughly enjoying himself. "Because your son's life is still of value to you, isn't it?"

"There are certain boundaries that I will not cross," Eyal said quietly. There was a dangerous glint in his eyes. "And it makes no difference what the price for that might be."

Guy put his cell phone down thoughtfully and entered the living room. Yariv and Ofer were listlessly playing a game of chess like two bored souls at the table. Chess it was, as there was nothing else to do, and playing the waiting game was even worse. By now they had been in Ukraine for three days and were still awaiting fresh orders from Bentzy.

"There's news," Guy said flatly.

"News! Finally!" Yariv said, looking expectantly toward Guy. "Where are we being sent this time? Berlin? Hawaii?"

"You wish." Guy went over to the wall, removed a painting, and opened the safe that was now exposed. "We have a rendezvous in ten minutes' time in a street off the E95 on the other side of the river. It's fifteen minutes away, and that means we're five minutes late. Time to get ready and go, guys."

Yariv and Ofer jumped to their feet without a moment's hesitation. They'd find out later what it was all about. For now, time was of the essence.

"Take these," Guy said, handing each of them a couple of guns, spare cartridges, and silencers from the safe. "Gear up and head outside."

"Who's directing this mission?" Yariv called out after Guy as Guy disappeared into one of the bedrooms.

Guy removed two rifles from a closet and returned to the dining room. Yariv and Ofer were already waiting for him at the entrance to the apartment. "Eyal is," Guy said, opening the front door. "Take these too."

"I forgot my license in the apartment," Ofer said. He was sitting up front next to Guy, who was driving, while Yariv was sitting tensely in the back seat. "So you won't drive, because if we get into trouble with the traffic cops, this story will not end well."

"I have my license with me," Guy said absentmindedly, his eyes on the road. Fortunately, at this hour the road was virtually empty. "We don't have time to get into trouble, so if either of you sees any traffic cops, you'll shoot out their tires."

They drove on in silence for several more minutes until finally

Yariv spoke. "Aside from the fact that we're supposed to magically find this boy and rescue him, do you know any other details?"

"No. All I was told is that Bentzy needs backup. And since we have no idea who the enemy is, we'd better gear up for a serious battle." They crossed the river, and Guy peered into the darkness. "The turn should be right here...yes. Got it. Ofer, call Bentzy and tell him that we'll be arriving in forty seconds. Ask him for an update. Or maybe he simply wants us to stand around and snap pictures of the scenery?"

Ofer whipped out his cell phone, but Yariv stopped him. "Wait. There's a car coming now. Maybe it's Bentzy."

Ofer turned around in his seat and saw the headlights. It was a huge car, something like a jeep. "Guy, stop," he called.

Guy killed the motor and the three of them jumped out.

"He got here quickly," Yariv said. They started to make their way toward the approaching vehicle, which slowed at it neared them. The car's windows were tinted, and that, combined with the evening's gloom, made it impossible to see who was inside.

Three men shot out of the jeep.

It took the three Mossad agents a fraction of a second to draw their weapons and open fire.

But sometimes even a fraction of a second is too much.

Bullets spewed out of rifles and submachine guns. Yariv was the first to be hit, and he instantly switched to hand-to-hand combat, letting his gun drop to the floor as blood trickled down his arm. He had the advantage of Mossad training, and his superior skills were evident as he tackled his adversary and brought him down. Within seconds the man's head slumped onto the hard tarmac of the road.

Meanwhile, Guy's third cartridge had jammed, and he quickly tackled his opponent, wrapping his hands around the man's neck and squeezing with his thumbs.

The third man was thrown off balance after seeing his friend killed, and all it took was two bullets from Ofer's rifle, and he collapsed on the ground.

The sound of an approaching vehicle caused Guy to lose focus for a moment, and he loosened his grip on his enemy's neck. Immediately the man utilized the opportunity to free himself of his grip and to kick out Guy's feet from under him, sending him sprawling to the ground. Ofer turned to come to his rescue, but it was too late. The man had already drawn a second gun from a holster in his belt and he shot three times, twice at Guy and once at Yariv.

Guy fell in a pool of blood, and Ofer shot the man a second later.

One second too late.

Only then did the car carrying Bentzy and Yonatan arrive on the scene.

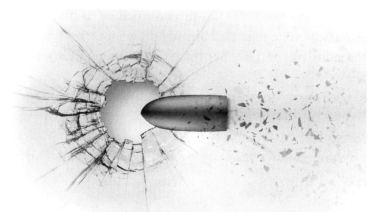

CHAPTER FORTY-SEVEN

Kiev, Ukraine

"W e have yet to see about your boundaries," X said coolly, looking at his watch as he spoke. "According to my
estimation, my men should be arriving here with your
son within half an hour. That should make it easier to find out
exactly which boundaries you won't cross and when."

"X, if your plans are to murder these men, then I will not cooperate with you." Eyal attempted to control the trembling note of
fury in his voice. "I refuse to be a partner to homicide, and that is
final, with no conditions attached."

X laughed. "Maybe I forgot to tell you this before, dear Eyal,
but I have a rule about people who say no to any of my orders. If
they want their words to be taken seriously, they have to give me a
better idea. So, let's hear yours."

"No problem. There are plenty of things you can do instead. For instance, you can leave everyone here, still bound, together with an explosive device attached to a timer. Once you're safely away from the area, you'll call the police and have them neutralize the bomb and free the men."

X shook his head. "Too complicated. And I have no intention of getting the police involved. If they manage to track me...no. Forget it. A few bullets will easily resolve the problem with no risk to myself."

"It won't solve the problem of my refusal to cooperate with you," Eyal said.

"We have yet to see about that," X said cryptically, turning toward his men. "Leave the hostages here for now. We need to go back up to the helipad to prepare the helicopters for our departure. Who was in charge of the motors? Jamal? Take whoever you need and get to work. And where's Ahmed?" At that moment the man reappeared. "Good. You'll stay here on guard. I need someone trigger-happy. Don't hesitate to shoot anyone at the slightest suspicion."

Ofer ran over to Guy and placed two fingers on his neck, feeling for a pulse. There was none, and the briefest of examinations revealed that Guy had been shot in the head.

No one said a word. No matter how many times it happened, one never acclimated to losing a friend in battle. Bentzy shook himself and turned to Yariv, who was bleeding profusely from two separate wounds and needed treatment urgently. As for the men from the jeep, they were beyond needing anything.

Yonatan bent down over Yariv and tried to stop the blood flow. Bentzy and Ofer watched with wretched helplessness.

"Too bad he was injured and not me," Ofer murmured. "He's the combat medic."

"Quiet," Yonatan said shortly. He groped around to try to locate the bullet in Yariv's body. "It looks like the bullet is pressing against an artery," he said. "I'm going to have to remove it. Bentzy, give him CPR in the meantime."

Bentzy bent down and did as he was told, overcoming his frustration at having to postpone their mission. Of course there was no choice. Saving Yariv's life had to take precedence. Meanwhile, Yonatan ripped a shirt off one of the corpses and handed it to Ofer. "There's an entry and exit wound on his arm, which means that there's no bullet to remove there. But I need you to use this as a tourniquet."

Yonatan bent down again, and his fingers groped around Yariv's chest, but he was unable to extract the bullet lodged there, and he knew that if he didn't succeed in doing so, they were likely to lose him.

"He needs a hospital," Ofer whispered, hands working at top speed to apply the tourniquet to Yariv's arm.

"Really?" Yonatan said. "And here I was thinking he needed a private yacht."

"He's losing his vitals," Bentzy said. "He isn't breathing."

Yonatan stopped feeling around for the bullet and began CPR with Bentzy continuing to breathe for Yariv.

Ofer finished with the tourniquet and straightened up, watching the other two agents still working on his friend. "You can't give up on him!"

Yonatan and Bentzy didn't reply.

"Is there a heartbeat?" Ofer pleaded.

"It's very slow," Bentzy said. "And it's fading."

"How did the hostages get away, Eyal?" The president's voice was low and hoarse. Ahmed was sitting nearby, smoking a cigarette and smiling at the wall. He turned toward the president when he heard his voice, but he made no objection to his speaking.

"I attached a bomb to the kitchen wall," Eyal said quietly. "I was forced to do it, but I guessed that I would be able to play it to my advantage, and I was proven right. The explosion blasted through the outside wall, which turned out to be their escape route."

"What about injuries?" The president's expression was one of concern.

"We had to leave two men behind," Eyal admitted. "They weren't conscious. I don't think they've recovered. They're actually over on the other side of the room." He shook his head. "There was no way they could take them with."

The president licked his dry lips. "And how many others were killed?"

"I still don't know." Eyal had no way of knowing if all of the hostages had managed to escape. They had certainly been shot at.

"Why didn't you escape together with them?"

Eyal's lips curved upward in a slow smile. "I committed to protecting you, Mr. President, and that's what I resolved to do." He paused for a moment, waiting for his voice to grow steady again. "And I admit that there's another factor involved. X's men are holding my son as collateral."

Yonatan continued his determined efforts at CPR, with Bentzy assisting as best he could, but Yariv's color was fading and the bleeding from his chest wound showed no sign of abating.

"Why aren't you doing anything?" Ofer burst out.

"We are," Yonatan said, sounding dejected. "Ofer, go to the car and look for tweezers, or something similar, in the trunk or the glove compartment. Maybe I'll still find a way to remove that bullet."

Ofer raced toward Bentzy's car, relieved to be able to do something, anything. He started to root through the contents of the trunk and then inside the car, but there was absolutely nothing there of use. His desperation mounting, he ran over to the terrorists' car, pulling open the door with all his might.

Then he froze.

Lying calmly on the back seat of the car, with eyes closed and an angelic look on his face, was Elitzafun Gilboa.

The large dining room was silent. Ahmed got up from time to time to wander around the room and check on the hostages, most of whom were too exhausted and dejected to even make an attempt at conversation. The president had sunk into deep thought, his eyes half-closed. To all appearances, Eyal, too, was in no state to do anything more than rest and recuperate. But hidden behind the inscrutable expression on his face was a mind that was churning, impatient, desperate to take action, however impossible it might be.

Eyal knew that the best time to act was before Elitzafun arrived at the scene. There was no way of knowing what would happen once his son was brought into the hotel. He hoped and prayed that Bentzy had somehow intercepted the car, but he couldn't count on that happening.

He needed to make a distraction to get rid of Ahmed. He needed answers and information from Eli, and he needed to know what had happened to Elitzafun.

A voice cackled out from the radio. "Ahmed?"

"Yes."

"Bring the president upstairs to the helipad. Thank you," X said, impeccably mannered as usual.

Ahmed's eyes flickered momentarily in hesitation. "Who will guard the hostages in the meantime?"

"Leave them," X said. "They're tied up, and this will be quick."

Ahmed walked over to the president and cut the cables around his hands and feet. "Get up, and don't try anything," he barked, shoving his gun into the president's back. Turning to Eyal, he added, "You'd better watch yourself too. You remember where your son is, don't you?"

"Ask X what he plans to do with the president," Eyal said.

Ahmed feigned surprise. "Has X signed some sort of contract with you in which he's undertaken to answer all of your questions?"

Eyal stared at Ahmed, trying to convey fearless resolve. "I want you to remind X that he promised not to kill the president. His plan, as you may be aware, was to have him kidnapped and later returned home safely."

"So now you're devastated because X has betrayed your trust. Would you like me to invite a psychologist down here so you can unburden yourself to him?"

"No." Eyal had Ahmed's complete attention, which was exactly what he wanted. "But if the president is about to be murdered, then I believe he needs to know that, so that he can defend himself. Because sometimes a person needs to take a weapon into his own hand."

Ahmed stared at Eyal, visibly confused. *Keep on looking; don't look away*, Eyal prayed.

"What are you trying to say?" Ahmed said. "That the president—"

An earsplitting shot.

Ahmed's face contorted with shock as he slumped to the floor, eyes glassing over almost immediately. The president's hand trembled as the gun that he was holding continued to smoke.

Eyal looked calmly at the president and nodded in approval. "Thank you," he said simply.

"You were talking to me and distracting Ahmed." The president was still shuddering from his experience, even as he did his utmost to regain a serene expression of authority.

"You were the only one with his hands free, Mr. President," Eyal said apologetically. "Forgive me."

"There's nothing to forgive you for. We have the same goal." The president walked over to Eyal's chair and cut open the cables around his hands and feet using a dinner knife from one of the tables, aided by a plier from Eyal's pocket.

With a tiny smile on his face, Eyal thought back to all the various people who had gone through exactly the same motions with him during the past few weeks.

Eyal bent down over Ahmed's body and took his cell phone. "The important thing right now is that the frequency jammer that was used earlier is no longer operative; it hasn't worked for a while now. X is in constant contact with his men. He must think that there's no longer a danger of anyone contacting the police."

"You're going to call the police?" the president called out in horror. "He said he'd kill anyone who—"

"I wouldn't dream of such a thing," Eyal said quickly, dialing a number even as he spoke. "I'm calling Eli."

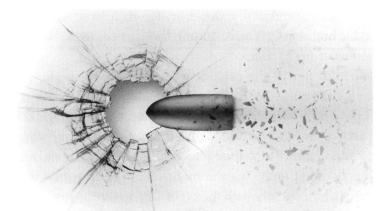

CHAPTER FORTY-EIGHT

Kiev, Ukraine

Chevreh," Ofer's voice sounded strange even to his own ears, so shocked was he at his discovery. "I think I've found what you're looking for."

"His pulse has stabilized!" Bentzy exclaimed suddenly. "What was that, Ofer? Yonatan, don't stop. He still needs support."

"I think I've found what you're looking for," Ofer said again, louder this time.

Yonatan lifted his head. "That's great. Bring me the tweezers."

"No," Ofer said, "not that. I found...I found Eyal's son. I found Elitzafun! He's asleep in the terrorists' car."

"What?!" Bentzy jumped up in disbelief and forced his trembling legs to take him over to the car as his heart pumped wildly in his chest. He pushed Ofer aside and stared wide-eyed at the boy, lying there as peacefully as if he had been at home and tucked in bed.

In fact the boy was so still, so motionless, that Bentzy placed a hesitant two fingers on his neck.

"He's alive, no doubt about it," Ofer said, struggling to overcome his emotions. "You're getting too carried away," he added, conscious of his hypocrisy.

"No, I'm not! I just can't believe it...how can he have slept through everything that happened here, all the noise and—"

"Look, he's obviously breathing. It doesn't take much skill to see that." Ofer left him and went around to the trunk, where he found a toolbox. "These little pliers can serve as tweezers, right?"

Bentzy didn't reply. Instead he lifted Elitzafun with one hand and stroked him gently with the other. Tears were streaming down his cheeks and he made no attempt to stop them.

Ofer understood him. To Ofer, Eyal was simply a name and a legend. To Bentzy, however, he was a friend – Bentzy knew the whole family. He walked away, giving Bentzy the space and privacy that he needed, and went back over to Yonatan. "Will this pliers do?"

"I think so." Yonatan bent over Yariv's body, groping around to feel the right place. When he found it, he inserted the pliers and, working quickly, managed to extract the bullet. Yariv's body trembled, but the blood stopped spurting out. Yonatan wiped the sweat from his face and looked at Ofer. "He'll need a blood transfusion and surgery in a hospital as soon as we can get him there, but he's going to be okay."

Ofer nodded, his feelings of anxiety and relief battling one another.

Yonatan stood up and headed toward the car. Bentzy was shaking Elitzafun's shoulders with force, having tried only a moment earlier to rouse him gently.

The boy had yet to respond.

"He's been sedated." Yonatan said.

Bentzy nodded. "Whatever he was given is actually working in our favor, because who knows what the psychological repercussions would have been had this child seen what just took place here."

"We need to hurry," Bentzy continued. "Ofer," he addressed him, "you're going to drive Yariv to the hospital in your car while Yonatan and I head to the hotel, to do what we can for Eyal."

"What about Guy?" Ofer said, the pain in his voice evident as he pronounced the name of his slain friend.

"We're going to have to leave him here and return when we're finished." Bentzy said, swallowing with difficulty.

"Are you crazy?" Ofer cried. "I'm not leaving him here."

"I'm sorry. There's no choice. I can't take him where I'm going, and if you leave him unattended in the car while you're in the hospital with Yariv, things could get very complicated. There's no time to lose, so please, don't argue about this, okay?"

Ofer nodded, though his eyes betrayed his feelings. Yonatan helped him move Yariv into the back seat of his car, and then they set off to the hospital.

Meanwhile Bentzy made a quick check of the jeep, just in case it had been booby-trapped with explosives. He found nothing, and by the time he was done, Yonatan was ready to leave. He climbed into the passenger seat, and Yonatan started the engine. They needed to reach Eyal quickly. With everything that had just transpired, time was not working in their favor.

"Eli." Eyal spoke quickly into the cell phone. "Do you have answers for me?"

Eli's deliberate voice was a marked contrast to Eyal's rapid-fire speech. "Bentzy has located your son, and I'm hoping he'll call with good news very soon."

A thin ray of hope pierced Eyal's heart. Once Elitzafun was

released, Eyal would be able to concentrate all of his energy on escaping together with the president and the rest of the hostages. "Use this number to keep me updated, okay?"

"Of course." Eli ended the call, and Eyal turned around to face the president. They didn't have much time, but this was urgent. If the president could help him piece together some of the many factors of the puzzle, the information that came to light might prove of crucial importance.

"Mr. President," Eyal said, his expression grave. "There's something I need to ask you."

"Of course."

"How much do you trust Paul?"

The president recoiled in shock. "He's the deputy director of the CIA. What are you trying to imply?"

"That doesn't answer my question." Eyal sighed. "I'm not trying to *imply* anything. I'll just tell you straight, that if I'm reading the signs correctly, he's the one who led you directly into this trap."

"The City Clinic emergency room is situated at 3 Bratislavka Street." Ofer was driving as fast as he could through the unfamiliar streets, guided only by Google Maps. "It says it will take me over an hour. I hope Yariv can wait that long." He cast a worried glance in the rearview mirror. Yariv's breathing was raspy but regular, and his eyelids fluttered occasionally.

Bentzy nodded, forgetting that Ofer couldn't see him. Most of the drive had been spent in the same cool silence. With the memory of Guy's death at the forefront of their minds, neither Bentzy nor Yonatan felt like talking. "Speed up, Yonatan. I don't know what we're going to find when we get there, but the sooner we know, the better."

"I think we've made a mistake," Yonatan said. "We shouldn't

have taken Elitzafun with us. Ofer, how far away from us are you?"

"Pretty far."

"I want you to come back and take Elitzafun with you to the hospital. It won't hurt to have him checked out too; and it's better than taking him to the hotel."

Ofer balked. "I can't," he said flatly. "It will waste almost an hour, and I can't take the chance with Yariv. He's lost so much blood – you know it yourself! Why are you suggesting such a thing?"

Bentzy grew thoughtful. "Fine," he said. "I mean, it's obviously not fine, but we really have no choice, because Yariv needs to reach the hospital fast. Yonatan, you'll stay in the car to watch Elitzafun while I approach the hotel. We're close now – I think it's about a ten-minute walk from here. Then I'll just have to find Eyal somehow, if that will seem possible. If I can get in, maybe I can do something. And if I can't, then we get out of here fast, with Elitzafun."

"Bentzy?" A thin voice from the back seat had both Bentzy and Yonatan spinning their heads around in shock. Elitzafun was awake, and it took Yonatan a full three seconds to turn back to watch the road – in another moment he would have lost control of the vehicle.

"Elitzafun," Bentzy said. "Wh..how are you?"

Elitzafun ignored the question. "Are you taking me to my father?"

Bentzy glanced sideways at Yonatan, who kept his eyes on the road. Yonatan shook his head, very slightly, but unmistakably. The boy was too young to be told the truth.

"No," Bentzy said. He was more than accustomed to lying whenever necessary, but for some reason he felt a pang of guilt at lying to this five-year-old boy. "First I have to have an important meeting with someone, and we'll take you to your father after that. In the meantime, Yonatan will take care of you. Okay, *motek*?"

"I'm not a *motek*," Elitzafun said, pouting. "And you *are* going to my father! You just said so. You said you have to find Eyal, and that's my father."

"Ah, well…you're right, I guess. But first I have to have this meeting, like I just said."

"But I want to see my father right now!"

"Soon, Elitzafun, okay? First I need to go to this meeting, and then I'll take you to your father. All right?"

Elitzafun shook his head, but Bentzy's attention was rerouted to the sound of a ringing cell phone.

Yonatan answered. "You continue on to the hospital," he told Ofer. "We're almost at the hotel now. Bentzy's going in, and I'm staying here with the boy." Yonatan parked the car in a narrow side street, and Bentzy shot out while Yonatan's gaze followed him anxiously. "Bentzy, make this as quick as possible," he called after him.

"What do you take me for?" Bentzy called back. "Just take care of the kid, okay?"

But Yonatan failed at his mission. Because despite the expression of sweet innocence on his face, Elitzafun was an obstinate five-year-old. While Yonatan was speaking to Ofer, keeping tabs on his progress through the streets of Kiev, Elitzafun opened the car door and slipped quietly out.

The president looked at Eyal. "Are you sure of this?" he asked. "You have to have some kind of evidence before you make such far-reaching allegations."

Eyal was silent for a moment. "To be honest, it's hard to be sure about this – or anything else related to this operation, for that matter – but from what it seems, six CIA agents betrayed you, here in Kiev, when they opened the gates of the hotel to X's men. It's illogical to conclude that all six of them became turncoats at the same time. It makes more sense to assume that their handler knew that they were traitors and therefore selected them for this mission."

"Tell me more." The president's face was ashen.

Eyal wondered how much more he could say before the president fell apart, but he quickly rationalized that the president was not a child and that he would be able to handle the questions that arose. "Earlier today, when I was in the parking lot, I took a look at some of the bombs placed by X's men."

"Go on," the president said.

"They were assembled using the same methods as those the United States Army used during battles fought in Afghanistan."

"And therefore?"

"And therefore, it seems to me that X and his men are not foreign terrorists, Mr. President. They are Americans, and traitors. Despite their talk of Syria, I don't know where their loyalties really lie."

The president, unlike Eyal, was unable to conceal his fury. The veins on his forehead bulged and his lips trembled with barely suppressed rage. "That's impossible."

"No, not impossible. Maybe improbable, but many things in life are. And there's another thing. One of their dead, a man called Stefan...his body is actually still in the kitchen. You can see for yourself. He has a Navy SEAL tattoo on his arm. That seems to suggest that at some point he was a fighter in Special Ops."

The president shook his head, more in disbelief than denial. "This is a big mess that needs sorting out," he murmured.

"Right, and I don't know who you'll find to do that sorting," Eyal remarked. "Looks like there are some crooked big guns somewhere who will be only too eager to stymy your attempts to drain this particular swamp." He was about to add something, but then stopped – but the president noticed his hesitation.

"What were you about to say, Eyal?"

"You're not going to like it," Eyal said slowly.

"I don't like anything about the situation I'm in, but I still want you to tell me."

"X and his men haven't come here to kidnap you. If I'm reading the signs correctly, they've come here to take care of a targeted killing."

"Me?"

Eyal drew his eyebrows together and an almost imperceptible sigh was all the confirmation that the president needed.

"Why? Who sent them?"

"I have no idea."

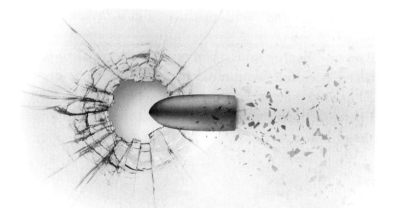

CHAPTER FORTY-NINE

Kiev, Ukraine

H ow far do you think you— wait…Ofer! The boy's gone!"
Yonatan almost dropped his phone in shock. "He's
gone!"

"You can't be serious," Ofer said. "Where could he go?" But
Yonatan had already ended the call and was frantically dialing
Bentzy.

"Bentzy, you won't believe this, but Elitzafun…he's gone,"
Yonatan stammered. "He just disappeared. The door's open. I
can't believe this…"

"What?" Bentzy stopped mid-stride, gazing around him in a
panic. "Gone? Where? How? What were you – asleep? What's
wrong with you, man?"

Yonatan was silent.

"Go and look for him!" Bentzy screamed, and then dropped his voice quickly. "Are you crazy? Out of your mind? Do something!"

"He could have gone in any direction," Yonatan said, trying to clear his head and think logically. "But it makes most sense that—"

"Exactly," Bentzy said. "You're right. No need to look. He must have been following me. I can see him in the distance. I circled around the perimeter of the hotel grounds looking for a good place to enter, but he just headed straight for the gates... and they're wide open..."

The president exhaled deeply, and his pallor turned from gray to white. "Okay, Eyal. What exactly do you suggest now?" Both of them knew that time was running out. Within the next few minutes X would realize that Ahmed wasn't appearing with the president, and he would send someone down to see what was going on when his calls over the radio went unanswered.

"All I can suggest – and it's really the only realistic option – is that you try to escape via the same route the hostages took earlier. It's going to be chaotic, and they will almost certainly fire on you. Are you ready to face that?"

"I'm ready for whatever is necessary." The president's voice was firm, but his eyes betrayed his fear. In theory, someone in his position had to be mentally prepared for such eventualities, but in practice, nothing could ever prepare a person for the reality of a life-or-death scenario.

"Your men will do whatever they can to protect you. The question is whether that will be enough. And there might be some bad apples in the barrel. I can't promise you that all of your men are truly loyal to you. But I think they are."

The president seemed to be in a state of shock, but he still struggled to focus on the salient points. And one of them was extremely salient for Eyal: "Tell me, Eyal," the president said. "What will happen to your son if I succeed in escaping?"

Now it was Eyal's turn to turn pale. This was the question that had given him no rest from the moment he learned of his son's abduction. Looking straight into the president's eyes, he said slowly, "I don't know."

"But you can guess, right?"

"Yes, I can." Eyal's voice cracked as his demeanor changed from brave soldier to brokenhearted father.

"I won't do it," the president said, sitting firmly back down on his chair.

"What?" By now, the remainder of the hostages had gathered around them and were listening in rapt attention. "You won't do it?"

"No. I won't do it. I will not sell my soul for the life of a young child." The president looked from one man to the next, almost as if he were bidding them farewell. "I will not attempt to escape on such terms, Eyal. Just as you didn't make any attempt to escape earlier even though you could easily have done so. I would be a coward, and worse, if I abandoned a sinking ship before rescuing a five-year-old child."

Eyal fell silent. He knew that the president was right. If he escaped, X would undoubtedly murder Elitzafun. Only his son stood between the president and his men.

The president looked at him, silent determination in his eyes.

"When X brings your son here, take him and leave," he said quietly. "I have already lived my life for seventy years, but your son is only five. I've lived out my dreams, while your son hasn't yet begun to dream. You, and only you, can make your way back to the United States and tell reliable, patriotic men what you told me earlier, and make sure that the right steps are taken. In fact, your life is more crucial than that of the president right now, and the information in your head is more important than whatever I have in mine." He laughed, but a tear spilled out of his eye at the same time.

The clock in the dining room ticked on in its ceaseless, monotonous rhythm. The president looked at Eyal again, eyes full of humanity along with unshed tears.

"Go, Eyal," he said softly. "Save yourself and your son."

Eyal didn't move.

"Go." The man raised his voice. "Do not turn this into an unnecessary drama. Go in peace, Eyal, and tell my citizens that I loved them." He looked around at the hostages in the room and said. "You're all free to go."

The men looked at the president, their expressions reflecting their lack of comprehension.

"Go. There's no reason for you to die, and X will be here in another minute."

"We will fight him, Mr. President," Louis said. "Eyal has to escape somehow, because he's the one who needs to pass on the information you just mentioned, but we will stay here to fight for you. We have a few submachine guns, and if we have time we can devise some explosives from the substances at hand. We won't give up without a fight."

Eyal got up, relieved the dead Ahmed of his gun, and handed it to Louis. The man took the weapon and saluted. "Go, General," he said. "Go and save America."

Eyal responded with a weak salute of his own, and headed toward the door of the kitchen. Blinded by the tears in his eyes, he stumbled on his way there.

"Eyal!" The president's voice was laced with rebuke.

Eyal turned around.

"Don't turn into a spineless wimp just because I sacrificed my life for your son. Fight, and be the man who you are! Do not surrender! I am sending you instead of me so that you emerge victorious from a battle that I cannot win. Do not disappoint me."

Eyal nodded, swiping at his eyes as he left through the open door.

The president, of sound mind, chose to surrender his own life.

"X, look at this." Teddy, standing on the helipad on the roof, handed the binoculars to his commander. "You're not going to believe it."

X looked into the binoculars and saw a small form running down the long, wide path leading up to the hotel. "What is the meaning of this?!" he thundered.

"I don't know! But I'm sure we both agree that something has to be done about it."

X turned to Leon, who was already in the pilot's seat of the first helicopter. "Get everything ready for takeoff within ten minutes. We need to finish matters up down there and then get away from here as quickly as possible."

Then he and Teddy raced down the stairs and into the hotel courtyard.

Eyal emerged from of the breach in the kitchen wall at exactly the same moment.

In front of him, just yards away, he saw the child for whom he had been yearning, praying, and battling, running toward the entrance of the hotel. Simultaneously, he heard the voices of X and Teddy as they approached. The two terrorists raised their weapons and aimed directly at the boy, and Eyal stopped in his tracks, his gaze flitting back and forth between Elitzafun and his two captors. Then he began racing toward his son, but Teddy was faster than him, blocking him with his body.

"Stop right there," Teddy shouted. "Don't move!"

"Elitzafun!" Eyal shouted, tears flowing from his eyes. "Elitzafun!!"

The boy stopped running, trying to figure out where the voice was coming from. He looked first to the right and then to the left, and it was clear that he wanted to continue to run. Again Eyal shouted, louder this time: "Elitzafun!"

Finally, Elitzafun saw him, and his face shone with a huge smile. He started running again, toward his father, who wanted more than anything else in the world to embrace him – if it hadn't been for the small matter of X, who now spun around and aimed directly at him.

"Let me pick him up," Eyal pleaded, but X shook his head.

"He'll wait," X said. "We haven't finished up here yet."

"Just for a minute, no more than that."

"No."

By then Elitzafun had realized that something was wrong, and he stopped running again and stared from one man to the other, his face a mask of confusion – just as someone else came running up from behind, panting and terrified.

Bentzy.

X was literally trembling with anger. His men had never seen such a potentially lethal and animalistic expression on his face before. He took two steps toward Elitzafun and grabbed hold of him with one hand. His other hand – his right hand – raised his gun and held it to the child's head.

"You breached our agreement." X's finger was on the trigger. "You killed my men and released my hostages. Instead of quietly handing the president over to me as we agreed, you brought your men into the hotel, and now you expect me to keep to my end of the agreement?"

Bentzy stood frozen in fear, his eyes flitting between X and Eyal. But he didn't dare to look Eyal in the eye. He had been responsible for taking care of Elitzafun, and now the boy was in more danger than ever before. He would never forgive himself if anything happened to Elitzafun, never. And would Eyal forgive him?

"X," Eyal said quietly, gathering every last ounce of emotional energy in order to force the words out of his mouth. "I know who you really are."

X turned toward him. "Oh, you do?"

"Yes, I do. And I sent all of the information about your handler to a friend in Israel just a few hours ago. He has orders to publish it to the web unless he hears from me otherwise, and I imagine your bosses won't be too pleased to find out that you exposed them, to say the least."

"You have no idea who sent me, nor do you know what my goals are."

"Oh, but I do. You aren't a Syrian, as you tried to pretend. You're an American. And you aren't a so-called freedom fighter either. You're simply a hired assassin, directing a group of hired assassins like yourself. If you still don't believe me, I can tell you exactly who your handlers are and describe their motives."

"You don't know a thing. You're bluffing."

"You'd like to believe that, but trust me – you really can't afford to take that risk. As I said, I already passed along my information to a friend back home."

His eyes black with rage, X dropped his gun hand, and his face hardened as he stood in silence, thinking. Without seeming to realize it, he let go of Elitzafun, who instinctively took a step away from him. Then, as though permission had been granted, he ran forward and fell into his father's arms, hugging him tightly.

Eyal bent down and lifted his son to his chest, hugging him with more strength than he knew he possessed.

"Ow," Elitzafun protested. "Stop, Abba. It hurts."

"Really?" Eyal said, his voice choked. "It hurts me a lot more."

"Why?" Elitzafun stared up at Eyal. "Why does it hurt you?"

A similar conversation had taken place just a short week earlier, and Eyal recalled it now. "When you're here, nothing hurts me anymore," he said, correcting himself.

By now X had recovered from his shock. "Get into the building," he barked. "Now!"

Bentzy looked at Eyal and nodded. They had no other choice.

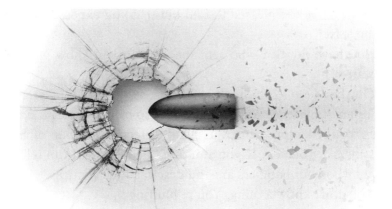

CHAPTER FIFTY

Ben Gurion Airport, Israel

Efrat had arrived with plenty of time to spare before her flight. It made little difference to her whether she paced the floors at home or in the huge airport terminal. She had purchased a ticket the moment she heard from Uri Shabtai that the saga was drawing to a close – a one-way ticket. There was no way of knowing how long she would be in Ukraine – or who would accompany her back home.

Several friends had offered to accompany her, but she had adamantly refused. Now she was glad to have the time to herself, without any perceived need to talk or to keep up appearances. She wandered absentmindedly around the duty-free area, part of her wishing that the time until the flight would pass quickly, another part relishing this space in time that was connected to nothing and no one.

A toy store with its colorful display window pushed its way into her conscious mind. She walked in, gazing at the cheerful, optimist décor, its vibrancy such a contrast to her gray mood. Her legs carried her through the aisles as though of their own volition.

"Can I help you?" A young saleslady approached her with an artificial smile pasted on her face. "Are you looking for a gift for someone in particular?"

Despite her misery, Efrat wasn't about to rudely rebuff the woman's inquiry. "Yes," she said. "I'm looking for a gift for a five-year-old boy."

It was a mistake. She should have realized. The moment she mentioned her son's age her lips began to tremble, and it was only with an incredible amount of self-control that she was able to regain her composure.

"A five-year-old?" The saleslady either wasn't perceptive enough to pick up on her mood, or wasn't looking closely enough. "What sort of toys does he like?"

"He likes lots of toys." The words only emerged with difficulty. If only she could just run away…

"Lego, maybe? Or Playmobil? A board game?" The saleslady rattled off her advice fluently. "Or maybe something that tests his mind, or perhaps something sports related, like baseball or Rollerblades?"

Efrat's eyes welled up with tears. "He likes Playmobil and board games."

"Okay, follow me," the woman said. "These shelves, up here and along the right. Would you like something that you'll play together with him, or would you prefer something that he can play with by himself?"

Would she ever let Elitzafun out of her sight again if he came home? Would she let him play by himself? Unthinkable… she would sit by his side, whatever he was doing, even if he was asleep, just watching, praying, loving. She would never take him for granted again. Even if he grumbled, nagged, or whined. But no one had asked her what she preferred. Not the evil kidnappers, and not the Mossad agents either, even though they were now doing everything they could to rescue him. And if she wanted to be totally clear-eyed, then she could even say that Eyal himself, who was waging a valiant battle in order to return her son to her, hadn't asked her about her preferences either. Where was he now? Was he able to do anything for Elitzafun, or was he engaged in a battle for his own life?

"I...I think I would prefer a game that I can play together with him."

"There are plenty of board games like that. Some of them are just sophisticated versions of the games we grew up with, like Rummikub, Sorry, and Snakes and Ladders. But they're perennial favorites." The saleslady led Efrat over to the newer versions of the games she had just mentioned, and Efrat picked one at random. It was an electronic version of Snakes and Ladders. When the die was cast, little soldiers moved the correct number of spaces, up ladders and down ferocious-looking snakes.

"I'll take this," Efrat said quietly, afraid to raise her voice for fear that she would break down in tears.

"Oh, you picked a great game," the saleslady trilled. "Is it a gift for your son?"

"Yes." Only the briefest answers possible now.

"He will be delighted with it, I promise you."

"I'm sure he will be," Efrat said, her voice leaden.

The saleslady stared at Efrat, and finally she seemed to realize that something was wrong. Not everyone who traveled aboard did so for happy reasons. She stood frozen for a moment before saying: "May he have a *refuah sheleimah*."

"*Amen*," Efrat said, accepting the conclusion the saleslady had drawn. It was a good *brachah*. It covered a lot of things. Gently, the woman wrapped the game in shiny striped paper and tied it with a pretty bow, adding a cute Playmobil keychain to the package without saying anything.

"Thank you." Efrat held the present tight and stroked the wrapping.

The saleslady looked at her strangely. "He'll be okay," she said hesitantly.

Efrat smiled with effort. "*Im yirtzeh Hashem*," she said.

The gift would remain with her. If she didn't end up playing with it together with Elitzafun, then it would serve as a souvenir of her son's life.

X and his men took Eyal, Bentzy, and Elitzafun straight upstairs to the helipad. Eyal thought of the president and his guards, armed and waiting for their showdown with X, which now would probably never come. If only he had been able to get a message to them, letting them know that they could flee – but it was simply impossible.

"Where are we going?"

"You'll see."

"You think you're still going to manipulate me into working for you, I see," Eyal said, his voice level. "What about the president?"

"We're finished with him," X said shortly. The fury was still evident in his eyes, but his manner was cool, even offhand. His mission was nearing its conclusion, and only a fine line separated dizzying success from searing failure.

"You plan to detonate the bombs with the president and his men in the building?" Eyal hoped that he had misunderstood, although he knew that he hadn't.

"You do catch on quickly." A thin, cynical smile.

Eyal drew a deep breath. "Over a dozen men will be killed without reason. You want to kill the president. That's understandable, from your perspective. But why do you need to bring about the deaths of so many others?"

"I didn't ask you to function as my conscience," X said. "Get into the helicopter. Now."

Eyal felt his body freeze. Downstairs, innocent men had mere moments left to their lives, lives that would be wasted due to the gratuitous cruelty of X. He had little or nothing to gain from their demise. And there was nothing Eyal could do to save them.

"How much longer?" he asked quietly.

"What difference does it make to you, or anyone, if it's ten minutes or fifteen?" X looked emphatically at his watch. "It won't be longer than that. But why are you so concerned? Your friend and your son are right here with us."

"Will you never release my son?" Eyal asked. "How long will you continue to use him to blackmail me?"

"Never is such a restrictive word." X said with scorn. "Stop wasting time, Eyal. Get into the helicopter. I will not repeat myself."

Feeling like a wooden soldier, Eyal climbed into the helicopter with Elitzafun in his arms. Bentzy followed close behind, and then X. Leon was already in the pilot's seat, and a moment later Teddy and Omar joined them.

X addressed Leon. "You can take off now. Get up to maximum speed as soon as you can." Then he turned to Teddy. "Bind their hands," he said. "Tightly. I don't want them to try anything."

So, the show's over, Eyal thought. X was no longer trying to impress Elitzafun with his supposed compassion. Now exposed as a common criminal rather than a pseudo-ethical freedom fighter, he had lost his incentive to make a favorable impression.

The helicopter's blades began to whirl. Bentzy fixed Eyal with a questioning look, and Eyal shook his head. He had no plan. Nothing. Only Elitzafun was unaware of the gravity of the situation. Although his hands were bound, he was so overjoyed to be reunited with his father that everything else paled into insignificance.

As the craft began to lift, Eyal stared blankly out the window, watching the doomed hotel building dwindle in the distance.

"You can start counting down now," X said, following Eyal's

gaze. "Ten minutes until detonation. In case you were interested."

"And ten minutes left of your own life," Eyal said casually. "You do appreciate that, don't you?"

X smiled with self-assurance. "Appreciate what?" he said. "You are so fond of exaggeration, Eyal. But this time you've really outdone yourself. You have no idea what you're talking about."

"Oh no? Don't you realize that as soon as the hotel explodes, the Ukrainian and United States' security forces will all be on your back?"

"What do I care about that? By the time they get themselves organized, we'll be across the border."

"X, you disappoint me." Eyal's gaze was scornful. "Are you really such a fool, or are you just pretending to be one? This helicopter belongs to Squadron One, and it will take the Americans less than a minute to locate you. And once they do that, they'll take over the controls and flip us into the river."

"Together with you and you son," X said with a celebratory smile. "Which means that they won't dare to do any such thing. And just in case they aren't aware that you're with me, I'll make sure to notify them."

"You really think that will stop them?" Eyal said. "I'm just insignificant collateral damage when it comes to avenging the murder of their president. And if it's left up to the Ukrainians, I won't even figure in their calculations. In fact, I'm willing to bet that the United States will pass the buck to the Ukrainian government to settle the score and deal with the diplomatic fallout – if there is any."

X was still smiling, but Eyal saw the hesitation in his eyes. His words were hitting their mark.

"You may be right, and you may be wrong," X said. "But as I mentioned earlier, if you shoot down an idea of mine, you have to provide one of your own in its stead. So, what do you suggest?"

"Cancel the detonation of the explosives and gain a few more minutes in which to escape the country."

"Impossible. I've set the timer already, and it can't be canceled. This isn't a sophisticated United States Army toy."

Eyal raised his eyebrows. "That's strange, given that the bombs I had a chance to inspect were all manufactured by Americans. But let's say you're telling the truth. Okay, so I have another idea for you. I can block the signaling and effectively drape an electronic cloak over the helicopter. That way, they won't be able to intercept our communications or to track us in any other way."

"How can you do that?" X said suspiciously.

"Remember that I was the chief of the president's security team. As such, I was given access to many of the security codes."

X fell silent, thinking hard. He still wasn't sure whether to believe Eyal – maybe the man was bluffing? But did he dare to call his bluff? Teddy was the technical wizard of his team; he would ask him what he thought.

"Teddy, you heard what Eyal said. What do you think? Can he really do what he says he can?"

Teddy glared at Eyal. "If he really has the codes, then I guess so."

"And there's no way to cover our tracks without those codes?"

Teddy shook his head. "If there is a way, I don't know it."

X turned to Eyal. "I'm going to let you try. But my finger is on the trigger and your son is in my sights. If I so much as suspect that you're doing anything other than what you said you'll do, I won't waste time asking questions."

"No problem." Omar stepped forward to untie Eyal's hands, and he approached the pilot's seat. Leon moved to the side as Eyal bent over the switchboards and began to enter a long series of digits.

X approached. "How long is this going to take?"

"I'm almost done." Eyal appeared immersed in the task at hand.

"Why's it taking so long?" X asked. "What's wrong?"

Eyal frowned. "We're flying too fast. I'm afraid the blades will stall," he said. "Take a look at the flight data and tell me what you think."

X bent down toward the screen – giving Eyal his opportunity. It was then, or never...

With lightning speed, Eyal grabbed X's second gun from his holster and shot him point-blank, straight in the heart. In the next split second, before Leon and the others had absorbed what was happening, he shot Teddy and Omar in the stomach, aiming to disable rather than to kill. They probably deserved to die, but the only person he could bring himself to murder was X himself. Then he turned to Leon, placing his smoking gun next to the terrified man's temple and warning him to keep flying steady.

Dumbfounded yet quick to react, Bentzy had placed his handcuffed hands over Elitzafun's eyes in order to protect him from witnessing the sight, and he kept them there, even though the boy was already squirming.

"Leon, turn the helicopter around," Eyal was saying. "We're going back to the hotel."

Leon shook his head. "I can't. First of all I need to—"

"Forget it." Eyal struck the pilot hard with the butt of his gun, and Leon slumped unconscious to the floor of the craft. "I can pilot a helicopter just as well as you."

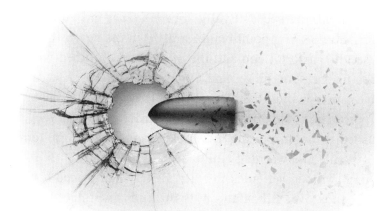

CHAPTER FIFTY-ONE

Kiev, Ukraine

E frat walked slowly out of the international terminal of
Boryspil Airport. She had no idea what her next step
ought to be. Somehow she had avoided facing this question during the four-hour flight, and now she stood there, her coat
tightly wrapped around her against the freezing wind, wondering
what to do next.

Her thoughts were interrupted by the approach of an unfamiliar woman who was clearly headed her way.

"Mrs. Gilboa?" The woman didn't look Jewish; judging by her
accent and apparel, she was probably American, and very smartly
dressed.

"Yes." Efrat looked at the woman in surprise, wrinkling her
brow. "Do we know each other from somewhere?"

"Not yet." The woman offered Efrat a pleasant smile. "I'm Sandy from the CIA. I was sent here to ask you to join me."

Efrat looked at her in surprise. "How did you know I'd be here?"

The woman laughed. "You're certainly aware of the fact that our agency does a lot more than just this."

Efrat blushed. "Well, yes. Obviously."

"So…would you be so kind as to join me? I have a car waiting."

A shadow of hesitation appeared on Efrat's face. Eyal had taught her to suspect everyone and trust no one, and by now it was virtually instinctive. "Thank you. But I'm fine. I've already made my own arrangements," she added, hoping she sounded convincing.

"Sounds to me like you don't completely trust me." The woman smiled. "And you won't trust me even if I show you my ID, will you? So what will convince you? Because we really are the right address for you, and I'd like to be able to help you."

Efrat considered for a moment. "Listen, maybe we have someone in common?" she suggested. "Someone who knows both of us?"

"That's an idea," Sandy said. "Actually, I do have your Mossad chief's number. Zev Avshalom, right? Should I call him?"

Efrat hesitated and then nodded. The woman scrolled through her contacts, pressed a number, and quietly gave someone on the other end of the phone a few instructions. A moment later a deep Israeli voice emanated from the phone. It was a voice that Efrat had, regretfully, been hearing far too much of lately.

"Shalom, Geveret Gilboa. From what I understand, you don't trust the agent who has been sent to meet you."

Typical secular Israeli bluntness. Efrat cringed. "I don't know this lady," Efrat clarified. "And there have been many…new people in my life recently. It's better to be cautious, no?"

"Absolutely. I see Eyal has trained you well. But you can trust her. Sandy is a senior CIA agent, and if they sent her, that means that they greatly admire your husband, which is no wonder. We admire him tremendously at the Mossad as well."

"Admired, past tense."

"No. Admire, in the present tense. He may have left the Mossad, but we still have the greatest respect for his capabilities."

"Will you never forget that he was once a Mossad agent?" Efrat had no idea where the words were coming from. Surely they couldn't be coming from her. She had never been the type of person to voice such thoughts aloud. "What will it take for you to finally let him live his life in peace? He doesn't owe you a thing, you know."

There was complete silence for five seconds before Zev Avshalom responded, in a shocked, but firm, voice. "Geveret Gilboa, no one forced Eyal to do anything. Let me make that crystal clear. We asked him to go on a difficult mission, but then—"

"But then it all went wrong, right? Then the mission failed, leaving Eyal to suffer for the rest of his life, with a microchip implanted in his arm so that he will forever be forced to fight on a thousand fronts. How can you wipe your hands clean of a story that all began with a request from you?"

Avshalom's silence this time around was even longer than before as he wondered how much Efrat had managed to deduce since her marriage to Eyal.

"Geveret Gilboa." Avshalom finally broke the silence, and from the changed tone in his voice, it sounded very much like he was about to change tactics, which was exactly what Efrat was hoping for. Perhaps now she would finally receive some explanations. "I am willing to admit that there is a certain measure of justice to your argument. The circumstances in which your husband has been asked to serve his country have not been…quite regular, one might say. He was indeed compelled to take on certain missions for hostile entities, against his will. I acknowledge these facts, which give me no pleasure. Nevertheless, please do believe me when I tell you that we are keeping track of Eyal's every move and providing him with backup every step of the way, even though he doesn't know it."

If the Mossad chief had been hoping Eyal's wife would accept his ambiguous tale, his hopes were dashed.

"Even though he doesn't know it?" Efrat repeated. Her tone of voice was neither challenging nor condemnatory. "That's exactly the point. Why doesn't he know what's going on behind his back? Why is he being manipulated by foreign powers and essentially abandoned by his own country? Eyal isn't a spy machine, Mr. Avshalom! He's a human being. He's…he's a husband. And a father."

Avshalom searched in vain for something, anything, to say to calm the distraught woman on the other end of the line. But no response, not even the vaguest of platitudes, came to mind, maybe because Efrat had no idea how right she was and how many agencies had indeed used her husband without his ever being consulted or informed.

Suddenly Efrat felt embarrassed. She hadn't planned on speaking so directly to the Mossad chief, and she didn't even know what she had thought she would achieve.

"You know what?" she said, trying to remember how the conversation had begun. "Never mind that now. I mean…it matters so much, but I don't know what you can do now. I hope you understand me."

Understanding was at least something he could make an attempt at. "Of course, Geveret Gilboa. We are very much with you in your time of trouble. We never imagined that things would reach such a point, and we admire Eyal for everything. We're doing our best to provide him with backup and to help him in whatever way possible." Avshalom cleared his throat, wishing he could be genuine for once. But he really did want to help. Probably. "Please do not hesitate to turn to us for help."

"Of course. Thank you."

Efrat ended the call and handed the phone back to Sandy. Her heart was beating wildly and she felt utterly drained. The heart-rending pain of Elitzafun's abduction, her hopes of being reunited with her husband, the tears at the airport, the exhausting flight, the strange woman who had approached her, and now the difficult conversation with the Mossad chief, had all left her exhausted, depressed, and depleted.

"Come," Sandy said gently. "My car is parked nearby. Where is your suitcase?"

"This is all I brought." Efrat pointed to her carry-on. "I wasn't exactly in the mood to pack, with my son in this situation."

"We're hoping that everything will end very shortly." Sandy flashed her a friendly smile. As they crossed the parking lot, she contacted Paul and heard that he and the other agents were on their way to the hotel where the president was being held with Eyal. They needed to be extremely cautious given the situation with the hostages, and they still had no idea what condition Efrat's son was in.

"I'm hoping so too." Efrat sighed, but she seemed outwardly calm and composed. Sandy eyed her with admiration, reflecting on the fact that there weren't many people who could manage to exercise restraint in the face of such an uncertain situation.

"Here's my car." She pressed the button on her remote and the car lights blinked. Sandy took Efrat's carry-on and placed it in the trunk while Efrat sat down in the passenger seat and fastened her seat belt. Sandy sat in the driver's seat and opened a small cooler on the floor by her feet. "Would you like some juice, or water?"

"Water, please."

Sandy handed Efrat a bottle of mineral water and started up the car. The vehicle sped forward, and Efrat gazed out the window, her heart constricted in fear and pain.

~∞~

After the initial shock of Eyal's actions had subsided, Bentzy's breathing slowly returned to normal, and he eyed his friend in disbelief. "You're going back to the hotel?"

"Yes." Despite the overwhelming sense of responsibility he felt for Elitzafun, Eyal couldn't ignore his obligation as an agent. He had been charged with defending the president, and he could not simply abandon him if the possibility of saving him still existed.

"But, what about Elitzafun?" Bentzy's hands were still trying to cover Elitzafun's face, and the boy was resisting with all his might.

"Stop it already!" Elitzafun protested. "Abba! Tell him!"

"Don't let go of his eyes, Bentzy," Eyal said sternly. He addressed his son: "Elitzafun, Bentzy is going to keep your eyes covered until...until we're out of the area. Okay, sweetie?" X's agents were unconscious on the floor and X was dead, lying in a pool of blood. It wasn't a sight Eyal wanted his son to see.

"But I want him to take his hands off," Elitzafun whined.

"No. Not now," Eyal said firmly. His children knew that voice, and they knew that when their father used it, it brooked no arguments. "You're going to go with Bentzy now, because I need to take care of something. You'll listen to whatever he tells you, and he will take you to Ima."

"To Ima?" Elitzafun sounded happy but confused.

"What's wrong?" Eyal said, astonished at his son's reaction. "Don't you want to go to Ima?"

"Of course I want to," Elitzafun said, upset that he'd been misunderstood. "But why are you sending me with Bentzy? Why aren't you coming with me too?"

"Because I..." Eyal began, and then he faltered, unsure of what to say. "I just can't."

"So when are you coming?" Elitzafun demanded.

"As soon as I can. I promise."

"Okay." Elitzafun clearly didn't think it was okay, but he knew when he was defeated.

"You have to daven now, *motek*. Hashem is listening to your *tefillot*, and I need you to daven for me."

Elitzafun was silent for a moment, thinking hard. "Chagelet said that sometimes Hashem saves our *tefillot* for something else. So I'll tell Hashem to take the *tefillot* that we prayed for our Abba, because he was *niftar* anyway, and use them now for you."

Eyal couldn't restrain his laughter. "I don't think it works like that, but all the same, you should daven as much as you can."

"Eyal." Bentzy interrupted the conversation in a voice that spelled trouble. "Our friends are beginning to grow suspicious."

"Whose friends?" Eyal asked, and his question was immediately answered by a voice coming from the radio.

"X, what's going on? You're on your way back to the hotel?" It was the pilot of the second helicopter in which were seated ten of X's men, awaiting further instructions as they headed toward the border of Moldova.

"That's right," Eyal said. "We have one or two matters to attend to back there."

A moment of shocked silence, and then the pilot's voice choked out: "X?"

"Not exactly," Eyal said calmly. "But let's just say that if you value your lives, I'd advise you not to get bogged down with the details of who I am and where your boss is, because I'm a person who greatly values my privacy. If you ruin my plans for me, I will have no choice but to make use of some of the sophisticated weaponry this helicopter has to offer. On the left of the main control panel are the controls for the Spike-LR missiles. As soon as I punch in code 563227 and fire two of those missiles, your lives will be history." Eyal glanced out of the helicopter window and saw the second helicopter turning to follow his path in the air. With a smile of satisfaction he turned the radio off.

"You're insane," Bentzy said. "You just supplied them with all of the information they need in order to make *our lives* history."

Eyal smiled his usual smile, and Bentzy felt slightly encouraged.

After everything Eyal had been through, he had feared that his friend would never return to his old self. But here he was, acting exactly like the Eyal he knew so well, and that included using that famous know-it-all voice of his. "That's exactly what I want them to do."

"I don't understand," Bentzy said slowly. "You want them to shoot a missile at us? Your thoughts are galloping away like a wild horse and I can't keep up with them. Why did you do what you did just now?"

"Bentzy, you need to reboot your thinking," Eyal said, still smiling broadly. "The three of us are going to bail out of here and leave everyone else to be eliminated by their friends. They have to be at a significant distance from us to fire this type of missile, far enough – I hope – that they won't notice us making a tidy exit."

Bentzy gaped. "You...your crazy ideas never end."

"Yes. I'm a genius. Admit it." Eyal laughed, but his euphoria quickly dissipated as he focused intently on lowering the helicopter as close to the ground as possible. "Bentzy, you're going to jump with Elitzafun and take him to his mother." He looked away. Oh, how he yearned to be the one to do exactly that. "Take good care of him, all right?"

"How about untying me first?" Bentzy said, indicating his still bound hands.

"In case you hadn't noticed, someone needs to fly this thing," Eyal responded. "You're going to have to figure that out for yourself."

Bentzy turned around and spotted a pocketknife dangling from Leon's belt. He managed to manipulate it to cut open the cables on his wrists, then he lifted Elitzafun in his arms. His eyes locked with Eyal's for a fleeting moment and his gaze conveyed wordless sympathy along with the strong bond of friendship that existed between them. "Will you be okay?" Bentzy asked, knowing the question was ridiculous.

"Leave already," Eyal said gruffly, before briefly turning to his son. "Goodbye, Elitzafun," he whispered. Emotionless as he became while on a mission, his eyes were full of tears as he gazed at his son.

By now the helicopter was just a few feet above the ground. With one arm around Elitzafun, Bentzy jumped and landed, safely, as Eyal watched. Then he sped off as fast as he could, waiting until he deemed it safe. The second helicopter was a speck in the distance, and then he saw a bright flash of light emitting from it. At that moment he jumped, tumbling to the ground and bracing his fall with his stronger arm.

That initial encounter with the earth was never pleasant. Eyal's breath caught in his throat for a moment, but then he recovered and got to his feet quickly as he regained his sense of balance.

He started to sprint toward the hotel, not stopping or looking back even as he heard the horrific sound of the two missiles shrieking through the air and then hitting the helicopter with precision. A fiery ending for X and his men.

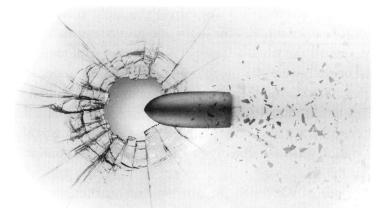

CHAPTER FIFTY-TWO

Kiev, Ukraine

E yal glanced at his watch. If what X had told him was true, there were only two minutes and thirty seconds left before the bombs went off and the building collapsed. He reached the perimeter fence, panting, and kept running toward the breach in the kitchen wall. Then he stopped. Something didn't look right. The breach seemed to have been blocked with rubble; there was no way in from there.

As he turned to search for another way to enter the building, a low rumbling sound shuddered through the air. A nearby wall collapsed, but nothing more serious than that – at least, as far as he could tell from where he was standing. Had X's bombs malfunctioned?

But there was no time to consider that question. Clambering over a partially collapsed doorframe, he managed to access the building, confronting a scene of devastation. By the looks of it, a series of minor explosions had systematically wrecked the building, floor by floor. There was not a square foot without broken glass, plaster fragments, or spatters of blood.

Eyal started to make his way through the ruins at an impossible speed. He passed through the lobby and headed toward the dining room, and all the while additional bombs were exploding around him. The walls were starting to collapse, and finally understanding dawned. In addition to the powerful bombs X had planted in the parking lot, his men had placed many others around the building in order to sow panic among his captives. Eyal wasn't panicking now, but he was undoubtedly in danger. Should he continue and risk his life, or…?

Eyal abruptly arrested the direction of his thoughts. He had known this would be dangerous, but his objective was to save the president and his men before the building collapsed – and he had exactly two minutes and five seconds left to do that. Nothing else mattered.

He needed to get to the dining room. From there he would be able to…

The dining room was empty.

Sandy's cell phone rang. She answered it, her even tone belying the stress she was under: "Give me an update, please."

"The boy's been rescued," Paul said. His voice was laconic. "He's in our hands, and he's fine. He's a bit shocked and confused, but otherwise he's okay. One of Eyal's friends brought him. Are you with Gilboa's wife?"

"Yes. What else?"

"We're going to take the boy to the home of the local rabbi as soon as possible. We should be there in about twenty minutes."

"What else?" Sandy repeated. She wasn't about to mention

Eyal's name when his brave, suffering wife was sitting right next to her, but she needed to know.

"If you're referring to Gilboa himself, he's still in danger. But there's no reason for you to tell her that, of course."

"Okay." Sandy hung up the phone and glanced at Efrat as she continued to drive.

"What happened?" Efrat asked.

"Excellent news," Sandy said, injecting a note of cheer into her voice. "Your son has been released."

Efrat neither cried out nor fainted. Instead, she drew a deep breath and asked quietly: "And my husband?"

"He hasn't been released yet." Sandy smiled encouragingly. "But you know him, and he'll be okay."

Efrat didn't answer. She twisted her hands together as her heart hammered in her chest. "When will I see my son?"

"They're leaving for the rabbi's house now. It will take about half an hour for them to get there. You'll see him there. Will you be okay?"

"I was okay, I am still okay, and I will remain okay." Efrat's voice was steady. "All with G-d's help."

They must have escaped, Eyal thought. That meant that he had jeopardized his own life for nothing – a bitter thought. The president and his men had fled the scene, acting as any sane person would. And now he too had to act like a sane person, not a crazy agent who thought that victory could always be snatched out of the jaws of defeat. There were less than two minutes left to get out of there.

That voice of cold logic was correct.

Instead, Eyal chose to follow his instincts. He had to check that the men really were gone. He had to know for sure.

Eyal sped back to the lobby. He stationed himself beneath the stairwell and forced himself to overcome his impulses and remain immobile, without breathing, listening in tense silence. The men were probably gone. But maybe they were still there, trapped by a series of explosions.

One second. Two. Three. Eyal gritted his teeth, sweating from tension and fear.

Four seconds.

They were still in the building.

Eyal heard the almost imperceptible sounds coming through the thick walls. He listened for another second to make sure he knew where the sounds were coming from and then he ran back out of the hotel, jumping over debris, making his way to the staff parking lot, one floor below ground level.

The door was locked. It was made of reinforced steel, but it was something the security men should have been able to breach with homemade explosives. Why hadn't they done so?

"Mr. President?" Eyal called out. "Are you in there?"

"Eyal!!" The voices emerging from several pairs of lips simultaneously expressed a mixture of hopefulness and despondency.

"How did you get here?" someone asked. Through the heavy door, Eyal couldn't tell exactly who it was.

"That doesn't matter right now," Eyal said, wondering whether he should tell him that they had just minutes to escape. "Why don't you break the door down?"

"We can't," the president replied.

"How long will it take you to reach the lobby and get out from there?" Eyal asked breathlessly.

"We can't reach anywhere. We were forced to retreat here when the bombs started going off. And then we were trapped. Is there anything you can do to get us out?"

"I'm going to try." Eyal looked around, wondering what he could possibly do. He pulled out X's gun, and after warning the men to stand clear, he shot directly at the doorframe, shifting the lock from its place. The door swung open. The men were free to leave the building.

Or so he thought.

As he looked through the doorway, Eyal froze in shock. Now he realized why the men hadn't gone anywhere. A huge hole blown in the floor of the parking lot exposed the floor beneath the men. Fourteen men stood between the destroyed walls just above an abyss that was over twenty feet deep and about ten feet wide, crammed onto just a few square feet of concrete, amidst debris and a few beams that had survived the explosion intact. They weren't going anywhere.

Eyal started to tremble with fear. The men were waiting to be saved by something, someone. They had no idea that in less than two minutes it would all be over.

Ninety seconds.

Without pausing to think, Eyal rushed out, returning ten seconds later with a metal ladder from a storage cupboard he had noticed the day before. Speed was crucial, but a single badly judged movement made by any of the men could prove fatal. It was an almost impossible combination.

Almost.

Eyal placed the ladder diagonally on the ground, creating a bridge of sorts between the place where the men were standing and the entrance to the lot. *And now*, Eyal thought, *you are to act without feeling, without emotion. Like a machine.*

The men looked at Eyal in confusion. "The president first," Eyal said.

No one moved. Eyal looked at them and knew the time had come for complete disclosure. "You don't have long," he said. "The whole place is coming down in less than a minute. There are massive bombs placed in the upper parking lot. So you're getting out now. One at a time, as fast as you can."

Hesitantly, the president began to straddle the ladder. As Eyal watched him climb, dragging one of his legs, he realized that the president had been injured by one of the blasts. His pants leg was soaked in blood, and Eyal hoped desperately that the wound would not prove to be fatal. He watched the president with concern. If the president could make it, maybe a few of the other men could too.

The president continued to scale the ladder cautiously. Twice he lost his balance, swaying and nearly toppling to his death, but he swung back at the last moment. But more men needed to get out after him, and judging by the president's current pace, they wouldn't make it in time.

Eyal glanced at his watch, and his lips moved in ceaseless prayer. Forty-five seconds. The president was almost there. Two more steps. One.

And then it happened.

The ladder slipped, sliding into the abyss beneath. In that very instant Eyal leaped forward and grasped the president's hands, preventing him from plummeting to certain death. The president remained hanging between the ground and the abyss, shaking as he held onto Eyal's hands.

"Run, Eyal," the president whispered. His breathing was labored. "I was injured by one of the bombs. I'm not going to make it. Leave me and save yourself." His voice was weak yet urgent. "You won't manage to get me out before the building collapses. Eyal, run and leave me. Don't sacrifice your life for nothing."

Eyal ignored the president's words and continued to drag him up.

"Leave me, Eyal." The president stopped demanding. His voice grew pleading instead. "Please, just run and save yourself. We're not going to manage to get out of here. But you need to go." A deep breath. "Go, Eyal. For your family and for the American nation. Stay strong for them. They need you more than they need me."

The president was heavy, but Eyal didn't give up. He pulled forcefully at the president's hands, dragging him upward until he was on firm ground.

The thirteen men still inside the building watched in silence. The ladder that had been their last chance of escape was lying twenty feet below. It was too late for them. But Eyal had another twenty seconds to save himself and the president.

The president had collapsed onto the ground, and Eyal realized that his wounds were worse than he had originally thought. There was no way he would be able to leave the building on his own – Eyal would have to carry him.

Thirteen pairs of eyes watched Eyal turn toward them.

"Eyal, take the president and run," Michael said. His voice was amazingly steady. "We're not going to make it out, but you and the president still have a chance. We can't let these evil people defeat our nation. The fight will go on without us."

For a moment Eyal stood speechless. He had evacuated wounded soldiers probably dozens of times during his career, usually under fire, but nothing had prepared him for a situation such as this. Drawing a deep breath, Eyal bent down and lifted the president onto his shoulders.

"I...you know I wanted to save you." Eyal stopped. Words were so woefully inadequate.

"Thank you, Eyal." Michael said. "Thank you for everything. Good luck."

Eyal turned and raced toward freedom.

Eight seconds later a massive explosion rent the air. Eyal didn't stop running. He couldn't bring himself to turn around and see the building collapse and bury thirteen sacrificial lambs beneath it.

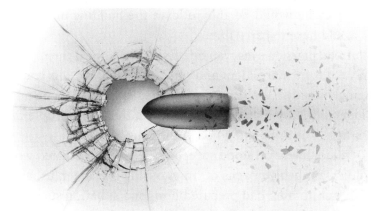

CHAPTER FIFTY-THREE

Kiev, Ukraine

I t was only when he was about fifty feet away from the building and nearing the hotel gates that Eyal allowed himself to stop running and lower the president to the ground. The wound in his leg was still bleeding, and his open eyes were glazed.

"Eyal," the president whispered.

"Yes." Eyal crouched down, his breathing labored, his face drenched in sweat. He had been injured by a bomb shard, and the pain caused him to wince.

"Th...thank you...Eyal..." The president was struggling to breathe. "T...tell everyone...tell the world what happened. Tell them to be strong and not give in to terror. We are stronger than they are. We are humans." The president's body trembled, and then he fell silent.

Eyal silently lowered his head and mourned. Millions would mourn the death of the president, but few would mourn the death of a man.

Eyal remained silently in his place for another moment.

And then he saw the lights.

Red and blue lights flickering on the walls and trees, casting shadows in all directions. The police were on their way, and that meant that someone was about to lose his freedom.

Again.

There was no one there who would speak in his favor. The police officers would arrive to find Eyal stooped over the president's body, the president's blood on his clothing. Even if he wasn't accused of his murder, he would be held culpable for the fact that the president had been murdered on his watch.

And there was nowhere for him to run.

By now the hotel grounds were swarming with police and the night air echoed with the wailing of sirens. Eyal covered the president's face with his torn jacket. Another chapter had ended in history's bloody book recording the war against terror. Eyal looked down one last time at the president and then turned away.

Almost immediately he was accosted by six police officers, weapons drawn and with fierce expressions on their faces. A bitter smile, laced with amusement, spread unbidden over Eyal's face. Again he would find himself in Ukrainian police custody. Always for assassinating someone important. Who would be the next victim? He could laugh – not now; the Ukrainians wouldn't appreciate it – because, and solely because, he knew that he wasn't the one pulling the strings. The Mossad had trained him to view himself as invincible, the master of his fate, the one setting the scene and deciding the outcome. But time and a greater Teacher had given him perspective. He could laugh or he could cry. And it didn't make any difference which.

Somehow, the police officers who had come to arrest him didn't strike him as being receptive to his profound insights on the meaning of life, the universe, and everything. They were reveling in their capture of "the criminal" and the praise that would be heaped on their heads for having pulled off that particular feat. Whether or not Eyal had actually shot the president dead was immaterial. The main thing was the headline in the newspapers tomorrow morning. Preferably with their pictures included – on the front page, of course. Promotions to follow, and a bottle of vodka on the house.

All this and more flashed through Eyal's mind in the few seconds it took the gang of Ukrainian police to yell: "Hands up! You're under arrest!" Eyal didn't respond. Mutely he submitted to being frisked for weapons and then handcuffed and tossed into a squad car. It could hardly be otherwise, and he didn't expect them to listen, let alone understand.

He would try to explain later. If they gave him the opportunity.

"Eyal's not coming back so fast, is he?" Efrat had contacted Bentzy as soon as things slowed down. If she had thought she would be reunited with both her husband and her son, soon to travel home as a complete family, she had been extremely naïve. But Efrat was nothing if not a master of adjusting to reality.

"Well," Bentzy stammered, "the truth is that we don't know yet."

"Tell me the truth," Efrat said firmly.

"The truth is that he was removed from the scene," Bentzy said, his voice unnatural. "But you know him, and he isn't someone who, once removed, stays that way. He tends to resist all efforts to—"

"—kill him," supplied Efrat.

"That too," Bentzy said, embarrassed by her forthrightness.

"I don't know of anyone who's immune to bullets," Efrat said. "And that includes Eyal."

"No, no," Bentzy protested. "I don't think we're talking about guns here." He tried to find the right words. "This is something else."

"What?" Realization dawned. "You mean he's been arrested?"

"Something to that effect," Bentzy admitted.

"Are you trying to tell me that not the Mossad, and not even the CIA, can pull the right strings to let him talk to me?" Efrat said, her voice incredulous. "You really expect me to believe that?"

Bentzy swallowed. "It's not that simple. We're working on it, but it will take time. As far as Ukraine is concerned, Eyal threw them into a diplomatic nightmare. He was supposed to be looking after the president, and he messed up, big time. This is a huge embarrassment for Ukraine, and understandably, they're only too keen to find a scapegoat. And the fact of the matter is that it was Eyal himself who let in the six terrorists, thinking they were CIA agents." Bentzy stopped. The truth was actually worse than that, but there was no need to scare Efrat out of her mind.

Efrat hung up the phone and looked at Elitzafun, playing with the toy that she had bought him. She smiled, recalling her thoughts while in the duty-free shop, tears in her eyes, as she contemplated never being able to play with Elitzafun again. Now Elitzafun was alive, happy, and unharmed, together with her. There was no end to her gratitude. Even though Eyal...

But Eyal's life wasn't in danger. No – it was just the threat of a life sentence in a Ukrainian prison that hung over him. The Ukrainians would not easily relinquish their scapegoat, and what evidence did Eyal have to prove his innocence?

"Why are you crying?" Elitzafun asked, his voice full of charming childish anxiety.

"I'm not." Efrat wasn't exactly crying, but her voice was choked with tears. What else would she and Eyal have to endure? Would Eyal ever manage to escape from a lifetime of "service" to whichever intelligence agency had a hold over him? Would he ever resume a normal life?

An unkind voice deep within Efrat's heart whispered that Eyal was clueless as to how to go about living a normal life.

"You're sad," Elitzafun announced.

"A bit," she admitted.

"Why?"

"It doesn't matter." There was no reason for Efrat to share her worries with him. He had been through enough of his own and needed to move on. "Do you want to play?"

"Ima, are you worried about Abba?" He was smarter than she had thought.

"A bit," Efrat whispered.

"That's why you're sad." Elitzafun climbed onto her lap, nestling comfortably against her, and examined her face. He lifted his small hands to clasp her around the neck. "I missed you, Ima."

Efrat stroked her son gently, and in a choked voice full of pain, she said: "I missed you too, my precious son."

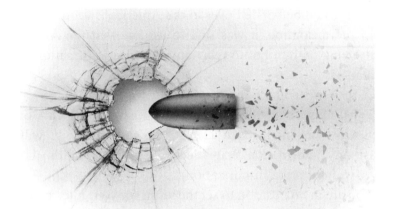

CHAPTER FIFTY-FOUR

Kiev, Ukraine

T he United States is mourning the death of its president. His casket will be brought to the United States tomorrow, where he will be laid to rest in Arlington National Cemetery alongside Michael Morris, the White House Chief of Security, Jim Corel, the president's private secretary, and Louis Moran, deputy chief of security. Also to be buried alongside these heroes are fifteen guards from the president's security team who were murdered in the same horrific act of terror. The United States government has reiterated its intention to see that justice is served against the perpetrators of this heinous crime against humanity."

The interrogator turned off the radio and turned to Eyal. "I will begin with a general, almost banal question: What do you know about all of this?"

Eyal was silent, trying to organize his thoughts. He had no interest in sharing what he knew with the Ukrainian police, but he had to figure out how to refuse to cooperate without making things worse for himself than they already were. He had no idea at which point he would be handed over to the Americans for questioning, but in the meantime, it was safe to assume that the Americans were relying on him not to relay any sensitive information to the Ukrainians.

So, they trusted him, did they?

"I will only divulge the information I have to the CIA or another American intelligence agency," he said finally. "I will not release any information that affects the security of the United States, without prior authorization."

"You are in no position to set the terms for your interrogation," the detective said. "As someone who is suspected of being party to a grave act of terrorism, it is in your best interests to cooperate."

"I did everything I could to prevent that act of terror from taking place." Eyal was exhausted and impatient, and he was in physical pain as well. Bentzy had managed to get word to him that Elitzafun was safe and was being taken to his mother, but the knowledge that Efrat was in Ukraine and yet unable to meet with him seemed only to make things that much worse. Emotionally he was a mess, even though he was still able to give the impression of being calm and composed.

The detective leaned back in his chair and lit a cigarette. "You were the head of the president's security team. You've admitted to letting six hostile agents into the building, providing an extremely flimsy excuse for doing so. You allowed certain hostages to escape, proving that you had the ability to manipulate the situation, and you failed to release either the president or those close to him. Yet you yourself emerged relatively unscathed. Something doesn't add up here. In fact, a lot doesn't add up, and if you don't start providing some explanations quickly, we will provide some of our own. And the results, for you, won't be pretty."

Eyal shrugged. The man was right, but it couldn't be helped. "I'll repeat what I already told you. I can only hand over information that will not damage United States security interests. So all I can tell you is this: Terrorists seized control of the hotel, taking many hostages. I was able to free some of them. I was not able to act freely, however, as they were holding my son hostage. The building was rigged with explosives, and when it blew up, those remaining inside were killed. The president died of his wounds. That's it."

"It says here that you have no children." The interrogator made a great show of thumbing through several papers in a folder on his desk.

Eyal knew that those papers were most likely either blank or contained crossword puzzles, but he swallowed his mirth and responded matter-of-factly instead. "That is correct. The boy is my wife's son, but when I married her I assumed responsibility for the boy's welfare. So I behave as a father would, and he relates to me as a parent."

"Fine. So you admit that in essence you collaborated with the terrorists." The interrogator gathered his papers together.

"If you call action as a result of blackmail 'collaboration' then you are right. But most normal people don't see things that way," Eyal said acidly. "I did my best, under the circumstances, to save the president's life, along with the lives of the other innocents put in harm's way. How else can you explain my returning to the hotel even after having escaped? I went back to try to save lives. Ultimately I failed, but that wasn't in my hands."

"Ah, that's what you say. Curious. You reappear on the scene, and the president then dies." The interrogator smiled. "As for cause and motivation, we only have your word for that."

Eyal gritted his teeth and managed to restrain himself from issuing another biting response. Really, it made no difference. The man would believe whatever he wanted to. If the CIA refused to step in and corroborate his account of things, he would be hung out to dry.

"Okay. That's enough for now. Igor!" The interrogator summoned a warden. "Take him to his cell. We're holding you until your trial. And that won't happen until we get the information we're looking for, so just bear that in mind next time you start your courageous speech about United States security interests."

"It's clear that you want a scapegoat," Eyal noted. "Bit of an embarrassment for your government that you couldn't even keep the president of the United States safe, smack in the middle of your capital city, isn't it?"

The interrogator colored. "It should be an embarrassment to your government that you are in a Ukrainian prison cell for the second time in a month. Maybe the Israelis should stick to exporting oranges rather than of troublemakers." He got to his feet and "accidentally" knocked the palm of his hand into the back of Eyal's head as he exited the room without a second glance.

A moment later Igor entered the room and laid a heavy hand on Eyal's shoulder. Eyal turned to him. His expression was pleading. It was an expression that he loathed adopting, but he simply had no choice this time. "Please, allow me to make a phone call. Just one." A phone call to Efrat to hear that Elitzafun was okay. To hear something from the outside world, the free world, beyond the confines of prison and the prison of espionage work. Would he ever be set free?

"No."

They didn't become prison wardens for nothing, Eyal reflected. Only a person who liked saying "no" would work in a prison. "You're a troublemaker, so all privileges are automatically revoked. You've done enough damage already."

A fine excuse.

Eyal was returned to his cell. He sank wearily onto the thin mattress on the concrete shelf that passed for a bed and let the waves of pain engulf him. Far greater than the physical pain was the emotional torment, and he felt sapped of his patience, fortitude, and power of restraint. All of the skills he had ever learned and trained for seemed to have dissipated. Perhaps this was the way agents felt when they reached the end.

The cell was dark and empty, and he was grateful for that. Dealing with other prisoners just then would have driven him to the verge of insanity. As it was, he felt as though he were on the brink of a breakdown.

As Eyal lay down he realized why he had been given a private cell. He was privy to no small number of government secrets, and the Ukrainians were obviously afraid that he might share information with others who could potentially use it for criminal purposes. Apparently it hadn't occurred to them to plant informants in the cell who would suggest an exchange of information for money. Probably they realized that he would immediately see through any such attempt. Or did they know that he couldn't be bought?

Eyal heard the mice squeaking as they scampered about his cell, but he paid them no heed. His current conditions were so much better than those of the Ukrainian prison cell he had last experienced. He tried to fall asleep, but he was in too much pain. His arm was still throbbing from the wound from Ahmed's bullet, especially after having strained it so much in his attempt to save the president, and he had three bomb shards lodged in his body from the final explosion that had brought the hotel down. Instead of seeing to it that he received medical care, however, the police officers arresting him had added to his injuries with several severe beatings.

Eventually, however, his exhaustion won out and he fell asleep.

Paul arrived in Ukraine on a charter flight. While Americans mourned the death of their leader, he had a series of emergency tasks to tend to. His first destination was the home of Rabbi Kagan, in order to meet with Gilboa's wife. He hoped that she harbored no unrealistic expectations of what the CIA could – and would

– do to expedite her husband's release. Although Eyal had been hired by none other than the president himself, he was still not an official US agent, and neither was he officially employed by the intelligence agency of any other country. As such, the Ukrainian government could legitimately decide to make an example of him for causing a diplomatic nightmare for them, counting on the United States government to choose to sacrifice the Israeli and wash its own hands of the entire business.

Of course, the Ukrainians had the additional motivation of being seen to achieve justice for the murdered Rubinov. Right now, the Ukrainians hated Eyal Gilboa even more than they hated Vladimir Putin, and that was saying something.

Paul would have to exercise all his diplomatic muscle in order to make things move even a fraction in Eyal's direction. If he couldn't get Eyal released from prison, he would attempt to at least have him transferred to an American prison, where he would be dealt with more humanely, and where Eyal could at least speak relatively freely about the details of his mission.

A mission that had ended in tragedy for the American nation.

Eyal awoke after just a few hours. The cold and pain didn't permit him to sleep for long. A brave mouse clambered over his feet, springing off as he sat up. He had no blanket, and the warden's forgetfulness in providing him with one seemed somewhat less than innocent. The temperature in the underground cell was intolerable, and Eyal bit the tips of his fingers in an attempt to warm them and restore sensation to them.

Eyal got to his feet and looked out through the cell's bars into the silent, dimly lit hallway. He was desperate to speak to his wife and son. He needed to see for himself that they were okay. Bentzy had told him that Elitzafun seemed fine, but after everything the boy had been through, "fine" was surely relative.

Eyal grasped the cell bars tightly with his frozen fingers. He grasped the bars so tightly that his knuckles turned white before he finally let go, defeated. How long would it be before the Ukrainians allowed him to see his family again? Two weeks? A month? A year? The police investigators would hound him until their interrogation produced its desired results – a full confession that would at least partially allay the international humiliation of Ukraine for its failure to protect America's president. And the United States would probably go along with it, if his suspicions were correct.

Eyal's thoughts turned to Efrat, and he wondered what she was thinking. He had surely suffered more than her, but she was suffering only because of him.

Someone approached his cell and Eyal instinctively took a step backward, simultaneously ashamed of his fearfulness. The warden flicked a light switch outside, turning on the light in the cell. Eyal squinted at the sudden glare, and three mice retreated to their holes. One brave mouse remained, sniffing the air and staring at him with unabashed curiosity. With mice too, it seemed, there were those that were more courageous and those that were more inclined to timidity.

"Eyal Gilboa?" the warden asked.

Who did he think he was? "No," Eyal said drily. Despite the mood he was in, he hadn't lost his acerbic wit.

"What?" the warden asked in confusion.

"I said I'm not Eyal Gilboa. Eyal escaped and I came to take his place."

The warden stared. The man before him was clearly the same person whose image had been plastered all over the media. "You..."

"You asked me if I'm Eyal Gilboa and I said I'm not. Were you expecting to see someone else?"

The warden could think of no response.

"You weren't, right? So don't ask me any more stupid questions. Your interrogator already did a fine job of that yesterday."

The warden looked at Eyal with an expression reserved for those who clearly were not in their right mind. Eyal noted his expression and thought how right the warden was. He really was on the brink of losing it. All it would take to drive him completely out of his mind would be another few days of loneliness and interrogations. "Follow me," the warden said as he unlocked the door.

"Another interrogation?" Eyal asked.

"No. You're free to go." The warden's voice was expressionless.

Eyal stared at the warden in shocked silence. "What?" It was his turn to be confused now. "Why?"

"I don't know," the warden said coolly. "If you prefer, I'll find out if you can stay." His sharp retort was a clear retaliation to Eyal's earlier practical joke.

Eyal left the cell, following the warden down the hallway and up the stairs to the ground floor. The warden unlocked and opened the front gate and pointed out a rusty metal bench just outside it. The outer gate to the prison was locked.

"Wait there," he said. "Someone will come to get you soon."

"The same person who arranged for my release?"

"A brilliant deduction. Wait here for him. Don't try anything clever in the meantime. Those are orders from above." The warden closed the door, leaving Eyal alone.

An order from above, Eyal thought. *How very impressive. Too bad Paul doesn't know how good I am at breaching orders from above.*

"Bentzy?"

There was static on the line, and Bentzy's words came over fragmented, but even so, the joy in his voice was clearly audible. "Eyal! Where are you?"

"Come and pick me up from Zhytomyrska Street. Get here fast, but there's no pressure. I'm not in the middle of a gun war or a dizzying chase, for a change. Do you think you can make it?"

"Of course. I'm on my way." Bentzy grabbed his keys and shot straight out. "Keep me posted."

"I can't or I'll be tracked. I'm throwing this phone away. Be there. All right?"

"Of course. May G-d protect you." Bentzy pressed down on the gas, bringing the needle on the speedometer up to 130 miles per hour. He hoped the roads would be relatively empty, as they should be at that early-morning hour. He would need to pull over somewhere in order to "borrow" a motorcycle from someone on the road, leaving a phone number for the innocent citizen so he could contact him later to arrange for its return...or maybe it would be a better idea to pinch something from a car dealership.

The motor roared, and Bentzy's heart pounded with happiness. Eyal had asked him to pick him up. Presumably that meant that he had made some progress in getting back home, or, more precisely, to the place where his family was staying.

Bentzy debated whether he should let Eyal's wife know that her husband had contacted him, but eventually he decided against it. Why should he test the woman's nerves? He would call when it was all behind them.

Thirty minutes later Eyal called again from a different number. "Everything's ready, Sergeant," Bentzy said. "I borrowed a motorcycle from a law-abiding Ukrainian citizen and left him a contact number so I can return the vehicle to him."

Eyal laughed. "How many vehicles did you exchange along the way?"

"Three cars and one motorcycle. I'm not in the mood to be traced. We'll meet up in a minute, and we'll save the thank-yous for later."

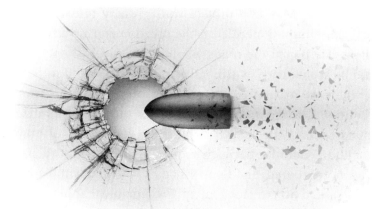

CHAPTER FIFTY-FIVE

Kiev, Ukraine

I 'd rather stay in a hotel," Efrat said timidly to the concerned
CIA agents who were with her in the room. Sandy was at her
side, ostensibly to shield Efrat from the pressure of having to
deal with all the official demands.

Rabbi Kagan was in the hallway outside, pacing nervously. He felt
it was his obligation to protect this woman who was having to contend
with American, Ukrainian, and Israeli agents, all on her own. No one
had invited him to the meeting taking place inside, but if he managed
to find even a whisker of an excuse to enter, he would certainly breach
the standards of etiquette and would do so even without an invitation.
In the meantime, he made do with listening in on the conversation.

"That's understandable," Paul said. "But I'm worried that it's a
bit...unsafe for you."

"Why?"

"Because…" Paul coughed. "Your husband hasn't returned yet, and we're concerned; we'd prefer to provide you with as much protection as possible."

"So station some of your agents in the hallway outside my hotel room, and outside the building too. You can even cordon off the whole street if that makes you feel better." Paul stared, not sure what to make of her sarcasm – or perhaps she was being serious? "You know what my son has just been through," Efrat continued. "What he needs now is a semblance of normalcy. He doesn't need to be surrounded by poker-faced agents with cocked weapons, itching to get a potshot at someone. If you don't believe me, then get some psychologist with fancy letters after his name to back me up."

Efrat was clearly overwrought, and her suggestion didn't appeal to Paul in the slightest, but he understood where she was coming from. "Fine," he said. "I'll send some people to the hotel where you'll be staying, but I will ask you not to go anywhere without arranging it with me in advance."

Efrat nodded, resigned.

Sandy parted from her with a warm handshake. "Bye, Efrat," she said. "It was a pleasure to meet you."

A convoy of CIA vehicles escorted Efrat to the hotel.

What an honor.

The Bontiak Hotel was located just beyond Kiev's city center, a hub of life that attempted to duplicate the best the Western world had to offer. The atmosphere was one of gloomy contemplation, and now, at three o'clock in the morning, the streetlights were already dimmed, saving the city money.

All of this worked to Eyal's advantage. But as he made his way through the silent neighborhood, pressing himself as close to the buildings as possible, he was overcome by a strange sensation of calm. He was injured, in pain, and still hunted – but he had a smile on his lips and a joyous feeling in his heart. He wondered what Paul would think when he turned up at the prison and found him gone – but the man was surely no fool, and he must have realized that Eyal was just about the last person to sit calmly and wait to be rescued.

The address of the hotel, which Eyal had received from Bentzy, was just beyond an empty lot. As Eyal sprinted past a building and toward the lot, he reflected on the injustice of the situation. All he wanted was to talk to his wife, and he had to go to such ridiculous lengths to achieve that. Even if he truly had nothing to fear from the CIA, at the very least they would, upon locating him, seize him and pump him for information for hours on end. He didn't have the emotional fortitude for that right now – and more importantly, he had other priorities.

"Be careful, Eyal," Bentzy's voice murmured from the cell phone that he had given Eyal before taking leave of him. "Paul has stationed his agents all around the hotel. There are two men guarding the front of the building, three others patrolling the street, another three men in the hotel lobby, and two guards in the hallway, all with weapons at the ready."

"At the ready?" Eyal said scornfully. "Really now, Bentzy. Have a bit of respect for my capabilities, and please don't bother to call me again unless you have something truly earth-shatteringly urgent to tell me, because the next time you call I will already be inside the hotel, and I have no interest in waking up anyone there."

The empty lot made things more complicated for Eyal. But he couldn't blame Efrat for her choice – naturally, she had no idea which hotel would best suit someone trying to approach undetected.

At least the hotel had pretty gardens outside, densely planted with colorful flowers and hardy-looking foliage. Eyal dropped to his hands and knees and started to crawl through the bushes, hugging the earth, making slow, deliberate progress. Haste was the enemy of speed. Eyal continued to make his way forward slowly until he was just a few paces away from the first guard. If time had been no object, he would have first staked out the guards' system for patrolling the area so as to figure out what his next move should be, but under the circumstances, he had no time to spare. And he was simply too impatient.

There was no way that he would be able to enter the hotel in silence. He would need to pull off a convincingly threatening performance.

The guard approached, and Eyal sprang up and lunged forward like a lion attacking its prey. It was a routine he had spent close to twenty years perfecting. He spun the man around and twisted his arms behind him before throwing him to the ground. Then he pulled the guard's gun out of his belt. Bending over the guard now, he pushed the man's weapon up against his forehead and pressed down with one foot onto the man's knees so that he would not be able to get up.

"Hi. I'm Eyal Gilboa. No, don't faint on me. I have no hostile intentions; all I want is to meet my wife and son without your commander finding out. Not for the next hour or two, in any case. Can I trust you to keep all this a secret?"

The man nodded in confusion. "Wonderful," Eyal said, letting the man's legs go free. "You can get up now and radio your friends. Now. Why aren't you moving? How many men are you?"

"We're ten men, but we've received orders."

"You received one order, and now you're receiving another. I may look like I'm calm and pleasant, but trust me when I tell you that I've been through too much today to accept being refused. I won't actually kill you if you don't take my advice, but I can certainly weave one of these pretty bullets into your kneecap. How does that sound?"

The man shook his head, fear glinting in his eyes.

"I didn't think it sounded good. And I'm really not interested in putting that bullet into your kneecap in any case, because I don't like to play dirty when I don't have to – meaning, whenever people don't force me to act that way. But unfortunately, most of the time people do…so call your dear friends down to the street. Tell them you need some backup because you think there are a few dodgy-looking men headed this way from a dark alleyway, and get the people in the hotel to come down here too."

The man's expression had become openly hostile. "No. I won't."

"Why not?" Eyal asked, amused. "Don't act like a hero for nothing. If there were a hostile party involved, then you'd be right to stand up for your ideals, but we're simply talking about games of honor here. You were sent here to protect my wife and son, but there's no need for that now. I'm here, and I'll protect them myself."

Eyal took the radio from the guard's belt, pressed a button on it, and shoved the device up to the man's lips. Eyal's eyes were brimming with fire and determination. He was clearly angry enough to make good on his threats.

"Johnny, Murray, I see some suspicious activity in the alleyway on the left of the hotel. I need backup."

Eyal turned the device off and smiled with satisfaction. "Good boy. That wasn't too hard, right? I'm going to hold on to this device for a while, because Paul's going to want an update soon, and I'll hold on to your gun too, so that you won't feel the urge to shoot me after I move on. Wonderful. Thank you, and enjoy the rest of your night." Eyal waited a moment until he could see some movement in the direction of the alleyway. He counted nine guards, including the guard whom he had tackled. That meant that one smart man had stayed behind, most likely the one right outside Efrat's door.

Eyal made his way cautiously through the vacant lot, entering the hotel quickly. A sense of calm filled his being. He had his own gun in his right hand and the gun that he had "borrowed" from the guard in his left. He checked the hallway carefully and saw a guard sitting on a chair outside one of the rooms with a pistol resting on his knees and wearing a bulletproof vest. How impressive. Eyal placed the radio on a table, fiddling with the switch so that it began to emit a series of random beeps, before retreating behind the door of the electric closet.

The man heard the beeps and got up, pistol in hand, to see where they were coming from. Slowly, he approached the table where the radio was, and Eyal saw the question marks and fear on his face. In one leap Eyal reached him, wedging his gun into the guard's ribcage. "Drop your weapon," he hissed.

Instead of complying, the man swung around quickly, wedging the butt of his gun into Eyal's neck in order to take him down, but Eyal dodged the maneuver and simultaneously caught the man in the stomach with the heel of his shoe. His gun clattered to the floor, and Eyal immediately retrieved it.

"Dear me, there's no reason for alarm," Eyal said, shaking his head in mock amusement. "I suppose I ought to thank you really, seeing as you've been keeping watch on my wife and son, but as I told the guard at the entrance, there's no reason for you to remain here any longer now that I've arrived. You can pack up your equipment and move on. And not a word about this to Paul."

"But..." The fear reflected in the other man's face dissipated. "But..."

"That's right. I'm Eyal Gilboa, and as you most certainly realize, I'm too annoyed with certain people to provide any explanations to you and your friends right now. So do as I said – pack up your gear and move on before you find out just how impatient I'm getting."

The man retreated with caution, stretching out his hand. "Can I have my gun?"

"No. That is the United States' gift to me." Eyal pointed down the hallway. "And now, I'd like to see you move on."

The man looked at him in confusion before slowly moving away. Eyal cocked his gun with impatience. "How about moving a bit faster?" he barked. He would have preferred to hurry the man along with a shot or two, but he was concerned that the door to one of the rooms might open suddenly and an unlucky guest would get in the way of the bullet.

The guard turned around and raced down the hallway. Eyal turned in the opposite direction, making his way down the corridor in search of room 245.

Soft knocking at the door. Efrat, who was trying to read by the light of the lamp, froze in fear. She knew that if whoever was at the door had malicious intent, he wouldn't have bothered to announce his arrival so pleasantly. But even so, after fear and tension had been her constant companions for the past few weeks, it was hard to let go. Her visitor had ignored the "Do not disturb" sign hanging on her door – evidence to the fact that it was not one of the hotel staff members outside but rather one of the security men. And she had no interest in being disturbed by any of them just then.

At least Elitzafun was asleep, but he was one of the reasons she could neither join him in slumber nor concentrate on her reading. She was too worried about her son's emotional well-being and the impression the kidnapping had made on his soul. What was he going through?

And aside from Elitzafun, Efrat was worried about Eyal. His condition was so precarious. Paul had promised that there was no great cause for concern, yet she was concerned for precisely that reason.

Efrat got up, scared. Even though Sandy had promised her that the CIA agents were keeping close watch on the hotel, she was still worried.

She put the safety catch into place and opened the door a crack.

Eyal stood there, clothing ripped and stained with blood and mud. A jagged cut next to his temple was still traced with congealed blood, but otherwise he was smiling.

Efrat stared at him, unable to get a word out of her mouth.

"I'm sorry to disturb you, especially as you have a 'Do not disturb' sign in place. Please open the safety latch." The sentence was meant to guide her, because she seemed too overwhelmed to perform even a simple act. She pulled the door in slightly, then slowly opened it wide. "I understand that my son is here."

Efrat didn't move. She was still in shock.

"How are you? How is Elitzafun?" Eyal approached the bed that Elitzafun was lying on and gently stroked his hair. Tears appeared in his green eyes. A long moment passed with him touching his son's hair, cheeks, and eyes, feeling the wonder and surrealism of the moment, the culmination of two weeks of war. It was only after a long moment had passed that Eyal turned back toward his wife, and an expression of concern, compassion, and intense regret appeared on his face. "Are you okay?"

She ignored the question. "Why didn't they tell me anything?" she managed to utter.

"Who is 'they'? And what should they have told you?" Eyal asked, taken aback. His wife had attacked him from an angle that he hadn't even considered, raising a completely insignificant issue as though that were the only one that mattered.

"Paul, Sandy, all of the other intelligence agents," Efrat said. "No one told me you were released from prison. No one let me know that you were on the way."

"No one knew. If I had wanted to get here via official channels, I wouldn't have arrived for another two days, at least. The CIA wouldn't have let me go before I told them everything I knew. I decided I didn't like that option. I wanted to see you first, so I evaded them."

"But what about the guards?" Efrat stuttered. "I mean…the guards that are watching my room…didn't they see you and then run to tell Paul you're here?"

"Hey, a bit of respect for my professionalism," Eyal said with a laugh. "If I can't deal with a few agents in suits, I'd never have gotten this far, right?"

Elitzafun opened his eyes. "Abba?"

"Yes, my son," Eyal gently stroked his son's hair again. "How are you, sweetie?"

"How did you get here?" Elitzafun asked sleepily. "Bentzy said you disappeared."

"What does Bentzy know?" Eyal said. "I'm right here."

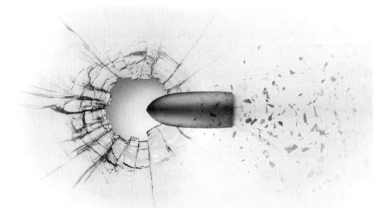

CHAPTER FIFTY-SIX

Kiev, Ukraine

E
yal set down the phone with a lengthy sigh, and Efrat looked at him curiously. "What now?"

"Debriefings." He stretched the word and sighed again. "The Americans and Ukrainians have a huge number of questions they want answered. The Ukrainians started putting on the pressure right away, while I was in prison, but it didn't get them very far. The Americans will use a different kind of pressure, and obviously I owe them real answers. They'll get them, in the end, but first...well, they were pretty shocked when I called from here." Eyal attempted to vanquish the smile from his lips, but it spread across his face, unbidden. "Am I really so childish that I'm proud of myself for having hoodwinked them? Paul nearly swallowed his cell phone when he realized where I was calling him from."

Efrat smiled. "They'll be more shocked by your appearance than by the fact that you got here," she said.

Eyal looked down at himself and took in his appearance. It would have been wonderful to take a long, hot bath and get dressed in clean clothing...but he had no clean clothing to speak of. Everything had gone up in smoke along with the hotel.

"I'm sure the CIA can stretch an expense account for one of its hired guns," he said. "Come to think of it, they should have done that in the first place." He sat down next to Elitzafun's bed and stroked his face. Elitzafun didn't wake up; he simply rolled over in his sleep.

"Don't," Efrat said. "He's tired after everything that he's been through. Let him sleep. You'll make up for lost time afterward."

"You're right, and I fully intend to, but – well, I don't know when that will be. Most probably I'll have to leave again tomorrow, and I have no way of knowing how long they're going to keep me there."

"I wanted to talk to you about that," Efrat said. "You'll be at the CIA's headquarters in Kiev, right?"

"Yes, although I might need to travel to Lviv to see some people there too. And don't forget that I'm still being closely monitored by several intelligence agencies."

"I see."

You have no idea just how much you don't see, Eyal thought. He knew that he was but a step away from a lengthy prison sentence if the American authorities decided to hold him accountable for what had happened. The cogs of true justice would turn very slowly, if at all. They liked scapegoats in the United States just as much as they did in Ukraine, or anywhere else, and Eyal was an extremely convenient scapegoat. They could paint him as a mercenary, a hired assassin, someone who had no personal loyalties to the president and no scruples whatsoever. Anyone who knew him would know how ridiculous it was, but the wider American public baying for bloody revenge didn't know him at all.

"I hope things will all get finished up here, in Ukraine," he continued, hoping he sounded convincing, "but there is just a possibility that Paul will want me to go to the United States to testify there." Eyal tickled Elitzafun's neck in an attempt to wake him, and he laughed at the expression on Efrat's face. "That's it. I won't try to wake him up anymore. Are you okay?"

"So when will you return to Israel? Even just an estimate?"

Eyal frowned. "Efrat, it's not simple. You know that. I was the head of the presidential security team. I was working in tandem with the CIA, but they're going to want to hold someone accountable, and I'm sure they would prefer—" Eyal stopped. He was sure the CIA would prefer to hold him accountable rather than someone within their ranks, but Efrat didn't need to know that. She probably wouldn't believe it anyway. And meanwhile he didn't even have any proof. It was only a series of hunches, based on instinct borne of long experience, but that was unlikely to persuade anyone to listen and take him seriously.

Furthermore, he didn't have all the puzzle pieces on hand. If they wanted they could drive a jeep through the holes in his account of events, and there wouldn't be a thing he could do about it. So he would have to lie, to brazen it out, to sound confident and convincing. And meanwhile, he would have to watch and listen very, very carefully to find those missing pieces and build a true picture, a factual account of what had gone wrong.

"You mean you might be arrested?" Efrat said, jumping to the conclusion without going through the motions to get there.

"Unfortunately, that could happen." There was no point in painting a picture of a glorious homecoming scenario. "But whatever the case, one thing is certain: I'm going to have to answer a million exhausting, complicated questions. I'll be okay, but my question is how you'll manage with everything." Eyal pointed to his sleeping son. "And with Elitzafun."

"He's okay," Efrat said quickly. "I've been speaking to him and playing with him all day long, and he seems fine."

A glint appeared in Eyal's eyes. "Did he…did he tell you anything?"

"What should he have told me?" Efrat drew a deep breath and then said quietly. "You mean in connection with everything he's been through?"

"Yes. Not everything he saw was all that beautiful. X and I—" Eyal paused and answered the question mark in Efrat's eyes. "X is the name of the kidnapper and, strange as it may seem, we both worked together to make sure that Elitzafun wouldn't witness anything too traumatic. Even so, certain things couldn't be prevented."

"Like what, for example?" Eyal's face was frozen.

How did you manage to box yourself into a corner like that? Eyal wondered. *Why did you so easily volunteer information that Efrat never asked for – maybe never even wanted?* "For example…I needed to kill Elitzafun's captor and incapacitate his staff members. Elitzafun was in the helicopter with us when that happened, and even though Bentzy covered his eyes, he heard what went on, and he may have seen some of it too."

There was a lengthy silence as Efrat's thoughts spun out of control. Her son had been witness to events that a child of his age – of any age – should never see. She couldn't get the words out of her mouth. Eyal looked down and remained silent. Was Efrat aware of the fact that her son had been left alone with strangers for an entire week? What had Elitzafun told her?

It was Efrat who finally broke the silence. "I can't know exactly what's going on inside of him," she said quietly. "But he seems okay. Of course he's been through a terrible experience, and we will obviously need to get him professional assistance to help him process everything, but *b'ezrat Hashem* he'll be okay."

Eyal bit his lip. "I'm sorry." Words that did absolutely no justice to anything that had happened, he thought, reflecting on the pain and fear that he had caused his wife, and wondering if there was any way he could ever atone for it. The words "not guilty" did nothing to alleviate the situation.

Efrat fell silent once again, thinking of everything Eyal had done to rescue their child, and the awful choices he'd been forced to make.

"I'm going with you," she said suddenly, her voice growing firm and decisive.

Eyal stared. "You? I mean…you can't, in any case. The CIA won't let you into their headquarters."

"No. Not their office here. I mean to the United States."

"The United States?" Eyal repeated in shock.

"Yes. If that's where they decide to transfer you, then wherever you go, I'm coming along."

"It's never a good idea to make hasty declarations," Eyal said, disguising his true feelings by injecting a laugh into his words, "because I may end up in an American prison."

"I said *wherever you go!*"

Eyal looked at her with open admiration. "Thank you," he said simply. Up until that point they hadn't spoken about themselves, neither as individuals nor as a team. That aspect of his life had been sorely missing for so long.

"Thank you? What for?" she asked.

"For not giving up on me these past few weeks."

Efrat smiled a watery smile. "As if I had a choice."

Eyal's heart stiffened. "I'm sorry," he said again.

There was a knock on the door, and a voice called out, "Eyal Gilboa?"

"Yes?" Eyal opened the door a crack.

"Mr. Ferguson is waiting for you downstairs in the car. He says that your presence at headquarters is urgent."

Eyal looked at his wife. Elitzafun was asleep, and she was stroking his hair over and over again as though she never planned on stopping. "Efrat…can I…can I go?" he asked quietly.

"There are five guards out here to keep watch on you in the meantime, Mrs. Gilboa," the man at the door said, and Efrat smiled at the irony of his statement. Men like her husband could overcome even ten guards, just as he had done earlier.

Eyal saw his wife's smile, immediately understanding its meaning. "Give me a minute," he told the man at the door.

The man left.

Eyal turned to his wife. "Efrat, if you don't want me to leave you alone, then I won't. I'll ask Paul if I can meet him tomorrow."

"Go." Efrat looked away and the tears that she had been working so hard to restrain during the last few awful weeks started to spill, unchecked, from her eyes. Her fears, the trauma that her son had endured, the threats to her husband's life... She pictured his spur-of-the-moment decision to shoot men point-blank inside a careening helicopter, only inches away from Elitzafun, and wondered how he was able to carry on afterward. "I'll be okay."

"I'm staying," Eyal said, sitting down theatrically on a chair for emphasis.

"No, Eyal. You're going." Efrat tried, without success, to hold back the tears that she had swallowed for so long. "You need to go. They're more likely to go easier on you if you cooperate with them."

"Probably," Eyal agreed, getting up from the chair with a sigh.

"Go then. I'll be okay."

Eyal wavered, one hand hovering over the door handle while his second hand opened the door. He followed the man down the hall as Efrat looked on. "Eyal?" she called out.

He turned around. "What?"

"Get them to give you a change of clothes, at the very least."

"I had hoped that you would respect my intervention," Paul told Eyal, taking in the man's torn, blood-stained clothing as he spoke. "I invested a lot to get you released, and I really didn't expect you to humiliate me like that. It's not even as if you tired of waiting for me to pick you up. Ten seconds. That's how long the warden said he turned away before you disappeared."

"Sorry," Eyal said, a look that resembled contrition in his eyes. "Let's just say I was in a rush."

"And just look what a state you're in," Paul added. "I'll have to get your injuries seen to first, I suppose, and a change of clothing. Pity you didn't see that as a priority. I'm surprised that you didn't mind your wife seeing you like this."

Eyal shrugged. "She would rather see me like this than not at all," he commented.

"Well, either way, let's get going. You've wasted enough time already, and the people waiting to speak with you have long since lost their patience. Bobby, take us to the nearest clinic, and while he's being treated, get hold of some clean clothes for him."

Ten minutes later they pulled up at a health clinic, and Bobby went inside. A few minutes later he reappeared. "There's a side door to the treatment room," he said. "This way – follow me."

Eyal followed him around the building, where a door already stood open. Inside, a white-coated doctor grimaced as he took stock of his wounds. Eyal lay down on the treatment table and the doctor got to work, removing shrapnel, stitching up partially-closed wounds, and cleaning off dried blood. By the time he was done, Bobby had returned with a parcel of clothing, and Eyal got dressed feeling appreciative.

"Feel better now?" the doctor said, smiling.

Eyal nodded. "Great, thanks."

He left the treatment room via the door he had entered and rejoined Paul in the car.

"You took your time," Paul said, drumming impatiently on the steering wheel as Eyal buckled his seat belt.

"I did? Well, it was you who wanted this meeting," Eyal shot back, affronted. "I'm sure you don't see it this way, but I'm doing you a big favor by conforming – more or less – to your timetable. My wife and son would certainly have appreciated seeing me again for more than an hour, you know."

Paul's eyes narrowed. "Eyal, quit the tough talk, will you? It's only thanks to my intervention that you even got out of jail in the first place. So far you've repaid that debt with nothing more than troublemaking, confirming the worst fears of those I overruled when I insisted you could be trusted. From now on, I'd like you to remember that."

Eyal was silent. However hard he tried – and admittedly, he wasn't trying very hard – he found it impossible to feel gratitude for being forced to take on a complicated, dangerous mission. Furthermore, the mission wasn't even over yet, and he had no idea how it would end. He would have to navigate the CIA's interrogation sessions without knowing who could be trusted and who was working for an outside, hostile agency. So far he only had suspicions, and somehow, he had to obtain hard evidence. Could Eli, or Bentzy, help him with that? He had no idea. Either way, he would have to tread extremely carefully.

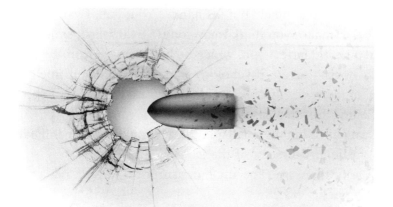

CHAPTER FIFTY-SEVEN

Litky, Ukraine

T he car stopped outside the gates of a nondescript building. Evidently, someone had been looking out for them,
as the electric gate immediately started to slide open
with a low hum. The car sped toward an underground parking
lot, and Paul quickly found an empty space. "Get out," he said
tersely.

"Where are we?" Eyal asked as he looked around.

"Some people call this a secret CIA base. Others are under the
impression that it's the location of the private library of a certain well-known philanthropist, after being repurposed from the
days when the KGB operated here. They're all wrong, though.
This building is the headquarters of the combined operations of
various intelligence agencies from several different countries." In

response to the unspoken question in Eyal's eyes, Paul added: "Not including the Mossad."

They took the elevator up to the main lobby, and Eyal looked around with interest. When they reached the front desk, Paul turned to Eyal and held out his hand. "Your gun, Eyal."

"What makes you think I have one?" Eyal asked, smiling drily. In fact, he did have a gun, which he had received from Bentzy.

"It doesn't take a psychology major or a brilliant intelligence agent to figure out that you would have found some way to procure one. Hand it over, please."

Eyal pulled out the small gun from his ankle holster and handed it to the deputy director of the CIA.

"I hope there won't be any more surprises," Paul said, a note of warning in his voice.

"Oh, there won't," Eyal said, uncharacteristically compliant.

"Good. Now give me your cell phone too."

"Why?" Eyal asked with surprise.

"Because."

Eyal put his hand into his pocket, pulled out his cell phone, and handed it over to Paul.

"Good boy. Too bad you didn't listen this well earlier this evening." Paul still couldn't forgive Eyal for the prank he had played on him. He handed the two objects over to Bobby. "Put these into a locker near the entrance and give me the key." He turned to Eyal. "You'll get them back when we finish up here."

Eyal adopted an injured expression. "I would appreciate being trusted just a little more," he said, knowing in advance what the response would be.

"So earn that trust," Paul replied, predictably. "It's in your hands."

They headed down a long corridor with many offices occupied even at this late hour. Several men nodded in greeting to Paul and Bobby, and some of them stared at Eyal with open curiosity. Eyal assumed they recognized his face and were wondering what he was doing in such a sensitive, secret location. Paul, unfazed by their unspoken reservations, led Eyal toward a locked room, which he opened with a key from his key ring. "Come on in," Paul said, walking inside himself.

In the room, the only furniture consisted of a huge, broad desk, three plain chairs, and one upholstered seat. On the desk was a mammoth stack of documents.

"See that mountain?" Paul asked, a gleam in his eyes. "It's all yours, in connection with your last mission." He gestured toward the upholstered chair. "This is yours too, so you don't claim that I'm not taking good care of you."

Eyal turned back toward the door of the room. "Forget it, Paul. I can't deal with a mound of paperwork now. I need to get back to Israel and my family. They haven't seen me for months, and we need to deal with the aftereffects of the kidnapping as well." Eyal made no mention of his arm, which was still throbbing with pain. He had chosen not to show the gunshot wound to the doctor in the clinic, knowing that he would be sent to a hospital for treatment – and he had no intention of stepping inside a Ukrainian hospital.

"You're not leaving this place," Paul said. "Some twenty people are waiting here to ask you questions."

"What do they want to ask me about? About X? Yesterday's events?"

"Most of their questions will be related to those things, but they also want to know more about your general performance during this operation. Our men are fascinated by the story." In answer to Eyal's stubborn expression of refusal, he added quietly: "Eyal, there's a reason you were released from prison. You're smart enough to realize that something is being requested of you in exchange for your freedom, and you will have to provide it."

Eyal exhaled slowly and settled into the padded chair. "Let's go then. Ask away, Mr. Extortion Artist."

"Just a minute." Paul pressed a button on his phone and called out: "We have his consent. You may enter."

Eight men immediately burst into the room, and Eyal eyed them in shock. "Paul, who are these people?"

"All sorts of people who are interested in hearing your answers to the questions I plan on asking."

"Names? Rank? Country of origin?"

"Nothing like that. Be a good boy and let us get going, okay?"

Eyal leaned back in submission. "I'm listening."

"When was the first time you met Rubinov?"

Eyal was taken aback by the question. He had been certain that the first question Paul would ask him would be related to events that had taken place at the hotel. "What's the difference?"

"If you ask questions about every question, we'll never finish."

"That's true." Eyal was grateful that he'd been provided with a comfortable chair, and soon refreshments were brought in too – bottles of water and juice, along with fresh fruit. "I met him at an event that he arranged."

"How did you manage to get in?" Paul asked the question, but the other men were clearly interested in Eyal's answer. Three of the men who occupied the chairs facing Eyal had laptops, which they placed on the table, two had recorders, and the other two took notes with pen and paper. Only one man leaned against the wall, arms folded, eyes focused intently on Eyal.

"I took over for someone else who had received an invitation. I interrogated him and received all the information I needed to get into the event, and then I turned up in his place."

"Why didn't you murder Rubinov right there? Wasn't that the reason you were sent to Ukraine?"

"I had no intention of killing him, and certainly not at the outset. I was concerned, however, that I might end up in a situation where I would have no choice but to do exactly that, and I was hoping things wouldn't turn out that way."

"What was the security like at that event?"

"Excellent. They wouldn't let even a shoelace in."

"If so, you wouldn't have been able to kill him in any case,"

Paul said. "You had no weapon, and you couldn't even slip in a pen with a hypodermic needle hidden inside."

Eyal laughed. "I don't want to sound coarse, but I don't need more than the tie around my target's neck to commit a murder."

"Describe his home."

Eyal's patience was wearing thin. "What for?"

"Eyal, be a good boy. We're asking the questions here, not you. We're trying our best to act nicely, but don't try our patience, because your status isn't exactly set in stone. You're hovering somewhere between freedom and prison; you're somewhat responsible for the tragedy, yet you're also the man who rescued several of our agents. It is clear to us all that you know too much, and we want to know what you know, even if it takes six, ten, or fourteen hours. Or days. So don't try to act like a smart aleck here. I hope I've made myself clear."

Eyal said nothing. Paul had no idea just what "you know too much" meant. Eyal knew plenty, but the interrogation would drag out only if they realized that he was withholding essential information.

Paul's gaze was accusing, and Eyal was shaken out of his reverie. "Give me a pen and paper, and I'll draw a diagram for you."

"With pleasure."

One of the agents in the room gave Eyal a transparent sheet and a dry marker. He began to sketch the building, floor by floor, hallway by hallway.

"Rubinov allowed you to roam freely around his house, I see," one of the men said. "How did you gain his complete confidence in such a short time?" All eyes focused intently upon Eyal with this question. "We all know that he was extremely paranoid. And you were a stranger. How did you manage what you did?"

"What is it that you want from me?" Eyal was getting angry. The room was overheated, and the number of people crammed into it just made things worse. Two of them were smoking, and Eyal was beginning to find it hard to breathe. His head began to pound, and exhaustion penetrated every fiber of his being. With the gunshot wound in his arm, along with the shrapnel wounds, he was much more short-tempered than usual. And he wanted to go home, more than anything else, more than he had ever wanted anything in his life.

"We want to understand you and to figure out what makes you tick," the man lolling against the wall said. "So, how did you pull it off?"

"My Mossad training," Eyal answered shortly. "We know how to use charm and charisma to achieve our goals. And it helps to be a prominent personage who is worth getting to know. I'm surprised that you don't know all this yourselves," he added acidly. "But more than all that, Rubinov, like every other human being, had something he wanted really badly. I promised to deliver the goods."

"Meaning that you knew that what Rubinov wanted most was to find out who killed his son, and you then used that knowledge to your advantage." A third man lit a cigarette.

"Exactly."

"What is the name of the pilot of the plane that brought you to Ukraine?"

"Are you going to ask about me about every single little detail? Because that will take – oh, around thirteen years to go through, seeing as it's been about that long since I first started working for the Mossad."

"We're focusing solely on your most recent mission. Naturally, we're curious about a whole lot more, but we can't do everything at once. Your most recent mission took place partly within our jurisdiction, and so your bosses have permitted us to question you about that. We're trying to break that mission up into segments now, with your assistance."

Eyal felt like making a run for it. His bosses? Who was manipulating him now? But he knew he was – at present, at least – powerless. Ultimately, he would be coerced into cooperating with the CIA, like it or not.

The interrogation continued, seeming to stretch on for hours. Without his watch – confiscated by the prison authorities and not returned to him at his release – Eyal had no idea how much time had passed. At some point he realized that the questions were repeating themselves, which Eyal took to mean that they didn't trust him and were asking the same questions again in order to check the veracity of his tale.

"Describe X's methods in the house where you were held before your first escape."

Eyal's photographic memory left the men open-mouthed. He described each of X's men, his house, his security procedures, and the information that he had discovered about the president and his security team. Not a single detail had escaped his notice.

"Hey!" one of the men said at one point. "We want you to work for us!"

"You're not the first person to say that," Eyal said tiredly. "Are we done now?"

"Stop asking that question every few minutes – it just wastes time."

Eyal later discovered that six hours had passed, during which Eyal had become more and more infuriated – with Zev Avshalom, with Paul and the CIA, with the Mossad, and with the Ukrainian security forces. Finally, he was given a short break. Someone entered the room with a double-wrapped meal and a small note that read "Bon appetit and *hatzlachah*. Yosef Yitzchak Kagan." The note brought a smile to Eyal's tired face.

"Your wife called your cell phone, Eyal," Paul said, stepping back into the room after Eyal's break. "And boy is it hot in here. I'd better turn down the heat."

"Really now?" Eyal said, but there was a flicker of emotion in his eyes. "How long did you tell her it would be before I'd be able to talk to her?"

"How do you know that's what she asked?"

"It doesn't take a genius."

"Ten hours," Paul said with assumed indifference, fiddling with the heating switches as he spoke.

"Another ten hours!" Eyal rose angrily from his seat.

"Yes. Why are you so surprised?" Paul smirked. "You've been through longer interrogations than this in the past, under far less favorable conditions. And if you behave well, we'll even shorten the interrogation by an hour or two."

Eyal sat back down. The interrogation resumed, although not all of the eight men returned to the room. If Eyal had identified the men correctly, it seemed that the Ukrainians had chosen to leave already, and only the Americans still had questions to ask.

Now Paul changed tack. "What we're interested in figuring out is the identity of the people who cooperated with X, passing on critical information to him."

"I'm interested in figuring that out too," Eyal replied.

The men exchanged glances. "Can you make a guess as to who may have been behind the leaks?"

"If you tell me how your units are formed, then I can try to figure out where the leaks came from," Eyal said. There was a note of despondency in his voice. "But it won't be easy, and I can't guarantee success. I also charge five hundred dollars per hour." He might as well milk the situation for all it was worth.

"We'll let it go for now. Maybe we'll come back to this later, but right now we'd like to discuss the main issue: the act of terror that led to such a tragedy for the American nation. You were head of security, and we want—" The phone in Paul's breast pocket rang suddenly, interrupting him. Paul looked at the screen, and his expression changed from curiosity to surprise.

"Eyal," Paul said, giving him his phone, "I have no idea how this person managed to access my personal cell number, but he wants to speak to you."

"Eli?" Eyal asked, taking the phone quickly.

"How did you guess?" Eli's familiar voice caused a shiver to race down Eyal's spine. Eli was just about the only person in the world whom he knew that he could trust without reservations.

"Who else could retrieve the private number of a deputy director of the CIA, other than a member of the Mossad?"

"Exactly. Got to thank Eran for that."

Eyal chuckled. "No one beats the agents back home."

"If my friend can't be bothered to call me, then what can I do? Obviously, I had to track him down and call him myself."

"Sorry. Debriefings, interrogations. You know."

"And you didn't have time to call me just to tell me two simple words like 'I'm alive' or 'I'm okay'?"

"I figured Bentzy would let you know that I was alive and well."

"Where are you now? Answering those snoopy CIA agents' million questions?"

"Tell him I can hear him," Paul said in flawless Hebrew.

Eyal smiled. "There are people listening in on our conversation," he said.

"Fine. What I want to tell you isn't classified. Um, I mean – I just wanted to say that I thought I'd never see you again. And I'm glad that things turned out better than my expectations."

Eyal was embarrassed. Only Eli could bare his heart in such a manner, but he was clueless as to how to respond to such a display of emotion. In the end, he decided to play it down. "There were times when I thought the same way," he finally said. "When I thought – well, you know."

"I'm very happy that you're alive. And now please make sure to keep things that way."

"To keep you happy, or to keep myself alive?"

"Both, if possible."

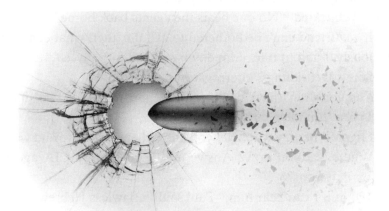

CHAPTER FIFTY-EIGHT

Litky, Ukraine

Eyal hung up the phone and stood in silence for a long moment, reflecting upon the man who had done so much for him and who expected nothing in return.

"Have you finished?" Paul asked.

Eyal shook himself from his reverie. "Yes. But please, Paul – have some mercy. Let's finish up already. Think about what my family and I have been through during these past two weeks."

"I'm well aware of that. But we have plenty more questions we want to ask you. We've only just gotten to the main topic, namely, the attack on the president, and it will take a long time to complete the interrogation. If you absolutely insist, we can let you go today and then start again tomorrow. Or we can continue now until we're done. You decide."

"I'll ask my wife."

Paul handed Eyal his phone.

Eyal looked around and saw three of the five other men in the room whispering, and he could guess what they were whispering about. They probably wanted him to figure out where the leak in security was coming from, but they could forget about that. If they chose to hold him in the same spot for the next week, he couldn't be held accountable for what would happen as a result.

"Which option sounds better to you?" Efrat asked after Eyal finished outlining his dilemma.

"It makes no difference to me. I'll go along with whatever you prefer. One the one hand, taking a break now will mean we have to stay here for another day, but on the other hand, we'll get to tour the city with Elitzafun a bit, and he deserves that." Eyal sighed as he recalled something. "And I promised him a trip to the zoo."

Efrat dismissed the idea out of hand. "We can take a trip to the Biblical Zoo in Jerusalem," she said. "But what about you? Aren't you exhausted? They've been interrogating you for about eight hours already!"

"I've been trained to survive twenty-four-hour-long interrogations, and under worse conditions," Eyal said. "This is really not a big deal, but the choice is yours, and I'll go along with whatever you decide."

Efrat laughed. "Okay. In that case, let's stay here for another day. I really would like to take Elitzafun out a bit."

Eyal ended the call and turned around to face his interrogators. "I'm going to call it quits now and come back tomorrow. So get me a car to take me back to my wife and son, and order another one to pick me up from the hotel tomorrow afternoon at half past four."

"Yes sir," Paul said in complete seriousness. Eyal had reverted to his usual peremptory style, issuing a long chain of orders with no regard for anyone who was on the receiving end. "Where do you plan to go tomorrow morning?"

"I haven't made any plans yet. What would you suggest?"

"I heard you mention the zoo. There's a great zoo in Kiev, and your son should enjoy it."

"Okay, thanks."

"Enjoy." Paul handed Eyal a slim black leather wallet.

"What's this?"

"It's called a wallet. Normal people put money inside it in order to pay for things, so that they don't have to requisition cars from law-abiding citizens."

"Oh, and that reminds me," Eyal said. "I'm not sure how much money I owe, but I definitely owe some money to the Metrobus, because I rode some buses there without paying."

"Perfect," Paul said, applauding. "So now you have some spending money. Uncle Sam's gift to you. Buy your son whatever he wants, all right?"

"Are you trying to bribe me?"

"Something like that."

"How are you doing?" Eyal lifted Elitzafun into the air, but an expression of pain flitted across his face, and he quickly put him back down.

"I'm fine," Efrat said, and Eyal wondered if Efrat was merely pretending to be a calm and serene wife or if she was truly made of steel. She looked at him. "But more to the point, how are you?"

"Me?" Eyal wasn't used to thinking of himself. "I don't know. I guess I'm okay."

She smiled. "You guess so?"

"Yes. No physical pressure was applied over the course of the interrogation, and that means it was tolerable." Almost tolerable. The tolerability didn't include everything Eyal had tried to conceal, his attempts to avoid mentioning certain things, and his tense, prolonged silences.

"Can you tell me exactly what it is they want from you?" Efrat glanced over at Elitzafun, happily munching on some of his beloved red Bamba. She turned back to her husband, and they settled down on a bench to watch Elitzafun together. He seemed so happy and carefree as he tossed Bamba to the fish in the lake.

"They're trying to figure out the series of events that took place during my last mission," Eyal explained. "They have millions of questions, which is understandable, considering the number of things that went wrong."

"Okay, I get that. But how much longer is this going to take?"

Eyal shrugged. "Paul promised me they'll finish up later today, maybe till late at night. And I'm not in a position to refuse."

"Why not?"

"Efrat, it's not as simple as you think. The mission was badly botched. Someone leaked sensitive information to terrorists, and someone is going to have to pay the price. A very visible price, in order to placate a lot of people in high places. The Ukrainians are asking for twenty-five years."

Efrat turned pale, and Eyal laughed. "There's no need to be so alarmed. If the Americans pressure them to drop their demand, they will have to do so. But I need to make sure that it pays for the Americans to do that. Do you understand?"

"Can't the Mossad or the GSS hush the story up?" Efrat was seething with rage at the idea that the men who had sent her husband on a mission refused to extricate him now that things had gone awry.

"They could, but they prefer not to. Like most of the world, the Ukrainians are quite rightly fed up with the Mossad's arrogant attitude, which takes nobody and nothing into account. Or at least that's the way they see it."

"But you weren't working as a Mossad agent," Efrat retorted hotly.

"That's exactly the point." he replied. "But sometimes it helps to keep a certain ambiguity. So I haven't been protesting too much in that direction."

"So how can the Americans help us?" Efrat asked.

"Let's admit that they have more diplomatic clout."

"I admit it! But what do you plan to do? How much longer are they going to hold you?"

"I don't know, but I've been through worse, no?"

"True." She didn't look at Eyal, when she said quietly, "I haven't even asked you yet where you were and what sort of awful things you've been through."

Elitzafun chose that moment to come running toward them. "Come, look! A huge goldfish is eating a Bamba! Come quick!"

Elitzafun was already running back to the lake as Efrat called out, "Don't go too far, Elitzafun. We're coming."

When Elitzafun was out of earshot, Eyal's expression turned serious. "You're better off not asking," he said.

Efrat eyed the wounds on his face and the bandage and bruises on his arm, and her heart filled with compassion. Yes, she was angry, hurt, and wounded, but there was no denying that he hadn't had an easy time of it.

She had no idea what he had been through.

Perhaps she would never know.

Paul left the building, which he had privately nicknamed the UN, very early the following morning. Eyal had been interrogated for ten consecutive hours, but he still needed to process the information and data, cross-checking it and trying to make sense of it all.

His initial impression, however, was that sense could not be made of it. Everything seemed to have become one huge jumble. Numbers that didn't add up, contradictory information, money transferred to obscure locations, and people appearing and disappearing at whim… Eyal's report was a complicated vortex of partially divulged secrets.

Deep in thought, Paul turned on his car engine and began to drive. He had the distinct feeling that Eyal knew much more than he was willing to admit. Maybe he needed to have him arrested again, this time on American soil, to keep the Ukrainians from meddling. There were things the Ukrainians didn't need to know, and it was just possible that Eyal was keeping his mouth shut due to their presence.

All the same, getting Eyal to talk was not going to be a simple matter. He was hardly the sort of person to be intimidated by even a brutal interrogation. Paul had studied Eyal's Mossad file at great length. Eyal had been subjected to interrogations where immense physical force had been applied and he had maintained absolute, total silence. But Paul didn't need Eyal's file to know that he would silently withstand even the toughest of interrogations; one look at the man's face and arm was all it took to know that he was steel in the face of his interrogators.

Paul parked his car in the hotel's parking lot and headed upstairs to get some sleep. His mind was churning. Eyal's version of events couldn't possibly be true. His tale was so riddled with holes that no logical picture could emerge.

Paul would need to approach the source directly and to demand answers.

"Eyal, Paul is making a call."

The Mossad had managed to infiltrate Paul's phone, using the opportunity opened by the call Eli had put through. Innocent as the conversation had seemed, it was not exactly motivated by the warm feelings between the two, though they certainly did exist. Rather, Eran and his team had managed to hack into one of the apps on the CIA agent's phone, and via that app, monitor all the activity on the device. Since then, Eli had been listening to every single conversation Paul had.

"What are you so surprised about?" Eyal said. "He must make dozens of calls a day, if not more."

"Actually, no," Eli said. "Your friend is not a big talker. His cell phone is inactive most of the day, and when he does talk on it, his conversations are lightning-fast. But now for the good news: Paul has arranged to meet someone at the Kunfoo restaurant at half past eight this evening. I'm going to venture a guess that if you listen in on that meeting, you'll find the answers to many of your questions."

"I'll be there," Eyal said shortly.

"Good. And I'm sure I don't need to remind you to take care of yourself."

Eyal stood at a safe distance, after making sure that he wasn't being tracked. He spotted Paul quickly and easily. From his confident gait it was clear that he did not suspect that he was being followed.

Paul entered the restaurant, and a moment later another man entered from the opposite direction. Given that coincidence, it was more than likely that this was the man Paul was meeting. Eyal trained his binoculars on the second man's features, and his face instantly turned gray. With disbelief turning to fear, he stared for a long moment, unsure how to react. Whatever suspicions he had entertained before, he hadn't expected anything like this.

The man meeting with Paul had a face, hands, and feet. The man was capable of speech, and he was wearing a smart suit and carrying an expensive attaché case.

The man Paul was meeting had a name.

His name was Dimitry Rubinov.

CHAPTER FIFTY-NINE

Kiev, Ukraine

S o, Paul had played him like the total fool he was. He had been willing to believe that the CIA, and no other organiza-tion, was behind this – he hadn't suspected for a minute that the plot was so much more complicated than that. Paul was just the front man – for who? When he had spoken openly to the man, how much further had the information gone? Which countries were involved?

And he had been angry at Yonatan, for letting himself be used! What a joke. Yonatan was a tiny fish in the scheme of things, one who probably had no idea what was really going on.

As the fury rose inside him, Eyal forced himself to consider the situation dispassionately. He was here, Paul was here, and Rubinov was here. Clearly the opportunity was too good to waste. He had to act now while he still could – while he was still at liberty to do something – anything.

Eyal walked up to the entrance to the restaurant, handed the security guard his gun, and stepped quietly inside.

Eyal's entrance into the elegant establishment was accompanied by delicate strains of classical music. A ten-piece ensemble was playing the notes of Shostakovich's Symphony No. 2, but for Eyal the music was merely so much background noise as he walked slowly, determinedly over to the far end of the room. He approached the table where the two men were sitting, dragging a chair over from a nearby table with deliberate disregard for etiquette. Absorbed as they were in their conversation, the two men paid little attention to the man approaching until he was literally under their noses.

Eyal sat down with aplomb and glared.

"Eyal?" Paul said, clearly appalled at this development. "What are you doing here?"

Paul might have been shocked, but Rubinov was absolutely horrified. He opened his mouth to say something, but then closed it again, unable to get a single syllable out.

"Calm down, honorable friends," Eyal said with a sneer. "I certainly didn't intend to ruin your appetites. The food in this restaurant is outrageously overpriced, and it would be a shame to let it go to waste."

The two men exchanged silent glances, and Eyal eyed the effects of his sudden appearance with satisfaction.

Paul was the first to find his lost tongue. "What do you want?" he asked.

"I'm sure you can guess." Eyal turned to the American, sparks of fury in his eyes. "But this time I want the whole truth, not just the parts you choose to reveal. Let me assure you that full disclosure is definitely in your best interests."

"Is that supposed to be a threat?"

"My, my, how swift you are to draw conclusions," Eyal

complimented the CIA's deputy director, his voice laced with contempt. "I may not be armed at this moment, due to the excellent security here, but..." he paused, gathering up the utensils on the table, "I can make do with what's at hand. I'm sure you know that already."

"You're threatening murder. That's a criminal offense."

"Wow, you're really scaring me," Eyal said. "Do you mean to say I could get put behind bars for hinting that I could do you both damage with a table knife? Maybe I'd even get a longer sentence than I would get for, let's say for example, murdering a mafia don? Or for collaborating with the enemy and allowing the president of the United States to be assassinated?"

Paul was silent. He and Rubinov stared quietly at the tablecloth.

"What do you want?" Paul said again, this time in a far more submissive tone.

"I already told you. The whole, unvarnished truth." The fire in Eyal's eyes was frightening. Instead of looking at Eyal, Paul turned to face Rubinov. There was another long moment of silence as Paul struggled to think of something to say to conciliate this very angry man.

"Eyal," he began.

"Just a moment," Eyal said, whirling around to face the waiter coming up behind them. The man held an order for two. "Thank you," he said. "And if you don't mind, we'd like a bottle of Glenmorangie Signet now, if possible."

The waiter headed to the bar with a nod, returning a moment later with the whiskey. "Thank you," Eyal said.

"Order some food for yourself," Paul said, attempting, unsuccessfully, to inject a friendly note into his voice. "Waiter, we have one more order to place here."

"Yes sir, what would you like?" The waiter's expression was inscrutable, but he was clearly trying to conceal his surprise. The Kunfoo wasn't the type of restaurant where diners appeared without advance reservations.

He handed Eyal a menu, which Eyal pretended to study. Out of the corner of his eye he saw Rubinov inching toward Paul. They clearly wanted to exchange some information, to find a way to rescue themselves from this predicament, but he wouldn't give them that chance. Besides, it was a shame to waste a perfectly good damask tablecloth.

"Mineral water in a closed bottle, a plastic cup, and a rare rib steak, with a proper knife." Eyal turned from the waiter to Paul, taking in his shocked expression. The man knew that he kept kosher. "As you know, I was already aware that I was a puppet in the hands of the American security system. So now, here's news flash number one: Deputy director of the CIA adopts an innocent expression while incriminating an Israeli agent for the murder of a mafia don. The murder, however, never took place. And news flash number two: This same deputy director of the CIA authorized the kidnapping of a five-year-old boy from his home in Israel in order to blackmail the Israeli agent – his father."

"I never authorized any kidnapping," Paul declared. "You're making unfair assumptions, and you have no proof of any such thing."

Eyal ignored the interruption. "We could put it differently, of course. We could describe how a cunning plot to capture a dangerous terrorist using the United States president as bait went horribly wrong and actually led to the death of the president. I'm sure the media would love that. I know my wife will enjoy reading it."

"Nobody will take you seriously, Eyal, and you know that," Paul said, trying to sound blasé. "You don't have a scrap of written proof, and much of what you suggest is simply wrong."

"You want to call my bluff?" Eyal said, taking note of the warning glance in Rubinov's eye. Clearly the man was worried about what Paul might let slip, though Eyal had no idea why he didn't have more confidence in the American's professionalism.

"We don't have to be enemies, Eyal," Paul tried. "We can cooperate. To our mutual benefit."

"Sounds like fun!" Eyal said. "When you don't have your neck in a noose, that is."

The waiter arrived with Eyal's order on a carved wooden tray. It hadn't taken long – a rare steak was, of course, the quickest to cook. The steak was accompanied with two small dipping bowls of sauce, two side dishes, and a sharp knife with a wooden handle.

Eyal picked up the knife and thanked the waiter. He ran a finger appreciatively along the blade, watching as the men across from him turned pale.

"Look here, Eyal," Paul said, hating himself for his fear of this unpredictable but undeniably talented agent. "You were the only person we could entrust with this task. We considered many agents, from a variety of countries, and ultimately decided on you. You ought to take pride in that fact."

Eyal looked down at the steak and ran the knife's cutting edge along it, leaving a jagged ridge behind. "Okay. If it makes you happy, I'll be proud. Check. What happened next? How did my son enter the picture?"

"Eyal, I told you when we met at the firing range: That was something that we never anticipated."

"Too bad you didn't," Eyal said cynically. "Funny thing, that. I mean, you seem to have thought things through pretty thoroughly in general. Oh, on second thought, maybe not. After all, the president was actually murdered in the end. I guess you didn't anticipate that either. Or maybe he was just collateral damage?"

"Do you want an apology, or explanations?" A crack appeared in Paul's self-confident veneer, and it started to widen.

"Both. Why should I settle?"

"Why? Because—" Paul was angry at himself for not being more in control, but he could not restrain himself from uttering his next sentence aloud. "Can you please leave that knife alone?"

"No."

Paul swallowed. He had underestimated just how angry Eyal was. "Okay, okay. I'll admit that I wasn't being one hundred percent accurate with you when we discussed things at the shooting range. This isn't a Syrian terrorist organization we're talking about, it's the Fraternity. You tried once, unsuccessfully, to destroy the organization, and that's what we decided to attempt here as well. We wanted to bring them down, and as someone who was harmed by the organization, and as an intelligence agent, I'm sure you can sympathize.

"The Fraternity has overstayed its welcome in the world. It's created too many problems. We asked Israel for help, and they sent us an agent who had previously failed at his mission and who was subsequently coerced into murdering Rubinov."

Eyal turned to face the frozen figure of the man in question. He didn't even blink when his name was mentioned.

"I see," Eyal said slowly. "Israel sent someone who was to be locked up in a Ukrainian prison cell for life, punished for a crime he did not commit, while the supposed victim of the crime was sitting pretty – where? Paris? Vienna? Canberra? At what point did you decide it was safe to return? When you heard from your good friend Paul that X was dead? I did you that favor, by the way. I think I deserve a thank-you."

"I need not thank you, because you didn't act expressly for my benefit," Rubinov said drily. "But I will express my admiration for your skills nonetheless."

"The Fraternity wanted Rubinov removed because he had begun to meddle into their affairs," Paul said, continuing his efforts at placation. "Rubinov's son crossed their path too many times when he was in America, and the Fraternity didn't blink before liquidating him. His murder, however, bought them a dangerous enemy, and they needed to do everything possible to have that enemy removed from the equation before he took revenge for his son's death."

A long moment of silence passed. Eyal stared at the dangerous enemy Paul had mentioned, and his mind went into high gear as adrenaline began pumping through his veins. The skeletal image in his mind morphed into a fully clothed form. "Let me tell you what happened," he said. "The Fraternity knew that one day Rubinov would succeed in discovering the identity of his son's murderer, and so they sent me to kill him, keeping their own hands clean. Rubinov, as a mafia man who likes to play tough – that's you, Dimitry, right? – was the perfect partner for an organization with a similar desire to destroy the Fraternity, and so he found you, Paul. Correct?"

"How did you—" Paul began.

Eyal lifted the steak knife threateningly, and Paul fell silent. "So Rubinov met with Paul, the deputy director of the CIA, who had a deep-seated interest in taking down the Fraternity, and offered to assist him," Eyal continued. "The CIA would cooperate with Rubinov in staging his own death, and Rubinov would help the CIA destroy the Fraternity. Staging his own death worked well for two reasons: one, simple self-preservation; and two, to let the Fraternity think that their sworn enemy was out of the picture and that they had nothing more to fear. And the plan was executed with precision. No one but Yabrov, who was devoted to his boss, knew that Rubinov was still alive. Instead, the suspected murderer was arrested, humiliated, tortured, electrocuted, and beaten, while Paul and Rubinov insolently celebrated their first victory. Of course, the suspected murderer could have ended up breaking and admitting to murder, landing him a life sentence in a somewhat less-than-luxurious Ukrainian prison."

"We wouldn't have allowed that to happen," Paul said quickly. "We would have intervened if things came to that."

"Wow. What would I do without you?" Eyal's eyes shot daggers. "Onward. The Fraternity now believes that Rubinov is dead, which means that Rubinov can start putting into action his plan to bring them down. His plan is a simple one. He hires someone to kidnap the president, and he suggests that this person turn to the Fraternity for assistance. The Fraternity will cooperate with the hired assassin because they're not too fond of the president, viewing his opinions as far too aggressive for their pacifist leanings.

And this will destroy the public image of the Angels of Peace, because they will finally be exposed as the violent thugs they really are."

"But…"

"Paul, hasn't anyone ever taught you to keep quiet for five minutes at a time? Allow me to be the first, then. So Rubinov hires someone who goes by the name of X, and suggests, via Yonatan, that X's men abduct the president. X is a Syrian who is very interested in his personal militia gaining fame for successfully changing the face of Syrian warfare." Eyal deliberately wove this piece of misinformation into the conversation in order to see how the two men would react, but neither of them seemed moved by it. *Paul and Rubinov really don't know the whole truth*, he thought. *They must actually believe that X was acting for the good of the Syrian people. They didn't know that he was an American assassin hired by some anonymous person with other interests at heart.*

"Amazing, isn't it?" Eyal said, passing his gaze between the men.

Rubinov looked as though he were on the verge of having a heart attack, while it took a minute for Paul to find his tongue again. "You told me to keep quiet," he said hoarsely.

"And what a good boy you've been," Eyal said, flashing the agent a sickly smile. "Yonatan responded to your joint request in order to prove his loyalty to the president and his men. He approached X, suggesting that he abduct the president. He also suggested that X turn to the Fraternity for assistance, and then he told X to blackmail me as well. The president was in on the plan. He wanted to become known as the president who brought peace to Syria. Both Paul and the president were unconcerned about my uncovering the plot to capture the president. X too was completely tranquil throughout the operation, unfazed even by the counter-espionage team following me around in Washington. Every last detail of the plan had been worked out in advance, and I was dumb enough to fall for it."

"You…" Paul began, but then stopped, carefully weighing his words. "How did you figure all that out? Again, I'm awed by your deductive abilities."

"Is that supposed to be a compliment?" Eyal hacked the steak in half, lips pursed together in controlled fury. "Because I'm not exactly in the mood for nice acceptance speeches."

Paul took a sip from his drink, trying to think of the words that would cool down, at least somewhat, the other man's fury. "You haven't fully understood, though. X took matters a few crazy steps forward, without coordinating with anyone. Instead of turning to the Fraternity for weapons and equipment, and forcing you to cooperate under threat of having you sent back to prison, he took drastic measures and kidnapped your son. We had no idea he would do that, Eyal. We really didn't."

The knife remained perfectly poised over the meat. "And what's been going on with you in the meantime, my dear deceased friend? How have your plans to destroy the Fraternity been working out?"

Rubinov eyed Paul with a beseeching look, and Paul took over the role of orator once again, changing tracks. "He hired a negotiator, not Yonatan. We used Yonatan only for you. Rubinov's negotiator told the Fraternity about X, a young Syrian militant with crazy ideas about kidnapping the president. The Fraternity was happy to assist X, and thereby gain a new president who would go along with their pacifist ideas. At the same time, X's Syrian goals would be achieved."

"But none of that happened in the end," Eyal pointed out. "The president was killed, and all X provided was hot air."

"We didn't think of that," Paul said quietly. "X wasn't the person we thought he was."

This time it was Eyal who was silent. He wasn't ready to reveal the fact that he already knew that X had not been a Syrian unfortunate seeking to bring peace to his war-torn country – that he was in reality nothing more than a greedy American thug hired to murder the president. After a long moment of thought, Eyal turned to Rubinov. "Tell me, Dimitry," he said softly. "What if I had really murdered you, due to my obligations to the Fraternity? Truthfully, I thought of doing just that on several occasions when you were well within my shooting range."

Once again Rubinov remained silent, and Paul answered the question for him. "We were relying on our assessment of your psychological profile and the Mossad psychologist's report, which told us that you are an extremely ethical person, who will never buy his own life or freedom at the expense of another. We knew that you could never go through with a killing unless you found an ethically justifiable reason to do so."

Eyal stared at Paul long and hard, and his green eyes sparkled with disbelief coupled with rage. When he opened his mouth again, his voice was full of venom. "Go and tell those oh-so-clever Mossad psychologists that what they consider to be ethical doesn't always conform with what I know to be truly moral. And you might add, while you're at it, that when they hand over a spy's personal details, not only are they betraying the trust of the spy himself, they are also endangering lives. The lives of people with whom I am far too intimately familiar." Eyal's eyes sparked, and he maneuvered the knife in his hand into a dangerous position.

"Let's go for a walk," Paul said hurriedly. "It's getting too stuffy in here."

Eyal closed his eyes, reining in his emotions with superhuman strength.

"Eyal." Paul took his hand gently. He understood the thought processes of undercover agents; he recognized their human frailties; and he was used to navigating the murky waters in which they swam. "Let's go out for a walk." When a spy reached the end of his tether he was liable to lose control, and it was vital that his handlers realized this before it was too late.

"No." Eyal drew a deep breath, opened his eyes, and said quietly, "I'm not going anywhere. Continue."

With no other choice, Paul carried on with his tale: "X planned the president's capture with Eyal like putty in his hands due to the presence of Elitzafun. I'll admit, however, that Eyal performed some heroic feats and attempted to escape despite his situation. In the United States, Eyal coordinated the mission with the CIA exactly as we wanted. The president would not be in actual danger at any point, because everything was perfectly planned. We would prove that the weapons used for the attack on the president had been provided by the Fraternity, and that would drag the organization down. X and his militia would be captured by the CIA as well, and everything would work out just fine."

"And here," Eyal said, his voice growing cold with cynicism, "is where things began to unravel."

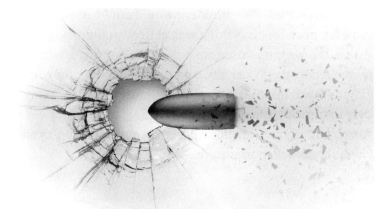

CHAPTER SIXTY

Kiev, Ukraine

E yal was a different man when he left the restaurant. The facts of the case had started to coalesce, and an astounding picture was emerging. Paul and Rubinov both knew what he knew, but what they didn't yet know was that X was not a Syrian freedom fighter who had willingly cooperated with the Fraternity and had, for some reason, later let them down. He wondered how they would react to the revelation that X was actually an American citizen who had betrayed his own country.

But Eyal still needed to verify Paul's loyalty. Despite their common interests, Rubinov was hardly an appropriate comrade in arms for a CIA agent. To put it bluntly, the man was a criminal. On the other hand, if not Paul, then in whom could he confide?

Eyal's exhaustion, coupled with the crushing weight of

responsibility that lay on his shoulders, was taking its toll. When he entered his hotel room, Efrat took one look at the expression on his face and knew immediately that something was very wrong. Eyal was the last person she would expect to break under stress, meaning that this was no minor issue.

"What happened?" Efrat asked, a note of alarm finding its way into her voice. How could things get even worse than they already were? They had been counting on a modicum of support from the Americans – were they being abandoned now, when they had no one else to turn to?

"It's not important," Eyal said, slumping down onto the couch and reaching for a bottle of juice.

"Eyal, don't do this to me," Efrat said, her tone rising in frustration. "It is important – I can see it on your face. And don't make the mistake of thinking that it doesn't affect me, or the children – not after what's already happened to us."

"That's exactly why I don't want to share this with you," Eyal said, fixing her with a tired gaze as he put down his glass. "Once was enough for both of us, wouldn't you agree?"

"What do you mean?" Efrat asked, a tremor racing down her spine. Was this a new threat to her children's lives? Anything but that...

Eyal sighed. "There's a cardinal rule in my line of work that goes something like this: When it concerns your spouse and your children, what you don't know can't hurt you. I won't say it's always applicable, but it has a lot of merit. I don't want you mixed up in this, Efrat. You won't gain anything from it."

Efrat shook her head. "It doesn't seem as though you have control over such things. Like you said, it happened once already. Please realize that what happens to you affects me and the children, regardless of whether we know why or not. I knew that when I married you – that's part and parcel of being a family. Hashem – not you – has willed things that way. So please, at least share with me what's going on now."

"Why?" Eyal had been trained to keep whatever he knew completely confidential. He knew how to disconnect completely from others and to share nothing. He couldn't imagine why in the world his wife might want to know what really took place behind the scenes of his job.

"I want to know for your sake," she said, surprised at having to explain herself. "I want to know what I can do for you."

Now it was Eyal's turn to look at his wife in surprise. "For me? Why?"

Efrat was suddenly overwhelmed with feelings of compassion for her husband. The man in front of her was clueless as to what a healthy interpersonal relationship looked like. He was used to serving his country while breaking confidences – and having confidences broken. A healthy spousal relationship – even a healthy parent-child relationship – was a foreign concept to him. Years of what was tantamount to abuse inflicted by his handlers had crippled him emotionally.

Suddenly, so many things crystalized in Efrat's mind. She had never seen her husband actually "in the field," but the thick screen that partitioned off that aspect of his life suddenly seemed to fall away, and her husband's exceptional prowess suddenly became clear to her. However greatly his Mossad bosses might sing his praises, it was obvious that his skills were built on unhealthy foundations. With bitterness, Efrat realized that this revelation should hardly have surprised her. After all, the structure of the Israeli army itself was based on abuse of power for the furtherance of goals antithetical to true Jewish values. Eyal was a product of that system, lauded and feted but ultimately abandoned once they had no more use for him.

She wanted to share his life, but even more than that, she needed to lead her husband toward a normal, healthy way of life that was still so foreign to him. A life that did not consist of mystery, denial, and secrecy. She needed to show him the possibility of living a life without the constant threat of danger and death at every turn. She needed to introduce him to people who didn't automatically scan their surroundings for possible sniper posts whenever they walked down a narrow street. To people who looked for the most pleasant table in the restaurant, not the one located in the most strategically safe position. And more than that, she needed to introduce him to people who knew that one's home was the center of one's life, not just a transit point between operations.

"Yes, for you," she said simply. "And you're not going anywhere until you tell me what you're going through."

Eyal was an intelligence agent – there was no changing that, or at least, not quickly. And so, in order to answer his wife's question he took out a pen and paper, placed them on a mirror he took off the wall, and wrote, *I have critical information to convey to the American security establishment.* He drew two lines underneath the word "critical," and then added, *Their president's murder is a part of a huge web spun by someone with dangerous plans for the US. The trouble is that I don't know who that person is. I tried to reach out to the deputy director of the CIA, but I'm concerned that he may not be trustworthy. I don't know who I can trust with what I know.*

Efrat read the note quickly and then scribbled her response: *Maybe you can talk to the vice president.*

Eyal smiled and wrote, *He's actually my main suspect, because he stood to gain the most from the president's murder. After all, he's now the acting president.*

Efrat thought for a moment and then wrote, *Maybe consult with Bentzy? He's someone you can trust, right?*

Eyal glanced at her with a pained expression before writing, *Not anymore.*

Why? Efrat wrote back, shocked. They had known Bentzy for years, and Eyal had never expressed the slightest doubt regarding Bentzy's integrity.

Because I'm surrounded by spies wherever I turn. One didn't need to know graphology to detect the bitterness clearly etched into each of Eyal's letters. *Even good men were manipulated into serving as spies without their knowledge – their information was extracted via devious means, with terrible results.*

Do you trust Eli? Efrat now asked.

Eyal nodded. Eli was the only person in the world who wouldn't pass on a single word, nuance, or expression without Eyal's explicit permission.

So call him down here. He'll come.

Paul returned to his hotel room and fell asleep the moment his head hit the pillow. The transatlantic flight, the meetings, the interrogations, the cross-examinations, and the fact-checking had all worn him down. He had been busy verifying data all night prior to his meeting with Rubinov, hoping to figure out what had gone wrong. In the end, however, before he had managed to exchange a single intelligible word with Rubinov, Eyal had shown up and taken him by surprise. The shock, coupled with Eyal's intimidating manner, had thrown him off and loosened his tongue, and now he needed to recoup as much energy as he could before the next round, whenever it came.

A sound at the door.

Someone was tampering with the lock on the door to his room.

Tired as he was, Paul's thirty years of intelligence agent instincts shot to the fore as he overcame his exhaustion and grabbed under his pillow for his gun.

Too late.

A powerful hand clutched at the wrist of his right hand while a second hand, extended from the other side of his bed, forced both of Paul's wrists into plastic handcuffs, snapping the cuffs shut. The window drapes had already been drawn, but now some kind of coarse material seemed to have been draped over the glass panes, dimming the light considerably.

"Who are you?" Paul asked, his eyes darting about in shock.

In the gloom he could only make out the forms of two blackened silhouettes. "Who sent you?"

One of the men leaned forward. Paul could smell the cheap vodka on his breath, and the scent was nauseatingly close.

"My boss decided that you've broken the rules of the game," the intruder said, his voice dangerously calm. "From what I heard, it sounds very much like he's made up his mind that your part in his plan will be written out very shortly."

Paul was not one to beg and plead for mercy, but at that moment he definitely found himself regretting his prominent position in the world's most formidable intelligence agency. Quietly, he wondered what to say, and how to justify his actions – no simple matter, considering he had no idea what it was that the man wanted of him.

"Aren't you going to ask the reason for his decision?" the man asked. He seemed surprised by Paul's indifference, but Paul knew that his demeanor was a sham.

"I'll grant you the honor of providing an explanation yourself," Paul replied coldly. Whatever fear he was feeling was expertly disguised in his voice. Despite his many brushes with death over the course of his chosen vocation, a sliver of fear was still present with every such encounter.

"How admirable of you to act with such decorum," the man said derisively. "But instead, I'm going to assist your recall. Try thinking back to your meeting at a certain restaurant. Are you seeing the light yet?"

"Naturally I recall the restaurant, but I don't remember any specific incident that transpired there that would make your boss, who I'm guessing is Rubinov, decide to kill me."

"In that case, dear Paul, you should try harder to remember," the man said, his voice dripping with disdain. "And I'll even give you a hint. Eyal threatened you, and even though both he and you knew that he would never act on those threats, you were quick to reveal to him the existence of the negotiator. The question is why you did that. My boss is very angry. Eyal knew nothing about the negotiator, and you handed him that information on a silver platter! What are you? A spineless wimp? You and the new president make a good team, it seems."

Paul's mouth turned dry, and the man continued: "I can see that you understand now. Very good. That's progress. And now my boss wants to know more about you and your connection to Eyal. I have a very simple question to start with. How did Eyal find out about this meeting?"

"I have no idea," Paul said, miserably aware of the fact that his response would only hasten his own demise. "I really don't know."

"Really now? I'll give you another minute to think about it some more, and after that we'll move on to the next stage, which you CIA men like to call 'gentle persuasion,' even if your prisoners don't always view it that way."

Paul was silent as fear clutched at his heart. He tried to formulate a response, but found that his words were stuck in his throat.

"My boss wants to know how you and Eyal came to enjoy such a close relationship. My boss pays you enough to cover the mortgage on your Washington home, but instead of aligning yourself with him, your true loyalties are with Eyal. The man may be charismatic, but he surely can't be charismatic enough to make you forget the source of your cash revenue."

"Cash revenue?" Paul's tongue loosened as he attempted a weak joke. "No one pays me in cash, aside from the CIA, and let's just say they're not exactly generous either."

"You really mean to say that my boss doesn't pay you?" the intruder said, donning an injured air. "Apparently, you're suffering from severe memory loss."

"I don't know where you've gotten your information from. I may have been in touch with your boss, and we share a common goal, but I've never been in this for money, and he knows it. As outdated as I may sound, I'm patriotic enough not to demand a bribe for serving my country."

There was a short whispered exchange in the room. The two intruders were talking quietly, and Paul decided to try his luck by asking his own question. "What made your boss think that I've betrayed him?" he asked.

The answer was quick in coming. "Someone who's loyal to him doesn't spy on him."

"I didn't spy on him," Paul stated, although his declaration wasn't exactly true. In fact, he had placed three CIA agents on Rubinov's trail and had them synchronize their moves.

"Really?" Despite the darkness Paul could make out the smile in the intruder's voice. "It looks like we have no choice but to make good on our word. Get up."

Paul pulled himself up from his bed, aware of the fact that the intruders were watching his every move. Something was going on behind the scenes, but he couldn't figure out what.

Something...

Paul's mind shifted into high gear. From these men's line of questioning it seemed that Eyal held the key to all the mystery in the case. During the course of his lengthy interrogation, the Israeli agent had withheld many details and distorted others. Everyone who was in the room realized that, and they had all raised the issue during their post-interrogation meeting. How Eyal had known to come to the restaurant that morning wasn't clear either, nor was it clear how he had so easily fitted together all of the puzzle pieces at that meeting in order to form a complete picture. The man's brain clearly functioned like an advanced computer.

A sack of some dark-colored material was pulled over Paul's head, and total darkness descended. Still, the thoughts running through his mind left him little room for distraction. He needed to figure out what was missing from the picture in his mind. The element would come to him suddenly, of that he was certain.

The door to the room opened quietly. Paul sensed the presence of someone new in his vicinity, and all of his senses went into high alert. With every question these men would ask him, he would gain half a response to the questions consuming his own mind. He wanted the men to get started already.

"About the bombs in the hotel lot, Paul. They were the same type of bombs put together by your soldiers in Afghanistan and Iraq, weren't they?" It wasn't the same man asking the questions anymore. Either the second intruder had taken over, or the new arrival was speaking.

"What?" Paul asked. "That's impossible."

"Those are the facts. We've had several of the components analyzed, and if not for the sack over your head, we would show you the pictures. So, tell me, what conclusion do these facts lead you to?"

"That…that the men who killed the president were Americans?" Paul found it hard to envision such a scenario.

"Bingo." Paul heard the smile in the man's voice.

"But that's impossible," Paul said. "X was a Syrian militant, and you have no way of proving your crazy assumption. There are other ways to explain the construction of those explosives." It was difficult for Paul to get the words out with the thick covering on his head, but his frantically racing thoughts wouldn't permit him to remain silent. "Besides, unless you can prove a motive, I won't believe it."

"You provide them with their motive, and then you ask me to prove it?" The man's voice dripped with sarcasm. "Their motive, and yours, is money. Simply put, they were someone else's hired swords. The question to ask is who, not what. And you're the one who's meant to supply an answer to that question, by the way. Now. Right now. Because having someone murder the president was not sanctioned by my boss."

"But I don't know who wanted such a thing," Paul said in confusion. "I thought that Rubinov…your boss…wanted to destroy the Fraternity, and that was why he arranged for X to have the president kidnapped. The fact that X left the president in the hotel to die, however, taking Eyal along as a defense while he ran away, tells me clearly that that my conclusions are off. Had Rubinov wanted to destroy the Fraternity he wouldn't have had X kill the president, for that would simply be too extreme."

"I want you to tell me all about your connection with the Fraternity." A hand was firmly wedged into Paul's shoulder blade for emphasis.

"Just a minute," Paul said. "Do you think I'm a collaborator with them? If that's what you think, then contact them via the negotiator and see if they know me. I have absolutely no connection with the Fraternity other than the fact that I despise them and want to destroy them. My attempt to do so, however, failed. But even if you're messengers of the Fraternity and were not sent by Rubinov, I'll still tell you about my feelings toward the Fraternity, regardless of what I myself may be risking."

The second man offered a dramatic sigh. "Time to pass him on to the boss. It's time for him to see that we're serious."

There was a rustle and a whispered exchange.

Paul's jaw locked into place, and his already taut muscles tightened further. The covering on his head was removed and a small flashlight was switched on, casting long shadows on the wall. Paul turned to face his interrogators.

He found himself standing before the man with whom he'd had the good fortune of becoming personally acquainted in recent days.

Eyal Gilboa.

"He knows more than you think."

"Maybe, but there isn't much that he can do with his knowledge."

The man fixed his boss with a penetrating stare. "I hope you know what you're talking about."

The boss lit a cigarette and said with assumed indifference, "When was the last time I made a mistake?"

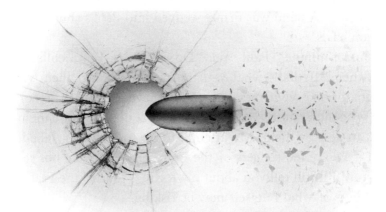

CHAPTER SIXTY-ONE

Kiev, Ukraine

P aul stared, incredulous at first. "I suppose I should have realized you were capable of that. The question is why. What did you do that for?"

"Come on, Paul. You're a pro at this game yourself. Besides, don't they say that imitation is the highest form of flattery? You should be proud."

"Proud? I don't think so. You're out of your mind." Paul had his anger on display and was keeping his fear firmly under wraps. Eyal had good reason to want revenge and was clearly capable of taking it.

"Actually, no. What I just did makes a great deal of sense, as you'll soon find out." Eyal spoke quietly, shining his flashlight into the CIA deputy director's face for a moment, and then turning the beam away and casting threatening shadows on the wall. "Because I know something that you don't."

"That was clear enough at yesterday's interrogation session. I knew you weren't speaking the truth. I saw it, and so did the others."

"Well, you got that wrong, then. I didn't lie. But I did hold some information back, for good reason." Eyal motioned for the other two men in the room to leave. Once he and Paul were alone, Eyal sat down opposite Paul and snapped open the cuffs around his wrists.

"What information?" Paul asked, his pulse slowly returning to normal. Eyal could be unpredictable, but his conscience was stronger than his emotions.

"First, I know exactly what my men just told you that I know," Eyal said, looking Paul in the eye.

"You mean those guys who so expertly neutralized me?" Paul asked, a note of amusement in his voice despite the fact that he was still angry at the deception. "Who were they, by the way?"

"Friends." Eyal said, without elaborating. "Anyway, as I was saying...X's men, those characters who turned out to be murderers and not simply terrorists, were Americans. Worse still, some of them – and possibly all – were former soldiers."

"And you can prove that?" Paul challenged.

Without a word, Eyal pulled a few sheets of paper out of his jacket pocket. It was the ballistic analysis of the fragments of explosives retrieved from the scene, and what was written there was more than enough to convince Paul.

The CIA agent was silent as he handed back the stapled pages to Eyal, who returned them to his pocket.

"If I'm reading this correctly, we have no time to waste. These men were a group of Americans whose goal was not to kidnap the president but to murder him, which is exactly what they ended up doing. At a certain point during the mission I began to suspect that this was their intention, though I couldn't prove it. Even after the president was already dead, it was just possible to believe that the operation had somehow gone wrong and that they had chosen to wash their hands of the whole business. In retrospect, however, that theory just doesn't hold water. X could have taken the president with him in the helicopter and no one would have shot them down. He knew that. But that wasn't his aim. He wanted the president dead, so he made sure that happened."

Eyal was carefully watching Paul as he spoke, but the man's expression was inscrutable. Studying his features, Eyal realized that the Americans were having a hard time recovering from the trauma of their president's murder. He could only hope that Paul, at least, would recover his wits quickly, because he needed him.

"Paul, you have to think hard. Who would want to murder the president, and why?"

"What a simple question to answer...the president – any president, for that matter – has enemies, including powerful ones. But..." His voice trailed off – he still couldn't quite believe it.

"Let's follow the old rule," Eyal said slowly. "Let's keep this simple. Who stood to benefit the most from this crime?"

"What do you mean?" Paul said, sitting up straight and staring directly into Eyal's face.

"Every politician's dream is to become president one day. And now one politician's dream has actually come true."

The blood drained from Paul's face, and even Eyal was taken aback by the intensity of the other man's shock. "You mean Marty Clifford? The vice president?"

"Well, why not?"

"They're meeting at the hotel now. The lights are off for an added dramatic touch. From the content of their conversation, I presume that they plan to send you off to Guantanamo for life."

"They can plan all they like. It won't get further than that."

"I would tell you that I've said my piece and that you're going to have to manage on your own from now on. But I care too much about you to do that. If those two men leave that room alive, you're finished. And I mean that literally."

"Oh, I'm sure you do."

"So, do you want me to take care of this?"

"Thanks for the offer. But I have the right people to deal with this. I'll manage just fine."

"You don't know Clifford," Paul said, grimacing at the very thought of the man. "He's a nothing. A loser. A total zero."

Eyal raised an eyebrow. "Whatever his qualities, or lack of them, this 'zero,' as you refer to him, has become your president. At least accord him the respect his position warrants."

"You don't understand." Paul got up and started to pace the room in agitation. "I'm really not exaggerating, and this has nothing to do with my political views. Marty Clifford is a newcomer to politics. He's a first-time senator, and no one expected him to make it into the Senate, let alone become vice president – and certainly not president! You'd be hard-pressed to find ten Americans who think he's ready to step into the role." Paul stood at the window for a moment, to calm down. "No one really knows why Jack chose him as his running mate. Like I said, he wasn't expected to win his Senate seat. He was up against the incumbent, Tom Jameson – a popular and charismatic man who was predicted to sweep the state. Then, at the last minute, literally days before the elections, this Jameson was implicated in a very unsavory matter and had to drop out. Clifford, an unknown quantity, was portrayed in contrast as whiter than white, and he was voted in. But the man's a complete idiot!" he exploded. "He was a loser all his life. He came out of nowhere, and if you ask me, he should go right back to where he came from."

Eyal, listening intently to Paul's diatribe, smiled in understanding. He asked his next question with visible excitement: "Paul, Jack Charleston was no fool. Why would he choose someone like that to be his vice president?"

"Like I said, no one knows for sure. But the consensus in the media was that Jack was so full of himself that he didn't want anyone near him stealing the limelight – not even a tenth of a percentage point of it. It suited his overblown self-esteem to surround himself with minor functionaries, yes-men who would follow him blindly and never challenge his 'wisdom.'"

"And what did you think?" Eyal ask.

"I thought, and still think, the same. I viewed Jack as someone who wanted to be a dictator, someone who thought he was born to rule. And what I saw throughout his presidency confirmed this assessment. He was careful to appoint compliant, passive figures to his administration. There wasn't a single person in the White House who dared to stand up to him."

"And you were one of them," Eyal said with a smile. "Did you ever contradict him?"

"No, I don't recall ever doing so," Paul admitted. "But there was a reason for that, and it wasn't cowardice. I considered him to be the right man for the job at this point in time, for the war against terror on the home front and abroad. The Angels of Peace are terror on the home front. And the president backed my every decision, despite the occasionally drastic measures that I took. He didn't try to run the show in the CIA."

"There's one drastic measure that I'm rather too familiar with," Eyal said coolly, his expression impassive. "Namely, using another country's former intelligence agent without his awareness of the fact."

Paul looked away. "I think we're even now, after that 'little' scare you gave me earlier."

Eyal's eyes sparked fire. "We haven't begun to get even," he said in a low, dangerous voice. "Whatever I think of you, I wouldn't wish it on you to go through what I endured in the last few weeks. But settling the score isn't my priority right now. We have much more important issues to deal with first."

"That's right." Paul seized on his words. "We need to hunt down the Fraternity and prove once and for all that they're nothing more than a bunch of criminals who don't stop short of murder. They're an immense threat to national security."

"No!" Now it was Eyal's turn to jump to his feet, jabbing an angry finger at the CIA agent. "Leave the Fraternity out of this! The United States has far bigger problems than the Fraternity right now!" He exhaled slowly, calming himself down. "We have to locate the man who was behind the president's murder. Don't you realize that this man is utterly ruthless? Someone who gets this far using such means won't suddenly stop and become Mr. Nice Guy."

"You're right." Paul sat down again, motioning for Eyal to follow suit. "What do you suggest? What about X's men? Are any of them still alive?"

"Yes. The terrorists had two helicopters. Bentzy, Elitzafun, and I were in the first one, along with X, his pilot and two of his closest men, who were all killed by a missile fired by the crew in the second helicopter."

"Why did they do that?"

"Because they thought Bentzy and I had thrown X and his men out and were using the helicopter to escape." Eyal preferred to keep from Paul the fact that he was the one responsible for leading the men to believe that to be the case. Although he and Paul were now working in tandem, he was still a foreign agent.

"How many men were on that second helicopter?"

"Ten, and they all managed to escape. I have no idea where they went, because those dumb Ukrainian police decided to arrest me and let the real criminals get away."

"So what do you suggest?" Paul asked, repeating his question.

"I suggest we head to the United States and start poking around the late president's papers. We might just discover how it was that this supposed zero Clifford reached such a position of power. Maybe a new name will come up; and maybe other new information will put the facts we already have in a different light."

"I'll take care of it." Paul stood up, exuding an aura of confidence and authority. All signs of his earlier stupefaction and bewilderment had faded. "But you are to remain in Ukraine, in your hotel, until further notice."

"Am I to understand that you're putting me under house arrest?" Eyal asked, calmly opening the hotel window and allowing the thick piece of felt that his men had placed over the pane to fall onto the carpet. A frigid wind hit the men's faces, sending a chill down their spines.

"Almost," Paul said. He was clearly trying to retrieve his trampled honor.

"Well, in that case I feel obliged to inform you that I intend to breach the rules and roam freely around Kiev, together with my wife and son," Eyal said.

Paul knew he couldn't draw the noose too tight. "As long as you answer your cell phone when I call."

Eyal offered an ambiguous nod. "No promises. But there's something else, Paul."

"Yes, Mr. Abductor."

"Someone needs to make a controlled detonation of the bombs I assembled in the conference hall before the Ukrainians unwittingly cause an additional act of terror. And if that happens, even you won't be able to secure my release from prison. The Ukrainians have been humiliated enough already, and they won't stand for being given another diplomatic black eye – especially if they find out that I had something to do with it."

"Well, having you back behind bars might not be such a bad idea," Paul said with a wink.

"Meaning?" Eyal wasn't amused.

"Never mind. Just don't get up to too much mischief, okay?"

CHAPTER SIXTY-TWO

Kiev, Ukraine

E yal? You have a tail. Actually, make that two."

"Thanks, Eli. Think you can deal with them? I have a few things to check out over here." Eyal was driving the car that Eli and Vitali had brought to the hotel for his use. Earlier that morning Eyal had called Eli and asked him to fly back to Ukraine after his week-long sojourn in Israel. Eli had protested the summons, but both he and Eyal had known that he would come.

Eli called Eyal as soon as his plane touched down, and after a few brief words of greeting, Eyal sent him straight to work. An urgent mission. Eli had recruited Vitali to join him on the job, and the two men had pinned down the deputy director of the CIA for an interrogation.

"I'll be fine. But what do you want me to do with them?"

"As far as I'm concerned, you can put them onto the Trans-Siberian Railway if it runs through this city."

Eli laughed. "You've just given me an idea. Travel by the main road so I can keep tabs on them."

Eyal glanced at his Waze. "I'll be at the Darnytsia railway station in ten minutes. Hold them at bay until then, okay?"

"Got it."

Eyal parked his car in the railway station's parking lot, got out, and walked inside through the rounded entranceway, flanked by wide pillars.

Eli, shadowing four men in two separate cars, kept up a steady report. "They don't seem to be armed," he whispered into his Bluetooth. "It shouldn't be too complicated to put them out of action."

"Two of them just entered the bathroom," Vitali reported. "Apparently they suspect an ambush."

"Very convenient," Eli said. "Because that's exactly what we're here for. I'm locking them in."

"You're insane. There are innocent people in the area."

"I'll lock their stalls and spray them with something nice that will put them to sleep for an hour or two. They won't feel a thing."

"Will you be able to manage on your own?" Eyal asked, walking quickly toward the platform that he needed, two trackers on his heels. "Because I need to be somewhere."

Eli quickly entered the bathroom, locking the two trackers there into their stalls in an elegantly quiet fashion. Addressing Vitali over the radio, he asked with mock resignation, "Do we have a choice?"

"Not really."

"We'll be fine, Eyal," Vitali said. "Trust your friends."

"I trust them too much. Please respect that trust."

Vitali, not far behind Eyal, now approached the two agents on their way to the train platform and bumped into one of them. "Sorry," he said, removing his syringe from his pocket and injecting it into the man's leg as he spoke. The man fell forward while his friend eyed him in shock.

In exaggerated horror, Vitali began to shout: "Help! Help! This man has fainted. Help!"

"He'll be fine," the fallen man's companion said hurriedly, anxious to dispel the unwanted attention. "He had one too many to drink, that's all. I'll help him get home."

"No, no! Just look at him. He's clutching at his left side! He's having a heart attack! Help! Call a doctor!" Vitali's hoarse yells drew more spectators to the scene.

"I'm a doctor," one man said. "Move aside. I'll take care of him." A second man also, claiming that he was a paramedic, while more than twenty onlookers added themselves to the crowd, curious to find out what would happen next. The man's companion stood and cursed quietly beside his unconscious friend.

In the meantime, Vitali remained close at hand, making sure the spotlight was hyper-focused on the two trackers. "Call an ambulance," he pleaded. "Help! Help!" The domed ceiling of the ancient building carried his voice well, and he was clearly enjoying the spectacle.

"Will you shut up," the doctor said disapprovingly. "We're taking care of him right here!"

Now Eli approached Vitali and whispered: "What's going on?"

"I got about a hundred people to keep their eyes on these two," Vitali murmured, concealing his satisfied smirk. "It's a little hard to go about tracking someone under such circumstances, as you'll appreciate. What did you do with your targets?"

"They're locked in their stalls, snoring away," Eli said, drawing Vitali out of the crowd of onlookers. "Eyal suggested we put them onto a train headed to Vladivostok. What do you think of his idea?"

"Good one. I just wish I could be there to see their faces when they wake up."

"It won't be long before Eyal lets the world know what he knows," Paul said. He was sitting in one of Rubinov's opulent mansions, smoking one of his host's cigars.

"I apologize that I can't wine and dine you in a more fitting manner," Rubinov said. "But this house really isn't quite up to par. It's far smaller than my customary residence, as I prefer not to attract undue attention before a few more months pass without incident."

"In that case, let me put your mind at ease by informing you that my own home, which I happen to be very proud of, is approximately the size of the ballroom of this 'small and modest home' of yours."

Rubinov smiled. "Down to business," he said. "What do you suggest?"

"We remove him from the scene," Paul said simply. "There is no other way to stop him, as you have surely noticed."

"I see." Rubinov carefully cut off the tip of his cigar and twirled it between his fingers. A long moment of silence ensued while he lit the cigar and took the first few puffs. "How urgent do you consider this to be?" he asked, leaning back against the soft leather of his armchair.

"You don't understand. You can't send a hired assassin to kill him."

"Why not?" Rubinov asked, puffing at his cigar and forming blue-gray rings of smoke in the air.

"Because even if he reports success, you'll never know if he really died or if he somehow evaded the hit man, using a double, or a dummy, or some other trick. The man is a consummate trickster, not to mention an expert escape artist. I don't know of anyone you could pit against him and be certain of the result."

Rubinov eyed his guest languidly. "What is your suggestion?" he asked.

"Kill him yourself," Paul said bluntly. "Invite him here, telling him that you want to share some information you obtained about who sent X. He'll come."

"No, he won't," Rubinov said. "He'll suspect me of setting up a trap."

"He'll still come, because he wants to solve this mystery. Agents like him will risk everything to accomplish their goal." Paul withdrew a pair of gloves from his pocket and put them on. Next, he took out a gun from another pocket and placed it on the coffee table between the two men. "This will be the instrument of murder."

Rubinov furrowed his brow with suspicion. "Why this?'

"This gun was the weapon used in a murder that received a great deal of publicity. Oleg Yalok, the criminal involved, escaped the scene leaving his weapon behind, covered with fingerprints. It was an incredible error for such a professional criminal to make, but other than that, his reputation as a highly competent assassin is impeccable. It makes sense that this 'whoever' whom Eyal thinks he is hunting down would turn the tables and kill him, and then we can kill two birds with one stone. Yalok has made a lot of trouble for certain people, most likely yourself included. The Ukrainians – if they manage to catch up with him – will be more than willing to accept that account of the affair. Understood?"

Rubinov nodded, slowly digesting the idea. "And if Oleg is actually caught, and he denies any involvement?"

"He will never let himself be captured alive. Unless the impossible happens and they both catch him and prevent him from doing away with himself before anything further occurs. In that case, I doubt he'll manage to get off the charges. I don't think there's a single lawyer, no matter how smart, who could clear his name. But the main thing is that the murder will never be able to be traced back to you," Paul concluded. "And, obviously, the plan will only work if I'm right and you're a sharpshooter."

A cynical smile. "I am."

"A single incriminating drop of blood and you will spend the rest of your life in prison." Paul stood up. "That's not something I can allow to happen, you understand."

"Naturally, I do." Paul was obviously concerned above all about his own safety, and Rubinov wasn't surprised.

"You will have to be very, very smart about this. There are a number of elements keeping tabs on Eyal, including my men, your country's men, and most likely his own gang too. He's back at his hotel right now, but I've told him to report back to the faculty in an hour's time, for some more questioning. Make sure to get hold of him before he leaves."

"I will."

"And remember to call me when it's all over."

CHAPTER SIXTY-THREE

Kiev, Ukraine

The knock at the door was strange. Efrat wouldn't have knocked; neither would Eli or Vitali. Eyal got up from where he had been sitting on the floor, playing with Elitzafun, and approached the source of the interruption.

"Who is this?"

"Shalom aleichem," a voice answered.

Eyal froze. He hadn't expected to hear that voice again – and in any case, what was he doing here?

Had the voice belonged to anyone else, Eyal would have made do with a few moments of shared banter before explaining that he was in the middle of spending time with his son. Now, however, Eyal was eager to set everything else aside. Squaring his shoulders, he opened the door.

"Yonatan! So good to see you!" he exclaimed, a broad smile on his face that did little to conceal the firm set of his jaw.

Yonatan's own smile of response was vague, as if he weren't quite aware of what his facial muscles were doing. "You're so pleased to see me, Eyal?" he said, walking into the room as Eyal stood aside and then shut the door behind him.

"Take a seat," Eyal said, noting that Yonatan had already done so.

Yonatan's face gave nothing away. He swung one foot over the other. "Would you like to tell me what's going on, Eyal?" he asked.

"I'm hoping you can share that information yourself." The hint of threat was clearly present in Eyal's voice.

Yonatan's attempt at a congenial expression faded and his face grew serious. "What do you mean by that?" he asked.

"I mean exactly what you think I mean."

Yonatan's right eyebrow twitched. An annoying tic. "What have you heard, Eyal?" he asked quietly.

"Why do you want to know? To help you figure out how much you can still keep concealed from me?"

Elitzafun looked up in surprise. Never had he heard his father use such a harsh and merciless tone of voice. That aspect of his personality was completely unfamiliar to him. "Abba?" He tugged at Eyal's sleeve.

Eyal looked down at his son and forced himself to smile. "Elitzafun, how about going to…" Where to send him? Elitzafun wasn't allowed out of his sight. Efrat had stepped out to do some shopping, and Eyal had promised to keep a firm eye on the boy. So there they were in the hotel room, and there was nowhere else for the boy to go.

Eyal looked at Yonatan, taking in the former GSS agent's frozen manner. "Use your words with caution, Yonatan," he warned.

"I just want to know what lies those friends of yours from your Mossad have been feeding you."

"The Mossad isn't mine," Eyal said slowly. "And don't refer to Bentzy and Eli as 'those friends.'"

"I wasn't referring to them. I was referring to Zev Avshalom, primarily. I'm assuming you know the man."

"How is he connected to you?"

"He's yet another hostile figure who thinks he's brilliant for trying to slap me with a seven-year jail sentence on the pretext that I passed on classified information to America – that and other, similar nonsense."

"And you really didn't do any such thing, Yonatan?" Eyal made no attempt to conceal the hurt emanating from every syllable he uttered. "You didn't contact certain elements in the American administration, friendly as they may have seemed, in order to share information with them? Is that idea really nonsense?"

Elitzafun tugged Eyal's sleeve. "Who came from America?"

"That's enough," Eyal said. "This isn't an appropriate subject right now." Eyal's phone rang suddenly. It was Efrat, telling him that she would be back in a moment.

"Efrat, someone came to see me. Take Elitzafun down to the lobby to look at the aquarium for half an hour, okay? He'll be waiting at the door." He turned to his son. "Elitzafun? Ima's coming upstairs. Run and open the door, and she'll take you down to see the fish."

Elitzafun jumped up from where he had been playing and raced to the door. A minute later a murmur outside announced Efrat's arrival, and she shut the door behind Elitzafun without entering the room.

Eyal got up and walked over to where Yonatan was sitting in silence, waiting for an opportunity to talk. Looming over him with narrowed eyes and clenched fists, he said nothing, waiting for the intimidating stance to bear fruit.

"I didn't betray you," Yonatan said, his expression grave, reflecting upon the many things that he had seen in his nearly fifty years of life. "I didn't betray you, Eyal."

Eyal shook his head. "It's because of you and you alone that my son was kidnapped and my family subjected to inhuman threats, terrified for the lives of their child and father," Eyal said quietly. "You are the reason I look the way that I do. And you are the one responsible for Guy's death."

"I am not," Yonatan said firmly, a stubborn but hurt look in his eyes. "You will not blame me for Guy's death, Eyal."

"Oh, really?" Eyal's voice was pained. Exhausted. "Yonatan, forget about the accusations against you for a minute and focus on the facts."

"The facts? The facts are not what you think they are, Eyal. If you knew, you wouldn't blame me for your son's kidnapping and the murder of the president."

"If I knew? So how about letting me know." His face had reverted to its usual expression of indifference, but inwardly he felt like pummeling the man before him.

"Eyal, I am not a traitor." Yonatan's voice was nearly pleading. "I was loyal to you throughout this story; but I simply didn't know…certain things."

"What didn't you know?" Hurt and rage made Eyal's whisper sound more like the hiss of a venomous snake. "What didn't you know, Yonatan? You didn't know that you were collaborating with the CIA? You didn't know that the CIA was collaborating with X? They may have been trying to arrest him, but I wasn't aware of any of that. The CIA used me like a pawn." Eyal stopped suddenly, swallowing the lava that threatened to explode. "At least don't try to tell me that you didn't know that Elitzafun was kidnapped."

"No." Yonatan said, and then he fell silent. Eyal stopped his monologue, and the two men faced each other in silence for seven long seconds before Yonatan finally spoke again. "I truly didn't know, Eyal."

"What didn't you know?"

"I didn't know that Elitzafun was kidnapped."

Eyal looked at Yonatan in shock. The man had given years of his life for his country. He had worked for people who trusted him, people he knew, and for an ideology that he believed in. It made no sense that he would discard all of that in order to collaborate with the CIA. There had to be more to the story.

"I wasn't aware that Elitzafun was kidnapped, Eyal," Yonatan repeated, looking down at the floor. He had been planning this moment for hours, dreading the confrontation, waiting for it to be over. "Let's start at the beginning, okay?" Yonatan looked at Eyal, and when he saw that the man hadn't thawed even a single degree, he lowered his voice slightly before continuing. "The people of Syria are suffering. Let's leave the fact that they are Arabs out of the picture. Their brothers may be terrorists responsible for the murders of dozens of Israelis, but let's focus on the Syrians them-selves for a moment. Think about their young children, thrust into a cruel reality. Normal daily life barely exists in Syria anymore. Finding out that a close relative was just killed is no longer shock-ing. The poverty and misery is unbelievable." Yonatan's voice grew choked. "And this is all happening because of a radical group with lunatic ideas whose leader decided to turn his fellow countrymen's lives into a nightmare."

Eyal was unmoved. "What does all of that have to do with me? When I go to battle, I do so for the sake of my country. It may hurt me to hear about the suffering that other humans endure, but none of that explains anything about our particular issue." He decided to refrain from telling Yonatan that X wasn't a Syrian citizen and that all of his sacrifices had been for naught.

Yonatan looked away and continued. "I didn't know that X was simply a murderer. The information that I received about him was misleading and false. I first met him at a field hospital that we set up at military post 105 in the Golan. Men arrive there in terrible condition. I interrogated X for the GSS, and a connection was forged. I viewed X as an ambitious individual who had some good judgment calls for the sake of peace. I knew nothing about the suffering you went through. And I absolutely did not know that he planned to kidnap Elitzafun."

Yonatan fell silent in the face of Elitzafun's father. Eyal's expression was completely closed, impenetrable. Only his green eyes looked at Yonatan in silence.

Ten long seconds passed before Eyal opened his mouth. "You didn't know that X was a terrorist and that he kidnapped Elitzafun. Those facts might work in your favor, Yonatan, but ignorance of the law is no excuse, and you did betray me."

Yonatan was silent, his fear all-consuming and nearly tangible.

"You're a traitor, Yonatan," Eyal said. "My son was kidnapped, and you will never know what he went through, or what his mother, and I, suffered as a result. That, however, is not what hurts me. What hurts me most is the fact that you acted with total awareness of your own motivations, betraying your friend and going behind his back, even though you knew that he was not to be informed of the true facts. You placed his life in peril, got him to cooperate with people he had no interest in cooperating with, and entangled him in an operation he had no interest in engaging with, all for the sake of your own bizarre ideology – and it makes no difference how righteous you might think you were."

Yonatan said nothing.

"That knowledge, Yonatan," Eyal continued, his voice nearly inaudible now, "cannot atone for your ignorance of other key facts, as well as the one stark fact that my own friend preferred to cooperate with the CIA rather than with me. The fact that my friend didn't hesitate before sharing what he knew about me with Paul Ferguson, without my knowledge. The man I viewed as a friend betrayed me."

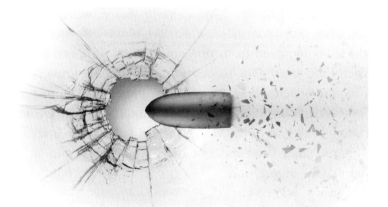

CHAPTER SIXTY-FOUR

Kiev, Ukraine

Efrat entered the hotel room and found her husband sitting at the desk with his back to her, staring blankly out of the window. "What was it?" she asked, motioning to Elitzafun, who was jumping up and down with one of his toys, to tone it down a bit.

Eyal turned around and looked up at his wife, a pained expression in his eyes. "I just had one of the men I most admired removed from my life."

"Yonatan," Efrat said. She had been in the lobby keeping an eye on Elitzafun as he watched the huge fish excitedly, when she noticed Yonatan leaving.

"Correct," he said shortly.

"Then I'm assuming you had good reasons to do what you

did," she said quietly.

"Correct again." Eyal stood up. "But that doesn't make it hurt any less." A long moment passed, and then his features morphed into an expression of strength and resolve.

Efrat looked at her husband in surprise, overwhelmed by the sudden change in his demeanor. The seemingly effortless manner in which he switched from one emotion to another astounded her each time anew. Her admiration gave way to curiosity, however, as she watched him remove his gun holster from his hip and his submachine gun from his shoulder. Curiosity gave way to heart-pounding fear. Why was he removing his weapons?

"I'm meeting…someone, in half an hour," Eyal said, answering her unspoken question.

"When will you be back?"

"Are you worried about me?" A gentle smile sneaked into his gruff agent's demeanor.

"Can I not be?" Efrat demanded. "When do you ever remove your weapons of your own accord? You were wearing at least two guns at our own wedding, and now…well, yes, it has me worried," she admitted. "And you won't tell me why, of course," she added, almost as an afterthought.

"Efrat, I'm a big boy."

"X thought so too."

Eli entered Eyal's hotel room without knocking politely to announce his arrival. He had noticed Elitzafun skipping happily down the steps to the lobby at his mother's side just a moment earlier, and he had waved fondly at the child. Elitzafun, for his part, had immediately left his mother and come running to him, and Eli had lifted him up into the air, causing the boy to yelp with glee.

"Where's Abba?" Eli had asked.

"In our room, getting ready to leave," Elitzafun had responded, unstinting with his information.

"So, I've gotten here in time." Eli had thumped the five-year-old loudly to the floor and raced toward the stairwell. He had taken the steps three at a time, entering Eyal's suite while Eyal was arranging the tie around his neck. Eli watched as Eyal removed a gun holster from his waist and placed it into in one of the drawers of the night table.

"Where to, your honor?"

"Are you my new chauffeur?" Eyal asked in surprise.

"I'm serious," Eli said.

Eyal offered his concerned friend a tiny smile. "So you're worried about me too."

"I'm assuming by your use of the word 'too' that your wife is also worried about you, and I think she's right." Eli offered Eyal a reproachful look. "You're going to a meeting with a man who's unafraid of bloodshed and about whom you know too many facts, without a single weapon. The meeting has been arranged without any advance notice. Anyone can see that it's a trap."

"I understand that just as well as anyone else can understand it." A strange glint flickered in Eyal's eye for a fraction of an instant and then disappeared.

"And you're about to enter that trap, with your eyes wide open?" Eli said with amazement.

"Yes," Eyal said, his voice carefully modulated. "Because I have no other way of receiving answers to my questions."

"You won't be able to share those answers with anyone once you're dead."

Eyal put on his jacket. "Are you trying to tell me to cancel this meeting?"

"Yes. Why should that be so hard to justify? Tell Rubinov that you have a meeting someplace else, and we'll get some backup ready for you. You can't go into his house, where he has all his people, without a single weapon on you."

"Rubinov isn't the type to allow me to bail out of a meeting at the last minute. Certainly not in order to attend a different meeting instead. Agreeing to this meeting is the only way I can see to receive any answers, and I'm not giving up the opportunity. If Rubinov wants to kill me, as you suspect, he won't stop until he accomplishes exactly that. Even if I don't show up at today's meeting, my life will not be spared. He has enough hired assassins working for him beyond the borders of his estate."

"Your choice of words and quasi-logical but dodgy deductions are making me more concerned by the minute," Eli said. "You too suspect that he has murderous intentions, yet you're going to meet him, because you believe he can kill you anywhere. I'm very concerned, and you'll appreciate that that's an understatement."

"You know what?" Eyal said, leaving the room with Eli hot on his heels, hand on his shoulder. "Come and back me up."

"How? By attending this meeting that I wasn't asked to attend? The repercussions of doing that will probably be worse than arriving at a wedding uninvited."

"No. Wait in a building nearby and find a good sniper spot," Eyal said calmly. "If I sense danger, I'll find a way to signal that to you." Eyal stepped onto the curb outside of the hotel.

"What are you doing?" Eli asked.

"Hailing a cab. Efrat took the car to go on a trip with Elitzafun." Eyal didn't mention Elitzafun's disappointment at not having him join them. Efrat, at least, had understood.

"I'll drive you," Eli said quickly. "Even though it appears that this will be the last time I'll be driving you alive in my vehicle."

Ivankiv, Ukraine

The gates surrounding the mansion hummed as they slowly pulled open and Eli's car entered the gravel path. Eli was astounded by the open vista, but Eyal, who remembered the ostentatious estate where Rubinov had been "murdered," wasn't overly impressed.

"Stop." Four men outfitted with submachine guns approached the vehicle. "Get out of the car."

Eyal and Eli stepped out of the car. Two of the guards trained their guns on them and another two checked them for hidden weapons. "Who is he?" the guard checking Eyal's body jerked his head in Eli's direction.

"He's my driver," Eyal said. He exchanged an amused glance with Eli.

"To the best of my knowledge, he hasn't been invited here. Have him get in the car and drive back out. He can wait outside the gates." The guard's expression was stony, and his tone of voice brooked no argument.

Eli bit his lip. He had been hoping to be able to remain at Eyal's side. Even without a weapon, the two of them could overcome plenty of obstacles. He turned to Eyal now, a pleading expression in his eyes.

"No problem," Eyal said calmly.

"Eyal, no," Eli began.

Eyal ignored him. "May I enter?" he asked.

"Yes. My boss is waiting for you."

Eli was led, expression grim, to his car and shown out of the estate. Meanwhile, two of the guards escorted Eyal into the magnificent building.

Eyal walked calmly along an expansive marble passage, taking in his surroundings. The two armed guards accompanied him, one on either side, but he appeared unconcerned. A selection of paintings from the Old Masters was hung on the walls, and chandelier prisms scattered light all around.

Eyal was led toward Rubinov's inner sanctum. A steel door, paneled with mahogany, opened to reveal a room that was almost entirely bare. Two simple chairs without upholstery and a carved wooden table greeted Eyal, who did not show his surprise.

An untamed thought entered his mind. Someone had cleared the room in order to prevent superfluous items from being stained by his blood.

His chest constricted with fear. Rubinov, sitting on one of the chairs, stood up as he entered. "Welcome, Eyal."

There was a new crease on the man's forehead, Eyal saw. It was a crease that hadn't been there at their previous meeting. Eyal overcame his fear, steadying his voice as he responded to the man's greeting with a smile. "It's strange to be speaking with the very man I was accused of murdering."

"It isn't your first time." Rubinov gestured toward the unoccupied chair. "Sit."

Eyal sat down and looked directly into Rubinov's eyes. "What's the issue?"

"I will get straight to the point, because it's clear to me that you know more than you told Paul during those lengthy interrogations, which I heard every word of, by the way, and during our unpleasant conversation in that restaurant."

Eyal offered Rubinov a thin smile.

"I'd like to find out exactly what you know," Rubinov said. His voice turned intimidating. "As you are certainly aware, I have a particular penchant for acquiring information that most people are not privy to."

"How poetic."

"What do you know about my connection with the Fraternity?"

Eyal was unfazed. "I reserve my right to remain silent."

A broad barrel appeared in Rubinov's gloved hand. His glove was of thin blue rubber, the type used by surgeons. "I didn't bother outfitting this little toy with a silencer, because no one will hear the shot beyond my estate, and those within the gates know how to keep a secret."

Eyal looked at the object in Rubinov's hand and stopped breathing. Rubinov chuckled. "What did you think? That I'd let you out of here in one piece?"

Eyal was silent.

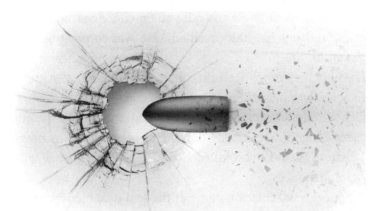

CHAPTER SIXTY-FIVE

Ivankiv, Ukraine

R ubinov stroked his weapon, savoring the fear he was in-
stilling in his guest. "I want answers to my questions."

"What do you want to know?" Eyal asked. His voice
was quiet and subdued.

"What do you know about my request to become a senior member of the Fraternity?"

Eyal breathed a little more easily. Rubinov was clearly desperate
for information, and also exceedingly sure of himself, which was
always a winning combination. The man had created an opening
that Eyal could widen, if he was both wise and intuitive.

"I know that you needed to accomplish things that were extremely difficult in order to receive such a prominent position,"
Eyal replied carefully. The statement he had just made was simple

for him to guess. "I do not, however, know what those missions were, although I will venture a bold guess that one of those missions involved murdering the president."

Rubinov's lips curved upward in a cynical smile. "I will confirm the accuracy of your guess and tell you that it's right on target. The Fraternity did not like the president. He was too aggressive and belligerent for them."

"I assumed as much...all the same, the notion that Americans would actually murder their president seemed too extreme to me."

"Go and tell that to John Wilkes Booth, who murdered President Lincoln because he didn't like his political leanings, or Lee Harvey Oswald, who killed President Kennedy under mysterious circumstances."

"Lincoln's assassination came at the end of a bloody civil war, at a time when the United States wasn't as politically involved in the world as it is today. And with regard to Kennedy's murder, we both know enough to understand that there was far more going on there behind the scenes than most people realize. But let those poor deceased presidents rest in peace while we discuss the current assassination. I believe someone urged the Fraternity to commit this murder, and that someone wasn't you."

Rubinov eyed Eyal with astonishment. "That is true. Like any other organization, the Fraternity needs money. As I said at the meeting that I was invited to before being sworn in, the Fraternity's policy of destroying vast quantities of dangerous substances, instead of selling them, is ultimately detrimental to the organization. Unfortunately, the Fraternity viewed my opinion as untenable, and they refused to even consider it. It was Russia who stepped into the breach and decided to support the Fraternity, viewing the organization as the quietest, most efficient means of weakening the United States. If the Fraternity can draw millions of pacifist Americans into its ranks, America will be forced to lower its international profile and Russia will extend its control over vast swathes of the globe."

"Russia, where there is no fear of citizens expressing any opinions against the government," Eyal murmured, as though talking to himself.

Rubinov laughed. "Naturally. I was chosen to mediate between Russia and the Fraternity. Russia views the Fraternity as a fifth column within the United States, doing battle with the current administration on the home front. The Fraternity, for its part, views Russia as a country with a belief system similar to its own. The arrangement thus suits both parties. Having a weak running mate chosen to join the ticket was not accidental. Russia believed that after the president died and the weak vice president took over, the United States would become embroiled in a series of internal crises, forcing it to retreat from the international arena. No more sanctions against Russia because of what might be going on in Crimea; no more fake peace deals between Israel and the Palestinians; and most importantly, Mother Russia would be left unopposed to strike some great deals with the Shiite Arab world. Understand?"

"Yes." Eyal enunciated the word slowly as he absorbed the information. "So it was Russia, and not the Fraternity, who sent X and his men to murder the president."

"Not exactly. Russia offered the Fraternity a pretty sum of money in exchange for their involvement in the affair. Russia didn't want to be viewed as the instigators. They have no interest in kindling another Cold War. The Fraternity came to me with the request, and I turned to the CIA, explaining that I wanted to destroy the Fraternity. I told them that I wanted to kidnap the president, and I had X hired."

"X is not Syrian."

"Correct. He is – excuse me – he *was* an American-born assassin who had previously conducted many similar missions in various parts of the world, albeit on a smaller scale. True, he demanded extremely high fees, but the results were well worth the investment. In the past, for instance, he caused several African villages in diamond-mining regions to…'disappear,' we might call it, allowing me to mine in peace. He was responsible for several assassinations of prominent politicians, leading to tensions between various countries…he was the natural choice for such a job.

"For this particular mission, he needed to adopt an identity to hide behind, and he settled on Syrian, proclaiming his wildly improbable goal of bringing the president to the battlefield in order to broker some sort of peace. The plot was always rather hazy, but that didn't matter. He slipped into the role of Bashar Hobeir, a friendly Syrian killed in November of 2014. The man was presumed killed together with the rest of his family, and his body was never found. There are plenty of dead Syrian men whose bodies were never located, but this man seemed to be the perfect choice due to his leftist credentials and, now, his personal agenda, due to the murder of his family. He was the right man in the right place. In the months leading up to his mission, he acted like the man he was impersonating, reading up on his life. Fortunately, he didn't miss reading the part about his meeting with Yonatan at that Golan military base, many years previously."

"Why is that fortunate?"

"Because when the CIA sent Yonatan to X, suggesting that he kidnap the president, X immediately realized who Yonatan was and was able to allay any fears about his reliability."

"Brilliant."

"Isn't it?" Rubinov smiled. "Yonatan suggested you for the job, and you, more or less, know the details of what happened next."

"More or less, as you say. Except that there's one thing that doesn't fit in with this portrayal of events, and it's the reason it took me so long to figure things out. If you wanted to become a senior member of the Fraternity, why did the Fraternity send me to kill you?"

Rubinov laughed, a laugh of scorn for those he deemed inferior to himself. "My second mission for the Fraternity was foiling an attempt on my own life and disappearing from public life for a short period, in order to better devote my time to the Fraternity instead of to my own affairs."

"What would have happened if you hadn't managed to outwit me?"

"That would have been my problem. The Fraternity doesn't give simple missions to those who want to reach the rank I was aiming for. But the Fraternity didn't know what I knew about you. Try to recall what Paul mentioned during our unpleasant meeting in the restaurant – about your psychological profile."

"I recall." Eyal felt his fury rise to an almost uncontrollable level, and he wondered why. He thought that he had managed to vanquish his feelings and would be able to appear indifferent. "You've answered my remaining questions, and all I'm missing now is X's real name and position."

"You won't receive an answer to that, and you do realize why I've told you everything else that I've told you now with such joyful abandon, do you not?"

"Of course." Eyal's voice reflected calm indifference. "Do not insult my intelligence. You are talking openly to me because you don't plan on letting me leave this place alive."

"I am rendered almost speechless at your superior powers of comprehension." Rubinov offered Eyal a look of true admiration. The man knew that he was about to be murdered, within minutes even, yet he was as calm as someone enjoying a stroll in the garden of his own home.

Eyal smiled. "You aren't the first. Can I ask you something else?"

"I am at your service."

"Who really killed your son? I'm assuming that if it actually was the Fraternity, you wouldn't have wanted to become one of their lackeys."

For the first time during this conversation, Rubinov's features betrayed his dissatisfaction. "I don't know."

"Incredible!" Eyal said. "For you, a man with billions at his disposal, a man who mingles with government leaders and who wields immense power even over the content of international treaties, to admit that there's something you don't know? I find this hard to believe."

"Incredible as it may seem, it's the truth." The pain was evident in the man's light-blue eyes.

Eyal seemed lost in thought for a moment, and Rubinov eyed him with interest. "What now? Is everything clear to you?"

"Almost. I have just one more question."

"Which is...?" Rubinov asked. What could interest a man who was about to die?

"Why did X need me? He didn't use the bombs that I placed along the walls of the conference hall, and with a bit of skill, which he undoubtedly had, he could have gotten his men into the hotel room. So why did he go through the trouble of capturing me along with my son? Didn't he have better things to deal with than a five-year-old?"

"I thought you would figure out the answer to that on your own," Rubinov said with derision. "Paul was involved in this story, right?"

"Correct. And so...?"

"Do you really need to be spoon-fed?" Rubinov said. "I thought you could deduce some basic information without assistance. The CIA had Yonatan ask X to attempt the president's capture. They were waiting for it to happen, and X knew that and wanted to get them to stop tailing him because he had other plans. So what did he do in order to shake his tail? He cast you their way as bait. And he held you firmly in place by kidnapping your son. The CIA thought you knew everything about the capture, while X diverted their energies to you, whom they believed had a similar goal.

"It was very simple for X to take over the hotel, because no one thought any of it would truly happen with the CIA's troops stationed outside the conference hall. There are plenty of similar stories about intelligence warfare. You surely know that wars need to be managed with wisdom."

Eyal smiled at Rubinov's last words. "Then you probably know that the Mossad changed its motto from 'For by wise guidance you can wage your war,' to 'Where there is no guidance, a nation falls, but in an abundance of counselors there is safety.'"

"For a former agent you're very up to date on the organization," Rubinov said. "Feel like going back?"

"That's not a very practical desire at this point," Eyal said calmly. "Not after I was just told that my moments in this world are numbered."

"Correct." Rubinov brandished his gun, gazing at the polished matte metal with pleasure. "As you can see, this room has been prepared. There is nothing here that will link me to your death. Not even this gun." He pointed the gun straight at Eyal's heart. "I am truly sorry to have to kill you. You are a man after my own heart, and if you were a little less burdened by morality, we could have accomplished a great deal together."

Rubinov pulled the trigger and fired twice. The first bullet hit Eyal's chest, and he doubled over in pain. The second bullet caused him to collapse, groaning, to the floor.

***

"Is Abba going to come on another trip with us?" Elitzafun asked his mother from the back seat of the car, gazing out the window at the brightly lit, Western-style city.

"I don't know." Efrat was more concerned than she dared show her son. Her fear was all-consuming, choking her. Eyal had told her that there was no reason for her to worry, but she didn't believe him. The fact that he had done the unthinkable and parted from his weapons was making her very, very nervous. Eyal never left his house without at least two guns.

Her phone rang, and she answered. This was one call that she wouldn't dare turn the speaker on for, as she had no desire for Elitzafun to overhear the conversation. "Mrs. Gilboa." It was Eli, polite as ever.

"Yes." A deep sense of dread filled her. "Has something happened?"

"Have you heard from Eyal?" Eli asked, his tone of voice impossible to interpret.

"No. Not in the last hour." Her breath caught in her throat. What did Eli know? She had seen him go up to their suite after she and Elitzafun had left, and he had presumably spoken to Eyal. What had they discussed?

"Have you tried calling his phone?" Eli asked carefully.

"No. He told me that he would be at a meeting and wouldn't be able to answer. Why are you asking?" Her voice rose shrilly.

"It's probably nothing." Eli's voice was light, but Efrat was familiar with the uncanny ability intelligence agents had to hide all true inflections from their voice. "I'll try again in half an hour."

"You didn't go with him to his meeting?" she asked.

"I drove him there. There is no reason for concern, Mrs. Gilboa. I'll call again in fifteen minutes."

He's just moved the time frame up by fifteen minutes, Efrat thought. There was plenty to be nervous about.

Rubinov placed the smoking gun on the table, and a triumphant expression appeared on his face. Another empire had crumbled beneath his feet. Captain Rubinov had vanquished the legendary Eyal Gilboa.

Rubinov eyed the crumpled figure with satisfaction. The murdered man had overcome the murderer. Gleefully he called out, "Yabrov, Sasha!"

The door opened, and Paul and five CIA men entered, weapons drawn. Rubinov's face turned white.

"Paul...what...what happened?" he stuttered. "Where... where's Yabrov?"

"Yabrov is under arrest, and so are you." Paul removed a small piece of paper from his pocket and smiled as he read: "It is my duty to inform you of your right to remain silent. Everything you say can be used against you in a court of law. I'm not simply reciting your rights – which you are surely aware of on your own – in order to be polite. I don't need you to talk, as you've spoken enough up until now...we have everything we need in order to try you for various offenses. We were only missing the final admission of your guilt, and you've just now offered that to us. Eyal guessed that you were behind all this, and he offered to act as the bait in order to extract the truth from you. He did his job exceedingly well."

"And paid for it with his life." As shocked and pale as Rubinov was, he still hadn't lost his wits.

"No. I don't think so...Eyal?"

Eyal slowly got up, massaging his chest with a twisted expression of pain on his face. "What did you put there?"

".22 caliber bullets. Not bad." Paul's voice was apologetic. "Sorry about that."

"Are you serious?" Eyal's voice rose in anger. "Why didn't you put in blanks? All things considered, the calibers aren't too dangerous, but they could have killed me in certain circumstances, and I don't remember volunteering for that..."

"That's what you wore a bulletproof vest for," Paul reminded him.

"Well, what if he had decided to shoot me in the head?" Eyal demanded. "You were meant to keep all bases covered."

"I had faith in your ability to improvise." Paul winked.

"The same faith that you've had for months now."

Rubinov's gaze flitted from one man to the other as he struggled to comprehend. "The gun...you..."

"No underrating the murder weapon. I put real bullets inside, but, no, I couldn't risk having you shoot at Eyal with any other weapon. I'll admit that I took a small risk, because you like chang- ing things at the last minute, but Eyal was okay with the risk, because he wanted to defeat you and conclude this chapter of his life." Paul turned toward Eyal, who was taking off his bulletproof vest and examining himself for damage. "Shall we leave?"

Eyal looked at the silent CIA agents in the room. "Where are you taking him?"

"Don't worry. He's going to a very secure facility." Paul offered Eyal a broad smile. "Do you need a ride home?"

"Give me my cell phone first. I need to place a call to my wife, and another to my friend. They weren't in on these plans, and I probably owe them an apology for giving them such a scare this past hour. Later, you can drive me and my family to the airport. I've already given far too many days of my life to the United States."

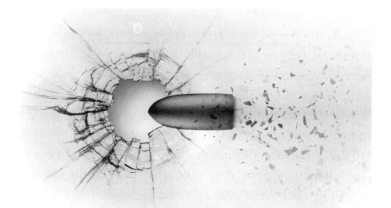

CHAPTER SIXTY-SIX

Boryspil International Airport, Ukraine

Y ou're coming in through the VIP entrance, Eyal my
friend," Paul told Eyal as he began pulling his suitcases
out of the car's luggage compartment. "There are far too
many reasons a security agent might be tempted stop you otherwise."

Efrat looked from Eyal to Paul. She noted Paul's open admiration for her husband and was unimpressed. The price Eyal had
been forced to pay for that appreciation had been too high.

"One of the fringe benefits of this line of business," Eyal said
with a chuckle.

"So, you're really going home?" Paul said, bending over
Elitzafun to unbuckle his seat belt so that the five-year-old could
skip happily out of the car.

"It's about time, isn't it?" Eyal said, piling his suitcases onto a cart.

"Absolutely." Paul handed Eyal five hundred-dollar bills. "This is just a small gift, so you can buy something for your kids back home. They deserve it."

"Thank you," Eyal said. His pride, however, would not permit him to accept the gift. "But really, I don't need this. If there was any way for you to somehow atone for all that my family has been through, it's by doing what you are promising to do – ensuring that I'm free to fly straight home rather than detour to the United States to give several months' worth of testimony."

"All the same, don't forget that you will have to answer whatever questions they pose to you, in whatever manner, as soon as the questions are asked." Paul pressed the cash into Eyal's hand. "Take it!"

"No."

"Don't be a snob. Buy a gift for your kids in my name."

"See this?" Eyal patted a huge suitcase. "It's full of gifts that Elitzafun received from all sorts of people."

"Those are his gifts, but you have another two children, don't you?" Paul pushed the money into his pocket. "Take it, for crying out loud. Don't be so stubborn."

Eyal sighed. "Give me a break. All I want is for you and everyone else at the CIA to get off my case."

"What makes you think we have no intention of doing any such thing?" Paul smiled. "You are an asset to the CIA. A very precious asset."

"That's exactly it. I'm not an asset." Eyal donned a menacing expression. "Write down that as of today, I swear never to serve as an asset to anyone in this world."

"Okay, I'll write it down. The question is what the agents in Langley will have to say about that." Paul's cheery voice turned slightly sober as he turned toward Efrat. "Thank you, Mrs. Gilboa, and sorry for everything."

Efrat said nothing. She wasn't sure if Paul was apologizing for Elitzafun's kidnapping, for the battles that her husband had been forced to wage, or for the past few days during which Eyal had risked his life for the sake of the CIA.

Paul bent down to Elitzafun's level. "What do you want your father to buy you? I'd choose the most expensive game in the store if I were you."

"Like what?" Elitzafun's eyes sparkled with childish joy. He was acting happily and spontaneously, and Eyal offered up a quiet and heartfelt prayer of gratitude. He turned toward Efrat and saw that the gratitude was reflected in her eyes as well. Yes, they would need to take Elitzafun to a psychologist to help him work through the ordeal he had endured, but his general appearance was that of a completely regular, happy child, and they were wholly grateful for that.

"Maybe ask him for a remote-control jeep."

Elitzafun nodded with excitement. "Yeah! Abba, can I get that?"

"Coming right up. At your service," Eyal said. Saying no to Elitzafun had always been a bit painful, and that was unlikely to change anytime soon.

"Looks like I managed to get you to change your mind quickly," Paul said, obviously enjoying himself. He gave a cheerful salute. "See you around, Captain."

Eyal nodded and began to walk away, but Paul called his name again. He turned around. "What now, you pest?"

Paul stepped forward and opened his fist to reveal a familiar chain dangling from his thumb and forefinger.

Eyal's heart skipped a beat.

"I understand that this amulet is a very precious object to you," Paul said

Eyal took the chain with the *kamiya*, and a shadow crossed his face. "Yes," he said shortly. "Very."

Paul nodded. "Tadiev asked me to relay his apologies."

"His apology has not been accepted." Eyal clasped the chain around his neck, and his eyes flickered with pain as he recalled the horrific time he had spent in prison. "Thanks, though, in any case."

Paul smiled. "Remember to expect a call from the president. He should be calling you in a day or two, and he'll be calling you from my number."

Eyal pretended not to understand. "His ghost will be calling me, you mean?"

"Don't be an idiot. I'm referring to Marty Clifford. He's going to want to speak to you."

"Then he'd better get in line."

Eyal settled into his seat, business class as he had requested, and made sure that his wife and son were comfortable. He put his hand in his pocket to check that the hundred-dollar bills were still there, and frowned. All Americans seemed to think they could solve any problem with money – it was just a question of how much. Even Paul, who knew him relatively well, thought he could manipulate Eyal's feelings with a few pieces of paper.

He couldn't allow himself to breathe until takeoff, nor would he relax entirely once they were airborne. He wouldn't allow Efrat to see his concern, but he feared that either a Ukrainian or an American security agent would suddenly realize that he wanted something else from Eyal Gilboa and that it would be a shame to let him leave the country before getting it out of him.

None of those worst-case scenarios played out in the end. Apparently Paul had pulled all the right strings. The airplane lifted off Ukrainian soil, and Eyal closed his eyes with relief. Only then did he notice the strong, throbbing pain in his arm. He hoped that his stubborn insistence not to tell anyone about this particular wound wouldn't result in any permanent damage.

Efrat noted his change of expression. "Is everything okay?" she asked.

"Almost." Eyal rolled up his sleeve, exposing his bandage, and Efrat looked at him in surprise. The bandage itself gave no hint of what was going on underneath. "A gunshot wound," Eyal said, in response to the unasked question.

"Didn't you have it taken care of?"

"Yes, but it wasn't tended to professionally. I'm afraid it might be infected." He chose not to mention the fact that he himself was responsible for the gravity of the injury.

Efrat's face turned pale. "You've been walking around like this for several days already." She knew exactly what an infected gunshot wound could lead to.

"More days than that."

"Why didn't you say anything to anyone?" she said. "I can understand your not saying anything to X, but why didn't you say anything after you were released?"

"Did you want me to have surgery in some hospital in Ukraine?" Eyal asked. There was a note of fury in his voice, although it was unclear who the object of his fury was. "They drove me crazy enough, as you probably noticed, and I knew that if I said anything I'd be delayed by another month, and I had no interest in that happening."

"But you're in pain!"

"Correct." Eyal chuckled at the urgency in her tone. "A lot of pain."

"How come you didn't say anything? You went through so many long, exhausting interrogations, and who knows what else, because everything is always so classified by you, and yet you didn't say a word to anyone about this?"

"I managed." Eyal decided not to add that he had also performed some physically demanding maneuvers with his barely functioning arm.

"Wouldn't it have been better to be held up for another month in order to receive the appropriate medical treatment?" Efrat knew she sounded like a strict schoolmarm, but she couldn't help lecturing him. "You acted really immaturely! That wasn't responsible."

"Thanks." Eyal didn't bother to hide the fact that he was insulted. He was exhausted, hurt, and wounded. His wife had suffered as a result of his actions, but it was he who had been subjected to endless tests of his physical, mental, and emotional capabilities. "Let's not talk about it, okay?"

Efrat fell silent, but it was clear that she had plenty more to say on the subject. Elitzafun fell asleep, and she closed her eyes and she too fell asleep.

Eyal closed his eyes and tried to doze off, but the pain was mounting by the minute, it seemed, driving all thoughts of sleep from his mind.

Efrat stirred slightly in her sleep and opened her eyes a crack, taking in Eyal's wan face and noticing for the first time that his teeth were gritted. "So take a painkiller," she said suddenly.

Eyal looked at her in surprise. "Weren't you sleeping?"

"I can't sleep when I see you this way. Take a painkiller."

Eyal bit his lip. "I already took one."

"And it's not helping?"

"No. It's not going to help something like this."

"We're going straight to the hospital when we land," she said.

"I had hoped to go home to see the children first, but I think you're right on this one."

"They'll be waiting for us at the airport in any case."

"Of course. Otherwise I might still be tempted to go home and leave the hospital for later. So you'll go home with them and I'll head to the hospital. Alone." The last word was said with distinct emphasis.

"No. I'm coming with you."

"The children need you, Efrat. Elitzafun needs you. I'll manage on my own."

"Just like you managed on your own up until now." Not for the first time since their reunion in the Ukraine, words of pain and accusation left Efrat's lips and Eyal turned pale in response. No one could hurt the super-agent. No one except for his wife. He opened his mouth to respond and immediately closed it. Thick, tangible tension filled the air, exacerbated by the air pressure in the cabin. Eyal's temples pounded, and he found it difficult to breathe. They both hoped that Elitzafun would wake up just then and ask for something, but the five-year-old didn't stir.

After several long moments Eyal broke the uncomfortable silence with a question. "What do you want me to say?"

She didn't answer.

Another few moments of silence passed. "Efrat," Eyal said finally, his voice quieter than it should have been. Efrat turned to him with a look of anger, pity, and loneliness all combined. That look, more than shouts or anger, threatened to shatter Eyal's fragile heart.

"Efrat," he repeated. "I...the whole time I tried to..." He stopped, unsure of how to continue and what to say.

"What did you try?" She tried softening her tone of voice, but instead of eking out a tone of understanding, her voice became almost belligerent and accusing. She stopped talking.

"Will you believe me when I tell you that I didn't want this?" Eyal asked, his lips trembling.

"My son was kidnapped." The 323 people in close quarters with the couple were the only reason Efrat managed to maintain a quiet tone of voice. Pain and utter helplessness, however, filled every syllable of her words. "My son was kidnapped, Eyal. Do you understand that?"

He wanted to say that *his* son had been kidnapped as well, but he knew that was a fallacy. Pained as he been over Elitzafun's kidnapping, Elitzafun wasn't his biological son. He was hers.

"For two weeks I was at home, alone and terrified, and there was nothing, nothing, nothing that I could do." Her whispered shouts were that of a wounded lioness, and Eyal closed his eyes. "You were there, at least. You were with him. You were able to do something. You fought and worked with his captors to have him released, but I was at home, Eyal, and there was nothing that I could do. There was no way for me to help my child! Can you understand that?"

Eyal was afraid to move a limb. Afraid to nod. Instead, he sat immobile, eyes fixed on the floor of the airplane.

"My son was kidnapped. And you know what else? You had also disappeared to who knows where, and my family was angry. They're not happy about this, and aside from them, I also had to put up with all sorts of tactless people who had questions about... about your having murdered someone in Ukraine. The Israeli media went wild with that trouble, and before I had time to recover from it, another even more horrific story hit me. I didn't know what to tell my parents. They had heard about the murder in Ukraine and were in shock. I couldn't think clearly, and then Elitzafun...it was way too much."

"He's been released, Efrat." Eyal had found his lost tongue at last. He had no choice. Efrat's accusations were coming thick and fast, leaving him wounded and defenseless.

Efrat looked up at Eyal as though seeing him for the first time. After a moment she looked down at the sleeping Elitzafun. His head was resting on her lap. "He was freed," she repeated, her voice full of bewilderment.

Eyal said nothing, and Efrat's expression changed. She bit her lips and chocked back the memories that still overwhelmed her. "You're not to blame for everything," she said.

Eyal turned to look out of the window. Had Efrat seen the pain in his eyes? Was that the reason she was backing down somewhat? He hoped not.

"You're not to blame," Efrat repeated, and Eyal wasn't sure if she was trying to calm him or if she was trying to convince herself.

He took a gulp of air. "Thank you," he said finally. "But really, you're right. Every word you just said is correct, and I have nothing to add."

"I'm sorry," Efrat said. She hadn't meant to say everything she had just said to the man who had struggled, been tortured, and suffered through so much in order to bring her son back to her. The man...her husband. Her children's loving stepfather.

Elitzafun shifted on Efrat's lap, and they both looked at him. "There's no reason to apologize," Eyal said quietly. "You're right, and I'm sorry. I know that my own pain makes no difference here, and I'm sorry."

Eltizafun opened his eyes and looked up sleepily at his mother. "We landed?" he asked.

"Soon." Efrat hugged him. "Soon we'll be home."

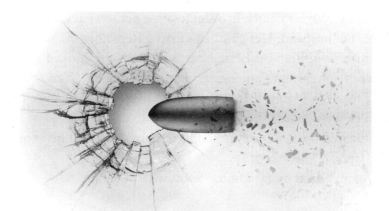

CHAPTER SIXTY-SEVEN

Ben Gurion Airport, Israel

The two children stood and waved. Their ecstatic expressions filled Eyal's heart with joy, and he lifted his own arms to wave in response. Immediately, the children broke into a run and came racing toward him.

The world seemed to stand still as he tried to absorb the fact that they were all together again. Efrat, standing beside him, was alight with joy.

"You're not going to leave us again," Chagelet said. "Right?"

Elishama tugged at Eyal's sleeve, and he drew in a sharp breath as a piercing pain sliced through his body.

Efrat saw and immediately understood. "Chagelet, there's nowhere Abba wants to be more than at home with us, okay?"

"Exactly that," Eyal said. "I'll be coming home as soon as I can."

Tel Hashomer Hospital, Israel

Efrat's heart raced as she paced the hallway outside the operating room. She was on her own, having left her children with their grandfather, Shemaryahu's father. And she hadn't told Eyal's father, Menachem, anything about what he was about to undergo, as Eyal had specifically asked her not to give him cause for concern.

"How ironic," she had said. "After all the worry you've caused him over the past months."

"I know," he'd replied. "But if there's something I can do about it, then I'll do it."

Now Efrat almost regretted her decision to come alone. Originally she had considered asking Giddi or one of her parents to accompany her. They, or any of her relatives, would have been happy to be with her, but she knew that they had all formed all sorts of opinions about her husband, and she wasn't in the mood to deal with those feelings just then. Certainly not with Eyal injured and in pain.

A tall man in a business suit and wearing glasses entered the waiting room. He could have been a clerk or a top specialist for all she knew.

"Geveret Gilboa?" the man called out.

He obviously wasn't there for another patient. He was there for her husband. "Yes?" Efrat asked, tension creeping into her voice.

"They've finished treating your husband's wound, and now they're about to begin the second stage of the surgery. We hope it will all go well."

"Please tell me, honestly – what are the chances of...of everything going according to plan?"

The man shifted from one foot to the other. "I will not deny that it's dangerous. We can't be one hundred percent certain that the formula we've come up with to remove the microchip is correct. Our team attempted to decode the original microchip that came into our possession, and we hope we've done so correctly. But hopefulness does not equate certainty."

"And if it doesn't go as planned…"

"There's a whole team standing at the ready in case it becomes necessary to resuscitate him. We are, however, hoping for the best."

"Who, exactly is 'we'?"

"I'm Dov Tal from the Mossad's technology department. I decoded the microchip's operating system and figured out how it's connected to Eyal's body." His demeanor was modest, almost apologetic. "I've come now to put my theory to the test."

He smiled, didn't wait for Efrat to acknowledge it in any way, and turned toward the operating room.

As he opened the door a guard barked: "No one's allowed in."

Dov showed the guard his authorization, and he was waved right in. The door closed behind him.

Efrat sat down, her hands clammy, trying to prepare herself for a long wait.

"What's happening now?" Dov asked, addressing his question to the chief surgeon.

"He seems okay," Dr. Regev said, a note of exhaustion creeping into his voice. "We've been working according to the method you outlined, but we needed you here before we began the actual removal."

Dov exhaled. "Okay. You can start." He flipped open his computer and accessed the program he had devised to link up to the microchip in Eyal's body, allowing him to fool the microchip into thinking that it was manipulating Eyal's neurons when in fact it was connecting to the computer instead.

The doctors worked quickly and in total silence. The computerized indices in the room began to beep, and the resuscitation team immediately sprang into action, with the doctors all taking up their designated posts. Eyal's blood pressure plummeted, his heart rate slowed, and for a single, awful moment, it disappeared completely.

"We're losing him," Dr. Regev whispered.

"We won't let that happen," Dr. Shiff said. "We're not giving up so fast..."

Eyal's heart had stopped. The EKG showed a straight line.

The medical team exchanged glances. One electrical shock. Two.

The line remained stubbornly straight.

"Again," Dov said. His lips were dry. If they lost Eyal now he would never forgive himself. Perhaps he had been too self-assured when he had cracked the code. His face was whiter than the hospital sheet. Had something gone wrong? Had he keyed in the correct code? He rebooted the program, manually entering the algorithm he had developed so that the computer could locate the cancellation prompt within the microchip.

"What did you just do?" Dr. Shiff exclaimed. "Whatever it was, keep doing it. I'll give him another shock."

"I think we need to lower the dose of his anesthesia slightly," Dov said cautiously. "The microchip has picked up on the anesthesia's presence and it's beginning to fight it."

"And if we lower the dosage then the microchip won't be able to sense it? By how much?"

"Not too much – well, as much as you can, to be on the safe side," Dov said. He knew Eyal had been through much more than this in his life.

They worked together in sync, with Dov communicating with the microchip via his computer, overriding the signals being sent from the microchip to Eyal's cells and brain stem. Meanwhile, the medical team kept tabs on all of Eyal's vitals, watching, waiting, hoping.

"You're making headway," Dov whispered to his computer. "Now we get to the main algorithm...how's he doing, Doctor?"

"Much better," Dr. Shiff said. "He still needs help breathing, but it's looking up."

Dov checked the synaptic transfers connecting the microchip to Eyal's body and realized that there was yet another security code he needed to crack. Whoever had devised this chip was clearly brilliant. "He's out of the woods," Dr. Shiff told him. His face was still pale, but he was smiling. "He's okay. His pulse is stabilizing."

"Ready to pull the microchip out?" Dov asked, his voice a combination of hope and dread.

The doctors looked at each other. If Dov's remote cancelation of the microchip had led to the collapse of Eyal's system, what would happen once the chip itself was removed? There was, however, no denying the fact that Eyal's condition had stabilized and that his connection with the microchip at this point was almost entirely physical, the electronic signaling having been reduced to almost zero.

"We're ready."

"Just a minute. I need to enter one more line of code. A long one." Dov looked over the program that he had written, making sure that all of the lettering was red. Negative. Disconnected. Eyes closed, Dov pressed enter and called out, "Now."

Dr. Shiff made a tiny incision and removed the microchip. In medical terms, it was an exceedingly simple procedure. The doctors all turned to focus on the screens. No response.

Dov's screen went blank, and he waited for the program to close itself. According to the computer, the microchip was ready to be implanted in someone else. He clicked on the desktop, closing all of the background programs before snapping his laptop shut. "That's it."

A chorus of cheers resounded through the room as the men exchanged high-fives and handshakes. Dov was sweating and exhausted from the exertion, but a smile of satisfaction spread over his face. He got up, computer in one hand, microchip in the other. "I'm going out to Gilboa's wife," he said. "She's waiting just outside."

"Good job," Dr. Shiff said.

"Thank you." Dov stepped out into the hallway, and Efrat rose immediately.

"What...what happened?"

"It was hard," he said. "We almost lost him, but he'll be okay now."

Efrat turned white. "What...what does that mean?"

"His body had a bad reaction when we disconnected the microchip remotely, but he pulled through. He needs lots of rest and recuperation – well, he needed that anyway. But he'll be back to himself. *Refuah sheleimah*," he added, before bidding her farewell. He preferred not to reveal his own role in the saga. It had been touch and go.

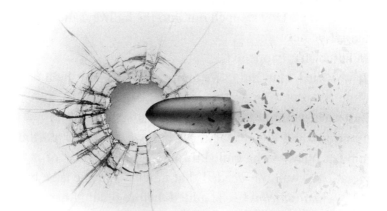

CHAPTER SIXTY-EIGHT

Tel Hashomer Hospital, Israel

Eyal woke up. He peered silently around the darkened room, taking in the beeping of the machines and the otherwise thick and blessed stillness. As an agent he was used to rising with caution, peering through the slits in his eyes in order to gauge what was going on around him before anyone realized he was no longer asleep. It was an unshakable habit.

Instead of Efrat, he saw his father resting on the armchair near his bed. A long moment passed before Eyal recalled having asked that his father not be told about the operation. How had he known to come?

Eyal closed his eyes. He was weak and lethargic, and he need-ed a few moments to plan what to tell his father. Even as a child he had often tried to placate his father, and as an adult he had maintained the habit.

One arm was still throbbing in pain, and he looked down at the bandages. The arm was still attached to him, and he was glad. There had been many moments when he had feared that amputation might be necessary.

His other arm was also bandaged. Had they tried to remove the microchip? How had their efforts fared? Questions raged within him, and he felt a burning desire for answers.

His father was dozing, and Eyal sat up impatiently and then softly stepped down from his bed. He realized, almost too late, that he was hooked up to an IV drip. He was obviously receiving vital fluids and antibiotics, and he had no idea how to disconnect the tubes. With a sigh of submission he lay back down. What time was it? He glanced at his wrist and saw that his watch had been removed. His souvenir from X. It was also proof that the whole thing hadn't been a dream. Or, rather, a nightmare.

Eyal reached to find his cell phone, guessing it would be in the drawer of the night table next to his bed. His father shifted in his seat and turned to him. "Eyal?"

"What are you doing here, Abba?"

"When are you going to realize that you can't hide things from your father?" His question was rhetorical, and Eyal could see the smile on his lips even in the darkened room. "I may not be an intelligence agent, but all it took was three questions to Chagelet and I figured out exactly what was going on."

"I'm sorry I didn't tell you anything, Abba, but I didn't want to worry you."

"If your statement wasn't so sad it would be funny," his father replied.

"I'm sorry."

"Stop," Menachem said softly. "How are you feeling?"

"Okay. In general."

"You're such an expert at saying nothing with few words."

"What do you want me to tell you?" Eyal was also a pro at hiding his thoughts and feelings, but it was difficult not to respond to the probing look in his father's eyes.

"The truth."

"The real truth? I'm tired. I have no energy and my arm is killing me. But tell me – where's Efrat?"

"She left. Or, rather, she was forced to leave by both her father and me. She had been here for twenty hours and was about to collapse. She hasn't had it easy these past few weeks either."

Eyal looked away. "I know." So his father-in-law had been at his bedside too. It was a good thing he'd been unconscious.

"Call her." Menachem handed Eyal his phone. "She made me promise that I'd tell you to call her as soon as you woke up, no matter what time it was."

"What time is it?"

"Four o'clock in the morning. You slept for almost a whole day." Menachem peered at his son's face. "Call her and speak to her. I'll go and get you some painkillers from the nurse's station."

Eyal took the phone hesitantly. His fingers played with the screen without pressing any of the numbers.

Menachem returned to the room and saw that Eyal still hadn't called. "Why haven't you called her yet, son?"

Eyal was thirty-five, battle-hardened, used, and much abused. People viewed him as a human weapon, a living intelligence legend, not a human being. His father was the only one who still saw the small child inside him, the boy who still, occasionally, wanted to be protected. "What...what happened to me? If you know..."

"I know. The microchip was removed and your body had a bad reaction. The doctors managed to stabilize you in the end, and they say you'll need a day or two of rest and that's it."

A beautiful feeling of freedom flooded his heart. Quickly, he dialed Efrat's number, and Menachem left the room "to see if the nurse is coming yet with those painkillers." Eyal knew he just wanted to give him some privacy.

He'd been given a private room. The government still regarded the information he held in his brain as highly classified. *They might want to use me again*, Eyal thought, but he forced the notion out of his mind.

The call to Efrat was brief. She was happy to hear her husband's voice, and she wanted to drive over to the hospital as soon as possible.

"It's four o'clock in the morning and the children are sleeping," he said.

"I'm not at home. They found me a room near the hospital."

"Good. But, Efrat, I'm really, really tired. Maybe come later this morning, okay?"

"No problem."

Eyal ended the call and closed his eyes. Waves of pain seemed to be engulfing him. There was no escaping the agony. He had sustained gunshot wounds in the past, but never had he experienced pain like this. His arm felt as though it were being hacked away with a knife.

"Go home, Abba," Eyal said, after his father returned from the nurse's station. It took all his strength not to show his father how much pain he was in. "I'm okay."

"I want to make sure that the shot they're planning on giving you has the desired effect." His father knew him too well.

"It's really not necessary, Abba. Thank you for coming. Go home and rest."

"Do you think I'm going to leave my wounded and suffering son, just so I can go home to rest?" his father asked. "You'd never do such a thing, nor will I."

Eyal didn't respond.

"Doctor's visit."

Eyal woke up. It was seven o'clock in the morning, and his father was still at his bedside.

"Yes. Eyal Gilboa." The doctor smiled. "How are you feeling?"

"I'm fine under the circumstances."

The doctor's expression turned serious. "How's your arm?"

"Which one?" A smile of amusement tinged with pain flitted across Eyal's face.

"Let's not make a big deal out of a two-centimeter-long incision." The doctor smiled again. "I'm talking about the arm with the gunshot wound."

"The truth? It's very painful."

"You were one step away from amputation. Did you know that?"

"I guessed it." A spark of warning appeared in Eyal's eyes as his gaze flitted back and forth between the doctor and his father. Eyal knew that his body was in horrible shape, thanks to the Ukrainian interrogators' beatings, and he had no interest in his father's finding out the truth.

The hint was well received. "I'd like to speak privately with your son," he told Menachem.

"I'll be waiting outside," Menachem said.

He left the room and the doctor turned to Eyal, speaking in an undertone. "You looked like you'd fallen from the sixth floor and bumped into all of the porches and air conditioners on your way down. How did your body get this way?"

"Never mind. It's classified information." Eyal smiled, despite his pain, at the doctor's vivid description. "What happened with the microchip?"

"It was removed. The surgery was complicated and there were some dangerous moments, but we got through those, and your arm is as good as new. No aftereffects. Regarding your other arm, however – how did you let it get to such a state?"

"It's been a while since I was shot," Eyal explained. "It couldn't be tended to earlier, and so things deteriorated."

"You're going to have to stay here for the next two weeks so we can pump you up with the heaviest dosage of antibiotics available, with the hope that your body will be able to overcome the damage caused by the wound."

"Two weeks?" Eyal repeated, stunned. "You said a day or two." In his mind's eye he could see the large bay window at home and the stunning view beyond it. He was dreaming of wandering through the fields and vineyards with his children, catching butterflies and counting birds. He longed to inhale clean, unpolluted air, away from the chaos of gunpowder and action. It was difficult to accept that it would be another two weeks before his dream would come true.

"One day for the microchip and two weeks for your arm. I'm assuming you don't want to lose it altogether, and the danger hasn't passed yet."

Eyal leaned back against his pillow. "Fine," he said slowly. "But consider yourself warned that I'm not accustomed to taking orders."

"You'll take them from me." The doctor smiled. "Your phone's ringing."

Eyal glanced at the screen. "He can wait."

"Who? The prime minister?"

"No." Eyal shrugged. It was Paul's number on the screen. "The president of the United States." In answer to the doctor's smile of disbelief, he added, "I'm serious."

"No kidding."

"Okay, so listen in." Eyal took the call, turning on the speakerphone. "Hello?"

"Eyal." Paul's voice reverberated through the air. "How are you?"

"Wow. I've never had so many people express an interest in how I was doing." Eyal chuckled. "I'm fine. More or less."

"There's someone here who would like to speak to you."

"I'm assuming I can't say no to this person, so, okay, to please you, I'll agree."

"Eyal." The president's voice was solid, and he sounded very young. Too young to be president. Eyal shook his head, trying to take his mind off the many derogatory things Paul had said about the man.

"Yes, Mr. President. Have you read through all the boring reports Paul gave you?"

"Boring would be the last word I would use to describe them. Eyal, I need you here more than ever."

"You're aren't the first person to make such a request."

"And...?"

"As I originally told your predecessor, the answer is a resounding no."

"Don't be so sure." The president issued a long and throaty sigh. "Take care of yourself, Eyal."

"That's an easy command for me to obey."

"I know."

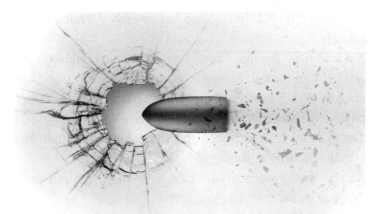

CHAPTER SIXTY-NINE

Tel Hashomer Hospital, Israel

E yal stepped out of the hospital's elevator with an expression of relief and longing. Wearing his own clothes, walking next to normal people, he savored his return to real life. He walked through the lobby and paused for a moment before opening the door and leaving the building.

Efrat was waiting for him next to the car, holding Elitzafun's hand. The older children were at school.

"What's that on your arm, Abba?" Elitzafun asked.

Eyal and Efrat exchanged glances, looking at the bandage and then at Elitzafun, who was hopping from one foot to the other, as usual. "It's nothing," Eyal said. "Really nothing."

Elitzafun tugged his father's arm, and Eyal lurched forward and gave a short moan.

"Why did you do that?" Efrat chastised Elitzafun.

"You said your arm doesn't hurt," Elitzafun said, lips quivering at the reprimand.

"Well, it hurts just a bit."

"It'll get better." Elitzafun smiled sweetly. "That's what Ima always says."

Eyal and Efrat smiled. "Yes," Eyal said. "Ima is always right."

Eyal got into the car, turned the key in the ignition, and opened his window. "Ah, there's nothing like the fresh air of freedom." He closed his eyes and inhaled the car's exhaust fumes.

Efrat grimaced. "If this were the Swiss Alps, you might be onto something. But this? Disgusting."

"So speaks the woman who hasn't recently been in captivity." Eyal's voice was free of all cynicism.

"I guess you're right."

A honk.

Eli jumped, and his hand flew toward his gun. A second later his hand dropped to his side in relief. The head sticking out of the window of the car behind him belonged to Bentzy.

Bentzy got out of his car and Eli stepped out of his. The two men approached each other, and Bentzy shook Eli's hand. "Good to see you," he said, drawing him into a bear hug.

"When did you get here?" Eli asked.

"An hour and a half ago," Bentzy said. He strode forward, taking in the deathly silence. Hundreds of still and silent gravestones stared up at him. "I came here straight from the airport, and I'm heading right back. My return flight is scheduled to take off in five hours."

"Strict boss?" Eli offered a short chuckle, even though he really had no desire to laugh. The silence and depressing atmosphere hardly called for shared banter, but still, it wasn't every day that he met up with a close friend he hadn't seen in a long while.

"No. Just paranoid." Bentzy walked down the narrow stone path, approaching the group assembled around the fresh grave. Thirty days old. "His predecessor didn't exactly end his job in the most celebratory manner." He paused. "Who are all these people?"

"Most of them are relatives," Eli said. A group of approximately fifteen people had gathered around the grave. "Ofer and Yariv are here. They were discharged last week."

"I know," Bentzy said. He didn't add that he had been the one who had arranged for Yariv to get an early flight back to Israel. "But one person is missing."

Eli glanced around quickly. "Two."

Bentzy didn't respond, but a wave of pain engulfed him. They approached the gravestone, where Guy's parents and two sisters were standing, hollow expressions in their eyes.

Two young men stood several steps away from the grave, and Bentzy placed his hands on their shoulders. In silence, Yariv turned his head around, and when he saw that it was his boss, he immediately looked away. Bentzy looked away too so as to avoid the boy's anguished gaze. He had caused it.

Someone handed Guy's father a siddur, and his voice grew choked as he enunciated the words of Kaddish.

Eli took in the scene in silence. He had been at the graves of dear friends dozens of times, and yet the feelings of pain and loss never diminished.

The stark etchings on the marble headstone stared up at him in silence: *Here lies Guy ben Fanya z"l*. But whatever was written made little difference. How could mere words ever do justice to the story of someone's life when it had been so brutally cut short?

The crowd began to disperse. Eli and Bentzy watched as Ofer and Yariv walked away. There was no farewell. Eli and Bentzy stared in silence at the gravestone for several long moments before making their way back to their cars.

"He didn't come," Bentzy said.

"Who?" Eli asked, though he knew the answer.

"Eyal."

Eli looked around again, taking in the entire cemetery, and his lips curved upward in a thin smile. "He's over there."

Forty feet away, Eyal stood up from a stone bench, his face an inscrutable mask, revealing nothing of the inner workings of his heart. Bentzy's and Eli's faces softened with understanding. It was clear to both of them why he had chosen not to join them.

As they watched, Eyal approached Guy's grave. The area was silent; everyone had left. The man who now lay beneath the tombstone had forfeited his life trying to save Eyal's son. There was no way Eyal could ever repay that debt. It didn't matter how many ways there were to explain what had happened; it didn't matter that soldiers knew that their lives might be sacrificed for the sake of others. There was no way for one to truly come to terms with the facts.

Eyal's posture was stooped. How many young men, commanders and friends, had he buried in his lifetime? His hand stroked the gravestone as he read the words again and again. Eyal had never met Guy, but this man had given his life for his son, and that was reason enough for Eyal to come and beg for forgiveness at his grave.

"Go over to him," Bentzy told Eli. The long silence at the gravestone was worrisome.

"No," Eli said. "Sometimes a man just needs to be alone."

They fell silent, and after several moments they returned to their cars. Even after they drove off, the image of Eyal's shadow over Guy's gravestone remained vivid in their minds. There were people who would never stand in the limelight, choosing to remain concealed forever, their only witnesses being the shadows and the silence.